MONDAYS

on the

DARK NIGHT

of the

MOON

MONDAYS

on the

DARK NIGHT

of the

MOON

Himalayan Foothill Folktales

KIRIN NARAYAN
in collaboration with
URMILA DEVI SOOD

New York   Oxford

OXFORD UNIVERSITY PRESS • 1997

Oxford University Press

Oxford   New York
Athens   Auckland   Bangkok   Bogotá   Bombay
Buenos Aires   Calcutta   Cape Town   Dar es Salaam
Dehli   Florence   Hong Kong   Istanbul   Karachi
Kuala Lumpur   Madras   Madrid   Melbourne
Mexico City   Nairobi   Paris   Singapore
Taipei   Tokyo   Toronto

and associated companies in
Berlin   Ibadan

Copyright © 1997 by Kirin Narayan

Published by Oxford University Press, Inc.
198 Madison Avenue, New York, New York 10016

Oxford is a registered trademark of Oxford University Press, Inc.

Library of Congress Cataloging-in-Publication Data
Narayan, Kirin.
Mondays on the dark night of the moon:
Himalayan foothill folktales / Kirin Narayan in collaboration with
Urmila Devi Sood
p. cm.   Includes bibliographical references.
ISBN 0–19–510348–3 (cloth).—ISBN 0–19–510349–1 (paper)
1. Folklore—India—Kāngra (District)
2. Kāngra (India : District)—Social life and customs.
3. India—Religion.   I. Sood, Urmila Devi.   II. Title.
GR305.5.K25N37   1997   398.2'0954'52—dc20   96–27891

1 3 5 7 9 8 6 4 2

Printed in the United States of America
on acid-free paper

For "Chachu" Jodha Ram Sood and "Tayi Sas" Nihali Devi Sood,
who told many of these stories,
and for
A. K. Ramanujan and Alan Dundes,
who across continents, decades, and languages
encouraged these retellings

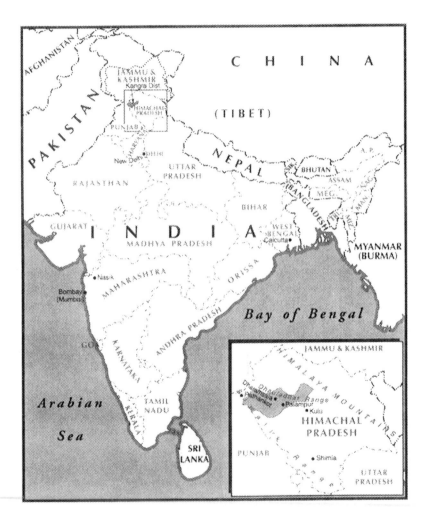

CONTENTS

Part II Winter Tales

PREFACE

"*Gale milnā*" is how Urmilaji always begins her letters to me: "Embraces."
Writing this preface with a New Year's card from her propped on my desk, I
think of how that opening greeting also speaks to what we've done in this book.
Gale milnā literally means "uniting the throats." In Kangra valley of the Himalayan foothills, where Urmilaji lives, women friends who are reunited after a
separation take one another in their arms in a leisurely, swaying embrace: pressing cheek against cheek (throat against throat) on one side, the other side, the
first side again. But *galā* "throat," also refers to voice; in this book, Urmilaji's
voice meets with mine. I am telling a story about her telling stories and about
the meanings she helped me see in her stories. Though I have tried to keep our
voices distinct, through dialogue, translation, and friendship we've inevitably
mingled.

In 1991, when I was living at the other end of Urmilaji's village, she gave
me the gift of every Kangra folktale she could remember. These were often
spell-binding stories but they were not just about set-apart worlds. Through
these Kangra folktales, I learned about people's relations to gods, to relatives,
to imagined historical pasts. I shared in Urmilaji's memories of the tellers who
had taught her these stories. I grappled with questions about the appropriate
relationships between scholars and the people whose lives they research. Sitting
together, the happy complicity of enjoying these stories drew Urmilaji and me
closer. I came to understand that oral stories arise out of relationships, are about
relationships, and forge relationships.

Here are the twenty-one stories that Urmilaji told. On her instruction, I have
divided the stories into two broad sets: tales associated with various women's
rituals and tales for entertainment on long, cold winter nights. Urmilaji used
the same word, *kathā*, for both sorts of stories, and I gloss this as "folktale."
Kathā is a term most often used for Hindu religious stories. Religious values

and beliefs are most explicit in the women's ritual tales, but they orient the winter's tales, too. For me, who wrote an earlier book on the folktales told by a Hindu holy man, it has been fascinating to see how the same general beliefs can be tilted away from ascetic male perspectives and toward the domestic lives of women.

The tellers of folktales are sometimes mentioned—usually in introductions or in footnotes—in collections of stories. They are not often given a sustained presence throughout a book. It is even rarer for them to be consulted about the meanings in their stories. Instead, it is usually the compiler, the scholar, who provides interpretations, trotting out his or her own favorite theoretical frameworks to elucidate the stories.

Certainly, all stories are not equally open to explicit interpretation, and all tellers do not have an exegetical bent. But the widespread notion that folktales express the unconscious and inexpressible in compact, symbolic form has shifted attention away from the conscious, articulable meanings that are also in stories. In this book, which is an experiment in interpretive collaboration, I explore the value of asking those who actually live with stories what they make of the tales that they tell.

Urmilaji and I talked about each one of these stories, either at the time of the telling or after I had digested it through transcription. Often, meanings that were perfectly obvious to Urmilaji and probably other women raised in Kangra needed to be plainly stated in order for me, an outsider, to understand. Other meanings seemed to emerge from Urmilaji's own prodigious ability to make connections between cultural realms. Sometimes Urmilaji had a lot to say about a story, sometimes just a little. I present her comments about each story and add my own. In the afterword, I expand on what this collaboration seems to have meant to her, what it means to me, and what it might mean for scholarship.

When Urmilaji sat opposite me, brown eyes fixed on mine, and when she sat among groups of her relatives or neighbors, scanning her audience, she was addressing people she already knew. Like most oral stories, her folktales emerged in specific, situated interactions. I wish I could say the same for the writing of a book! Sending these stories out into print, I have been overwhelmed whenever I think of the multiple, transnational audiences that books today increasingly have. It is a daunting task to write a nonfiction book that will hopefully be acceptable to the people described, accessible to any curious general reader, and also of interest to scholars, especially when all these readers are mixed and scattered across continents.

Putting this book together, I have had to keep in mind that Urmilaji's English-speaking relatives in Kangra are as likely to evaluate the ways I have presented these tales as are friends in Bombay, Tunisia, and Madison, or scholarly colleagues in Delhi, Jerusalem, Tanzania, and London. I have also been aware that different readers will come to this book with different expectations:

for entertainment; to learn about Kangra Valley or the Himalayan foothills; to reflect on the nature of Hindu stories, women's stories, or folktales in general; to interrogate the methodologies of folklore and anthropology, and so on.

Trying to keep sight of these multiple audiences, I've structured this book in the following way. First, I present a narrative introduction, setting the scene and giving readers a background on the cultural life of Kangra. Then, through the body of the book, are Urmilaji's tales. Finally, in the afterword, I return to the larger issues that these stories as a body, and this project as a whole, might speak to. To maintain a smooth flow of readability, I've confined scholarly references to footnotes.

Through the last decade, Hinduism has become increasingly identified with nationalist movements. Images of men battering the dome of the Ayodhya mosque and of saffron-clad women making inflammatory speeches have tended to eclipse the serenity of earlier associations with Hindu India: gurus absorbed in meditation, Gandhi's nonviolence, old-age homes for cows. Having worked so closely with two very different people—Swamiji and Urmilaji—whose stories are steeped in Hindu values, I believe that it is important to remember that the confrontational aspects of contemporary Hinduism should not be mistaken as the whole religion. Multistranded and polymorphous, the complex of practices and beliefs that have been lumped together as "Hinduism" can also bring meaning and connection rather than conflict to many people's lives.

Urmilaji has generously showered this project with good wishes in person and through letters. One of her reasons was simply to help me. But also, she has expressed the hope that the wisdom of these traditional tales, which she perceives as endangered, might be preserved in trust for future generations. I have set the stories down in English, the language central to my own storytelling. This does not preclude future translations into Indian regional languages, and I hope this book might even stimulate collaborative collections elsewhere.

A Note to My Colleagues

Many of us who are trained as scholars end up writing just for other scholars. My choice to address a more general audience comes partly from the material: these folktales that Urmilaji tells will, I believe, bring pleasure to many kinds of readers. The choice to write accessibly also grows out of deep convictions. I think that scholars trained in academic disciplines would do well to dismantle the wall between vivid stories and intellectual conversations; between narrated insights we would share with friends and families and rigorous analyses we would address to fellow specialists. Yet, to integrate personal and professional modes of communication, one has to proceed cautiously, with a continual, critical interrogation of relevance.

Some personal experiences are clearly relevant to the professional situations we write about: we need to know who the scholar is to understand why they did or thought a particular way. But there are other personal experiences that don't really add insight to what is being described, and we may end up hogging attention to ourselves rather than sending it out to understand the people and issues about which we are trying to write. Similarly, some kinds of professional analyses are relevant to the human situations that we study; theories and methodologies can illuminate the particularities of lives and empower us to draw larger connections. But we have to be on guard against the impulse to carry on in long-winded displays of theoretical virtuosity and name dropping that can be just as narcissistic as disquisitions about ourselves.

All too often, I fear, the people we have sought to represent have ended up as a faceless mass of informants spouting materials for the researcher's professional gain. Acknowledging the impact—both personal and intellectual—of remarkable people met "in the field" more accurately conveys the source of scholarly insights than such distanced depiction. Ironically, moving beyond generalizations to a careful account of the individuals and conditions from which insights emerge can be dismissed as being too precisely empirical, even positivistic; alternately, it can be dismissed as overly partial and personal. Yet I believe that this is a necessary move in today's interconnected, inegalitarian world to grant the people who are the sources of our written works respect as mentors, interlocutors, collaborators, and even friends.

Struggling to find an appropriate form for this book, I started from my commitment to Urmilaji and drew on my training as an anthropologist, folklorist, scholar of South Asian studies, and writer of fiction. I find that I have written my way beyond the simple definition of a collection and into a hybrid genre.

With one person and her narratives at the center of the book, writing it has carried some of the rewards and pitfalls of the close collaboration between two people which has characterized the anthropological genre of life history. The subjects of life history have occasionally insisted to anthropologists that the wisdom of their elders—passed on through explicit instruction or didactic stories—are part of their lives. The folktales that Urmilaji tells are part of her life too, and sometimes they symbolically mirror lived situations with which she has had to contend. Foreseeing that personal and familial revelations might prove awkward if broadcast in printed form, Urmilaji has requested that I not disclose important aspects of her life story. While Urmilaji's tales point to the ways that wisdom crystallized through the course of a life may take the form of stories, this book really cannot be termed a life history.

Alternately, including myself as an active participant in this relationship might give the impression that it is a fieldwork memoir. Looking through these pages, I am reminded afresh of what my life was like in 1991: at home in India, yet in "the field" of anthropological research. I think of the trouble my mother was having with her knees; the excitement of batches of mail; the soaring pleasure of finding material relevant to my project; the nagging burden of unwritten fieldnotes, and untranscribed tapes; and the sad sense of being a failure brought on by all the endless questions about why I wasn't married. But this book is more about Urmilaji's stories than my own. Abiding by my own argument for relevance, I omit a good part of my experiences in Kangra which might have found their way into a more deliberately personal story.

Attempting to weave a larger story about life in Kangra around these folktales, I have written a narrative ethnography. In retrospect, I see that I must have been inspired by the model of past literary folktale collections in which a frame story links separate tales. This is not to say that I invented any of the events framing these tales; rather I tried to selectively structure what happened with a sense of rhythm, setting, character, and even suspense where possible. Including only what Urmilaji or I perceived as relevant to understanding the tales and the field situation in which they are set, this book does not aspire to be a full-blown ethnography of Kangra Valley.

The influence of A. K. Ramanujan—folklorist, poet, linguist, translator—has shaped the form and content of this book. In April 1991, soon after Urmilaji started telling me her stories, I left Kangra for a few weeks to attend conferences in the United States. A. K. Ramanujan was also present at a conference in Minneapolis. We had first met after he served as a reader for the press publishing my first book, and our connection remained suffused by a delight in Indian folktales. I was excited to report having met Urmilaji. Sitting in a hotel lobby, I spilled out the stories I had already heard from her. Raman listened carefully, and with his expert, quiet precision, he too told folktales that he was reminded of. "How many stories does this woman know?" Raman inquired. "Do you think you might put them together in a book?" Back in Kangra, when I asked Urmilaji the same question, she smiled to herself, covering her mouth with the end of her scarf. Later, we withdrew into an inner room where she spoke about the wisdom in these stories.

Raman was a generous mentor when I returned to Madison that fall. When I visited Chicago to seek his counsel, he always made time for lunch. One storyteller's repertoire, he assured, would make an unusual, interknit collection. He suggested that I organize Urmilaji's tales according to a model that he had used in his own translation projects: introduction, texts, afterword. He alerted me to themes in particular tales. Also, he stressed the value of a colloquial, aesthetic translation, advising that I steer away from the standard anthropological practice of liberally sprinkling a text with indigenous terms. Sadly Raman died in 1993. I never had the chance to offer him the written fruits of his kindness. I wish that he too could have held the volume that you now hold.

At first I thought I would dash off this book in a summer. After all, the stories had already been translated while I was still in Kangra and could ask for clarifications. I assumed that adding further context and relevant scholarship would be straightforward and quickly accomplished. But I had not factored in my aspirations to artistry. It was Raman who cautioned that a book one cared about could take a long time. Five years and multiple drafts later, I have had to acknowledge his wisdom.

As I finally prepare to send this book out into the world, I hope that a wide variety of people whose lives are separated from Urmilaji by space, time, or language will be able to share what I enjoyed: the serene pleasure of Urmilaji's company, the beauty and insights of her stories.

I also hope that the publication of this book and the resources that it generates will bring Urmilaji satisfaction. I have tried my best to consult her, to abide by her views and her wishes. For all the many shortcomings of this final text, I ask her forgiveness.

A Note On Transliteration

When I first got help in making transcriptions from Kangri (Pahari) to the Devanagari script, I learned fast there did not seem to be clear spelling conventions in Devanagari for this dialect. Sometimes, when I hired assistants to help me with the laborious process of transcribing tapes of songs, the way that words were pronounced would be corrected to follow Hindi spellings, while at other times, the distinctive hill accent—which to my ear seemed to slur or foreshorten familiar words—would be maintained. Furthermore, Kangri is an unstandardized dialect, so a speaker from one village would have a distinctive speech style than someone a few villages away. Similarly, English transliterations of the Kangri dialect I found in various books seemed to range between representing words as they are spoken, and as they might be recognized by the ear of a Hindi speaker.

On the whole I have opted to transliterate very few words. Where I have done so, I have striven for readability for the non-specialist reader. I have dropped the common ending "a" which is usually present in Sanskrit transliterations. So, for example, *dharm* rather than *dharma*. I use *ch* and the aspirated *chh* instead of the more common *c* and *ch*; *sh* for both *ṣ* and *ś*.

A should be pronounced as in "but"; *ā* as in "car"; *i* as in "lick" and *ī* as in leek; *u* as in "put" and *ū* as in "soon." A *t* is soft, as in "path" while *ṭ* is hard, like *pat*. In all cases, an *h* following a consonant means that it is aspirated. An *ṛ*, *ṇ* and *ḷ* involve a retroflex flap. For most words, an *n* at the end involves a nasal stress to the preceding vowel, rather than an outright voiced *n*.

ILLUSTRATIONS

1. Urmilaji telling stories among her relatives

2. Urmilaji and her sisters, Nirmalaji and Kamalaji, 1982

3. Kirin and Urmilaji sitting on the ledge beside her courtyard

4. The Dhauladhar range of the Northwest Himalayas

5. Working in the fields

6. Worshipping the pipal tree on a Monday on the Dark Night of the Moon

7. A pipal tree on a raised platform

8. Worshipping Saili indoors, at Urmilaji's neighbor's house

9. Worshipping the Berry Bush

10. Baby Krishna

11. The Bujru visiting on a Saturday

12. Urmilaji's extended natal family doing a ritual to honor the sun, 1988

13. Palanquins of a bride and groom being taken between villages

14. Kirin and Urmilaji, 1994

MONDAYS

on the

DARK NIGHT

of the

MOON

Urmilaji telling stories among her relatives
(Photo by Kirin Narayan)

"There's wisdom in these stories," observed Urmilaji in June 1991. Cross-legged on a burlap sack spread on the floor, she addressed me over a mound of her ram's white shearings. "These stories are about love," she said. "They are about deluded infatuation, possessive attachment, and nurturing affection."

Afternoon light slanted in through the open window. A hazy shimmer of summer heat illumined Urmilaji's face from one side, picking up the glint of gray at her temples, the gleam of the small gold stud in her left nostril. As she spoke, Urmilaji's hands continued to work through the shearings before her. Brows puckered with intensity, brown eyes fixed on mine, she added, "Television can't teach you these things! Wisdom is ebbing with every generation."

"*Ji*," I agreed, using the same term of respect that I appended to her name. I sat on the floor opposite her with my hands unoccupied. I had intended this to be a social visit after a brief trip abroad, so I hadn't brought along my notebook and tape recorder. Instead, I had asked Urmilaji if we might put together a book of the folktales she told. This had inspired her to reflect on the value of the stories.

Moha, deluded attraction; *mamatā*, possessive attachment; *prem*, nurturing affection: as Urmilaji listed these types of love, images from tales she had already told me flickered in my mind. A king besotted by a beautiful demoness; a mother anxious about her daughter's unmarried plight; a poverty-stricken sister sharing her meal with a mysterious visitor. Yes! I thought. Stories were ultimately about human ties, dramatizing cultural wisdom about how people live out their lives in relation with each other.

But perhaps because Urmilaji sometimes talked, hand pressed lightly over mine, about the affection growing between us, I also could see and feel that stories were not just *about* relationships; they also *made* relationships.

3

Linking up with Urmilaji

Urmilaji's brothers, who run a tea and provisions shop on the main road of the village, had been among the first people my mother and I encountered when we emerged, dusty and bewildered, off a bus for our first visit to this Kangra village in 1975. It was April, and the Dhauladhar mountains looming to the north were still dazzling with snow. We had come on the invitation of friends from Delhi who made this their summer base. As our bags were handed down from the roof of the bus, Urmilaji's brothers and a local schoolteacher greeted us and pointed out the cobbled path. I was fifteen: mortifyingly self-conscious, burdened with studying for the exams that loomed ahead. I had no thought then of writing about Kangra village life. Yet, many of the ties we made that summer later became entangled in my life as an anthropologist.

For example, through those summer months, we showed our allegiance to Urmilaji's brothers by always sitting on the wooden benches of their tea shop as we waited for buses, drinking their glasses of sweet tea. Also, we visited the schoolteacher, who had rented part of Urmilaji's house. I vaguely recall being introduced to Urmilaji and have an image of a slight woman with a scarf looped over her head and shoulders, small children tugging at her clothes. She joins her palms, shrinks back . . .

"You seemed like such big people," Urmilaji reminisced, taking my hand over fifteen years later. "I thought: what can we say to each other? I felt shy to speak." To her, my mother and I must have clearly been outsiders: people with the resources of city dwellers and with visible associations to foreign lands.

My mother, who is American, has lived in India since 1950. She met my father, who is Indian, at the University of Colorado at Boulder. Leaving her home in Taos, New Mexico, for my father's family home in Nasik, western India, family lore has it that my mother staunchly said, "If Margaret Mead can live in Samoa, I can live in a joint family." (It was she, I should add, who bought the anthropological paperbacks that later sat beside the sea-mildewed murder mysteries on our bathroom shelves in Bombay: *Patterns of Culture, The Children of Sanchez, Male and Female, Sex and Repression in Savage Society*.)

In 1978, several years after our first visit, my mother moved to a dilapidated adobe house on the hillside at one edge of Urmilaji's village. My father remained in Bombay. Like other houses nearby, this house which my mother rented was built on land that had once been part of an estate belonging to an Irish actress and admirer of Gandhi. The house had been named "The Mirage" by its own-ers. It had an overgrown garden that was a cool haven in the summer, yielding mangos, leechees, guavas, pears, plums, and persimmons. But it had no indoor toilet, no running water, damp foundations, and only two hours of direct sunshine in winter. (In the mid-1980s, my sister's in-laws, visiting from Pasadena, California, assured my mother that they were comfortable since they already had camping experience). Out the back gate was an open meadow with a spectacular view of the Dhauladhar range.

By 1990, when I came for a year's fieldwork, my mother had lived in Kangra twelve years. Throughout this time, she had kept up neighborly ties in the village. Urmilaji's extended family was among the many families whose rituals and feasts my mother regularly attended, sometimes taking along a camera (and so, setting the stage for my own appearance as anthropologist). She had also designed a solar cooker that could be made with bamboo, mud, rice husk, flattened tin cans, and a single, store-bought sheet of glass. This invention took her to many remote parts of the valley and made her a variety of friends.

During the same twelve years that my mother lived in the village, I attended college and graduate school in anthropology and then taught in the United States. I visited India almost every year, taking long train trips across the subcontinent to be with both my parents. In 1982, as a graduate student, I spent the summer in Kangra informally taping wedding songs from a range of my own and my mother's friends and acquaintances. To write my Ph.D. dissertation though, I turned to another set of family ties in Nasik, my father's hometown. Swamiji, a genial and garrulous holy man I had known since I was a child, regularly told stories to the people who came to him for counsel. I taped these stories, using them to reflect on the use of storytelling as a form of religious teaching. The book I wrote is called *Storytellers, Saints and Scoundrels.*[1]

When I finished writing that book, I was in search of a different project. Building on my earlier interest in wedding songs, I decided to return to Kangra for a full year of research. I received fellowships and was granted leave from my new job as Assistant Professor at the University of Wisconsin. Taking off for fieldwork, I arrived at my mother's home.

Now, it is hardly standard anthropological practice to go home to one's mother to do fieldwork! Anthropologists have traditionally set off for strange and distant places where they might live with a family or set up their own household. Though it has become increasingly acceptable for anthropologists to do research "at home,"[2] this is usually taken to mean the society that the anthropologist is from, rather than literally moving in with one's immediate family.

At first I planned to move out of my mother's house as soon as I found an appropriate local family with whom to live. My staying with my mother, I thought, would be viewed askance by my colleagues: What sort of confused anthropologist would mistake going to "the field" as retreating home? But I soon realized that moving out would make me lose credibility in Kangra: What sort of shameless, heartless unmarried daughter would choose to live apart from her mother? Torn between these conflicting identities, I gradually came up with a compromise: I would make my mother's home my base, while taking off for research forays that might range from several hours to several days.

This idea of setting jauntily off to talk to people was not as easy as it might seem. It would have been easier if the friends I had made through years of visiting the village hadn't all been married away: only one of them, Vidhya Sharma, had married close enough for an easy visit. Each time I bravely set out to rekindle rapport in households where I was slightly known, I felt awkward about barging in, uninvited and unannounced. Also, I felt lacerated by well-meaning interrogations, "Not married? When will you get married?" And then the asides, "How old is she? Whose age-mate did you say? Poor thing! And she's so weak and skinny...."

I started to experience myself through local eyes as a walking anomaly: a pathetic, thirty-year-old girl who had not followed the right course of marrying and who was so overeducated it seemed unlikely that she ever would. When I was with my friend Vidhya, she defended me, telling inquisitors that in America people regularly married late. When I was with my mother, she took the tack of reminding people that I was a professor and that in America I had a car. Somehow, mention of the car was very effective. I was never sure if this shut people up because it was such a bizarre response to questions about marriage or because it evoked images of such fabulous success that it established me as being beyond the bounds of regular village womanhood and its expectations.

Lacking the self-confidence to tell people that I would marry late, reluctant to boast that I had a car, I had to struggle with myself everyday to go out and be an anthropologist. My mother did her best to get me started. She fed me nourishing breakfasts and tantalized me with choice leads. Among the people she urged me to go talk to was Urmilaji.

Over the years, my mother had become friendly with Urmilaji's extended family who lived in the village. She had observed Urmilaji leading other women through songs at ritual gatherings. She had also once heard Urmilaji tell a beautiful folktale associated with Mondays that fall on the dark night of the moon. Knowing my passion for stories, my mother spoke with high praise of the "assurance and artistry" in Urmilaji's retelling. She said that the tale, which I just had to go out and reelicit, was like the best of the fairy tales we had once, long ago, read together.

But I hesitated. It wasn't that I didn't know who Urmilaji was: after all, she and her two sisters had taped two of the longest and loveliest songs the summer I had worked with wedding songs. A slide my mother had taken of them, standing around the sacred basil shrine at the center of Urmilaji's courtyard, had accompanied me to talks and class presentations through the years. I had seen Urmilaji at village events on my vacations when I cast my anthropological persona aside and was just a daughter visiting home. But I felt rebellious, even sulky, about trotting off on a research route that my mother had traced out for

Urmilaji and her sisters, Nirmalaji and Kamalaji, 1982
(*Photo by Didi Contractor*)

me. Who was supposed to be the anthropologist here? And anyway, I was supposed to be studying songs, not stories!

Through the fall of 1990, I concentrated my research on the songs that village women sang whenever they gathered together for ritual events. I became particularly interested in a genre of song called *pakharu* which tells stories about suffering in married life. I became a regular visitor at several households and even stopped by a few times at Urmilaji's house to visit her schoolteacher sister. It wasn't until March 1991 that I seriously followed up on my mother's suggestion that I get to know Urmilaji.

By this time, I felt more confident in my role as researcher and was more fluent in the Pahari dialect. I had learned by now that most women were flattered and amused to be consulted; my bursting in upon them with my notebook and tape recorder was not a dreadful imposition as I had feared. Old

7

ties of affection were being rekindled, especially in the households where I had been friends with the daughters now off in their husband's homes. Also, I had become more skilled at deflecting questions about my unmarried state. I now briskly informed anyone who asked me that, for the moment, astrological afflictions barred my marriage. This usually brought cross-examinations on the subject to a speedy, sympathetic halt.

One cool afternoon in March, on a day when I was feeling exceptionally outgoing, I stopped in at Urmilaji's courtyard on a walk between villages. Urmilaji sat outdoors, knitting. She was sitting cross-legged in a patch of sunshine, her freshly washed hair spread about her shoulders. Seeing me, she stood up in greeting. She was then in her mid-fifties, about five feet tall, almost ethereally slight and fine-boned. There was a gap in her mouth where her front teeth had once been. Her hair, which she usually wore pulled back in a braid, was graying around the temples. Like other Kangra women—and myself when I was visiting—she was wearing Punjabi dress: a loose, sleeved tunic (*kurtā*) down to her knees; baggy pants (*salwār*) tied with a drawstring around the waist and tapered inward at the ankles; and a long piece of gauzy material (*dupaṭṭā*) worn looped over the breasts, the shoulders, and often also the head. On her forehead, a tiny, red felt dot signified her status as a married woman.

At first Urmilaji was reticent. Her bashful, deferential manner only emphasized my own awkwardness. Trying to fill the difficult silences, I took the tack of disclosing myself rather than trying so hard to draw her out. I chattered bravely on about what I had been doing: the places I had gone, the people I had visited. She pricked up her ears when I said that I'd spent that morning in a nearby village visiting a Brahman priest and astrologer. I later learned that this charismatic man, with hooped gold earrings, a crown-like Kulu cap, and a booming laugh, was also her family priest. She wanted to know what we had talked about: I said our topic was women's rituals. Urmilaji asked what precisely had been said about which rituals. She listened with great interest, adding her own comments.

The next time I came by, I brought an offering that I thought might interest her: a sheaf of various song texts that I had transcribed into the Devanagari (Hindi) script. Urmilaji brought out her spectacles and read slowly. She mouthed or hummed the words of each song, offering commentaries and variants. She was especially intrigued by the songs she had never come across before, songs that I had taped from women of other castes in other villages. She pored over these songs with apparent suspense, wanting to know what happened to the characters described in them. Her original reticence seemed to be flooded over by wellsprings of warmth, interest, generosity, and humor.

In this way we began our friendship through a shared fascination with local songs and stories. Though fascination linked us as kindred spirits, there were also vast differences between us. Urmilaji had spent her entire life in Kangra

Kirin and Urmilaji sitting on the ledge beside her courtyard (*Photo by Nirmala Sood*)

villages. Born into the Sood trader caste as a middle child among nine children, she had received only a primary school education. She had been married off at fifteen and, after she turned twenty-five, had given birth to five children. Her life, as she said, had "passed in work": by this she meant domestic labor and service to the gods. Her time was at least partially structured by the daily, weekly, monthly, and annual rituals that would please assorted deities and contribute to the well-being of her family. In contrast, I was about twenty-five years younger. My Indian ancestry associated me with a different region of India and my background allied me with a Westernized, urbanized class; my American ancestry made me foreign. Education had been of central importance in my upbringing, carrying me toward professional life in the United States (which Urmilaji confused with England and "German"). While I too could look back on my life and see it in terms of unrelenting work, this was mostly of the scholarly sort. My time had long been structured around the rituals of classrooms, semesters, conferences, and publication deadlines. At first, it seemed very hard to explain to each other what our lives were about.

After a few visits, I ventured a request for the story my mother had described. This is where the first chapter of this book begins. I had expected just one story, but Urmilaji went on to tell five more that afternoon, stopping only because it was time to prepare the evening meal. As we parted, she invited me to come back again, promising more.

9

It so came to pass that Urmilaji and I ended up sharing each other's company through many afternoons in 1991. We sat in the courtyard, enjoying the sun, when there was a glimmer of cold to the spring; indoors, cross-legged on a double bed, when the heat descended in a haze of sun and sweat; on the floor beside an open door when rain splattered from the eaves. Sometimes, members of her extended family sat in for a story or part of a story. Around us, the world heaved. Prices for market-bought goods soared dizzyingly at the local shops. Heated enmities between supporters of the Congress party and the Bharatiya Janata party made for ongoing tensions in village life. Rajiv Gandhi was assassinated, train passengers were slaughtered in Punjab just before the national elections, Narasimha Rao came into office along with pledges to liberalize the economy. The rupee was devalued on the international market, local prices shot up yet again. The Gulf War ended, oil fields burned, Kurds were stranded in muddy fields. Cholera raged in Latin America, violence in the West Bank dragged on. Yugoslavia shattered into the beginnings of a ghastly war. Listening to the BBC with my mother on the mornings when I was at home that year, I felt tense, filled with foreboding about all that was happening in the world. Yet Urmilaji, in her stories, seemed to spin an imaginative space in which dire events became threaded together by golden filaments of fate, justice, and order.

The Lived Setting of the Stories

Imagine the Indian subcontinent as a robed figure with outstretched arms, hovering above Sri Lanka. Kangra would then be roughly around this figure's right neck, beside Punjab and fairly close to what is now Pakistan. (Before Partition in 1947, Kangra served as a hill station for Lahore.) Lying at the foot of the massive Dhauladhar—"white-bearing" mountains—Kangra is a hilly green expanse of terraced fields, settlements, and forests. Culturally, Kangra mixes features shared with the North Indian plains with others from the higher Himalayas. Though various aspects of Kangra life have been described by other ethnographers,[3] and there are a few collections of Kangra's folktales in Indian regional languages,[4] to my knowledge this book is the first English publication of folktales collected exclusively in this region.[5]

Today, a visitor can fly to Kangra in an unpressurized, sixteen-seat propeller plane from Delhi. Heading north across the north Indian plains, one crosses the wooded Sivalik hills to behold the Dhauladhar mountains, first among the range upon range of Himalayas stretching north. These mountains rise from the valley floor, at roughly 3,500 feet, clear up to 15,000 to 18,000 feet. In other parts of the Himalayas, peaks are often crowded together or ascend more gradually from the foothills: the mountain vistas from Kangra are of an unusual stark grandeur. Stretched across the northeastern horizon, these mountains preside, grand and

The Dhauladhar range of the Northwest Himalayas (*Photo by Eytan Bercovitch*)

stately, over life in the valley below. Looking down from them, the valley is a swirl of terraced fields—in dry seasons, like grained brown wood; in wet seasons, a mosaic of greens.

Most people unsupported by foreign exchange cannot afford to fly into Kangra. Instead they take the narrow gauge train up from Pathankot junction in Punjab or they cram into one of the buses that lurch along the mountain roads. As the air thins, cools, and sweetens, the roads grow less packed. Flat-roofed, cement architecture gives way to houses of mud and slate, glimpsed across fields or through clusters of bamboo. Yet, since the mid-1980s these mud houses increasingly bear television antennae; furthermore, many of the houses made of local materials are being abandoned in favor of Western-style buildings of prestigious, expensive cement. Upon each of my visits, the landscape has been more visibly crowded with houses of cement.

External influences are not new to Kangra. Like most places, this valley too has a long history of interaction with the outside world through trade, pilgrimages, and political change. Rajput Katoch kings once governed Kangra as a hill state, but these rulers were brought under Mughal rule in the mid-sixteenth century, submitted to Sikh domination in 1809, and amid struggle became part of the British colonial state in 1846. Kangra remained an administrative district of Punjab under British rule and for almost two decades following Indian Independence in 1947. When post-independence Indian states were rearranged

11

on the basis of language, Kangra's local dialect—evaluated in colonial linguistic surveys as *Kāngṛī bolī*, a subdialect of Dogri, "intermediate between standard Panjabi and the Pahari of the lower Himalaya"[6]—was politically construed in favor of a hill, rather than plains, identity. In 1966, Kangra merged with the adjacent northern hill state of Himachal Pradesh.

A mix of different kinds of people was apparent in the village where Urmilaji and my mother lived. According to the 1991 census, the village was composed of 790 people living in 168 households. Though these were mostly locally born Hindus (some tracing distant ancestry to other regions of India), there were also a few Hindu and Sikh families who had settled in the last few decades. There was one Gujar Muslim family, annual migratory visits from nomadic Gaddi herdsmen with their sheep, occasional visits from Tibetan nuns, and the enduring presence of an Irish woman who had granted her land for use by artists (some of whom became local residents, others of whom came from cities in the summer months).

Kangra's population—over a million according to the 1991 census—is largely Hindu. Though Hindi is the official vehicle of state business, the mother tongue of these Hindus is locally termed *Pahāri* (*pahāṛ* means mountain, which evokes a wider mountain-based identity), or more precisely *Kāngṛī* ("of Kangra," to distinguish the dialect spoken here from the many other mountain dialects). Many of the local people who now speak the same language can point to genealogical roots in other regions of India such as Kashmir, Punjab, or Rajasthan. Urmilaji's Sood caste—also written as "Sud"—is one of merchants, clerks, and money-lenders, and is headquartered in the Punjab plains.[7] Soods are part of a larger subdivision of Vaishya traders. Strict Brahmanical *varna* theory, ranking castes into a fourfold hierarchy, would place Soods below local Brahmans and Rajputs, but above agricultural and service castes. However, Brahmans, Rajputs, and Vaishya castes were generally grouped together on account of being "twice born" or "clean" castes. In the local negotiation of status, I found that Soods were respected for a pure, ritually observant lifestyle, even as local folklore characterized the men as shrewd and avaricious "*kaṛāṛ*" traders.[8] Yet, like other castes in the area, Soods were influenced by the dominant caste of Rajputs, whose ethic of honor pervaded the regional culture.

Among the friends I'd grown up with in Bombay—middle-class, elite, secularized, Westernized, city children—caste seemed unimportant. To this day, I am not sure of the caste of my closest friends from childhood. It was something of a shock when I first visited Kangra to see how central caste was to local identities and interactions.[9] Caste identity is determined by birth. It goes on to structure allegiance in village factions, the kinds of rituals one performs, the sort of people one can eat with, and above all the choice of a mate in an arranged marriage. (Caste influences but no longer codes male professions.) I found that people regularly referred to each other in terms of caste. In Urmilaji's village, for example, there were at least two other in-marrying women with the name Urmila: one a Rana Rajput and another of the Turkhan or carpenter caste. While these women were directly addressed by kinship terms, behind their backs they were kept distinct by references to caste or the name of their husband. "Urmila the trader," "The Rana Urmila, Rajinder's wife," "That carpenter Changa's Urmila," and so on. In Urmilaji's stories too, the caste of the characters is often used as an identifying marker: the Merchant, the Oilpresser woman, the Brahman, the Sweeper, and so on.

Despite the efforts of post-Independence India to eradicate caste divisions, these clearly persist, structured into many people's consciousness and their visions of the social world. This was powerfully dramatized when I was beginning fieldwork in the fall of 1990. The Prime Minister, V. P. Singh, announced the decision to implement further affirmative action in government jobs based on the findings of the Mandal Commission. Kangra—as much of the rest of India—was rocked with widespread violence protesting the decision: for days buses did not run, markets and town-based schools were closed. High-caste households I visited were filled with indignation over what was perceived as sons' thwarted futures; lower-caste households I visited were somber and anxious about violence that could turn their way. In Kangra, the turbulence died down within a month or so: life seemed serene once more, but with a wariness beneath the surface.

Amid these emotionally and politically charged caste distinctions, I found that women sometimes jokingly referred to "the woman's caste" (*janāsān dī jātī*) or the "brotherhood of women" (*janāsān dī birādarī*). "Don't ask me what party I'm for," I heard an upper-caste Rajput woman say after V. P. Singh was forced to step down and elections were being held. "I'm a mother. I'm against every government that makes prices high. All I want is for prices to go down and to have enough food for my family." She also talked about how, at the hospital where she had given birth, she had befriended a low-caste woman who had also come to deliver. "We were both women, after all," she said. To some extent, then, despite caste differences, women see each other in terms of their common experience: expected deference to male relatives, the transition of marriage, childbearing, and the care of children. Once, at Urmilaji's sister's house, the family priest was holding forth about various life cycle rituals for "twiceborn" upper castes. A woman whose name I never learned spoke out: "What you're saying is for men. For women, there is only one rite-of-passage—marriage—and that, too, it's one full of sorrow!"

Across castes, marriage for women is seen not as a choice but as a necessary, natural destiny. Urmilaji once commented, "A girl is goods that belong to her husband's family, not to her parents." Women are almost always subject to marriages arranged by their elder relatives and so have little control over the choice of a partner. Also, because of the principle of village exogamy—marrying out—women are routinely married into families far from the home of their birth. (Urmilaji was the one woman I knew who was married into the same village, with her parents' home just up the road—she explained that this was partly because she had grown up outside the village, at the tea gardens where her father was employed, and partly because of the intervention of her husband's saintly aunt.) Due to caste hypergamy—women's marrying up—increasingly practiced in Kangra, in-marrying women mostly come from families of slightly lower social standing, compounding their inferiority as daughters-in-law within a joint family.

It is no surprise that a newlywed bride would find moving in with a husband's extended family and joining a household of strangers to be difficult and disorienting. Many of the women's tales that Urmilaji told featured newly married daughters-in-law. The sorrows of married life in a joint family were also richly described in the women's songs I was researching. In the stories and songs, many characters were identified not by name but by kinship: the mother (*māu*), the father-in-law (*sauhrā*), the brother (*bhāī*), the daughter-in-law (*nū*), and so on.

In everyday life too, people often addressed each other in fictional kinship terms. In fact, there was a taboo on speaking the name of elders. Introductions were often not made at all or were phrased in terms of kinship. This meant that I found it difficult to learn the names of the older women I met. I would hear them referred to as "sister," "aunty," and so on to their faces and in their absence as "so and so's wife" or "so and so's mother." Sometimes I would know a woman for a long time before I felt comfortable enough to elicit her name; having a notebook in which to solemnly write this down helped me overcome the breach in etiquette, but I still was occasionally reprimanded by others looking on: "Didn't you know, Kirin, that among us we never take the names of elders? It's a matter of modesty and respect!"

Within and between castes, and even within and between families, there are growing class discrepancies in Kangra. Yet the polarity between the garishly rich and the starving poor that one can see elsewhere in India, particularly in cities, is not visible here. If anything, there is a labor shortage from the long-term trend of men seeking work in the plains. Even landless laborers can usually be assured employment in others' fields and it is unusual to see families that are visibly malnourished. Within my mother's village, I observed an informal system by which people looked out for members of their own caste, helping them find ways to earn. In Kangra towns, I noticed that the most economically marginal people were invariably recent migrants: Rajasthani peasants displaced by drought and now living in tents beside the construction sites at which they worked, orphans from Bihar serving food in hotels, lepers from Karnataka seeking alms by the roadside, and so on.

Most Kangra village families are involved one way or another with farming:

Working in the fields. (*Photo by Rahoul Contractor*)

as owners of land, as laborers in their own fields, or as laborers in others' fields. The most common crops are rice and maize in the summer/monsoon and wheat in the winter. In addition, most families have vegetable gardens. But nobody lives off the land alone; everyone has ties with the market economy. A crucial part of most families' income hinges on remittances from men working elsewhere. Limited land resources coupled with a burgeoning population has accentuated the old pattern of men's migration in search of work. Following the British policy of recruiting men from hill states for the army, many Kangra men continue to join or try to join the Indian Army. Other men find other sources of employment: for example, as I was growing up in Bombay, my best friend's servant was from Kangra, as was my father's favorite taxi driver.

This is also limited local employment. Among traders of Urmilaji's caste, many men own shops. Though they might travel, they mostly live at home. Teaching is another favored occupation that can allow people to live at home, even though there is a perpetual threat of being transferred far away. Many men retired from the armed forces early bringing a pension with them, to join the government schools as teachers. Teaching has also been a respectable profession for educated women for several decades: Urmilaji's sister Nirmalaji, for example, is a schoolteacher.

In the last ten years, women have begun to take up jobs in banks, post offices, and law offices. Paid employment is locally termed "service" and women who do such work are called "service *walis*." To my dismay, I observed that women who worked outside the home were often a source of tension in joint families. Other women in the joint family could be resentful that the wage-earning women were gone all day, had more prosperous lives, and did not do the same amount of housework. Unable to spend leisurely time with other women for events like songfests or ritual gatherings, these women also faced charges of being snobbish.

Urmilaji sometimes reflected on the many changes that had come to Kangra in the five decades since she was born. She recalled the days when there were few roads connected by bus, no water taps, no electricity. She reminisced about how women used to wear a heavy skirt (*ghaghru*) over baggy *salwār* pants and plait their hair in a myriad of tightly bound braids (*mindīyān*). She reported that when she was growing up, each child among her eight siblings had only two sets of clothes. Laughing, she described the days when men came back from their shops for lunch and the daughters-in-law from a cluster of related households would take off for the village well to draw cold, fresh water. She spoke of how Gaddi tribespeople, related through loose ties of exchange with houses in the village, used to come through and stay during their yearly migrations with their flocks. She told of the days before land reform when lower-caste people were bound as laborers to upper-caste households. "I'll tell you openly," she once said. "I won't hide things. Our caste was one of moneylenders. Poor people became like slaves. They could not break away."

Electricity came in the 1960s and more roads and water taps in the 1970s. But the most drastic change of all in terms of folk traditions was the arrival of television in most villages by the mid-to late-1980s. Again and again, storytellers shook their heads, saying that since television had arrived, folktales were on the wane. As Urmilaji said, "In the past, there was so much storytelling! The children would sit down together wheedling, 'Te-e-ell a story, te-e-ell a story, te-e-ell a story.' Now we can't find the time to do it. These days, after we've eaten dinner we come in and the television is going, the drama is on!" Shaking her head with a laugh, she said, "The pictures play, that's all."

Kangra's increasing integration into the Indian nation-state also means that school education emphasizes Hindi for formal interchanges, while the regional dialect is confined to domestic contexts. Such changes can also lead to a devaluing of local tales, since any knowledge purveyed in Hindi is seen to have greater prestige than knowledge phrased in the Pahari dialect. Urmilaji's own polyester-clad and literate sons could not repress their amusement that I was so earnestly documenting these "old stories." When I reappeared with typewritten pages in English, though—a language seen as associated with bureaucratic and cosmopolitan clout—her sons read them haltingly aloud, appearing to be impressed. Yet, however prestige-laden the language in which an anthropologist writes may be, it remains unnerving when the people one describes review one's work. Reading a description of Urmilaji's missing front teeth, her eldest, Raju, looked up to inquire, "So you'll make our mother famous in America without her teeth?" (In subsequent years, Raju has arranged for Urmilaji to be outfitted with dentures that make for smiles of dazzling resplendence).

Storytelling in Kangra

The folktales that Urmilaji told were at once hers and not hers: she associated them with the people from whom she had learned them and the rituals that they accompanied. I, in turn, found that other people in Kangra—particularly those who had not received extensive formal education—told variants of many of the same stories. Back amid libraries, I gained a sense of the wider geographical distribution of the tales by looking through other Indian folktale collections, as well as folklorists' classification tools of tale type and motif indexes.[10]

As I have already indicated, Urmilaji divided the stories she told into two categories: tales told to accompany high-caste women's rituals for family well-being,[11] and tales told by men and women in any setting, particularly winter evenings. She subsumed both these kinds of stories within the word *kathā*,[12] which I am loosely translating as "folktale." The ritual stories tend to be explicitly didactic, laying out templates for female virtue and devotion. To some readers they may be less enjoyable than the winter's tales, which are generally more akin to fairy tales, stories of adventures full of strange marvels.[13]

Throughout India, observant Hindu women are thought to sustain familial well-being through their rituals (called *vrat, nompi,* or *nonpu*). The rituals involve a gathering that often extends beyond the joint family to women of related castes.[14] The stories (*vrat kathā*) that are told as part of the rituals usually make reflexive mention of the ritual and its rewards.

Mostly, it is upper-caste women who perform such rituals. In Kangra it was women of Brahman, Sood, and high-ranking Rajput families—those that had traditionally observed women's segregation—who were most steeped in women's rituals and so had the most elaborate ritual storytelling traditions. Women of lower castes who did not perform the rituals did not know the stories. So, while it is tempting to see Urmilaji's stories that are associated with women's rituals as representing a "Kangra women's point of view," I must emphasize that they are specifically upper-caste women's traditions.

All such women's rituals, Urmilaji explained, could be reduced to two aims: a long and auspicious married life (*suhāg*) and the long life of one's relatives (*lammī āyu*). Performed collectively, the rituals seemed to join women across stereotypically hostile kinship roles, across squabbling branches of extended families, and across the outlooks and values of different generations. Depending on the ritual, it might be performed weekly, monthly, yearly, or according to an irregular pattern. At some point, a woman might perform a grand, expensive finale (in Kangri *maukh*, in Hindi *udhyāpan*) for her performance of a particular ritual. She might then stop performing the complete ritual in her own home, but would continue to join other women to worship in their homes. Since the gatherings involved telling and listening to the appropriate stories, this meant that a woman who no longer performed a ritual in her own home could still circulate to "give" the right story.

Respected female elders were usually turned to for ritual stories. This meant that a younger woman who also knew ritual stories would usually defer to her elders. Only in rare cases, when the elders present knew that a younger woman was a particularly gifted storyteller, would she be urged to tell a story. Among the older women, ritual storytelling could involve tense status negotiations. On one occasion, when the senior member of one household began a story but was interrupted halfway through by the senior member of the neighboring household, I observed outrage among the daughters-in-law of the first storyteller; they later took me aside to insist that the second storyteller's rendition was all wrong and I should consider erasing the tape.

The stories, told year after year, were also part of women's lives. I found that the stories were retold outside demarcated ritual contexts, particularly to instruct and entertain children. The first time I heard the stories associated with the Five Days of Fasting, for example, was just before bedtime when I was spending the night with a family. The grandmother of the household was begged for stories by her young granddaughters. Urmilaji also first told me all her ritual tales outside the ritual context, and it was only a few years later, in 1994, that I had a chance to hear her retell some of the stories in association with ritual.

I have now taped variants of Urmilaji's ritual tales from twenty other upper-caste female tellers of assorted ages, from different villages, and with different performative styles. There are also other ritual stories which Urmilaji does not tell.[15] The corpus of stories associated with the Five Days of Fasting is especially popular in Kangra. Three men, all Brahman ritual specialists, learned of my interest and also retold variants of a few of the women's ritual tales. Trying to tell the women's stories, two of the male tellers got the plots and characters hopelessly garbled, to the stifled amusement of women listening in. Though the men were experts on some Brahmanical ritual, it was women who were the authorities on women's rituals and associated stories.

If the stories accompanying women's rituals were widely known, carried forward each time rituals were performed, the stories that both men and women told seemed rarer. I did not encounter variants of any of these tales from the lips of other storytellers. Urmilaji had mostly learned the other sorts of stories from her father. Some she learned from a female neighbor at the tea garden where her father had been employed when she was a child. I have since encountered six other tellers (three male, three female) of elaborate stories associated with winter evenings. Yet there was no overlap between the repertoires of any of the storytellers.

As teller upon teller recalled, before the advent of radio and television in Kangra the main forum for transmitting nonritual tales was around a fire on winter evenings. A popular proverb ran:

kanakā bāiyān	When wheat is sowed
tā kathā aiyān	then stories come,
kanakā nisariyān	When wheat grains form
tā kathā bisariyān	then stories are done.[16]

Urmilaji and her sister Nirmalaji explained that, unlike the monsoon crops of rice and corn, which required constant tending, wheat grew of its own accord and so people could rest and tell stories from the time the wheat was planted in the furrows of the fields in November until the time the harvest came, in April or May. Also, with the nights falling chill and early, people had more time together, huddled around a source of warmth.

Another saying associated with stories goes like this:

kathā kathākaṛī	The stories are finished
nav gīdhaṛ gae panāparī	Nine jackals went to Panapari.
tinhānde liṇḍ pai aḷī aḷī	Their tails got shriveled and dried
[jo bole] khāde talī talī	[Whoever you name] eats these fried!

This used to be said to young children, said Urmilaji, when they wouldn't stop pestering you for stories. The child's name was inserted as the eater of the fried jackal tails. "No one is going to eat jackal tails!" Urmilaji assured me, lest I mistake this as ethnographic fact. Panapari is a village where many jackals live in the surrounding areas, making mournful howls at night.

In the Kangri dialect, to tell a story is to "give" it (*kathā denī*). During rituals, women might ask an experienced teller like Urmilaji to give them the right stories. I came across no opening formulas, though most stories had variations of the introductory statement "There was a . . ." (merchant, Brahman, king, old woman, and so on). But there were a few ending formulas, most marking a return from involvement with characters in story worlds back to the here and now of listeners' lives.[17] These formulas included:

sai tithu kanne ahān ithu
They are there and we are here

sai rahe tithu raste baste kanne ahān chale āye
They've remained there, settled and flourishing, and we've returned here.

19

ahan apne ghare jo chale āye kanne sai tithu rah giyā
We've returned to our own home and they've remained there.

Urmilaji acknowledged these other tellers' ending formulas but said that she herself finished a tale with a gesture: "a gentle bow of the head" (*dhol mathā thekhnā*). I observed that she often ended her stories by saying, "That's it" (*bas*) or "Finished" (*hoi giyā*). In the setting of an actual ritual, she often ended a ritual tale with the exclamation "Victory [to God]" (*jai ho*) or something more specific to the tale such as "Oh Goddess Berry Bush, just as she found fulfillment, so may it be for a-a-all of us!" (*barairiye paramesvariye jīyān tinhānde santript hoi tiyān sa-aa-aariyā hoiyān*).

Different tellers had different performance styles. Urmilaji's own manner was exceptionally measured and soft-spoken. Though she sometimes shifted the pitch and tempo of her voice to portray characters or generate suspense, she rarely used gestures beyond the light flick of a hand. She often punctuated episodes by declaring "*Bas*": "That's it." Sometimes she was tentative, saying that something had probably happened in a particular way, so extending the sense that her stories had a reality larger than her knowledge of them. Sitting cross-legged, scarf looped over her head, she would often hold the microphone as she spoke, brown eyes locked to mine. I nodded, affirmed, checked the tape recorder's functioning, and occasionally interrupted for clarification.

Urmilaji is the teller I know best and with whom I felt most comfortable discussing interpretations. Certainly, my very presence and my questions elicited her commentaries. But she also seemed to be a person with her own reflective bent, closely scrutinizing and finding connections between aspects of traditional wisdom. She issued the most detailed exegeses of meanings for women's tales associated with rituals. Such stories, after all, are an explicit forum for transmitting ethical values and have rich reflexive resonances with the symbols employed in the ritual: it is no wonder that for Urmilaji, explicating these texts was a familiar cultural practice. Indeed, talking with other women, I found that they made very similar comments on the same tales. Urmilaji's interpretations, then, appeared to be set within a wider shared horizon of expected meaning.

For the winter's tales told by both men and women, however, my questions invariably led Urmilaji to retell the tale. The meaning, she seemed to say, was in the act of telling, not in standing outside of the text to comment on it. Such retellings were valuable to me, for she often elaborated sequences slightly differently, deepening my understanding of how Urmilaji perceived the plot as being driven. Occasionally she issued morals like "stepmothers shouldn't be like this." On the whole, though, this second set of tales, used mostly for entertainment, simply did not seem to be locally subject to the same sort of explicit reflection.

Stories Connecting People

For Urmilaji, telling stories seemed to rekindle memories of the people from whom she had learned them. Tears often welled up in her eyes as she spoke of the two storytellers most influential to her: her father and her aunt-in-law. It was as though, for her, the stories were valuable partly because they were pervaded with the presence of the two people death had taken away.

When Urmilaji gave me the stories, she was as an older woman educating me. Accepting the stories, I too have become linked to this chain of oral transmission and concern. On a recent visit, Urmilaji informed her relatives with visible satisfaction that these stories now appeared to be "stored in my stomach" (*peṭech pai giyā*); that is, they had become part of me. If the stories are part of me, that means, I think, that Urmilaji herself, and the impressions of past tellers, are in me too.

These twenty-one folktales encompass Urmilaji's repertoire of stories as it stood in 1991. Yet a teller's repertoire is neither static nor fixed; it exists in interaction with, and is kept in trust by, others. Indeed, it was often the prompting of Urmilaji's family members that reminded her of tales she had not yet shared with me. For example, when her son Raju mentioned a barber who finds a desolate forest where a palace had stood hours earlier, Urmilaji was inspired to retell this tale and several related ones. When her visiting sister Kamlaji hummed a verse about an astrologer from Kashi, Urmilaji retrieved from memory her father's tale in which childless cowives connive against the wife who bears a son. When her married daughter Rama mentioned a girl whose wicked stepmother transformed her into a singing bird, Urmilaji launched into a retelling of that story. It was clear, then, that Urmilaji's siblings and children recognized and remembered these tales as passive bearers[18] even if they no longer seemed actively interested in listening to them retold.

I wanted Urmilaji to approve what I had written about her, and so I read earlier drafts of this introduction and afterword to her, retranslating from the English. Her comment when I read this last paragraph aloud was, "It's not that they've altogether lost interest! It's a question of time." Using the English word "time," she continued, "There's no time these days. Children go to school and do homework in the evenings. People with jobs are gone from morning to night. And parents too, they want their children to read books rather than listen to stories—after all, there is such an expense in education. Everyone is constantly busy. When are they going to ask for stories? They have no time for worship, for getting wisdom through stories. Whatever time is left over, you know, it's all spent before the TV."

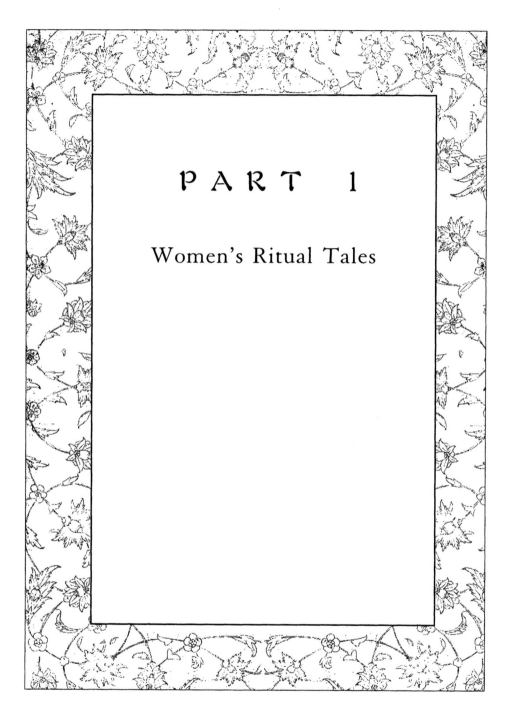

PART 1

Women's Ritual Tales

Mondays on the Dark Night of the Moon

Savāriyo amavans is a Pahari rendition of *somāvati amāvās*—*somāvati* from Monday (*somvār*) and *amāvās* for the last day of the waning half of a lunar fortnight, when the moon does not light the sky. Such a dark night occurs once every lunar month, but it rarely falls on a Monday. When it does, upper-caste Kangra women worship the pipal tree (*varh*). The worship is usually performed in the morning. Women begin by offering water to the tree—twelve brass pots for the welfare of every male member of the family and six pots for every female, including oneself. This water is first made into sacred Ganges water (*gangā jal*) by sprinkling into it a few drops of actual Ganges water (which is routinely kept in households) as well as a little milk.

Next, the tree is worshipped with offerings of frankincense, vermillion, flowers, scraps of yellow cloth, fried flour balls, and handfuls of unhusked barley (again, twelve handfuls each for a family's males, six for females). Women also tie a white thread around the circumference of the tree's broad trunk. This thread is called a *janeu*, like the sacred thread worn by high-caste men. In other words, the tree is symbolically male.

At the base of the tree the women place a dough figurine of Sunna the Washerwoman. She is offered such tokens of a married woman as red bangles, red hair ribbon, and scraps of red cloth. Women then circumambulate the tree 108 times. When they finish, they sit together on the raised platform around the base of the tree and ask a senior story-telling woman to tell the appropriate story.

25

Worshipping the pipal tree on a Monday on the Dark
Night of the Moon (*Photo by Brigitte Luchesi*)

ONE

Across the Seven Seas

The March weather could not make up its mind. Clouds massed, dark and dramatic, around the snowfields and glaciers on the mountains to the northeast. But sunshine kept breaking through from the west, bringing out the brilliance of young green in the fields. Fruit trees fluttered, delicate ensembles of white and pink as the wind rose. My visitor, a sprightly older woman from another village, who that morning had appeared unannounced, looked out at the sky. She decided that she had better take the afternoon bus home. Since Urmilaji's house was near the village crossroads where the bus stopped, I tucked an umbrella into my bag and told my visitor that I would walk partway with her.

Chatting, we set out together. We passed terraces of wheat, water springs under concrete canopies, a young pipal tree growing from a raised stand. We passed tawny adobe houses with slanted slate roofs and newer, gray cement houses. We must also have passed some of the people who were usually out at that time of day: the long-faced postman, groups of children returning in navy and white uniforms from the village school, the hunched man from the electric husking mill. Cars, buses, and trucks rarely came along this byway, which was unpaved in portions and eventually crossed a stream. When we reached the worn cobbled stones of the main village settlement, my visitor proceeded straight toward the intersection with the main tarred road, where tea shops clustered, their benches filled with passengers awaiting buses. I turned off on a path to the right.

Over the last two weeks I had occasionally dropped in to see Urmilaji on my rounds between villages. Today, I hoped that she might tell the story my mother had urged me to record. The last time I had visited, when I suggested this taping, Urmilaji had smiled, her lips pressed together. "Come back sometime," she had said.

The whitewashed exterior adobe wall of Urmilaji's home stretched beside the path as I walked. A raised stone ledge ran along the base of this outer wall.

I turned in at the house's main entrance. Two stories tall and as deep as the rooms inside, the entranceway opened out into a courtyard.

This house had been built after the Kangra earthquake of 1905 leveled the earlier structure. Three wings of rooms formed a U around the courtyard: the entranceway I had just come through would be at the right hand base of that U. There were knee-high stone ledges all along the sides of the house and steps leading up to the doors. Some of the wooden doors were intricately carved. Delicate arched moldings were traced on the whitewashed walls. The courtyard itself was plastered smooth with cow dung and festooned with lines of drying clothes. At the center, a waist-high, square, stone stand held a growing green plant. This was Saili, the sacred basil goddess, who is cultivated and worshipped in most upper-caste Kangra households.

Urmilaji had been out grazing her ram. Her return from the other side of the courtyard, wrapped in a shawl and leading the ram, coincided with my arrival. When we saw one another, we each joined our own palms saluting, "*Namaste jī.*"

Urmilaji disappeared for a moment to tether the ram in a back storeroom. She then ushered me into the formal sitting room in the apartments of her schoolteacher sister Nirmalaji. (Due to a son's health problems, Nirmalaji had relocated for several weeks to the nearby town). I had been in this room before, visiting Nirmalaji. The walls were painted a bright, aquamarine blue. The bed on which I sat was covered by a spread with a leopard-skin pattern. To my right was a tall steel cupboard; to my left, a television set. Aluminum chairs lined the opposite wall. Framed family snapshots, assorted plastic bric-a-brac, and a dangling string of greeting cards decorated the room. Drawn low on the wall by the door were ritual drawings in red ink which commemorated male birthdays.

When Urmilaji sat down beside me, cross-legged on the bed, we confronted each other awkwardly. Within a few weeks I was to fly to the United States for several conferences. I had already learned that one of the ways to overcome our mutual shyness was by telling her about my work. Trying my best to express myself, I told her my idea for a paper I was planning to deliver on Kangra women's songs. Urmilaji listened closely and courteously. Speaking rapid-fire Pahari, she suggested choice songs I might use.

After a while, I reminded Urmilaji about the story my mother had said I should tape: the one about Mondays that fall on the dark night of the moon.

"You want to hear *that* story?" she asked, as though bemused and not entirely convinced I would be interested.

"I do."

"Alright."

With a faint nod of the head, Urmilaji began to speak, her eyes on my face as I bent toward her, extending the microphone.

28

❋ ❋ ❋

There was a Brahman man. There was a Brahmani, his wife. She had five sons and one daughter. She herself, poor thing, was probably a widow. Actually, I haven't heard anything about her husband; I haven't heard about the father of the daughter. Anyway, this Brahmani had five sons and one daughter. *Bas.*

A Sadhu once came by the house to ask for alms. The old woman told her daughters-in-law, "Go give him alms and bow before him."

All the daughters-in-law went out to the holy man. One stepped up, she touched his feet, and he said, "May you be an auspicious married woman." The second went before him, and he said to her, too, "May you be an auspicious married woman." He said the same to the third, fourth, and fifth daughters-in-law.

Then the mother sent her daughter out. All that the holy man said to her was, "Blessings."

The old woman asked, "If you gave each of my five daughters-in-law the boon of a long married life, why did you only bless my daughter?"

He said, "Mother, she's not going to have a married life."

When the mother heard that her daughter would never be a married woman, she felt pain. Now, what could she do? Very distressed, she said, "If you're in a position to know that she won't have a married life, then you should be able to find a way out of this too. Tell us what to do."

He said, "Well, there is a remedy, but it's a very difficult one."

She said [*indignantly*], "Go ahead and say what it is! If it's possible to do, I'll do it: this is my one and only daughter."

He said, "Across the seven seas, there lives a washerwoman called Sunna. She's the one who can set this right. She has the water of immortality that revives life. This will revive the girl's husband's life: this and nothing else."

The old woman, poor thing, was beside herself with worry. Her sons began to ask her what was wrong. The first asked, the second asked, the third asked, the fourth asked. They all said [*muttering*], "We can't do anything about it, we don't have the time."

The fifth son said [*in a fresh, enthusiastic voice*], "Fine, brothers, I'll make the trip there and back."

So both the brother and sister got up and started off. The mother sent them off together, saying, "Go cross the seas!"

They walked as far as the sea. But how could they cross over? There was a big tree there, and they settled down to sleep beneath it. The brother fell asleep at once, but for some time the sister, poor thing, was unable to sleep. She stayed awake.

In that pipal tree there lived some geese:[1] a male and female, for geese are always in pairs. They had gone off, leaving their children in the tree under which the brother and sister lay.

That night, a black snake slithered out from the fields nearby. He climbed up the tree. And the gosling children began to twitter: "Chan chan chan chan!" He was all set to eat them up.

That's it. The girl woke up her brother. She said, "These children are all agitated because a snake is about to eat them."

The brother took out his sword and hacked the snake to pieces. He cut it apart into four pieces, and then everyone went back to sleep.

When it was morning, the male and female geese returned. They came back and their children were . . . fine! The geese tried to feed their children bird food. But the children refused to eat.

The geese asked, "Why won't you eat?"

They said, "You've given birth to other children in the past, but to this day where are any of your children as full-grown geese?"

The parents agreed, "Whenever we got back from a trip, we had no children left. Today, we're overjoyed to find you here."

The children said, "Ask these travelers who slept here last night about the terrible difficulties they are dealing with. What brings them to camp here? We're only going to eat after you've helped them with their problems. They saved us. Look down, that thing lying there would have eaten us up!"

So the male and female geese talked to the travelers and the travelers said, "That was a snake and it had come to eat up your children."

The geese asked, "What are the difficulties that you're dealing with? What can we do to help?"

The brother and sister said, "We have to cross the seven seas. So you could take us across."

The geese said, "Fine. We'll take you across, and then we'll bring you back too."[2]

Fine. So the two of them, the male goose and the female goose, bore both brother and sister across the seven seas. When they arrived at this distant place, they began to look for Sunna the Washerwoman. They asked who she was and where she lived. They inquired here and there, they listened to see who was wise and if she was Sunna. This was how they proceeded. Finally, someone told them, "That house there, that one is Sunna the Washerwoman's."

Then they probably set up camp somewhere in the bazaar. The two of them, the sister and the brother, began to live there.

The Washerwoman used to wake up in the early morning, and then she would set off to bathe before she worshipped her gods. When she left, the girl would go to her house and polish up the brass implements for ritual. She would use cow dung to plaster a sacred square on the ground. On this square she would draw an auspicious geometrical design and scatter flower petals. In this way, the girl performed the Washerwoman's work for the gods.

30

The Washerwoman noticed this for a few days. Then she asked one of her daughters-in-law, "What's come over you these days that you come do my work for me?"

The daughter-in-law said [*in a high-pitched voice*], "I never do your work!"

She had two or three daughters-in-law and she asked them all, and they all said, "No, we haven't been doing this."

Then, one day when the Washerwoman was sitting to worship her Gods, she called out, "Who is here? Why have you come here to me? Whoever it is that's been doing my work, come out and stand before me!"

The girl came out. She came out and told her the whole story.

Sunna the Washerwoman called for the brother. She instructed, "This is what you have to do. When her wedding is underway, just as she is about to make the fourth round of the sacred fire, then her groom is going to develop a stomachache and he'll die. Nobody should weep. Just think of me, Sunna the Washerwoman, and I'll come to you. I'll be there at once. Just don't weep. Cover him with a white sheet. Sit down to remember me and I'll be there. [*Whispering*] Then I can save him."

Poor things, they turned around, and at the coast of the sea the male and female geese were waiting for them. Once again the geese carried them over for the crossing.

Then they got home. Their mother asked, "What did she say? What happened?" They told her the whole story, "We went there and this and that happened. She said, 'When her wedding is underway, that's when I'll come. When the bride and groom are circling the fire for the fourth time, then the groom will get a stomachache and he'll die. But no one should weep. He should be covered with a white sheet, and everyone should remember me, Sunna the Washerwoman. Then I'll come.'"

So preparations for a wedding began in the poor thing's house: they set to looking for a groom. The mother was thinking, "Let's get this marriage performed quick so we can deal with that moment." Fine, so the engagement took place, the date for the marriage was set. The poor girl was worried, "Who knows what's going to happen and how it will all turn out?"

Then, truly, in the middle of the marriage ceremonies, as the bride and groom were circling the fire for the fourth time, the groom got a pain in his stomach and fell down dead. They covered him with a white sheet and everyone sat down to remember Sunna the Washerwoman.

She came at once: she knew everything right where she was. She sprinkled the water of immortality on the groom, and he stood up. Then the marriage ceremonies were completed, and the poor things set off for his home. The day that this happened was a Monday on the dark night of the moon.

It was a Monday on the dark night of the moon, and Sunna the Washerwoman turned around to go home. Where she lived, whenever a person died she would bring him back to life. She had left instructions: "If anyone dies while I'm gone, don't cremate him."

Bas. As she was going along, someone asked, "Hey there, old woman, help me lift up this basket of grass." She said, "Today is a Monday on the dark night of the moon. First I must go home and perform my worship. Until then I can't touch grass."

Then she passed another woman who carried a basket filled with cotton. "Help me with the basket," she called. Sunna the Washerwoman said, "No, until I've performed worship for a Monday on the dark night of the moon, I won't touch your cotton."

By the time Sunna the Washerwoman got home, a lot of people had died. She went and performed the full worship of the *pipal* tree: she did the worship that's done on a Monday on the dark night of the moon. Then she circled the tree 108 times. As she went around the tree, those that had been lying dead all stood up. *Bas.*[3]

❊ ❊ ❊

Urmilaji paused, smiling at me. She went on to explain, "The reason that worship is performed on this day, the reason that the tree is worshipped, is so that married women will have a good married life, and those who want sons will have sons. The meaning is that the pipal tree is Brahma, the Creator. So when it is worshipped, everything can be achieved."

Pipal trees are tall, with pale bark and leaves like elongated valentines.[4] When these leaves fall into water, they decompose to leave fragile veined skeletons. Some handmade Indian cards feature paintings on these skeletal leaves. Through years of walking to and fro between my mother's house and the main road, I also knew that there was a magnificent pipal tree (its trunk fused with several other kinds of trees, like mango) on the path that continued past Urmilaji's house. This tree invariably bore traces of worship: bits of cloth, string, earthen oil lamps. I had noticed these traces of worship, but had never seen the ritual.

Urmilaji explained that this ritual for a Monday on the dark night of the moon was especially prescribed for married women, although widows and unmarried girls could participate if they had an interest. She said that there was an irregular pattern to this observance, since the dark night of the lunar month rarely coincided with a Monday. "It could be once a month, it could be once a year, it could be once every three years," she said. She went on to contextualize this by referring to another story that featured the five Pandava brothers of the Mahabharata epic: "It's said that they waited twelve years for a Monday that fell on the dark night of the moon. Then they dispensed the boon that in our

A pipal tree on a raised platform (*Photo by Kirin Narayan*)

era of time (*yug*) there would be many such days, but it wouldn't have the same power as it had in their time."[5]

As Urmilaji spoke, on the wall above her was a large calendar featuring Lakshmi, The Goddess of Wealth. Lakshmi presided, cross-legged, from a pink lotus. She wore a gold crown and a pink sari. SOOD GENERAL STORES was emblazoned in English above her, and the twelve months were lined up underneath. These months were at first glance arranged according to the Western calendar: January, February, March, and so on, and divided up into weeks. But on a second look, the calendar also displayed the standard Hindu lunar calendar in smaller Devanagari lettering: January, for example, spanned lunar *tithi* days from the waning fortnight in the month of Paush to the waxing fortnight in the month of Magh. In addition, fine print at the right-hand corner of each day marked the regional, solar-based *sankranti* calendar. A Monday on the dark night of the moon, then, would fall at the intersection of weeks and lunar months.

Mondays—called *somavar* (or in Pahari, *savariyo*)—are "moon days"; that is, associated with the moon and its life-bestowing ambrosia (*soma*). A dark night of the moon occurs between waning and waxing cycles and is thought to be saturated with dangerous power. It would make sense, then, that if a Monday, already filled with the moon's power, should fall on a dark night just as the moon is being reborn in the sky, this day would be related to re-generation.[6]

A few months later, when I had translated the story, I brought it back to Urmilaji for further discussion. She pointed out that geese were important to the story since "they always come in pairs." As a married "pair" (*jori*) they stand for the enduring bond between a husband and wife. In many songs, when a husband laments his dead wife, he speaks of "my goose pair" (*hamsa di jori*). As all my work with women's oral traditions in Kangra underlined through the years (and as clucking commiserations over my then unmarried plight re-minded me daily), marriage is of central, defining importance to village women's lives: marriage is considered to be women's destiny. So, to be of marriageable age but unmarried is to be an anomaly, and to become a widow is catastrophic tragedy. Seven rounds of a sacred fire are key parts of Hindu wedding rites. By dying on the fourth round, the husband in the story leaves his bride stranded, both virgin and widow, at the shores of auspicious married life.

I asked Urmilaji why suhag, the state of being auspiciously married, was so valued. She said, "No woman wants to be a widow. No matter how bad a husband is, no woman would prefer to be a widow." She was speaking from the high-caste perspective, for upper castes vehemently prohibit widow remar-riage. An uppercaste woman who loses her husband is likely to spend the rest of her life celibate, unadorned, marginalized, and subject to strict ritual pre-scriptions like bathing in cold water before dawn. Only a widow with grown sons—like the mother in this story—might hope for a secure position in her husband's family. The mother in this story displayed her authority by instructing her daughters-in-law to greet the visiting holy man, by chastising the holy man to reveal what remedy there might be for her only daughter's predicted plight, and by exhorting her sons to help find a solution.

Though Urmilaji likened husband and wife to an enduring pair of mated geese, it is worth noting that the geese in the story bore a brother and sister, not a husband and wife, across the seven seas. In Kangra, as in most of India, a brother and sister form another central, idealized pair.[7] Rituals for a brother's welfare are performed by women of all ages at various moments through the year.[8] Also, during Kangra women's observances of various divine weddings, the goddess bride always has her brother beside her. Such brothers have no counterpart in mainstream Hindu mythology and seem to be women's folk elaborations that emphasize a brother's importance.[9]

In this story, it is the brother's presence that enables the girl to cross the seven seas. It brought to my mind how, in Kangra, a brother has the ritual responsibility of escorting a bride to her husband's house for the first time, as she crosses the enormous emotional gulf between her homes of birth and of marriage. In subsequent years, it is also his responsibility to fetch his sister from her in-law's home to her original home for visits. (Though this is the ideal, I observed that with many brothers employed in distant places, it was not always possible for them to fulfill this role of escort for married sisters).

In this story, the brother accomplishes what his sister cannot do alone; he is an active extension of her desires. It is on account of her brother's presence that the respectable unmarried girl can go wandering off on her quest; it is the brother who kills the snake that his sister has spied; it is the brother to whom Sunna the Washerwoman dispenses instructions after the sister has won her boon.

"Why a washerwoman?" I asked Urmilaji. "Could it be that a washerwoman like Sunna washes out the dirt of bad karma?" Urmilaji considered my suggestion, then noncommittally agreed that perhaps this was so. She mentioned that in a woman's lavish final observance of this ritual, the clothes she wears during the performance must be gifted to a washerwoman, though everything else must be gifted to a male Brahman.[10]

I asked Urmilaji whether the washerwoman's name, Sunna, might be related to "golden" (*sonā*)? Or might it perhaps imply "listening" (*sunnā*)? Urmilaji wasn't sure: it was just a name, she said, like my name was Kirin and hers was Urmila. In versions of the story from other parts of India—as well as in another version I heard in Kangra—the washerwoman is called Soma. As I've mentioned, *soma* refers to the life-bestowing ambrosia of the moon, akin to the nectar of immortality that the washerwoman dispenses.

Urmilaji explained that the droplets of immortality (*amrit kundu*) which Sunna had in her possession were some sort of fluid associated with the gods. "Flies have this," she said, "Have you noticed that if you swat a fly, sometimes it lies dead for a while and then starts to move and buzzes away? In the same way, when this water was sprinkled on the dead men, they all stood up saying 'Ram, Ram' [repeating God's name]."[11]

Urmilaji went on to say, "All this is a matter of a past era of time. At that time, Mondays falling on a dark night of the moon were rare. At that time, there was the Washerwoman, there was the water of immortality. Now, we are in a different era of time."

While the best-known Hindu perception of time features four progressively declining eras, folk perceptions in Kangra often reduce these to two: Satyug, a primeval golden time when many paradigmatic events occurred, and Kaliyug, the present dark and degenerate age.[12] Contrasting these eras reminded Urmilaji of a story set at their watershed, a myth explaining the origin of death.

❀ ❀ ❀

In the past, when it was the era of Satyug, there weren't many people, and they all had enormously long lives. At night, there were lights only at great distances. Say an oil lamp was lit here, then the next lamp and house would be at least a kilometer away. Some people used to light oil lamps, others would light fires. You'd have to walk at least a kilometer and then look around for light before you could spot another house.

At that time, people lived lives that spanned hundreds and hundreds of years. They couldn't see well as they walked around. This was because they had become so wrinkled that their eyelids had folded over their eyes. To see anything, they had to lift up an eyelid [*Urmilaji demonstrates, pulling her lid away from her eyeball, and craning her neck*], and when they'd done whatever they needed to do, they'd let the lid flop down again.

They were suffering and unhappy. So they went to God and said, "Look we're in this state and we're miserable. Do something about it."

God said, "Now if you die, don't say that God killed you. Don't say that this was an excuse for me to exterminate you all. You can say that someone had a fever, that someone's "heart failed" [*Urmilaji uses the English words*], that someone felt pains. If you're asked why a person died say things like "the fever rose." Don't say that God ended his life."

So that's why we now say that someone died of a particular pain, or a particular illness.

After this, people began to die, and also their numbers began to grow. In Satyug there were very few people. Now Kaliyug is on, it's a terrible dark time. It's hard to understand now how a person can be sitting well one minute but be struck dead a minute later!

❀ ❀ ❀

This myth emphasized the physical suffering that old age could bring, characterizing death as a necessary release. Yet as the story of Sunna the Washerwoman showed, death could also come importunately, and could then be reversed through the power of women's rituals.

Sunna the Washerwoman Urmilaji explained had also lived in the primeval era of Satyug. In the present era, Urmilaji said, not only was the effect of worship less powerful, but no women matched Sunna's powers. Nonetheless,

36

by continuing to worship their household gods and to observe the ritual of Monday on the dark night of the moon, women linked themselves back to the powerful Washerwoman.

I could not fathom why Sunna refused to help the two women who needed a hand lifting their baskets; in the logic of folktales, it seemed to me, helping strangers was usually a good idea, leading to unexpected boons. Urmilaji explained that grass and unspun cotton are both taboo on the day of worship: they should not be touched until after the worship is done.[13] If sacred *drub* grass is used for worship, Urmilaji said, a young girl may go fetch some blades and lay them out. The wick of an oil lamp must be twisted the day before worship so that a woman need not touch cotton as she prepares to light a lamp under the tree.

Why should cotton and grass be taboo, I pressed, mystified. "It's because cutting grass and spinning used to be part of everyday work for women," Urmilaji said. "Of course not so many women spin now that you can buy everything in the shops, but this was in the past. God's work is different from household work. The meaning is that you should do God's work first, and then do your own work. Sunna the Washerwoman still had to do God's work and make all the men come back to life. When she worshipped at the tree, they all stood up, saying 'Ram, Ram.' That's why she didn't help those people with the baskets before."

"This story is about worship (*pujā*)," Urmilaji summarized. "Through worship, the worst afflictions of the planets can be overcome. By performing this worship, women can have a long and auspicious married life. In the story, an auspicious married life was miraculously achieved. It was all accomplished through worship."

A central message of this story, then, is that women's worship bears the capacity to change destiny, grant boons, and raise up the dead. The holy man in the story could discern destiny but he deferred to the pious Washerwoman to actually transform it. Though of a low caste that performed impure services for others, and a housewife with daughters-in-law, Sunna was a devotee. Her daily worship and observance of Mondays on the dark night of the moon had given her powers to overcome death and to hear entreaties from afar. Just as Sunna served God and gained powers, similarly, the girl gained the boon of a living husband by serving Sunna in her ritual work. Because of Sunna's power, a representation of her is made from dough and put out under the tree during the Monday worship. "We worship the tree," said Urmilaji, repeating the closing section of the story in which Sunna brings men back to life, "and we worship her, too."

The afternoon that I first heard the story, my head was still reeling with images from this other world, and I hadn't yet formulated all the questions that struck me in the following months. At the time I simply asked, "Where did you learn this beautiful story?"

Urmilaji replied, "The thing is that this story is given, it's told, while the worship is being performed, right there under the tree. I heard it from some old woman in the past. Now I remember it and I tell it to others."

"So this way it's passed along."

"Right," said Urmilaji, "this way a story goes on into the future."

The Five Days
of Fasting

The Five Days of Fasting are celebrated by upper-caste women in Kangra from the eleventh day to the full-moon day during the bright half of the lunar month of Kārttik (October/November). These five days are thought to be so sacred that even if a woman has not performed any other form of worship, she can observe this ritual and gain enough merit to last her the whole year.

Panch Bhikham—the Five Days of Fasting—appears to be a corruption of Panch Bhisham (in Sanskrit, Bhishma Panchaka)—the Five Days of Bhishma. I was told by two other women that during this sacred time the five Pandava brothers of the Mahabharata epic came to their wise uncle Bhishma who lay dying on a bed of arrows: they performed austerities themselves and distracted Bhishma by telling him stories. Urmilaji was puzzled when I suggested that there might be a connection to Bhishma, and so here I follow her designation of these days as associated with fasting rather than with Bhishma.

On the eleventh day of Kārttik, the gods are thought to awake from their monsoon slumber. Since slumbering gods should ideally not be invoked at weddings, this eleventh day also opens the marriage season for the winter months. From the eleventh day to the full-moon day, Goddess Saili—or Tulsi, the sacred basil plant—is married off to Thakur, a form of Vishnu.

During the Five Days of Fasting, pious women bathe every morning, preferably in swiftly moving cold water. They may scrub themselves with a paste from sour *ānvlā* berries. They worship Saili morning and evening.

They ideally should not eat wheat, rice, potatoes, or salt. They should keep five oil lamps, called *diye*, burning continuously for five full days or visit households where such lamps are installed. Such households attract women's gatherings and become a setting for group singing or requests that an older woman "give" stories.

TWO

Daughter, My Little Bread

"My children sometimes wouldn't let me sleep the entire night!" exclaimed Urmilaji. Having just finished the story for Monday on the dark night of the moon, she was reflecting more generally on occasions for storytelling.

"Before television?" I prompted. I had already heard Urmilaji elaborate on this theme several times.

"Before. It was all, 'Tell a story, tell a story!' Even the night before last, something came up and my eldest son said, 'Mother, we used to hear an awful lot of stories from you!'" Urmilaji laughed. She paused, as though viewing some happy memories. "He said, 'You used to tell a story in which a barber left his satchel hanging near a window, and when he returned to get it, there was nothing else there.'"

As though an evoked story could not be contained, its force to burst out into telling too strong, Urmilaji started headlong with "There was a woman." Then she stopped herself and instructed me, "This is a story for The Five Days of Fasting. Turn off your tape recorder and let me remember it properly."

After sitting in silence for a few moments, Urmilaji indicated that she was ready to start. She also announced that this was a story told on the fourth day of the Five Days of Fasting.

❈ ❈ ❈

There was a mother and a daughter. The mother, poor thing, would go off to work in other people's houses. After earning something, she'd bring it home and give it to her daughter saying, "Cook this up." Then the two of them would eat.

Bas. The daughter would roll out and cook up two breads: a big one and a small one. She'd give the small one to her mother and eat the big one herself. But when she grew more mature, some wisdom came into her head. "Look, my mother goes from house to house to earn something. She brings home whatever she earns and gives it to me. Then I eat the big bread myself and give my mother the small one. What am I doing?"

41

That day she ate the small bread herself and left the big one for her mother. When her mother came home, the daughter gave her the big bread. But the mother wouldn't eat it. She cried, "Daughter, my little bread!" She understood that her daughter had taken the little bread. Now a mother, if she's sane, would hardly feel upset about this! But she began to search everywhere, "My bread! I must eat that very piece of bread."

The daughter had already eaten it up, so how could she give it back? When the mother said, "Give me my little bread," she said, "I've eaten it." But the mother said, "I must eat that very one." There was nothing else stored in the house: after all, every day food would be brought home by going out, then cooking, then eating, then going again the next day and eating that, and doing the same the day after. There was nothing else in the house. But the mother kept on reciting, "Daughter, my little bread. Daughter, my little bread."

The daughter slipped off with a clay water pot and went to the spring nearby. When she got there, she placed her water pot to fill under the jet of water, and she sat down beside it. Just then, the King's servant arrived with a brass pot. He too wanted to fill water. The brass pot was filthy. So the girl took the pot from the servant's hands and gave it a good scrub until it gleamed. Then she filled the pot and returned it to him saying, "Take this, take it to the King to drink"

When the servant gave the water to the King, he asked, "Why does this brass pot shine so much? This isn't your doing, for you only fetch water. Yet this brass pot has been transformed. It's become really beautiful."

The servant said, "King, there's a girl sitting there by the spring. She took the brass pot from my hand and scrubbed at it."

"Let's go," the King said. "I must take a look at her."

When they went there, he saw that the girl was very beautiful. "Come along, you must marry me," said the King.

Now she was unhappy at home anyway. So the King took her. She went off with him.

When she went off with the King, the mother went really crazy. She kept repeating this one line [*in a frantic singsong chant*]: "Daughter, my little bread. Daughter my little bread. Daughter, my little bread."

Bas. Repeating this line, the mother set out searching for her daughter.

Who knows how many years had passed before the mother reached the King's palace. She arrived there, still crying out, "Daughter, my little bread. Daughter, my little bread."

The Queen's serving maid came in from outside and reported, "These days there's this woman who's come to town. She wanders everywhere calling, 'Daughter, my little bread. Daughter, my little bread.'"

When she said this the Queen remembered her mother, "Oh-ho! [*in a la-*

menting tone]. If she makes her way here I'll be dishonored. This is a catastrophe. Where is a King, and where is she: covered in dust, unkempt? The poor thing, in her mad state. . . ."

So the Queen called for someone, and who knows, she probably gave them some money too. "Discreetly kill that woman and bring her to me." So that person finished the mother off. In the past we had huge trunks. She put her mother in the trunk and thrust it high up in the beams.

Bas. The Five Days of Fasting came around. Where the Queen slept, there the King probably slept too. All of a sudden, his gaze fell on that trunk. "What do you keep in that?" he asked.

She said, "Women's things, like rags that I've put away."[1]

"Bring it down," demanded the King. "Open it up!" Some sort of obstinate whim had come over him.

She, poor thing, didn't want to bring it down. "What am I going to show him now?" She lit the lamps, and she began to pray to them, "Oh God, protect my honor." Who knows what she'd planned to do with the contents—maybe float it downstream or something—but she hadn't yet had the chance.

Bas. She bowed before the lamps [*Urmilaji demonstrates, palms joined, eyes closed, head lowered*]. "Eternal Goddess Lamps, keep my honor!" Then she brought the trunk down and set it on the ground. She opened it up.

Inside, there was a necklace worth nine hundred thousand.[2] An incredibly gorgeous, fabulous necklace studded with gems and diamonds.

"Where is this from?" asked the King.

She said openly, "This was a gift from my parents."

The King's eyes grew big. "If you have parents that give such a precious necklace, then they must be wealthy and powerful people. I want to visit your parents' place. I must see where they live!"

So the poor thing was filled with anguish. After all, what was there to see, what was there to show? Once again, she bowed before the lamps. "Oh Eternal Goddess Lamps, keep my honor."

Then the King issued the command for a certain date: "On this date we will go to your parents' place." He was such an important person, with such enormous wealth, he traveled with a whole army of attendants to make his arrangements: hordes of men. And she kept burning the lamps, making the vow. "Just as you preserved my honor here, do this there too. You must definitely keep my honor for me."

Bas. So they all got ready and set off. Her heart was thumping: "What am I going to show as my parents' place when we arrive? Who knows what the grace of the lamps is, and what we will find there?"

When they arrived, there was a huge palace! [*Urmilaji's voice is tinged with awe.*] She led the King into it. A huge, huge palace with a kitchen filled with workers and all kinds of arrangements for the King, arrangements for his horse-riders and for their horses, arrangements for his elephant-riders and their elephants. There was room for all the attendants: places to sit, places to wander. There were arrangements made for everything.

Bas. Now the Barber had accompanied the group. Everyone ate and drank, they did this and that. And the Barber hung from a hook his satchel with all his things for shaving. Then after much eating and drinking, they all turned back.

As they were proceeding, when they were halfway home, the Barber said, "Oh no! My satchel has been left behind." All of his things were in it. "It was left behind," he said.

Now she had asked for a parent's place for just two-and-a-half days. Before the two-and-a-half days were up, they had all set off. The Barber returned along that same path. But there was not even a blade of grass there. There was a withered tree that had been a window, and there hung his satchel. Otherwise, not even a blade of grass.

When the Barber came back with his satchel, he told the King, "This is a hugely astounding matter!"

The King said, "What?"

The Barber said, "It's an enormous puzzle."

"What?"

"When I went to fetch my satchel there wasn't even a blade of grass: just one tree with my satchel hanging on it. Otherwise, nothing, not even a blade of grass."

The King said, "You're lying."

"No, sir, come along and take a look. What would I get out of telling a lie? There's not even a blade of grass there."

Then the King asked her, "What is this? What's going on? Tell me the full truth."

She said, "Just don't ask me the truth about this matter. Otherwise, that will be the end of me. I'll die."

He said, "Whether you live or you die, I must know the truth of this matter. Tell me, what illusion did you set dancing?"

Bas. Then she told him everything that had come to pass for her. How she had such and such a mother, how there was nothing to eat, how the mother would fetch materials and they would eat. How she had thought that if the mother recognized her, they would have to go out collecting food all over again. "I had my mother killed. Then I put her in a trunk, but you wanted to see it. I prayed to the lamps that I light, making a vow, asking them to protect my honor. When you opened the trunk there was a necklace worth nine hundred thousand inside. You asked me 'Who gave this to you?' and I said that my parents had. Then you were possessed with the whim: 'We must go there.' I made a vow to the lamps, asking them to give me that place for two-and-a-half days."

Bas. She told him the whole story, and that was the end of her.[3]

❋ ❋ ❋

Urmilaji regarded me somberly. I was obviously showing distress on my face, for to me this story was inexplicably morbid. I had heard variants of the tale before (and heard more later) but this did not make the tale any less disturbing.

"So could this mean that blessings can't dissolve injustice?" I hazarded, struggling to make sense of this tragic end. "That with God's blessing the results of bad actions might lessen a little, but that in the long run one's karma catches up with you? That you shouldn't kill your mother? Is this the meaning?"

Urmilaji pondered over my badly articulated instant analysis. Then she said, "This was a wrong thing to do. She did it partly for her own happiness, partly out of bashful modesty, poor thing; partly for her happiness, partly out of something or the other, but she murdered her mother. Then, she was narrating all this and was finished off herself. She had warned the King, 'Don't ask me about this or I'll die.' But the King had a whim, who knows how many other Queens he had, after all. He said, 'No! Whether you die or not, whether you stay or you go: you have to tell me everything about this matter.'"

This is an immensely popular story among storytelling women. All the variants I heard had begun with the sharing of bread between mother and daughter, with the mother unable to adapt to a new system of division when the daughter came of age. Living with my mother at the time, I heard one of the main messages in the story as being the need for mother and daughter to change their relationship as a daughter grew. The story seemed to say that for a mother to doggedly hold to "the way things were" was to drive herself crazy and to incite violent aggression in her daughter.

A childless Rajput widow in her seventies, who was universally known as Tayi (Aunty) first suggested this theme of intergenerational conflict to me. It had been a morning during the Five Days of Fasting, and Tayi had invited me to come by and hear some of her stories. She sat by the hearth, continuing with the cooking and the overseeing of a crawling baby boy as she talked. Other women in the joint family were out in the fields, older children were at school, and Tayi was cooking the midday meal for them all. Her variant on the story started with a single piece of bread that was usually shared, but one day was eaten by the hungry growing daughter. Tayi said that the story instructed that when people got older they should eat less so there was more for the young. She also justified the daughter's killing the mother by saying that the mother had shamed her. Furthermore, she declared, anyone who died during the Five Days of Fasting would go directly to heaven! In Tayi's variant, the daughter was called Saili and told her whole story at the end with many praises to the

Worshipping Saili indoors, at Urmilaji's neighbor's house
(*Photo by Kirin Narayan*)

worship of the Goddess Saili. She did not die. This retelling, then, rationalized the violence in the tale along the conventional lines of most ritual tales in which worship bestows lasting fruits.

The specific ritual associated with this tale involves the making of two flat breads, one big and one small, on the fourth day of the Five Days of Fasting. The breads should be offered to the Sacred Basil Goddess and then given to a mother-daughter pair of a lower caste: the daughter must be an only girl and unmarried. Urmilaji said that it was good to give such gifts to God and to the poor. "If you give in God's name then you get more," she assured.

Also, this story—like many others in the set associated with the Five Days of Fasting—extols the benefits of burning oil lamps. As Urmilaji explained, "For five days and five nights these lamps should be kept burning. You shouldn't sleep. You should wake up again and again to look them over." At the same time, Urmilaji acknowledged that this discipline was difficult and that

46

few households still did it. She herself had lit lamps in the past, but had already performed the lavish final ceremony that marked the end of her observance of this particular aspect of the ritual.

Households in which the lamps were kept lit became a gathering place for women. Through the years, I have had the chance to visit several of these households during the Five Days of Fasting. Typically, Saili, the sacred basil goddess, is brought indoors and set under a canopy with her tiny brass groom Thakur (a form of the crawling baby Krishna). Five oil lamps are set burning beside them. In addition, fruits and berries are laid out, and women coming by bow their heads to the ground and offer coins. In the late afternoons or evenings, pious village women with the inclination to do so gather by the lamps to sing and tell stories. The lamp soot collected on a brass tray may be shared out as a consecrated offering. In 1990, in Chaudhrer, I joined women using their little fingers to scoop up soot and draw it over the lower eyelid as beautifying *kājal*. But given the lack of mirrors, and the general tendency of soot to smear, we all soon had large blotches of black around our eyes, lending us a comic, raccoon-like appearance.

Chaudhrer is a mostly Brahman village about a forty-five minute walk away from where Urmilaji lives. I had become friendly with families there in the early 1980s. Sometimes I squeezed into the crowded buses, but mostly I would walk there along the tarred road, through the fields and under the mountains. Hearing the same story from several Brahman women there, I learned that they sang a little ditty as part of it. In their variants, when the daughter first ran off, she went to the forest and hid inside a hollow sandalwood tree. Later, when woodcutters came to the tree she sang:"Slice from below, cut from above, but take out gently from the middle" (*heṭhe bhī baṛeyā, upare bhī kaṭeyā, bich kore kaṛeyā*). This singing tree incited the King's curiosity, and he came to see for himself.

These same Brahman women also stated that the daughter's vow (*sukhaṇ*) before the lamps caused her mother's head in the trunk to turn into a golden peacock. (In one macabre variant, this disembodied head floated around after the daughter, insisting on helping out with the cooking!) When the King asked where this golden peacock came from, the Queen answered that at her parent's place, such birds were always flying about. Evoking this story, women in Chaudhrer add peacocks to the symmetrical designs which they draw with powder in their courtyards during the Five Days of Fasting.

There is a related story, also told in Chaudhrer, which I heard from a primary school teacher in her sixties, Bimlesh Kanta. One hot afternoon when I was visiting her relatives, Bimlesh Kanta stopped by. Learning of my interests, she briskly set to "filling up my tapes" with all the stories associated with the Five Days of Bhishma that she knew. In a story I perceive as related to this one, a holy man ceremonially bathed in the river during the Five Days of Fasting, clutching at his staff for balance. He was reborn as a King. The staff became a beautiful Princess, perfect to look at except for her wooden neck, where the holy man's tight grip had blocked the transformative touch of water. At the time of the Princess' inevitable marriage to the King, the Barber's wife was combing her hair and spied the wooden neck. She told the Barber who told the King. The King (who had forgotten his past life) rushed in and ordered that his wife pull off her veil. He looked at her wooden neck and demanded to hear the story. His bride wept, saying that she'd die if she told her story. "If you die, where is the shortage of Queens?" inquired the King. The bride told her tale, and when she finished, she became a walking stick and fell over on one side.

A look at these other variants helped me sort out the troubling violence and tragedy in Urmilaji's tale. First, the daughter kills her mother for appearing at the palace still crazed and visibly poor, so threatening her status as Queen. Second, the King kills his Queen by insisting that she retell the story of her origins. Both deaths, it seems, are linked through the wife's reluctance after marriage to reveal embarrassing truths about her past. While she can live with her own embarrassment when it remains silent—distant or dead—she can no longer live with it when the truth is publicly disclosed.

Like the girl in this story, upper-caste women ideally marry up, to men from families with greater status.[4] In marriages involving "the gift of a virgin" (*kanyā dān*), it is generally thought that a bride's parents detract from their meritorious gift if they take something in return. For many upper-caste Kangra women, this meant that their parents rarely visited them, and if they came, would accept no hospitality. (If a father accepted tea in his married daughter's house, for example, he would immediately take out change to pay for it). The crazy mother following her daughter to her married home violated the notion that a woman's parents have no place in the married home. I wondered if the story might perhaps play upon the feelings of inadequacy that a woman might have about her natal home as inferior compared to the home of higher status into which she married. As Urmilaji said, "She killed her mother for her own honor; this was a King's mother-in-law after all!"

Another time, Urmilaji observed, "The daughter did a wrong thing in killing her mother. She felt bashful modesty in a King's house, bashful about the kind of mother she had. She was bashful in front of the servants, the laborers, and everyone else. Her veil was pulled off by telling the story. She had warned the King that she would die if she told her story and she did."

For Urmilaji, then, the crucial motivating explanation was the woman's bashful modesty (*sharm*). This ideology of modesty associated with honor (*izzat*) pervaded women's lives in Kangra and was explicitly linked to the practice of veiling.[5] *Sharm* involved hiding one's sexuality, showing deference to males and elders, and all in all upholding the honor of one's family. I heard *sharm* invoked as the reason that unmarried girls should behave circumspectly and not adorn themselves; the reason for married women to veil in the presence of their older male in-laws. I knew women who hung up their undergarments to dry in damp cupboards "from *sharm*" when men were around, women who were mortified as their stomachs ballooned out in pregnancy from the *sharm* this caused, women who cringed with *sharm* in doctor's offices when other women undressed. A much-repeated scandal (in which a Rajput girl eloped with a boy from her school) always emphasized that the girl's mother took to her bed, ill with *sharm*. As a powerful prescribed norm, *sharm* seemed to connect social ideals with emotions lodged in minds and in bodies.

Urmilaji's comment about the Queen's "veil being pulled off" when she revealed herself (matched also by Bimlesh Kanta's story in which the King ordered the walking-stick Queen to remove her veil) led me to reflect on how women's veiling could create a private female space in which women might hope for refuge from unwanted intrusions.[6] Being stripped of a veil was to stand defenseless, overwhelmed by *sharm*. Just as the King insisted on seeing what was in the trunk, though the Queen warned that it contained women's things "like rags" (indicating menstrual rags), so he had no regard for his wife's privacy and desire to keep her story to herself.

Worse yet, the King had no regard for his wife's life. In both Urmilaji's and Bimlesh Kanta's variants, the King did not care if his Queen died, for, as he said, there were always other Queens to be had. In making explicit the devaluing of women's lives and the easy replaceability of wives, these upper-caste women's tales also seemed to set a cultural double-standard in ironic relief. For among the upper castes, men were allowed cowives (particularly if one had not produced a son and heir). Further, if a wife died the man invariably remarried, needing someone to serve him and his children. Yet, upper-caste widows like Tayi were required to live a celibate life, hemmed in by ritual restrictions.

While wives were considered replaceable, they were valued, too. Men's need for women's labor—and also perhaps their reproductive powers as "vessel"—was highlighted in Urmilaji's explanation for why the King had been attracted by the sparkling brass pot his attendant brought him after the girl polished it. In response to my question about this, Urmilaji said, "He saw the pot, and he saw that this was a woman who worked well. Then, later, he saw that she was beautiful, too."

As I saw through my visits in Kangra, relations between husbands and wives could not really be typified: I saw rejecting distance, simmering attraction, amused camaraderie, and matter-of-fact coexistence, in different households and even in the same relations through time. The tragic end of the story, then, seemed partially to be a threat to men who claimed indifference to their wives, putting their own whims first. In a sense, by dying, the Queen forced to tell her story also had the last word. As Asha Devi of Chaudhrer said, shaking her head after listening to this story on one of the occasions it was told:

"So then that King must have really repented, he must have repented a lot!"

49

THREE

First Sour, then Sweet

Sitting cross-legged opposite me on the same bed, Urmilaji asked if I was interested in hearing yet another tale.

"Oh yes!" I said.

Urmilaji pulled her thick gray shawl closer around herself with a quiet smile. Then she announced that the next story was for the first day of the Five Days of Fasting, that is, the eleventh day of the bright lunar fortnight of Karttik (October/November). Correspondingly, the two sisters in the story bear the names of the eleventh and twelfth days of the lunar fortnight.[1]

❋ ❋ ❋

There were two sisters, Eleventh and Twelfth. Eleventh was very rich, and Twelfth was very poor. So Twelfth would go work in her sister's house. And what would she be given in return? Just food and drink. She worked this way for many years. Also, she did all the right worship, all the right rituals.

One day, God took the form of an old man and visited her house. He had come to test her, to see if she had full devotion or not.

Bas. So he appeared, and he said, "I want a place to stay overnight. It's dark outside and I want a place to stay."

She said, "Come in, sir, come and sit down." She showed him great respect. Now inside, there wasn't even anything for her to eat. Truly, how could she have invited him in? But no! She had sympathy inside her. So she asked him, "What would you like to eat?"

"I'll eat whatever you're eating," he said [*in a relaxed voice*].

Poor thing, she collected some sour berries. At that time of year there are these sour berries. She broke them open and boiled them up. Poor thing, she fed this mixture to him, and then she ate some herself.

When the night was half through, he said [*slowly and hesitantly*], "Listen. . . . I've got to shit."

She said, "Sir, how will you go anywhere in this black darkness? Just squat right here in the corner."

50

So he shat. He was God and he was testing her. After another two hours, he said, "I have to shit again." She said [_turning, and pointing behind her_], "Squat on the other side." In this way, he shat in all the four corners. Then once again he said, "I have to shit." "Go ahead and squat in the middle," she instructed. She didn't get upset, and she kept speaking to him with affection.

Then when it was morning, there was no Brahman, no old man: he had completely vanished.

[_"Where are you off to?" Urmilaji gently asks her daughter Sello, who has sidled in. Sello is fifteen, the youngest in the family. She has large and penetrating eyes and two long braids. I turn off my recorder as mother and daughter chat. Sello settles down on the edge of the bed to scrutinize me and my machine. Then Urmilaji resumes where she left off_].

In the morning, when she began to look around, he was nowhere to be seen. The Brahman had gone.

In the meantime, her sister waited, fretting, "She hasn't come to work. She hasn't come to work today."

So she went to her younger sister's house to find out why she hadn't come. When she got there, she looked in and saw invaluable riches spread out. Emeralds, diamonds, gold, silver: the whole room was full! She asked [_in a sharp, high-pitched voice_], "Where did you get all this from?"

The poor thing, she had no sins in her mind. She said, "Dear sister, last night this Brahman, this old man, had come here, and he did this and that. At night he said he had to shit, and I said, 'Do it here, do it here.' In the morning he went off, and this was what was left inside: wealth and wealth." This is what she said.

The older sister became terribly jealous, thinking, "She works for me in return for just enough to eat, yet look at all this wealth she's collected!"

She said aloud [_in the same fast, high voice_], "Well when that old man comes back, send him to my house. Be sure to send him to me as well."

The younger sister had no sins in her mind, right? She said, "Certainly, I'll send him to you."

Bas. Two or three days went by. Then the old man came by again.

[_"This was a form of God," puts in Sello_].

Before he came, the older sister had asked, "What did you feed him?" She said, "I boiled sour berries and fed the mixture to him. He had said that he'd eat whatever I was eating, and I only had sour berries to boil."

So then, three days later, the old man returned in the evening. He said, "I've come to spend the night."

The younger sister said, "Today, my sister has invited you to her place. She left instructions that when you come again, you must go to her house."

He already knew that he'd been summoned there. Otherwise he wouldn't have come again, he had no need to sleep! So he went to the sister's house.

51

"Sister, I want to spend the night here."

She was delighted. "Come on in! Come on in! Come on in!" [*with the same comic pitch*].

She sat him down inside. She boiled up sour berries. She fed him this mixture, and as for herself—she probably ate good food!

Bas. Halfway through the night, he said, "I have to shit."

"Squat right down!" she said. She had asked her sister, and was doing exactly as she had described. After a while, he had to shit again. In this way, he left mounds of shit in the four corners. In the middle of the room too.

[*"Latrine," states Sello with a grin, using the English word to make sure I get the picture.*]

When it was morning, she began to look around, and in all four directions there was shit, shit, and shit! [*We laugh*]. The old man had vanished.

She went to her sister. She said, "That day he gave you gold and silver, and because of you I invited this shitting man into my house!"

Then she began to hit her sister and make a scene. The younger sister said, "I'll clear it all up. I'll clean up your place."

So she cleaned up her sister's house, and in her own house, the wealth doubled. And the other sister became the poor one.[2]

※ ※ ※

Urmilaji stepped out of the story frame to comment. "One should honor a guest. The first one, though she was poor, fed him what she could. If you have good things, she should feed these to a guest. But the second sister ate fine things herself and just boiled up sour berries for the old man!" Urmilaji laughed. "She did the wrong thing, didn't she?"

"Right," I said.

"If someone is eating two or four things oneself, and there is someone else to entertain outside, they should also be fed fully. This is the wisdom here."

The same moral was repeated, in almost exactly the same words by Urmilaji's neighbor, an elderly woman with thick glasses, when Urmilaji retold this story in its ritual context in November 1994. I was visiting and had been invited by Urmilaji to come along with her Sood relatives as they went down to the village commons to perform the appropriate worship for the fourth day of the Five Days of Fasting. The women's bright clothes and spangled scarves worn for the ritual were resplendent in the afternoon sunshine. When little boats had been launched and the berry bush had been worshipped, we all sat in a semicircle in the grass. Urmilaji's relatives urged her to tell various stories. The request "Give us the one about the sour berry (*ānvlā*)" brought out this tale. Urmilaji told it in much the same way as she had told it to me. Her audience, familiar with the tale, began to laugh expectantly as the second sister encouraged the old man to squat right down.

Later, as we were walking along the beaten track back toward the central area of village shops, Urmilaji's neighbor commented, "If someone is wealthy and eating fine food themselves, they should feed this good food to others."

Urmilaji's youngest brother's wife, a fair young woman wearing bright pink lipstick observed, "She probably thought that you *had* to feed him sour berries."

"That's it," agreed Urmilaji. "That's what was in her mind: that you had to use the same things."

Another woman whose identity I knew only insofar as the village post office was lodged in her home, made another comment about the second sister, laughter bubbling between her words, "Look at how she was waiting expectantly but when morning came—"

"—there was a lot to clean up!" grinned the woman walking beside her.

"A *lot* to clean up!"

"It was gold and silver she'd wanted to clean up," muttered someone from the back of the moving group.

Our next destination, it turned out, was an *ānvlā* tree in a patch of forest behind the shops on the main road. Women bowed their heads and made offerings to the roots of the tree before we all went home for the day.

Sour, smooth, and a pale greenish yellow, *ānvlā* berries are in season when the Five Days of Fasting take place.[3] These berries are also known to have medicinal properties when eaten or applied to the body or hair. Their tangy vitamin C–like flavor means that on first bite one's mouth puckers with sourness, but later—especially after drinking water—a pleasant sweetness suffuses one's taste buds. During the Five Days of Fasting in Kangra, a branch laden with berries, or just a handful of berries, are offered to the Goddess Saili in worship. Some women make the berries into a paste and use this to bathe during the five days, not allowing soap to touch their bodies. As Subhashini Dhar explained, "This gives you a beautiful form." Observant women may also restrict their diet (no salt, rice, wheat, lentils, or vegetables) and eat the sour berries.

When I asked Urmilaji what the significance of sour berries might be, she replied, "They are auspicious. When a canopy is set up for marriage, then stalks of the banana tree, the berry tree, and sugarcane are used at the four sides." She sat twiddling her hands in her lap, brows furrowed. Then she brightened up. "There's a saying: 'Eating a sour berry and the words of an old person: sour at first and sweet afterwards' (*ānvle dā khādiyā kanne siyāṇiyā dā gilāyā pahale koṛā kanne picche te miṭhṭhā*).[4] When you first hear something from an old person, you might not like what they say. But you should listen, because it can come to use later. Old people understand a lot about life."

Urmilaji herself had learned many of the rituals and accompanying stories from her old Tayi Sas, her husband's father's elder brother's wife. As Urmilaji reminisced:

That Tayi Sas—she was already old when I was married here. She had enormous wisdom. Whoever she mixed with, she gave them wisdom. Whatever wisdom there was, she had it inside her. When we would sit together, then she would talk about wise things: good talk. Then we lived together for fourteen or fifteen years. I learned a little wisdom from her: these stories and other things.

She would say, "Speak good words. This is one's own, nothing else is one's own. Even one's body isn't one's own: at one's last minute, it must be left behind. Act toward others without selfishness." For example, when I tell you these things [*Urmilaji indicates me*], they are matters of interest to you. This is work of your interest. So you feel enormously happy with me. You feel, "This is meaningful. These are good words." In this way, she'd say, "act toward others without selfishness."

If she saw that someone's clothes were torn, in a flash she'd go to sew them up. She would take out her needle and thread. If someone's button was off and she'd see this, she'd bring out a button and sew it on for them. "Is there anything I can do for you?" she'd ask. She'd help others first, and then do her own housework later. She was a very wise woman. A great souled woman.

The younger sister in the story—generous, patient, attentive to others—seemed to exemplify the virtues that Tayi Sas embodied and preached. There appeared then, to be a parallel between Urmilaji's Tayi Sas who told this tale and the kind sister in the story.

"Was the old man a holy man?" I asked Urmilaji.

"He was just an old man," said Urmilaji. "She didn't know what he was, except that he was poor and that he was old. So she felt compassion in her heart. She was full of affection for God. And when there's love for God, there is love for others too."

In Kangra—as in South Asia generally—guests (*parouṇe*) are treated with enormous, self-effacing respect. Admittedly, this is tinged by values of caste. It is considered meritorious to feed high-caste male Brahmans at all times, and auspicious occasions such as the Five Days of Fasting are particularly good times to feed them. It is worth noting that the old man in this story is not just *any* destitute wanderer but a Brahman. (In other versions, though, he may be a "Baba" or holy man).

While male Brahmans were those most often sought out to be honored, within interacting castes, routine hospitality could often be overwhelming. As I experienced again, and embarrassingly again, the best that a household can offer is often brought out for a guest. Meals feature delicacies that would not be part of everyday food, and sometimes other members of the household may approvingly watch you eat what they themselves forgo. Every visit—even down the road—invariably involves the exhortation "today spend the night here" (*aj ithu rahā*), a holdover from earlier times when there were fewer buses and people routinely walked long distances. In 1978, soon after my mother first moved to Kangra, we were out in the fields by a crossroads awaiting a bus. Here we received a memorable invitation, in English, from a chatty young man who chanced upon us and struck up a conversation: "What is there if bus does not come? My house is here only. Come live with me."

Though such hospitality is especially found among interacting castes, a low-caste person coming to a high-caste household is likely to at least be offered tea and perhaps also a meal. Lingering ideas about caste pollution can mean, though, that lower-caste people may not be invited to sit inside, and members of the household will instead bring them food or drink on the ledge just outside the door. At feasts held by high-caste households, when most guests were seated in the courtyard in parallel lines to be served, I often observed that low-caste people arrived with their own containers to take away food to their homes. Increasingly, low-caste people, particularly those whose economic lot has improved, understandably feel no desire to enact their caste inferiority like this over food and may not attend such occasions at all.[5]

For women, pride taken in the care and feeding of guests is also subsumed within the larger framework of "service" (*sevā*). To serve others, particularly those in one's husband's family, is seen as a central part of women's role. Deities are served through rituals. Elders and men are served through caring for their personal needs. Families are served through daily feeding. Service is a central aspect of a moral woman's identity, and from selfless service, merit (*puṇ*) is gained.

In serving the old man, the kind sister goes out of her way to indulge his age and presumed weakness. Until very recently, outdoor spaces like forests or rocky ravines served as toilets for all households; it has only been in the last ten years that there is a growing move toward having cement latrines and septic tanks constructed a short distance from the house. For an old person, a sick person, or a child, a trek outdoors to relieve him or herself at night could be difficult. Urmilaji explained that children especially were told to squat down indoors and that a mother would clean up in the morning. In a retelling by Judhya Devi Avasthi, an old Brahman woman who lived with her husband beside the goddess temple at Chaudhrer, the kind sister is portrayed as an old woman. She addresses the old man as though he is a child: "Child, squat right down in the corner," she urges. In a variant told by Mira Devi "Chachi" Dogra of Badoo, the kind sister not only makes this invitation, but later offers her clothes for him to wipe himself. (Later, these clothes also turn to silver and gold, causing admiration at the village spring. When the other sister goes down to the village spring in the morning, though, she is mocked by other women for her smeared and smelly attire). Since men in upper-caste families would most certainly not be involved in the business of cleaning up dirty and ritually polluting feces, this action shapes the story as being peculiarly about women's experiences.[6] The subtext would seem to be that for women toiling through the daily routines of serving others, there may yet be sweet rewards.

There are two related stories associated with the Five Days of Fasting. One is linked to the *ānvlā* story through the motif of hospitality and *ānvlā* berries offered to a stranger; the other is linked through two sisters, one rich and selfish, the other poor and selfless.

In the first story,[7] an old couple is very pious, performing all the appropriate rituals for the Five Days of Fasting and hosting feasts at this time as well. The couple's son and daughter-in-law are annoyed by the inconvenience of all these observances. In some variants, the son and daughter-in-law abandon the parents by hiding in a haystack (which in November, after the rice harvest, is a familiar feature across the Kangra landscape). In other variants, the son and his wife lock the door so the parents cannot enter. The parents go off into the forest and camp under an *ānvlā* tree. They have nothing to eat when an old man comes to them at night, but they share with him the sour berries they have boiled. When they wake up, the old man has gone but they are in a magnificent palace, with everything that could be needed. In the meantime, the fortunes of the son and his wife dwindle (as Judhya Devi Avasthi poetically put it, "all the water in the house turned to blood, all the food in the house turned to worms"). The son starts to make a living selling wood. He comes by with wood but does not recognize his parents. The parents recognize him, but do not reveal their own identities. When the Five Days of Fasting roll around, the mother asks if this man's wife might come by and help her wash her hair. The wife does come to help, and she spies a mole (in some versions a golden hair) on the neck of this rich woman. This reminds her of her own abandoned mother-in-law. Hot tears drop onto the mother-in-law's back as the daughter-in-law confesses the wrong that she and her husband did to his parents. The mother-in-law reveals her true identity and welcomes the son and daughter-in-law to share life in the palace. In this story, then, the tension between kind and unkind relatives is not between siblings, but across generations.

In a second, related story,[8] an impoverished younger sister is not given any food, not even sweets by her elder sister at whose home there is a wedding. Filled with despair that she was returning home empty-handed to her children, the younger sister picks up a dead snake, thinking that its poison should be the perfect remedy for the family's dire straits. She announces to her children that she has brought fish. She cuts up the snake, pats it with turmeric, and then throws it into hot cooking oil. Instead of snake flesh, she finds hefty chunks of gold clattering in her pan. When the greedy elder sister arrives, wanting to know how her younger sister became rich, she claims a chunk of gold. On her way home, this becomes a snake and kills her.

The respective husbands of the two sisters were never mentioned in any variants. It seemed apparent, though unstated, that the root of the financial inequality lay with the families that the sisters had married into. On account of the Kangra pattern of "repeated alliances"—that is, women being married into families or villages where their relatives have earlier married—women related by birth might also end up in the same village after marriage. In other parts of India, though, this same story tends to feature the wives of two brothers.

Urmilaji actually lived beside her youngest sister Nirmalaji, too. This was very unusual, since they were both in the village of their birth. Nirmalaji was about ten years younger, a confident, good-looking, modern schoolteacher. The changes that had come into the valley during Urmilaji's lifetime meant that the ten-year age gap between the sisters had allowed them very different choices. Urmilaji was educated only as far as primary school before being married as a teenager into a family in the same village. Nirmalaji, though, was one of the first girls in the village to finish high school and gain a teaching certificate. She had taught for several years before she married. Her husband's family lived in Kulu, across another mountain range, and Nirmalaji mostly conducted a commuting relationship so she would not lose her professional seniority in the Kangra school system. She stayed for long periods of time in a wing of Urmilaji's house. It was in her front room that Urmilaji and I were sitting when this story was told.

I was often struck by how intelligent both sisters were, even as their agile minds roamed through very different landscapes. Urmilaji was an expert on the symbolic resources available to her as a pious, Pahari-speaking woman: she knew the appropriate songs, ritual actions, and stories for various auspicious events that involved upper-caste women. Nirmalaji, on the other hand, spoke several languages, including English, and followed political events closely. She spoke with glowing animation about the challenge of every class she took on, the compliments of school inspectors who observed the order in her classrooms, the number of students she was able to guide toward scholarships. Standing somewhat apart from the expected constraints on local women's lives, Nirmalaji was also critical about local traditions. If Urmilaji was like a theologian, speaking as an intellectual steeped in belief, Nirmalaji was like an anthropologist, shifting between closeness and distance as she reflected on the social setting of those beliefs.

Between the sisters was a strong support system. Once when Nirmalaji walked me home, she observed that if a woman earned, she was in a position to make decisions about what to do with money and was less subject to her in-laws' control. For example, if she chose, she might aid a sister. She also said that without Urmilaji's help it would have been much harder for her to pursue her profession. "When my boys were young, she looked after them when I went to school," Nirmalaji exclaimed. Eyes unexpectedly brimming, she said, "She even fed them at her own breast." For sisters so interdependent, then, a story like this could partly function as a model for how sisters should *not* interact.

Urmilaji summarized this tale: "It's a question of serving with affection. The younger sister served both her elder sister and the old man with affection. She served her sister though her sister did not care for her, and she served the old man though she had nothing. It's all a matter of affection, of the feeling in the heart."

FOUR

The Daughter-in Law With No Groom

Having told these first three stories, Urmilaji was warming up. Sello had slipped out at the end of the last story. Now Urmilaji reminisced again, a smile playing over her face, thinking of how her children used to beg for stories.

I followed suit and asked Urmilaji for another story.

"There was a merchant, and there was no son in the house," Urmilaji began. "Though there was no son, he arranged for a daughter-in-law to be married into the family. Have you heard this?"

I shook my head. "Is this a story about Saili?" I asked, thinking about the Sacred Basil Goddess whose marriage I associated with the Five Days of Fasting.

"It's *for* Saili," said Urmilaji. "This is a story about burning oil lamps in her honor. You can tell this story on any of the Five Days of Fasting. It's a story about the effects of keeping oil lamps lit. It was believed that if you kept the lamps lit with a true heart, then the wishes in your heart would be fulfilled; the desires in your mind would be granted."

❊ ❊ ❊

There was a Merchant, a very rich Merchant, with much wealth: like a King. He had a wife who used to light oil lamps for the Five Days of Fasting—

[*"One minute," I say, suddenly worried that with this unexpected bounty of stories, my batteries are running low. I change to freshly charged batteries, then set up the tape recorder again. Urmilaji starts afresh.*]

There was a Merchant's wife. She used to light lamps during the Five Days of Fasting. Now during those days that she lit the lamps, she had a lot of work. Those who live alone have a lot of work. If women live together, if a woman has a daughter-in-law, then the daughter-in-law helps by her side and all the work is done. But this woman had to keep performing her tasks all by herself. [*Urmilaji lapses into a sing-song voice that seems to underline the repetitiveness of all the routine duties.*]

59

> She had to look after the lamps,
> she had to perform the worship of Saili, too;
> then in the house, poor thing,
> she had to look after her husband,
> to cook for him
> and feed him
> and do all the work.

One day she said to the Merchant. "Everyone else has a daughter-in-law in their house. Get a daughter-in-law for us too. Then she'll do my work for me."

The Merchant said, "Wife, what are you saying? If we don't have a son, how are we going to get a daughter-a-law?"

She said, "Just bring a daughter-in-law. Get her married, and have her brought here."

The Merchant, poor fellow, was really perplexed. He said, "Alright," and he called a Purohit, a Brahman ritual specialist. He said to him, "Listen, my wife says she wants to have a daughter-in-law married."

Now Brahmans are very clever. He said [*in a shrill, crafty voice*], "No problem! I'll be the go-between. I'll have a daughter-in-law married and brought to you."

The Merchant said, "Do this if you can. Then her wish will be fulfilled. She says, 'Everyone else's daughter-in-law helps them out with work, and I'm all alone, working away all day long.'"

He said, "No problem. During the Five Days of Fasting we'll have the marriage performed. I'll bring you your daughter-in-law!"

Bas. So the Brahman set off. He traveled two or three different roads; this means he traveled two or three regions away from this one. Then he went to this other kingdom where there was another Purohit, for in every kingdom there were different Purohits to do the work. So this Merchant's Purohit came from one kingdom, and he met another Purohit from this other kingdom. He had set out to find a groom for a girl. The two of them met on the road: Brahman and Brahman.

They began to talk among themselves: "Where are you going? Why? What for?"

The second Brahman said, "There is a certain Merchant who has a daughter. I've set out to look for a groom for her."

He said, "Then the matter is settled! I too have set out for a Merchant, but to find a girl."

"Fine. No problem."

"But there's one condition," he said, "It's like this . . . the son won't come to the marriage.

"There will be a dagger. This dagger will be brought in the groom's palanquin, and this will be married and come back with the girl. The son won't come to be married himself."

The second Brahman said, "What's there in that? He said [*in a singsong voice*]:

"There's a Merchant there,
there's a Merchant here;
a Merchant's daughter,
a Merchant's son:
marriage among Merchants.
There's no problem if the dagger is sent to the wedding!"

He thought that there was a son at home and this was just an engagement. [*Urmilaji laughs*]. How was he to know that he'd gone ahead without there being a son?!

[*Urmilaji laughs again, extending a palm toward me; I touch it lightly with my fingers, so sharing the joke*].

"No problem," the first Brahman said. They set the date for the wedding, they made all the arrangements. "We'll arrive on such and such a date for the wedding. But we'll come along with a dagger."

[*Urmilaji pauses to make sure I understand that daggers are frequently sent with a groom at the time of marriage. At a Rajput wedding I'd attended, I'd seen such a dagger, wrapped in pink gauze to match the turbans of the men in the groom's party.*]

"Well, that dagger will be brought to be married."

"No problem."

So this one set off for his Merchant, and that one went off to his Merchant. The first arrived. "I made the betrothal," he said, "I set the date for marriage." The Merchant and his wife were happy. The other went to the girl's side. "I offered vermilion for the the betrothal to a certain Merchant's son."

Fine. A Merchant found a Merchant. What more could they want?

So they took and they gave [ceremonial gifts] and the day of the marriage came. The dagger was sent off to the wedding. This was how the girl was married.

When she was married, poor thing, she looked around, and wondered where "he"[1] could be. She was always busy and working. There was no son to be seen, and his mother now just lazed around. They had deceived her, saying that on the day of the wedding feast he had gone off to work somewhere and that sometime he might return. But how long could they keep deceiving her?

Now, poor thing, she kept working away, she was always busy. In her mind, she kept thinking, "When will I see him? These eyes have never seen him."

Bas. The old woman used to light lamps. When they were lit, they stood up in a cluster, each flame like a peacock. Then she'd take them off the tray and put them away in the cupboard. Then she'd go off to bathe, having shown the daughter-in-law all the work there was to do. That's it. On one bank, the old woman was happy, now that she had a hardworking daughter-in-law. But on the other bank, her daughter-in-law was unhappy. "She's showing me just what she wants to show, but when will she show me her son?"

Whenever she took off she'd say, "Bride,[2] don't open this cupboard."

The daughter-in-law would wonder, "What's this? What could this old woman have in there except the soot of oil lamps?"

Bas. One day the daughter-in-law thought, "Look at this, she never gives me instructions about anything else. All she says is, 'Do all the work, and don't open the cupboard.' Today I absolutely must open the cupboard."

When she opened the cupboard, there was this very handsome boy inside.

[*"Really!" I exclaim.*]

Yes. Very handsome and with the look of a Prince. She said, "You've been deceiving me by hiding in here. To this day you were never shown to me. This is why the old woman tells me not to open this cupboard." She blamed it on the old woman, "She sat her son down here and wouldn't show him to me."

Bas. He climbed out. They spoke nicely to each other. They talked, they chatted, and they were happy.

Then she said, "Come on outside."

He said, "I won't come out like that. What you must do is tell the Merchant that on the full-moon day he should sponsor a big fire ritual[3] and a big feast. Then everyone should be seated to eat. There should be no man appointed to serve the food, and that's when I'll come out." That's what he said to her.

"No problem," she said.

So then the old woman came back. She saw that her daughter-in-law was tremendously happy. What could this be about?

The daughter-in-law said, "Mother!" She said, "On this full-moon day we must sponsor a big fire ritual!"

Now, whatever the daughter-in-law said, the mother-in-law, poor thing, would try to do: she wanted her to stay happy and have no sorrow. So she said, "Tell this to the Merchant."

[*Sello has appeared with steaming cups of tea in steel glasses. In response to my whispered thank you, she interjects, "Among us, we don't say thank you." "Among us, we do," I reply, "And it's become a habit." "Yes, it's become* your *habit," says Sello bluntly. Urmilaji pauses to laugh.*]

And she said, "We'll do just as you say. We'll have a fire ritual, there's no problem."

Bas. So the Merchant returned. His daughter-in-law told him, "On this full-moon day you must have a feast."

He said, "That's no problem, child, we can have a feast."

So they began to prepare for the feast. They got all the ingredients together:

rice, lentils, all sorts of ingredients were collected. They announced that they would have a big ritual and feast on the full-moon day. Then, when all the rice and everything had been cooked and was ready, she said to her father-in-law: "Now go stand beside Saili and call out three times:

> If anyone is listening, come out to serve.
> If anyone is listening, come out to serve.
> If anyone is listening, come out to serve.
> [*jo sundā gundā hai tā priye denā chalā aur*]."

Now the people there had been seated for the feast at the same time. Everyone: the cooks, their helpers, everyone. The Merchant stood beside Saili and he said those words: "If anyone is listening, come out to serve."

And from inside, wearing draped, yellow garments,[4] he came out in a flash. He came out and served everyone. And all the assembled people[5] were happy. "There is a son in the home of a childless couple! There is a son in the home of a childless couple! There is a son in the home of a childless couple!"[6]

❀ ❀ ❀

"Did you like that?" asked Urmilaji, shifting from her authoritative storytelling persona to a more shy and deferential version of herself.

"It's very beautiful," I replied, turning over the images from the story in my mind. I wondered whether, to a virginal bride, a groom might be identified in a metonymic way as "dagger." Could growing intimacy without the constant supervision of a mother-in-law demanding domestic labor allow for a disembodied dagger to fill out with the substance of a human being with whom one could talk? But I hesitated to air these thoughts.

"There's another story similar to this," said Urmilaji, "in which there's a frog."

"What happened?" I asked.

FIVE

The Frog Groom

Urmilaji continued:

❊ ❊ ❊

A woman rubbed at her foot when she was spinning [*Urmilaji reaches down to touch her bare foot*]. She rubbed her foot, a blister formed, and a frog came out.

[*"Like Ganeshji," I suggest, thinking of how the Goddess Parvati once rubbed at the dirt on her body and had a son who was later to become the elephant-headed God, Ganesh. "Yes!" Urmilaji smiles at the mention of this well-known myth, "Just like that; Ganesh was formed that way too."*]

So in this way the frog emerged. As she sat at her spinning wheel, he would jump around beside her. She raised him as a son. "This is my frog, this is my frog" [*swaying back and forth, hands cradled at her breast*]: she really loved him.

Now she too used to light lamps. After a few years she said to her Merchant, "Let's get our frog married!"

The Merchant said to her, "Is a frog ever married? Among frogs are there weddings too? How will he set out for his in-laws' house? How will he bring a wife home?"

But she was really adamant. "There's a daughter-in-law in everyone's house and I just have a frog. I must have him married."

The Merchant called his Purohit, "Go, brother, go fix an engagement for the frog!"

[*Urmilaji pauses. "And then?" I coax. Urmilaji's voice fills with droll amusement.*]

Then the Purohit went off! He set out to betroth the frog. When he came to the next kingdom he said to a certain Merchant there, "We want to fix an engagement for the son of a Merchant."

This man had just one daughter who had come of age. "No problem," he said, "We'll do it." So they arranged the marriage.

The Purohit said, "But there's one thing. At the time of the wedding, a dagger will be sent, the boy won't come himself."

64

"There's nothing wrong with that," the man said. "The dagger can stand in for him."

So the Purohit came back and told the Merchant that he had performed the engagement in the next kingdom. The Merchant was still pondering, "How can one get a frog married? How will we explain this to a daughter-in-law?"

Bas. So the daughter-in-law was brought. She came and she looked here, she looked there, she looked everywhere. All she saw was a frog jumping around at her mother-in-law's side. Nothing else. She thought, "They have no son. This frog is all they have." And she was always terribly sad.

Bas. When the mother-in-law went off to bathe in the mornings, she would leave the frog jumping inside, where she had lit the lamps. She would tell her daughter-in-law, "Don't open the door."

The daughter-in-law thought, "She always tells me not to open the door to the inner room. Today I must definitely open it up and take a look inside."

When she opened the door she saw that the frog had taken off his skin and hung it up. He was sitting there, with beads to chant with in his hand.

She said, "So you've been deceiving me, have you? I've been looking around in all four directions for you, thinking 'Maybe he's away, where could he be?' And all this time you've been right here?!"

Then she grabbed at the frog skin and she said, "I'm going to burn this up!"

He stopped her. He said [*mildly*], "No. Don't burn this today. Tell the Merchant that he must hold a feast on the full-moon day. He shouldn't get any men to serve at the feast. Then standing in the courtyard he should call out for me. Only then will I come out from inside. Don't say that you're going to burn this now."

So they played pachisi together for a long time. Then when the old woman was due back, the daughter-in-law closed the door again and sat down. She returned to her own work.

When the old woman appeared, she saw a happy daughter-in-law!

"You seem to be very happy today," she said.

When the Merchant came home the daughter-in-law told him, "We must hold a feast. There should be no servers. At that time in your house, in our house, you'll have a son."

The Merchant thought about this. He said, "If we didn't have a son before where is one going to come from to serve the food? Certainly, we'll hold a feast, it's a matter of joy to hold one. If we could have a son, what more could we want?"

"You will have a son," she said. "You are to have your son."

So with great happiness they organized the feast. They organized it, all the food was prepared, and everyone sat down to eat.

Then the father-in-law called out, "If anyone is listening, then come out to serve." And the young man emerged from within.

In this way, for these people too, the lamps gave them a son. *Bas.*[1]

✳ ✳ ✳

"Just as in the other story, a dagger was married without there being a son; in the same way, a frog is married in this one," concluded Urmilaji. Given the similarity between the two stories, she seemed to have glossed over some of the details when she told the second one.

The image of a cuddled and coddled frog has always seemed to amuse storytellers and their listeners whenever I've heard this tale told. To Urmilaji, the link between a frog and a child was straightforward. "Frogs jump around," she explained, "They're always hopping and jumping, just like children."

In other variants, this frog is a King or even a divine King in disguise, and the story is known as "The Frog King" (*mīnakū rājā*). Born from the blister to a childless woman (usually a widow living with a widowed mother-in-law), the frog is cherished as a son. When he hears that there will be a gathering of princes for a Princess to choose her husband, he sets hopping off. The Princess does indeed choose him, to the dismay of his surrogate mothers. They worry about whether a Princess will be comfortable in their humble home, and what kind of husband their little frog could make. Yet the Princess flourishes, visibly content. Eventually, the mother spies on the bedroom and is amazed to find that the frog takes off his skin at night to play pachisi with his wife. She asks what can be done, and the Princess requests that a second big gathering of princes be held for her to choose a mate. Then, the mother calls, "Frog King, emerge!" (*mīnakū rājā bāhar ā*) and the frog comes strutting out in his regal human form.

Both of Urmilaji's stories start out with a couple experiencing the sorrow of childlessness. In Kangra—as in India generally—a childless couple is thought to be terribly unfortunate. The woman who creates a frog seems to find some companionship in his hopping about and comfort in lavishing affection on him. Like her counterpart in the dagger story, she also yearns for a daughter-in-law. In the dagger story, where there is no groom altogether, and so no vindicating rationale for the surrogate son to be married, the mother-in-law's desires for a daughter-in-law are blunt. She wants the daughter-in-law at her side to help out with the unrelenting housework. She is willing to trick a girl in order to gain her labor.

These stories underscore how marriage in a joint family is not just a relationship between a husband and wife. Other stories in this collection describe the rivalry between a man's wife and sister, but in these two stories the relationship between a mother-in-law and daughter-in-law is highlighted. In a joint family, a mother-in-law and daughter-in-law are together responsible for accomplishing women's work; the mother-in-law can delegate or share tasks according to her inclinations. In a given day, the mother-in-law and daughter-in-law are likely to spend more time together than husband and wife. (When I visited Kangra in 1994 after getting married, Urmilaji and other older women all asked me in far greater detail about the temperament and habits of my mother-in-law than of my husband!)

The ties between a mother and son in South Asia are notoriously intense.[2] In these stories, the mother-in-law's control over her son seems dramatized by her ability to lock him away from his wife. It is only when the wife disobeys orders, building intimacy on her own terms, that she finds a way of luring him from the womb-like space (cupboard/inner room) and form (absent dagger/ flaccid frog) in which he was concealed.

The inner room (*obarī*) in traditional Kangra houses is a place of fertility and auspiciousness: it is here that the gods are kept in an alcove, grains are stored, new brides are ushered in for viewing by their female relatives, marriages are consummated, and childbirths occur. In this powerful arena, where the lamps are burning, the daughter-in-law finally meets her mate in human form. The rosary in his hand would seem to indicate his spiritual, even ascetic, pursuits. Emerging from this womb-like space and from the skin of the frog, he is reborn into a different form appropriate to his married life.

Both the dagger and the frog, which stand for the groom, would seem to have phallic connotations. Urmilaji was always sedate and circumspect on such matters in my presence, and to this day I have not mustered the gall to ask if she would agree. But I knew other women in other households and villages who found drawing connections between pointed objects and phalluses a source of giddy amusement. There is even a prescribed setting for this amusement: the *giddā*, an occasion when women of a groom's family are left alone in their household, along with all the female relatives and neighbors gathered for the occasion. (The men all set off to escort the groom to his marriage in another village, where they stay overnight usually returning in the late afternoon of the next day). The women who have gathered for festivities but who are now left behind turn to "putting on a *giddā*." They lock themselves into a room to dance, sing, cross-dress, and perform bawdy skits late into the night. At these events I have seen women proffering long ladles with imaginary "clarified butter" toward each other's crotches; brandishing bats for beating out clothes; and thrusting rolling pins through holes torn in flat round breads. Even my six-inch microphone could become an object of helpless hilarity. It seems to me, then, that a dagger wrapped so carefully and sent along with a groom could easily be connected to these other symbols. For the frog, too, which crouches small then extends to hop, there might be such associations. But this is my own guesswork, and lacking the nerve to ask Urmilaji, I have no evidence that this is a widespread association.

What did the bride and groom do when they met? They talked happily to each other; they played *chaupās*—a form of pachisi—or as Urmilaji later added, "you could call it chess (*shatranj*)." All this implied a concentration on each other and on a shared task. Fieldworkers from other parts of India have observed that playing pachisi as well as "talking" (*bātchīt*) often serve as a euphemism for sexual relations.[3] I learned from other older Kangra women that "talking" (*gilānā*) in Kangra, too, could have the same connotations. In another context, as Urmilaji explained the frequent motif of oil lamps in songs about marriage, she said that in the past, when the codes of joint family etiquette were even stronger, the only time that a husband and wife could be together alone was at night. Lamplight meant that they could talk freely, she said. The joint family taboo against a husband and wife talking openly during the day, then, charged the very act of talking alone at night as implying intimacy at several levels.

The oil lamps in these stories are sacred, unlike the utilitarian lamps in songs. Yet, the association of lamplight in inner rooms with intimacy seems to hold. The worship of lamps and meeting by lamplight also perhaps reaffirmed women's sense that success in their marriages depended on supernatural intervention stemming from their own piety. So lighting lamps during the Five Days of Fasting would appear to yield results that carry over into more prosaic evenings.

It also struck me as significant that it is after this encounter alone with the husband that the daughter-in-law in the frog story tells the Merchant "in your house, in our house, you'll have a son." Making the transition from "you" to "our," this experience of intimacy seemed to have cemented her loyalty to the family to which she has been given in marriage.

Yet, this is my interpretation, rather than Urmilaji's. To Urmilaji, the central message of this story, like the others in the same corpus, was the power of devotion, expressed through the burning of the lamps.

I asked Urmilaji just whose devotion was being rewarded when the son/husband in her stories took human form: the mother-in-law's or the daughter-in-law's? Urmilaji reflected a moment. "All this happened because of the mother-in-law's devotion," she said. "It was her who kept the lamps lit." In a sense then, the mother-in-law created the setting for the transformation of her son.

A charming parallel story featuring a cat daughter rather than a frog son is also told in Kangra.[4] In this story a childless woman adopts a cat as her daughter. She ties a bell around the cat's neck, and since the bell tinkles—*chun chun chun*—the cat is known as "Tinkling Kitty" (*chunako billī*) or just plain "Tinkling." After a while, Tinkling's mother wants to marry her off. Tinkling is married into a household where the mother-in-law also dotes on her. The mother-in-law lights oil lamps for the Five Days of Fasting. One day, she leaves

Tinkling with the lamps, and Tinkling piously raises up the wicks from the oil with her paws. Then, when she cleans herself, licking and using her paws, her fur turns to skin. She becomes a beautiful woman, all human but for a patch of fur on her back. The mother-in-law returns and is stunned to find a lovely stranger sitting with the lamps. She demands to know where her adored Tinkling Kitty is. It is only by displaying the patch of fur that the woman convinces her mother-in-law that this is indeed her. And of course, the husband (who is never mentioned until this point) is delighted too.

Urmilaji's sympathetic portrayal of the mother-in-law in her stories seemed to echo her desire to receive a daughter-in-law into the family. Already considering Sello's marriage into another family, and Nirmalaji's possible move back to her husband's home in Kulu, Urmilaji more than once emphasized how important it was for a woman to have other women working along with her in the house. Yet, marriages being so expensive, her hopes for her sons' weddings had to be temporarily delayed. The wedding of a daughter is notoriously expensive, especially if a dowry is included. But the wedding of a son should not be underestimated as another major expense, also requiring gifts of gold ornaments and clothes, and several feasts for the entire village and assembled relatives.

"Why did he only come out to serve at the feast?" I asked, thinking of the many Kangra feasts I had been to that celebrated festive occasions in a community setting. Line upon line of people sat cross-legged in the courtyard, leaf plates before them, as servers moved up and down the rows, systematically dispensing water and a subtly flavored progression of courses: some with mustard oil, some sour, until the grand finale of sweet orange rice. "Is there something special about serving?"

"Serving is often done by men who belong to the family," Urmilaji replied. "Also, at the time of a feast, everyone is together. The whole village and all the relatives are present. This allows them to recognize the son together. If he just come out at any other time, people would have been suspicious, asking: "Who is this person?" But this way, they understood."

SIX

The Fragrant Melon

Having finished the last story, Urmilaji humored a few of my queries, but then she briskly moved on. "Have you heard the story about the melon?" she asked. "The daughter-in-law ate it—"

"Yes, and then the mouse," I put in. I had heard this story in several variants. But I drew back, remembering that if I was too anxious to parade my knowledge, I would not hear what Urmilaji had to say. Years before, I had interrupted Swamiji when he started in on a story about a holy man who reforms a fierce snake, saying I already knew it. Later, I often regretted that I had missed the opportunity to record Swamiji's version of this well-known tale. Swamiji himself reprimanded me on a separate occasion: "When you tell people you already know something, you lose the chance to learn something from them." So now, with Urmilaji, I cut short my own display of knowledge to inquire: "And then?"

"So have you heard it or not?" Urmilaji asked, bemused.

"Well, a little," I said foolishly, turning off my recorder to fumble my way into a speech about how many women told stories, but everyone told them differently and few told them so well as her.

Urmilaji listened, but did not comment. "What's the time?" she asked.

I glanced at my watch. "Four thirty," I said. Living through so many different lives and predicaments that afternoon, time seemed to have meandered off its regular course.

"I'll tell this story about the melon and finish up."

❊ ❊ ❊

There was a father-in-law and a daughter-in-law. *Bas.* The father-in-law came from his shop bringing a melon with him. He brought this and gave it to his daughter-in-law, saying, "Take, bride, put this away." She probably took it and set it aside.

Now, melons have a powerful, inviting fragrance even when they are tasteless

70

inside; it's a beautiful fragrance. She was pregnant. Her heart longed to eat it, to eat the melon. But she was scared of her father-in-law: "When he returns, he'll ask where I put the melon." So how could she eat it? But her heart insisted: sometimes one's heart does this, insisting on eating a certain thing. She took the melon, gouged out some flesh from one side [*with her index finger*], and ate it. She ate just a little and then she left the rest of the melon just as it was.

Probably it was the next day when the father-in-law said [*forcefully*], "Daughter-in-law, bring the melon! I'll cut it up."

She was scared, poor thing: "I've eaten a little, now what will I say?"

So she brought it and he demanded [*in a brisk tone*], "What's happened here?" Inside it was half gone.

She said [*matter-of-factly*], "I had put it away and the mouse ate it."

She told a lie, poor thing. She was protecting herself—right?—saying "I didn't eat it." That's why she didn't just say right then, "I ate it, now it's gone, now what can we do?" The daughters-in-law here, you know, used to be really innocent and naive, and they were so timid, too. These days, a daughter-in-law would say in a flash, "I had the whim and I just ate it up!" [*"Isn't it so?" Urmilaji inquires with a laugh, echoing the refrain I often heard from older women that daughters-in-law today were extremely bold. "Yes," I agree.*] So she said, "The mouse ate it up."

The father-in-law, poor fellow, didn't say anything. He peeled it and sliced it, and probably ate the rest of it himself. But the mouse was enraged: "She has falsely used my name and implicated me in this matter."

What he did was this: he went to her while she was sleeping at night, poor thing. In the past women used to wear a short blouse up to here[1] [*Urmilaji indicates her midriff and forearms*]. These used to be taken off at night and kept by the pillow before going to sleep. So the mouse took her blouse and pulled it out to the main entrance where the Watchman was sleeping and threw it on the Watchman's bed.

Then he took the Watchman's cap and put it on her bed.

The Merchant got up in the morning and went out. As he went through the entranceway he began to wake up the Watchman. Now in the past, servants wouldn't appear before their masters with an uncovered head. When the Watchman looked for his cap, it wasn't there. He looked here, he looked there, he looked everywhere, but he couldn't find his cap. The father-in-law saw that her blouse was lying there.

So the father-in-law quietly turned around. He came back and went to the inner room and began to wake up the daughter-in-law. When she opened up the doors of the inner room, she couldn't find her blouse. And the cap was lying right there.

He said, "This daughter-in-law has become immoral. How can his cap come

71

here and her blouse go there? These two must be having an affair. She's bad." He ordered, "Take her off and burn her alive! She's no longer worthy of being kept in this house."

The poor thing: silent, no way she could object. She said, "If you are going to burn me up then burn me up. But let me light my oil lamps the way I usually do." She lit the lamps the usual way she did, but instead of oil, she put in water. She lit these lamps and set them in the inner room. Then as she was taking off, she put a stalk of rice hay into the lock.

Led by her father-in-law, the local men made a stretcher, they put her on the stretcher as though she was a corpse, and they probably also sent a telegram to her husband. First they sent the telegram, "Your wife has died." Then they took her off to be burnt.

When they got there to the cremation grounds by the riverbank and set her down, she said, "Sirs, I usually set little boats with lamps on them floating in the stream. Let me set these afloat and then you can burn me up."

They said [*nonchalantly*], "Go ahead, set them afloat."

Very quickly and efficiently she made some little boats [from bamboo bark] and put everything [*that the ritual demands*] into them and set them afloat. [*"In the water," adds Sello.*] In the water. Then they laid her down on the slabs of the cremation pyre and began to wait for the husband so he could be the one to light the fire. They had sent him the news, "Your wife has died."

So he, poor fellow, started home along a route that had a stream flowing across it. The stream was flowing, and these little boats were coming along, talking among themselves.

"Look here, these times are really astonishing!" one boat was saying. "A certain Merchant is burning his daughter-in-law up alive."

He heard their talk. He kept listening and thinking about their words.

[*Urmilaji explains to me in an aside, "When we launch those little boats we say to them.*

bere o bere jānde jāniyo	Boat oh boat, go along.
merī gal gilānde jāniyo	Speaking on my behalf, go along.
gurhe dā dhelu khānde jāniyo	Eating a nugget of brown sugar, go along.]

So the boats were speaking about the daughter-in-law of this certain Merchant, saying that she was being prepared to be burned alive though she was not guilty. He heard this and he dashed ahead, thinking, "Let it not be that she's burned while I'm on my way!"

He saw from afar that she'd been placed on the pyre. He had an umbrella with him, and he waved this to motion that they shouldn't extend their hands to light the fire. Some people saw him, and said, "He's come, he's come. If this is to be done, the fire should be lit by him." They stopped.

They stopped, and he reached there. He asked. "What's the matter? What's going on here?"

Then his father spoke. He said, "Her way of comporting herself wasn't any good. She's a disgrace to our house. This is why she's being burnt up alive."

He said to his father, "No, there's nothing wrong with her. It was like this: you had brought a melon, and she ate it, and then she said to you that the mouse had eaten it. It's the mouse that plotted this mix-up. She's not to blame. The little boats went along saying all this, and I heard this from them."

The father understood. "This must be right if the little boats said it, else how would he know what had happened? That this and that happened?"

Then she said, "If you doubt that I'm good and true, then go look at the lamps that are burning in the inner room with a stalk of hay serving as a lock—go see if these are still burning or not."

So all the people went there. But the lock wouldn't open. No matter who tried, this lock of mere hay wouldn't give way.

[*"This was of hay?" inquires Sello. "Yes," her mother affirms.*]

It just wouldn't open up. Then he said, "No, this is true. She is a devotee. This is why."

Then they brought her from the cremation grounds in a palanquin, with a lot of pomp as if it was a wedding. They brought her, and then she undid the hay lock. It sprang open. When they looked inside, the lamps were still burning after all this time.

She bowed before the lamps, saying "Eternal Goddess Lamps, you are true. Those who serve you with devotion are certain to be rewarded."[2]

❀ ❀ ❀

"This is the story of the little boats (*bere*)," Urmilaji concluded.

"Told on which day?" I asked.

"This is told on the day when the little boats are floated."

On the fourth day of the Five Days of Fasting, observant women come trooping out in clusters of relatives to meadows beside streams. All of them set little boats afloat, but the materials of which these boats are made and the steps of the ritual are variable. Brahman women and some Rajputs build little cottages (*tapru*) from rocks for the Goddess Saili, outfitting these houses with an extra shed for the cow, packets of spices for cooking, oil lamps, and a tiny red flag to proclaim that a deity lives there. Rajput women who work in the fields may build houses from clods of earth. These houses are built directly adjacent to each other, sharing walls, much like the houses of extended families. Sood women like Urmilaji, however do not build these houses at all. (My question "why not?" was met with the simple answer, "It's not our practice.")

The boats used in this ritual are most often a sheet of parchment-like bark peeled from bamboo. Alternatively, flat cardboard boxes otherwise used for packaging sweets are increasingly set to use. This choice is especially popular among women of the Sood castes, for often their male relatives own shops where such boxes are readily available. Bowls of green leaves sewn together with twigs used for feasts may also be adapted as boats.

Each woman loads up her own boats, usually two or three, for the boats need to be able to talk together. Soods for example, tend toward just two boats, but then light a wick on a petal in the grass which serves as the *sakhī*—translated variously as the "girlfriend" or the "witness" (in Hindi *sākshī*). Brahmans, on the other hand, may have three: two plus one as the "caretaker" (*jāmun*) who watches over them as they proceed. The loads in each boat include a few aluminum coins, almonds or walnuts, coarse red thread, flower petals, a scatter of rice grains, a lump of brown sugar, a piece of red cloth, some frankincense, and, finally, a lit clay lamp. As each woman floats a boat downstream, she recites some version of the same incantation that the woman in the story repeated. This incantation is recited again for every boat, asking it to float downstream while speaking on her behalf. After the boats are launched, the berry bush may be worshipped. Alternatively, women settle down directly to the business of telling stories appropriate to the occasion.

I had been present at such boat launches in the past. In 1994, I had the good fortune of visiting when Urmilaji and her relatives were performing the ritual. Urmilaji's retelling on this occasion was very much the same as what she had told me before, though this time she was occasionally interrupted with prompting or comments from her relatives (for example, her sister Nirmalaji insisted that in this retelling, the telegram sent to the husband was incongruous, since the story was set in the past). Urmilaji also made explicit what was assumed in the earlier retelling: that the Father-in-law and daughter-in-law were living alone since the son had migrated off to work elsewhere. She also switched from the father-in-law waking up his Watchman and daughter-in-law, to them waking up earlier, each frantically searching for blouse or cap. (In local logic, it was always inferiors like servants and daughters-in-law who should wake up first.) So when the father-in-law came to inquire about what was delaying his daughter-in-law, he found her wrapped up in a sheet.

In this retelling Urmilaji also elaborated on the miraculous nature of the lamps that were lit indoors: wicks of hay, floating in water. This added to the miracle of the lamps still burning hours later in the room locked away by the magically strong stalk of rice hay. And, while she had finished her earlier retelling with a salutation to the Eternal Goddess Lamps (*paramesvariye diye*), here she ended by saluting the Boat Gods: "Oh Boat Gods, just as you protected her honor, so preserve it for all of us too" (*paramasvareyo bereyo paramasvareyo jīyān tinhānde lāj rakheyo tiyān sārediyā rakhiyā*). "And that," concluded Nirmalaji briskly, "is why women float these boats."

Explaining why such boats are floated, Urmilaji reminded me that they are set afloat in other places too; for example, down the Ganges river in Haridwar, a sacred pilgrimage site. I thought immediately of little clay lamps I had floated myself down the Godavari river in Nasik, lights borne along with the current, bobbing hopefully in the gathering darkness. "When you float a boat," Urmilaji said, "you are asking that your family be happy, that it neither dwindle nor degenerate. By filling a boat, you ask that your family has everything it needs. Being a householder is like being on a boat. So you request, 'May our family lineage (*kul*) float along to the future, growing bigger.'"

Urmilaji's words resonated for me with the Sanskritic imagery of the "ocean of worldliness" (*saṃsāra sāgar*) that individuals must cross. Even a pilgrimage site is seen as a point of "crossing" (*tīrth*) toward the shore of salvation. In Brahmanically based traditions, the ultimate crossing is that of the soul moving through the whirlpools of karma, death, and countless rebirths to reach a place of merging with divinity and the end of rebirths. On a less grand scale, in both colloquial Hindi and Pahari, to hope that someone's "boat crosses" is simply to wish that they successfully achieve a desired project. As Urmilaji said, "One message of this story is that boats take you across, they accomplish what is best for you."[3]

A boat then, might stand for the trajectory of a particular individual. In the ritual of boat launching, each set of boats was explicitly asked to represent a particular woman. Yet, in Urmilaji's explanation, a boat was equated not just with a certain woman, but an entire patrilineage. By propitiating the boat deity with sweet offerings and requesting it to float onward, representing the woman's best interests by speaking for her, the ritual can be seen as an in-marrying woman's attempt to secure her position in the family of her husband. While codes of male precedence, female modesty, and deference to elders would seem to prohibit young in-marrying women from speaking for themselves, boats are enjoined to do so on their behalf.

For example, the daughter-in-law in the story did not protest to her incensed father-in-law or the group of village men who backed him in the task of punishing her by burning her alive (evoking bride burnings over dowries reported from contemporary Indian cities). Rather, the daughter-in-law continued with her ritual of lighting lamps and requested the boats to speak on her behalf. Her husband, overhearing the boats, was able to intervene and rescue her from death.

The boats bore forward the woman's best interests yet it was the husband who ultimately had the authority to save her. Similarly, in Kangra joint families, it seems that a new daughter-in-law can successfully achieve what she wants in terms of the larger family only if her husband acts as her intermediary. As another woman of my own age once fondly reminisced, when she was a new bride, her husband had said to her, "Don't worry what anyone says to you. Know that I am here for you, and don't worry about anyone else. If you need anything, just tell me!"

Yet, in the local interpretation of marital relations, a husband's goodwill and protection is achieved not just through a couple's intimacy but also through merit accrued by a woman's virtue and piety. As Urmilaji said about the woman in the story, "She did the right things. She was a chaste woman. It was the power of her practice that saved her." The woman's pious practice was what led the husband to arrive at the right moment and to rescue her. Just as she had inwardly "locked" herself into devotion to her husband and away from association with other men, so her stalk of rice hay miraculously locked the inner room where ritual lamps were burning and where intimacies between husband and wife first occurred. Taken away like a corpse on an open stretcher, she was brought back with renewed affirmation in a bridal palanquin.

"One of the messages of this story is that you shouldn't tell lies," said Urmilaji. "Especially lies about mice. The mouse is an attendant of Ganesh after all! He's right there beside Ganesh, and so if you worship Ganesh you're worshipping a mouse too." Ganesh, the elephant-headed deity who removes obstacles and is saluted at the beginning of all ventures, is indeed usually represented with a mouse beside him. This mouse is his animal vehicle (*vāhan*). A Ganesh was carved, in his customary cross-legged pose, on the stone stand from which the sacred basil plant grew in Urmilaji's courtyard. On Urmilaji's altar, built into a niche in the wall of the house's front room, was another small Ganesh. Framed by spangled red curtains and seated beneath a low-wattage blue bulb, this Ganesh and the other deities with him seemed to radiate benevolence on all who passed through the room.

Before I took off with my haul of six stories, I asked Urmilaji with earnest ethnographic curiosity what work she would now turn to. She replied that she was about to start cooking the evening meal for her sons who were due to return home from their jobs as tobacco agents in town (her husband worked at another end of the valley and was rarely around). While on the subject of work, she told me about how, in the past, there had been workers from lower castes tied to upper-caste households through exchange relations: they came around to help in fields, cut grass for livestock, plaster the house, grind the spices, and other manual tasks. The only work that women like her had to do in the past, Urmilaji said, was attend to the cooking. But now that lower castes made good wages by working outside too, they asked for daily wages that were hard to afford. So upper-caste women had had to learn all kinds of work they had not known before.

The differences between the past and the present was a recurring theme in people's conversations in Kangra. It was as though, in instructing me about their lives, beliefs, social arrangements, and economic circumstances, adults also needed to let me know that the present moment of rapid social change was peculiar, strange even to them. Urmilaji went on to talk about how in the past people had fewer things: only little boys were given sweaters while girls made do with shawls. New clothes were given to children twice a year, in the spring and in the fall.[4] "Not like today!" Urmilaji said, "Look at all the things in the markets, all the things that children must have."

This theme of a past era (*pichhleyā jamānā*) ran through many of the folktales too. As Urmilaji commented as she told the story, daughters-in-law *used* to be innocent and naive, women *used* to wear blouses they took off at night, lower castes *used* to never appear with their heads uncovered before superiors. This perception of a past era could sometimes be challenged by audiences listening to stories: for example, when Urmilaji retold this by the river's edge, her sister wondered aloud whether there would really have been telegrams in that past era. Similarly, after a Brahman woman once told this same story, her younger female relatives took me aside to say that she'd got it wrong when she said the Merchant had put out mouse poison after the melon incident: who had ever heard of mouse poison in those times?! At other times, though, the present could be effortlessly slipped in, as when a young Rajput woman retold this story inserting a ring in place of the blouse, which needed to be explained.

Urmilaji walked outdoors with me. The sky was fading, the evening mild and cleared of the earlier meteorological drama. "Come back another day," Urmilaji invited as we parted at the crossroads. "Whenever you have time, come back. I still haven't told you the story about the lion."

I walked homeward, mind swirling with the stories I'd heard. I took deep, happy breaths, anticipating the stories to come. I stopped in for a brief visit at Tayi's household on my way. Women of this Rajput family were squatting outside with stainless steel platters before them, picking and cleaning piles of black lentils for a forthcoming village-wide feast. I sat down beside Tayi, who had first told me some of these stories, and said that I had been visiting Urmilaji and listening to stories.

A smile broke out over Tayi's kind and freckled old face. Urmilaji, she said, was very knowledgeable, very wise. Tayi extracted a leaf cigarette (*biṛi*) from the pocket of her undershirt and lit up, reminiscing about what fun Urmilaji's wedding within the same village had been. "We went to both houses," said Tayi. "We danced a *giddā*, we said good-bye to the bride [at her family's home], then we walked just a few steps with the palanquin and welcomed her from the other side!"

I resisted the standard exhortation to spend the night chorused by all members of Tayi's family with my standard reply within the village: "My mother will be waiting." The dusk was thickening as I continued along the winding road. It was unusual for a woman to be wandering about alone after dark, and I picked up my step.

At the spring near the summer home of our friend the Sikh potter, trained decades ago in Japan, I turned to the left. I proceeded along a beaten path that traced its way up the hillside between a high hedge and terraced wheat fields. It was almost dark when I arrived in my mother's overgrown garden. Crickets whirred up to a sprinkle of stars. A dim light shone from the porch beside the front door. I knew that the door would be locked, and I went around to the back entrance near the kitchen.

Ma was cooking dinner in her small, smoke-tinted kitchen with crowded walls. A print of Saptashring Nivasini Devi, the many-armed goddess who Swamiji used to worship, presided above the hearth. The shelves were lined with old Nescafe bottles now filled with the textures and colors of Indian spices and home-grown Western herbs. Above the rickety table where my mother worked, a small, flour-smeared shortwave radio crackled with the brisk accents of the BBC news. Every now and then, the radio had to be twiddled and coaxed from slipping a millimeter that could be a continent away: Korean music, Soviet broadcasts in Hindi, an Arabic program. Speaking over the radio broadcast, I jubilantly reported on my afternoon with Urmilaji. This was the reality I was holding to that evening; this and not the blazing oil fields of Kuwait.

"I'm so glad!" said my mother. "So glad! I had always thought you should go talk to her."

We spooned up our soup in the yellowed light of low electricity. My mother listened, beaming, as I retold Urmilaji's stories, handing them immediately on-ward.

After supper, Ma continued with her usual schedule of "rat-proofing" the kitchen, which meant putting all food, even fruit, away. Field mice and rats burrowed in through the adobe walls and came through open drains. Even catching them and transporting them across the stream, as my mother did, never lessened the influx. At times when we didn't have a cat, we tried to adapt out lives around these visitors in as hygienic a way as possible.

I switched on my portable computer and set to writing field notes. *"March 18, 1991. . . ."*

SEVEN

Under the Berry Bush

The next afternoon, I was back again. It was a bright cool day—what in Pahari is called *nimbaḷ*, making me think of a nimbleness in the light and air. To catch the sun's warmth, Urmilaji and I sat out in the courtyard. She spread burlap sacks and a folded tarpaulin over the cold stone ledge and we sat down, cross-legged, facing each other.

Urmilaji offered to instruct me on two lengthy ballads. The first was about a King who unwittingly murdered a cow, the other was about King Bharthari, who killed a deer and was cursed by his does:[1] both ended up as wandering ascetics. My pen raced across page after page of my notebook as Urmilaji sang reflectively, unfolding these long and tragic tales. Sello, who should have been studying for her forthcoming exams, emerged from indoors as her mother began to sing. She stood wrapped in her shawl beside me, keeping a watchful eye on my transcriptions.

When Urmilaji was done, we chatted more about songs. Sello disappeared into the kitchen at the other end of the courtyard. As she reappeared with tea, Urmilaji announced that she had remembered another story related to the Five Days of Fasting.

Urmilaji's young nephew Sumit had been playing with two other boys under the canopy of mango trees at another corner of the courtyard. They came up to listen in as the story started, their black eyes large, their chatter suddenly quiet. Between sips of tea from the steel glass, Urmilaji started this story.

❋ ❋ ❋

There was an old woman: you can think of her as an old woman, or you can think of her as Krishna's mother. On the fourth day of the Five Days of Fasting, when we go to float the little boats, then we also worship a wild berry bush. The old woman's daughter-in-law was due to deliver a baby on that very day.

The old woman, you see, had one daughter-in-law and one son. Earlier, in her pregnancy the daughter-in-law had said to her husband Krishna—you could call him Krishna—"Maharaj,[2] my heart longs to eat something sweet. Any

79

sweet thing." He heard this and sent out for some milk. He gave this to his mother to make rice pudding.

Now mothers-in-law of the past were extremely strict and cruel. What the mother-in-law did was this: she went to the potter and got a pot made with two different sides and a partition in-between. On one side she cooked sweet pudding, but on the other side she used buttermilk for a sour pudding.

So she said to Krishna, "Eat."

The two of them, husband and wife, sat down together to eat. When the mother-in-law served Krishna, she served him sweet pudding. When she served the daughter-in-law, she gave her sour buttermilk. The daughter-in-law ate it, but she didn't enjoy it, for she had craved something sweet. *Bas.*

Then her husband asked her, "So, did you eat your sweet pudding?"

She said, "No Maharaj, that's not what I ate. What I had was sour."

Inside his mind, he reflected, "It was served from just one pot, and then she sat here beside me eating the same thing. She must be lying." He said, "Well, alright."

After two days he ordered milk again. He gave it to his mother, saying, "Today, make pudding again."

He said to his wife, "Don't touch the dish in which your food is served." In the past, women didn't touch men's food, or the men wouldn't eat it. This was the custom among the ancients. If they were to eat anything boiled by woman, it would have to be after she stripped down and wore special clothes [*"and a pure space was demarcated," I add, having already been instructed about these past practices*]. And a pure space was demarcated. Only then would men eat, otherwise they wouldn't. "Today, don't touch your dish," he said. "I'll eat from your dish and you eat from mine. Then I can see whether you're telling a lie or the truth."

"I'll do just that," she said.

At night when they sat down to eat, he grabbed her dish and gave her his. She ate the sweet rice pudding. He ate the part made with sour buttermilk. He asked, "Did you eat rice pudding?"

She said, "Yes, Maharaj, today I ate rice pudding."

So he came to know that his mother was doing this to her.

Then she said, "My heart longs for oranges."

In their garden there were a lot of oranges. What the mother-in-law did was this: she called a crow. She squeezed juice from a sour variety of citrus fruit into a small pot and poured it into his beak. "Make these all sour," she said [*sharply*]. And every sweet fruit he touched with his beak became sour.

The mother-in-law then said to Krishna, "These oranges are sour, how did they become sour?"

Bas, so the mother-in-law kept up with this sort of dreadful behavior. Then

80

the day came when the daughter-in-law was due to deliver a child. It was during the Five Days of Fasting. They were setting off to worship the berry bush when the daughter-in-law began to have labor pains.

[*The boys at this point appear to decide that this is a women's story they're not interested in, for they wander off whistling for the dog.*]

When she felt the pain coming on, she said, "I don't want to go out."

The mother-in-law said, "No, no! We all must go. We must definitely go if we want offspring."

In those days, the bushes and shrubs were far away. *Bas.* Krishna was God, he knew all about the dramas of the world! So she went along. When she got there she began to have terrible pains. She felt the pains and the mother-in-law tied a band over her eyes. "Keep your eyes bound up, and then later you can take a look."

She gave birth to a son. The moment the son was born, the mother-in-law hid him beneath the berry bush. She presented a rock to her daughter-in-law, saying, "You made such a fuss. You wanted to eat sweet things, sometimes you demanded oranges from the garden, sometimes you wanted pudding boiled and fed to you. And look what you've given birth to: a grinding stone!"

The poor thing believed her. "Truly, I must have given birth to a grinding stone. How would I know?"

So the mother-in-law took her home. And under the berry bush God [Krishna] looked after the child for an entire year. There, beneath the bush, he brought up and nurtured the child.

A year went by. As the time for the ritual approached, all the women began to say, "Come let's go worship the berry bush."

The mother-in-law said to her daughter-in-law, "You stay home. We'll be back later."

She said, "Last year I was in such an awful state but you forced me to come along for the worship. Now, when I'm fine, you're telling me to stay home! Why shouldn't I come this time? I'll come and do the worship too."

"Come along then!" said the mother-in-law [*in a shrill, impatient voice*].

When they arrived, the son was playing there. He was playing and gamboling. All of the women gathered around him. The old woman was scared: she had previously told everyone that her daughter-in-law had given birth to a grinding stone, not a son. She was scared.

When they saw this boy playing, then all the other women were overwhelmed. "I'll take him" one said. "I'll take him" said another. All of them were crazy about this boy.

Now there was an old woman there. She said, "All of the women should press milk from their nipples. The woman whose milk falls in the boy's mouth can take him."

Worshipping the Berry Bush (*Photo by Kirin Narayan*)

They all pressed their nipples, and the daughter-in-law's milk squirted straight into the boy's mouth. So then she took him as her son and she was happy.

When she came home and was so happy, God said, "I looked after this child for one year under the berry bush. You gave birth to him, and he is yours." *Bas.*[3]

※ ※ ※

Urmilaji went on to disclose that the *barairi* (also sometimes known as *jarairi*) is a bush with a tiny yellow berry. She added that such bushes grew in the pasture behind my mother's house: she had wandered out there as a child. Later, when I wandered in the pasture, I could not see any special bushes, just thorny scrub. It turned out, though, that this was the *barairi* bush. These bushes grew wild all over the valley, blending into the landscape in thorny clumps until the Five Days of Bhishma when tokens of worship marked them as special. Women poured water at their roots, lit incense beside them, and scattered scraps of cloth, red ribbons, flower petals, and rice around them.

Urmilaji explained that a *barairi* bush is worshipped by women because it has many berries. "In the past, women wanted many children, it's only now that people want two," she observed. "We worship that bush saying 'just as you protected that child, protect my children too.'"

82

Baby Krishna (*Photo by Didi Contractor*)

The November that I was tagging along with Urmilaji and her relatives as they did their rituals, I observed them launch their little boats and then squat beside a thicket of berry bushes to offer worship. After this, they sat in a semicircle in the grass. The berry story was one of the stories that Urmilaji retold as her relatives prompted and interjected comments (unfortunately, I was never formally introduced to most of these women, so, though they were familiar faces, I cannot identify them here by name). Before this, I had told Urmilaji that in my readings I had found that many variants of this story featured cowives. With a glance at me, she began her retelling by saying Krishna had two wives. Then, she retracted, saying, "I'll tell the story the way I've heard it." Apart from inverting the order of the sour orange and the sour pudding sequences, her retelling was very similar to what I'd heard before.

When Urmilaji reached the scene of the daughter-in-law being told she'd given birth to a grinding stone, her sister Nirmalaji interjected, amused, "OK, but when a child is born doesn't it cry?" That is, wouldn't she have heard her son cry and known she hadn't given birth to a stone? Others laughed too.

"It might cry but what could she do?" inquired one of the women. Urmilaji echoed, "What could she say? What could she do? What could daughters-in-law of the past ever say? They just had to accept what they were told."

When Urmilaji described the scene of the women squirting milk, Nirmalaji laughed again, asking, "So there would have been milk in everyone's breasts?!" "Probably," assured Urmilaji. "Women in the past used to spend their entire lives giving birth, so of course they'd always have milk. It wasn't like now when you have had two and you don't want a third!" Urmilaji ended this retelling with a prayer, the other women joining in and bowing low with folded palms: "Oh Goddess Berry Bush, just as she found fulfillment, so may it be for a-a-all of us!" (*barairīye paramesvariye jiyān tinhānde santript hoi tiyān saa-aa-aariya hoiyān*).

When this story was over, literate and rational Nirmalaji continued her interrogation. Perhaps she did this partly to instruct me, the earnest scholar, not to take the tales so seriously. In any event, her comments displayed that there may be more than one view of these stories, which to Urmilaji were cherished fragments of divine intervention in the past. At the same time, even the dissenting voices seemed to concur in associating these stories with the past rather than imaginary realms.

"These tales from the past are really nothing but idle talk," Nirmalaji asserted. "How can one have faith in empty talk of this sort? Certainly, a mother-in-law was strict then. But how could anyone think that they'd given birth to a grinding stone?"

"Grinding stones were said to come out of many people," replied Urmilaji, "It's happened in more than one story."

"The thing that's wrong with this grinding stone is that when a baby is born it definitely must cry!" Nirmalaji said, repeating her earlier objection with amusement.

"How can the two parts of the grinding stone be born?" asked a younger woman, giggling. (The two parts of a grinding stone, I should add, may also have sexual connotations).

"The women, poor things, couldn't open their mouths," Nirmalaji continued. "The main reason is this—"

"—they couldn't speak," put in someone.

"They couldn't speak up—"

"—that's exactly it," said Urmilaji.

Nirmalaji's voice was drowned out as many of the women rushed to speak their thoughts. The voice of the woman who lived beside the post office emerged from the hubbub saying, "Their hands used to be burnt. Mothers-in-law used to burn daughters-in-law's hands, people say they used to press their hands to hot griddles and do all sorts of things."

"Absolutely," said Urmilaji, persevering despite further interruptions. "Isn't that just what they did?! That's right, a daughter-in-law couldn't speak up. Even a son couldn't speak up. He ate that pudding, he looked after the boy, but he couldn't tell his mother off."

"Look, there's this story for Calf's Twelfth,"[4] said Urmilaji's neighbor from across the way, an older woman with heavy glasses and eyes reddened by glaucoma. "In that, too, the Mother-in-law said, 'Daughter-in-law, prepare the fish (*macchī*) to eat,' and what the daughter-in-law heard was 'prepare the female calf (*bacchī*) to eat.' " Urmilaji nodded and assented as her neighbor went on, "The thing is that as a daughter-in-law you weren't supposed to ask to hear something a second time."

"If she didn't hear something right, poor thing, then that was a problem," said Nirmalaji sympathetically.

Urmilaji urged her neighbor, "Give us this story from the beginning." Other women urged that she "give" this story too. Even though it was not related to the ritual at hand, the neighbor told the story for Cow's Twelfth in which the obedient daughter-in-law performs the terrible sin of killing a cow after mishearing her mother-in-law's instructions. The mother-in-law is horrified and arranges for the dishes of calf meat to be buried at a distance. Then the mother-in-law bathes and sits down to worship her gods, requesting that daughters-in-law of the future be allowed to ask to hear something a second time. Meanwhile, the distraught cow uses her horns to dig up the area where her calf is buried. The calf emerges whole. Mother-in-law and daughter-in-law worship the cow and calf, offering them garlands.

"Under the Berry Tree"—like the story of Cow's Twelfth that it evoked—highlights the relationship between a mother-in-law and a daughter-in-law. Beginning with the character of the mother-in-law ("there was an old woman . . ."), this story seems to point to the perspective of the mother-in-law who, as the daughter-in-law grows in household influence, may recede in influence herself. The theme of competition between the two women comes into sharper relief in light of other Indian variants of the story, in which it is jealous cowives who substitute the grinding stone for the newborn child.

The mother-in-law resents the special attentions the daughter-in-law receives when she is pregnant—she seeks to sour the young woman's anticipation of the forthcoming birth. *Khaṭṭā* (sour) implies not just literal taste, but also unpleasant emotion, not unlike the English expression of "a bitter taste in one's mouth." The play on sourness as an emotional response was highlighted in Urmilaji's proverb about the sour *ānvlā* berries, which were likened to the words of elders in first seeming sour and later sweet. The mother-in-law dispensing sour food, then, seems to be a case of emotion being literalized in narrative action.

85

An important ingredient that is soured in this tale is the milk: a special food when bought, a special food when produced. Krishna, in this story, "sends out" for milk; he gives it to his mother and asks her to make a sweet pudding for his pregnant wife. Here he is undercutting his mother's authority by ordering a special food especially for his wife (this, too, when his mother had previously fed him her own milk). In addition, by asking his mother to cook it and serve it to them, he is inverting the assumption that a daughter-in-law serve her husband and other elders in his family. While the mother-in-law is happy to serve milk to her son, she balks at serving it to her daughter-in-law. I thought of the partitioned pot the mother-in-law commissions as perhaps symbolic of partitioned emotions: loving milk for the son, sour buttermilk for his wife. That milk binds mothers and sons is reaffirmed at the end of the story when it is only the true mother's milk that spurts directly into the mouth of the baby boy.[5]

So partitioned is the mother-in-law's mind here that she does not seem to grasp that her daughter-in-law's child is also her own grandson. In a joint family, a daughter-in-law is usually seen as accomplishing something important when she produces a son; it would seem to be an occasion for a mother-in-law to rejoice. Yet, this folktale accentuates ambivalence on the part of the mother-in-law, who with the birth of a grandson can foresee the day when her daughter-in-law will be the central female authority in the household.

The Krishna in this story, like the Krishna in many of the women's songs, stood for an understanding husband. He was stripped of the biographical details with which epic and Puranic mythology had endowed him to become domesticated, a figure in a local kinship system. Similarly, his mother and wife lost their specificity to become more standard representations of a mother-in-law and daughter-in-law within a joint family.[6]

This is not to say that Krishna's philandering side was altogether overlooked within women's lore. On a previous occasion, Urmilaji had explained why Krishna had so many wives:

> Krishna was always falling in love with women. Before he was born as Krishna, he had taken birth as Ramchandra. At the gathering of princes when Sita chose her groom, it was Ramchandra whom she got. All her girlfriends were absolutely incredulous. 'Where did you get this groom from? Look at him! He's incomparable in looks, incomparable in wisdom, incomparable in every single thing. Where did you get this for yourself?' They were all aflutter, ensnared by desire for him.
>
> So Ramchandra gave them a boon. He said, 'In my next life, I'll marry you all.'
>
> Radha is one of them, and there are many others that he married too. The real one is Radha, and he married a lot of others too: 108, it's said.
>
> God, you know, is one. God is Shiva [the Destroyer], he is Brahma [the Creator], he is Vishnu [the Sustainer]: he comes in all sorts of forms.

These stories and songs, then, cast Krishna in the role of a husband in the joint family. This insertion points toward a fantasy of the idealized husband as a thoughtful nurturer of a woman and her concerns. He sides with his wife against his own mother, he seeks to feed her fine things, and he single-handedly tends the baby boy for a year. Since Krishna himself is often worshipped in the form of a baby (who miraculously survives the endangered circumstances of his birth), his care of the son has a special poignancy.

Urmilaji's final comment emphasized the imaginative porosity between everyday family life and the concerns of the gods. I asked why, if Krishna knew what his mother was up to, he allowed her to substitute the newborn baby for a grinding stone. "God made such [ugly] situations with his creation," Urmilaji said. "So, when you know that this sort of thing could happen in God's house too, it brings peace to your mind."

EIGHT

The Female Weevil
Who Fasted

Computer heavy on my shoulder and suitcase filled with sheaves of notes, at the end of March, I took the narrow-gauge Kangra train down to the plains. After months in the village, the hubbub of Delhi seemed disorienting. Even more disorienting, though, were all the glossy, reflecting surfaces and open, uncrowded spaces of the United States. I returned to India in May. During my absence, Rajiv Gandhi had been assassinated while campaigning for the elections. A woman associated with Sri Lanka's Tamil Tigers had stepped up to Rajiv Gandhi with explosives strapped around her waist, blowing him (and herself) to bits. I came back to Delhi to find an almost eerie calm and many clusters of khaki-clad police. Trouble was predicted in the state of Punjab where Sikh separatists had been campaigning for a separate homeland. Since the train to Kangra went through Punjab, for the first time I used the recently introduced air service from Delhi to Kangra, lurching along in a low-flying, sixteen-seat propeller plane.

During my absence, the valley had physically transformed. The wheat crop, which was ripening when I left, had been harvested. The landscape was now brown and bare. From the air it looked like grained wood. From the ground, I saw it was crowded with women in brightly colored clothes, swinging mallets to break clods of earth. Whenever I saw the backbreaking work performed with these mallets, it made me think of a Delhi visitor's polite inquiry to my mother several years earlier: "What are these people playing? Is it some sort of hockey?" My old friend Vidhya had laughed hard when she heard this story. Speaking Hindi, she said, "Yes, to city people we villagers must seem to have such a happy life! Playing hockey in the fields, sporting with bullocks. . . . No food shortages, nothing to worry about. What happy, happy people we villagers must be!"

Exhausted, in poor health, it took some time for me to regain my gregarious fieldwork persona. The first time I came by to see Urmilaji after my travels, it was the second Saturday of the month, and government offices and schools were closed. Not only were Urmilaji's grown sons, both tobacco merchants, at home, but so was Nirmalaji, the school-going children, and some of their friends. They were taking refuge from the summer heat in a closed, darkened room. I came in through a swinging cane curtain to find them arrayed on chairs and mats before the television, watching a video about the Hindu boy-saint, Prahlad.

My arrival was an interruption, but I was greeted warmly. The video was turned off, but an afternoon Hindi soap opera continued to play, half engaging everyone's attention. I was plied with fruit and for news of my travels. I reported that at one of the conferences I had attended, A. K. Ramanujan had suggested that I put Urmilaji's stories together in a book.

"Do you think I might put them together in a book?" I asked, echoing his words.

Nirmalaji's laughter was filled with pleasure: "*Le!* Look at this!" she said, turning to her sister. Urmilaji's sons focused their attention away from the television long enough to give me bemused looks. Raju, the older one with close-set eyes, teased his mother, "You can become famous in America!" Urmilaji covered her mouth with an end of the gauzy pink dupaṭṭa looped over her head. She clucked, shaking her head but smiling to herself.

On the television, a steamy romantic scene was in progress, creating visible embarrassment across this mix of generations. Then the electric current gave way and the tension was released. The group dispersed. Urmilaji led me to her own family's room next door. Here two beds were pushed together to make a larger double one. The walls were painted a pale green, with electrical wiring zigzagging across and two colorful calendars displaying gods and goddesses. A screen window and locked door ran along the cobbled path. We settled on the floor below this window. Urmilaji set to work on cleaning shearings from her ram as we chatted, catching up on this and that, talking more about the book. Urmilaji told me that while I was gone her afternoons had seemed empty.

A few days later, I once again found the family and neighbor children clustered on mats and chairs around the television. This time they were watching an old historical film *Noor Jahan*, which Nirmalaji periodically turned off to catch up on election returns flowing in from various parts of India. I sat and watched, too, wondering what I was doing there in the stifling heat, watching the fuzzy images of a film I wasn't interested in. Shouldn't I go home and transcribe my backlog of songs or write field notes instead? What about those photocopies from the Madison library that I should read? As the minutes ticked by, I argued to myself that this was, after all, immersion in "the field." Even if I wasn't particularly interested in the viewing of videos or television, this was another aspect of contemporary life in Kangra. Here was Urmilaji's rival, the television, displaying all its seductive charms.

Urmilaji sat cross-legged, straining before the screen. She seemed to have trouble following the plot and the Hindi dialogue. Nirmalaji's son, student at an English medium school in town and fluent in Hindi, patiently gave her updates on what was happening. He appeared to be enjoying this role of interpreter negotiating cultural horizons unfamiliar to his aunt.

After a while, Urmilaji turned to me and asked: "Would you like to do some work? Write something?"

"Absolutely," I said. We left the gathering for her own quarters next door and settled down on the double bed, facing each other.

"I've been thinking about stories while you were gone," Urmilaji announced. "I've remembered some more. Would you like to tape them?"

"Yes!" I said.

Urmilaji sat quiet, recollecting. The video clicked off next door. The television ran on instead, its sounds louder and clearer, piping in the latest in election returns through the adobe wall. The announcer's voice was male and British-accented: I wondered which political party was ahead, whether the Congress Party would win the election as projected. Sello came wandering in, yawning and seemingly bored, to lay her head in her mother's lap.

When Urmilaji announced, "There's a story I'm going to tell you," she had our attention.

"Wheat, you know, wheat . . . ," she began.

"Yes," I assented.

"Well, wheat grains can get infested with a small, black bug."

"*Kuṇ*!" shot out Sello.

"This is a story about a male weevil (*kuṇ*) and a female weevil (*kuṇṇī*)."

"Who live in wheat grains," I prompted, trying on my earphones.

"Weevils that live in wheat grains. I am going to tell you their story."[1]

❀ ❀ ❀

There was a male weevil, and there was a female weevil. The female weevil used to fast on the eleventh day of the lunar fortnight. On that day, she would climb out of the bamboo bin[2] within which the grain was stored. They used to live in a bin in a Merchant's house. So, on the eleventh day, she used to climb out of the bin and go to the churn. Women churn butter, you know. She would sit by the churn. And when droplets splattered, she would eat and drink. She wouldn't eat any wheat at all. She would fast.

This went on for a long time. She used to tell the male weevil: "You should observe the fast too."

He'd say, "No. I'm going to eat wheat. You can go die of hunger. A splash of buttermilk isn't enough for me. I'm going to eat my wheat!"

Time went by and they grew old. They both died. The male weevil died, and then the female weevil died too.

The female weevil, the woman, was reborn as a daughter in a King's house. The male weevil was reborn as an elephant. They both arrived in the same King's house. Alright, so the girl was really pampered—she was a Princess. And the elephant, he was tied up in the stables! [*We laugh.*]

Bas. So they lived near each other. Giving and taking [gifts], time went by and the girl came of age.

[*"And the elephant stays behind," murmurs Sello in anticipation.*]

Then the King said, "Now we must find a groom for her. She's come of age and we must get her married." He told his Purohit to look for a good home to which she could be married off: "Go look!" So the Purohit went somewhere or the other, and he arranged an engagement to the Prince there. Then he came back and told the King that the wedding was to be set for such and such a date.

The King's workers toiled away with preparations for the wedding. Time went by, and the wedding came. The King had the wedding performed with pomp and festivities. He also gave a dowry: an enormous dowry and lots of gifts that included the elephant.

The elephant said, "Oh-ho. . . . She was a Princess here, and she'll be a Queen there. But I'm in bad shape. It's better that I stay put."

So, as they were all proceeding with the dowry, the elephant sat down on the road. He sat right down, and everyone tried to get him to his feet. "Come on, get up!" They hit him and struck him, but he didn't move. So they were in a fix. How could they just leave him behind halfway along the road? If he had refused to come at first, he could have been left behind, but now it was impossible.

The Princess heard about this problem. She said, "Set this bridal palanquin of mine down beside him. I'll make him stand up." So they put the palanquin down near the elephant. She said into his ear, "We've each earned our own karma. Because of this, we must each experience rebirth from a particular sort of womb. I used to urge you, 'Keep a fast.' But you'd say [*in a defiant, hostile voice*], 'No, I want to stay in the grain bin.' 'I just want to eat wheat,' you'd say. I used to observe the fast. I used to worship God with a true heart. And you—why have you come and sat down halfway along the road? [*Sharply*] Get up and come along quietly! I'm experiencing my karma, and you're experiencing your karma."

Bas. He got to his feet and proceeded.

When the elephant got up, the groom—he sat down! He said, "What's this about? Everyone hit him, struck him, did this and that, but that elephant didn't get up. What did you say in his ear that made him get up and go?"

She said, "King, don't ask me about this!"

He said, "No, I must definitely ask you about this. It's an absolutely astounding matter: you just whisper in the ear of the elephant and he gets up and goes!"

She said, "No, don't ask me about it."

91

He said, "I must hear it."

She said, "It's nothing...." But then she told her whole story. "In our past lives we were weevils. I would fast on the eleventh day, and he would stay put in the grain bin. I told him again and again, 'Let's observe the eleventh day fast together, we'll sit on the churn and lick buttermilk together for a day.' But he wouldn't take heed. After this, he became an elephant and I became a king's daughter. When he sat down here and said, 'You live in a castle and I...,' I said to him, 'Each of us performs his own actions. If you'd listened to me before, why would you have had to become an elephant?'"

Bas, finished.

※ ※ ※

"So how did she remember her past life?" I asked. This angle had immediately caught my interest.

"She remembered it," said Urmilaji. "She remembered her past life."

"Do ordinary people remember past lives too?"

"Yes," Urmilaji nodded, "some do."

At this point Sello, who had slipped out at the end of the story, reentered to whisper that there was an unknown visitor outside. Adjusting her scarf over her head, smoothing down her top, Urmilaji went out to see who it was. In a little while she was back and resumed with three other tales.

"What's a *kun*?" I asked when I got home that evening. Laughing a little at my latest odd question, Savarna, the carpenter's teenage daughter who helped my mother in the afternoons, explained in Hindi, "A *kun* is a tiny black bug that lives in wheat." She left the dishes she was washing to swing open the door of the wooden cupboard built into the kitchen wall. The shelves were lined with old tin cans and plastic canisters, relabeled with my mother's indelible black marker. Savarna pulled out a can in which my mother stored wheat that hadn't yet been sent to the mill. Sure enough, there were a few black bugs crawling around among the golden grains. Savarna put one of the bugs on the palm of her hand for closer examination. Pointing to its long snout, she said, "They have a face like an elephant." The association between weevils and elephants, obscure to me, seemed fairly obvious to people who had to regularly deal with such insects infesting their wheat.

More precisely, a *kun* is a male weevil, while his female counterpart is a *kunnī*. The *kunnī* in the story is a pious creature not unlike a high-caste woman, intent on observing the right fasts and gaining good karma. In Mira Devi Dogra's variant of the tale, the female weevil crawls out of the bin in order to bow before the burning lamps for the Five Days of Fasting; in Asha Devi Sharma's variant, the female weevil clings to a woman's clothes in order to join in a meritorious morning dip in the river.

"So, is it true that women tend to fast more than men do?" I later asked Urmilaji.

"Yes," agreed Urmilaji. "Men are often busy: they work outside the home. Women can stay home and do the fasts and the other kinds of worship and rituals."

"What's special about fasting on an eleventh day?" I asked. Growing up, I had always been aware of the eleventh day of the lunar fortnight as an important day for fasting. In Maharashtra and Kangra, as elsewhere in India, fasting did not usually mean eating nothing at all, but rather, abstaining from certain everyday foods.

"The eleventh day has great importance," Urmilaji instructed. "You can't eat rice, and you can't eat wheat for this fast. There are twenty-four such eleventh days in a year. In these, there are three especially important ones: the Eleventh Without Water in the month of Jeth (or Jyesth, May/June); the Eleventh of Sesame in Magh (January/February), when you make sweets of sesame seeds; and then the Eleventh of the Five Days of Fasting, (in October/November). Everyone pays attention to these particular eleventh days even if they ignore the others."[3]

Urmilaji's blanket "everyone" was, of course, upper-caste men and women only. In particular, upper-caste women who did not do extensive agricultural work were the most devoted to fasting. As a lower-caste woman who'd done much work in the fields once said, her eyes twinkling, "Fasts and all that aren't for people who work in the fields! You'd have to lie in bed resting for the next two days if you tried anything like that!"

Urmilaji herself was punctilious about observing fasts. She fasted on the eleventh day of both waxing and waning lunar fortnights. In the past, she had also fasted for full moon days and for the Five Days of Fasting, but she had already performed the rituals marking the end of these observances. Though thin and fragile, she seemed to take pride in her capacity for being able to go without food. As she said, "I do drink tea. If milk is available for me, then I drink milk too. Or fruit or something. If my sons remember that I have a fast, then they bring me something, like bananas to eat. . . . I eat and drink if I get it. If I don't get it, it's not necessary to me. I can go to sleep like that, without eating."

She felt that this fortitude was a divine blessing. "Somehow God protected me, otherwise who knows how I'd have the strength to do this? God gave me this kind of power, to fast even when all my children were small. Even at that time I could do all the fasts and look after them too."

I had been struck by the sharpness in Urmilaji's voice as she took on the persona of the Queen addressing the elephant. This seemed to be a case of "I told you so," uttered in anger a full lifetime after the preliminary, weevil-based events had occurred. The story seemed to emphasize that even if women's words were disregarded or if their pious actions did not bear immediate fruits, there was always the possibility that in a future life they would be proved right. I was reminded of a time when I was visiting a different household where assembled women of the joint family were discussing a willful eldest son (whose wife was absent). He was planning to build a pretentious cement house next door, blocking the path to the old adobe house. During the course of the conversation, one of his sisters-in-law fiercely remarked, "Men just do what they want. But the karma isn't going to leave them!"

In Mira Devi Dogra's retelling, the Princess urges the elephant to get up and come along, for then she will light lamps on his behalf. The elephant rises to his feet and proceeds. As Mira Devi Dogra summarizes, "The meaning is this: she gives him wisdom, doesn't she? 'Come on with me. Then you'll be relieved of this body and you'll get the body of a human being. I'll do this worship on your behalf.' "

Like Mira Devi Dogra, Asha Devi Sharma also ended the story with the weevil/Princess telling the weevil/elephant off. But two other variants, both from ancient and vigorous old women, end the story with the Princess's death. In the variant told by Sita Devi Sharma, a Brahman woman in her eighties, this was not a Princess and an elephant, but a common woman and a bullock. When the groom demands to know why the bullock listens to his bride, she tells of their past lives and falls down dead. Similarly vigorous, ninety-five-year-old Mati Devi boomed to a gathering of Rajput women that the Princess warned her husband that she would die if he insisted on learning the truth. He threatened that he would leave her stranded on the road, refusing to take her with him unless she explained the event. When she told of her past, she died. Mati Devi dramatically ended, "The groom went off empty-handed, the bride went off to her death."

Thinking of these other variants, I subsequently asked Urmilaji, "So did the Princess die when she told this story?" I wondered whether I might perhaps have missed something, have cut Urmilaji off with a question at the end, or whether we had been interrupted. This time, Urmilaji stated, "Yes, she died."

"Why?" I asked. I had understood the point of the Queen in "Daughter, My Little Bread" dying from mortification over her lowly past when she had to confess her tale, but it wasn't clear to me why the Princess should be ashamed. Yet, in this case too, Urmilaji stated, the woman died from *sharm*—bashful modesty. "But why?" I persisted. "She had to admit to one man that she had had relations with another one, that elephant," said Urmilaji. "Wouldn't she feel *sharm*?"

In all the variants, men who ignore women and scoff at their piety receive a comeuppance. Whatever the story's end, it seems to emphasize the importance of women's worship in a world of less observant men.

NINE

The Dog-Girl

"There's another story from the Five Days of Fasting," Urmilaji continued that June afternoon. "A story about a dog. It's for the full-moon day."

Sello began to grin, eyes bright and naughty. She muttered something that I didn't catch.

During my absence, my mother had acquired a half-Apso puppy, as fluffy and white as an angora bunny crossed with a lamb. She was named Steffi, for her energetic wagging had reminded my mother of Steffi Graf's tennis skirt. Wherever Steffi went, people would stop to pet and admire her. I had recently walked her over for a visit with Urmilaji. So I smiled too at this mention of a dog.

In the background, a flock of parrots must have swooped down upon the ripening mango trees in the courtyard, for their calls competed with the dialogue pouring from the television in the next room.

❄ ❄ ❄

There was a woman who used to light oil lamps for the Five Days of Fasting. She probably lived alone, poor thing. Whenever she turned her back to do something else, a female dog would come into the house and lick at the oil in her lamps. The old woman would be really upset by this. But by the time she'd get there to see what was happening, all the lamps would already have been licked up.

So this continued. The female dog would come and lick the lamps.

[*Urmilaji demonstrates how the dog licks—"aaaah"—her mouth wide open, moving her palm back and forth before her exposed tongue.*]

The old woman would be troubled by this.

After a few years, the female dog died. Because she had encountered the lamps, in her next life she was born to a human womb. She became a girl. She was a girl for sure, but she still had that habit of licking! That didn't go away. If any food was prepared, any food was cooked and set aside, she'd immediately have to take a lick.

Bas. At first she was in her mother's house. Her mother, poor thing, would scold and chide, "What's this habit you've picked up?! If anything is cooked and set aside, you promptly take a taste. Whether it's special food or consecrated food for the gods makes no difference to you. If you see that something has been prepared, then you immediately rush at it."

Bas. This kept happening. Then, giving and taking, the days flew past, and the girl was married into the household of some Merchant. She was married, and in that house, her mother-in-law, poor thing, used to burn lamps. For five days, she burned lamps. On the final full-moon day, the father-in-law said that he wanted to invite Brahmans for a feast.

The mother-in-law said, "Everything can be prepared, but the problem is that she'll lick at it first. We have to find a solution for dealing with her. Let's give her some work that will keep her occupied and won't let her get anywhere near the kitchen. Else she's going to lick at everything we cook, and what will we feed the Brahmans then? Tainted food? We'll all be in a fix if she does this."

The father-in-law instructed the girl, "Keep filling water. It'll be your responsibility to fill water."

She said, "Water is fine." So she started filling water, and she kept filling water. She filled and filled and filled.

Then the Brahman cooks, poor fellows, had cooked rice pudding and set it aside in a covered vessel. Poor fellows, they were occupied with other things. They had to prepare the vegetables and the lentils too. The girl promptly set down her pot of water, scooped up some rice pudding [*Urmilaji demonstrates, with a cupped hand*], and stole off behind Saili [*the goddess of sacred basil, on a raised stand*]. She sat down to have a good lick. [*Again, Urmilaji demonstrates, tongue vigorously outstretched.*]

So she sat down to lick, and Saili thrust out her hand. "Give me some!"

"Get away!" she said [*fiercely*], "I haven't eaten anything since morning. I was hungry and had to sneak away with this pudding. What makes you think you can just demand some?"

Bas. She ate and drank it all in a hurry. Then she went off, and Saili's hand was left sticking out just like that [*Urmilaji stiffens her right hand with the fingers closed, palm thrust upward*].

A lot of people had gathered there. Someone noticed that Saili's hand was sticking out. When everyone came to look, they saw that her hand was indeed outstretched. People were confounded: how could this have happened? Everyone began to repent inside their minds: 'Who knows what we've unwittingly done that she sticks her hand out like this?'

[*Urmilaji lapses into the sing-song voice she always uses for rote or repetitive actions.*]

> They offered frankincense,
> they bent their heads,
> they offered all kinds of things:
> but the hand remained outstretched.
> Everyone was terribly distraught.

Then from the back of the crowd, the daughter-in-law asked, "Shall I make the hand withdraw?"

"If you can make it withdraw, then make it withdraw," they said [*in a rude, disbelieving voice*].

So she stepped forward. She took off one slipper. She said, "Do you want me to smack your hand? All these people are putting on this spectacle for you, do you want a smack?"

Poor Saili quietly withdrew her hand. "She'll hit me, she'll touch me with her shoe."

So she withdrew her hand, and everyone set to bowing their heads. "Who knows why Saili stuck out her hand, poor thing, who knows how we'd unwittingly offended her."

No one had the least idea what went on in that daughter-in-law's mind!
[*Urmilaji laughs.*]
That's it.
[*"So did she keep ... ?" I demonstrate the licking motion.*]
She kept licking away.
[*We all laugh..*][1]

❉ ❉ ❉

I asked where Urmilaji learned this story. She said that it was from her Tayi Sas.

"What could the meaning of it be?" I asked. I was confused by the story: the dog-like daughter-in-law getting away with licking and polluting food didn't seem to fit in with the moralistic tone of most of the other tales associated with the Five Days of Fasting.

Urmilaji paused, reflecting. As soon as the words left my mouth, I wondered if I was forcing a moral onto what was essentially a comic tale.

"The meaning ...," she began. "What could the meaning be?" Then she stopped short and began again. "It's this: that after cooking, a woman should not taste what she's made. First it must be offered to the gods, then it should be given to other people and they should eat, and finally, you can eat yourself. This is the meaning."

"And one should do this at all times? Or just during the Five Days of Fasting?"

"Every day! Whatever you make you shouldn't taste yourself first. First serve it out, feed it to others. If there's no one around, then feed the gods first, bow your head before them, and then eat yourself. But she just took what was freshly cooked and rushed to lick at it. This is the meaning."

"You should never taste food then?" I asked. I knew very well from my own upbringing that if one's saliva came into contact with a utensil, it would be *jhuṭā*—polluted and tainted, unfit for anyone but a very close person. When I first came to America, seeing people taste a dish and then continue stirring with the same spoon had made me uncomfortable. But I imagined that using a clean spoon to taste, then setting that spoon down to wash rather than back in the pot, might be within the bounds of acceptability.

Urmilaji shook her head.

"Not even to see whether there's salt or not? You have to remember everything you put in?"

Urmilaji still silently shook her head.

Awkward about divulging my own cooking practices, I observed that in America people often cooked by sampling: tasting what was left out, what flavor could be sharpened. Urmilaji shook her head, clucking with visible horror. She began to speak about low-caste people, who she felt did not keep up the correct standard of purity in their kitchens. She especially targeted people of the Chamar caste, of which there was a large settlement adjoining the village. (Though caste literature identifies Chamars as untouchable cobblers, members of this caste were actually employed in diverse occupations, ranging from field help to farming their own fields, from army employment to bank management).

"Those people, you know, they used to be ignorant," said Urmilaji. "That's why we don't mix with them. We people never eat at the homes of the cobblers. We don't let them into our kitchen either. If any strange person enters our kitchen, we clean it out completely."

This story of the dog-girl supplements the one about the fasting weevil; here, too, women's virtue is tied up with her attitudes toward food. To restrain one's hunger is depicted as meritorious, whether through fasting or simply eating after others are served. The meticulous handling of food, and the ingestion of only certain categories of food in relation to ritual cycles, is in turn seen as an index of a virtuous woman's caste status. Urmilaji continued in regard to cobblers:

"In the past, those people used to do really low jobs. They'd skin animals and eat their meat. That's why there was a big dislike of them. That's why there was no mixing. They had no fasts, no special days observed, no worship, nothing. Now these people do a lot of worship! They grow sacred basil in their homes. They perform fasts. One says, 'I fast on Fridays,' another says, 'I fast on Mondays on the dark night of the moon.' Now they observe all kinds of fasts and special days. Watching others, they've improved. Before they would just cook and eat: no idea of polluted food or anything. That's why we didn't go inside their houses."

As Urmilaji made this statement, I recalled that she, like other upper-caste people of the village, had recently visited a man of the cobbler caste who lay dying from mouth cancer. When pressed, she admitted that if someone of a lower caste was ill one might go to visit in their house, but not to eat.

Urmilaji's depiction of the slovenly handling of food among lower castes is a common feature of high-caste stereotypes justifying the separation between castes. Whether there is credibility to this statement is not something that a high-caste person, who never enters such kitchens, would actually be in a position to judge. (The cobbler kitchens I saw, I should add, were as clean as upper-caste ones). Her statement about cobbler women striving to adopt customs like fasting from higher castes also was, to my knowledge, only partially true. I never saw Saili, the Sacred Basil Goddess in any low-caste courtyard. But I did know some younger women from the cobbler caste who in the last few years had started to observe fasts for their husband's welfare.[2]

Urmilaji always referred to this story about the dog-girl with laughter gurgling in her throat. Similarly, when I mentioned this story once in the company of Urmilaji's brothers, sisters-in-laws, sons, and nephews and nieces, everyone burst out laughing. With vigor, Urmilaji reminded them of the last sequence, in which the girl threatened to hit Saili with a shoe.

This story seems to emphasize behavior appropriate to a virtuous upper-caste woman, but through comic inversion rather than direct moralizing. The impudent dog-girl is simply unable to control her appetites.[3] She gets away with tasting household food, tainting food meant for Brahmans, and even withholding food from the Goddess Saili. Further, in direct opposition to the practice of removing shoes or slippers in the presence of a deity, this girl threatens to swat Saili with her shoe. Saili meekly acquiesces. There is no hint of future retribution for the girl having behaved in this inappropriate manner. If anything, the fellow villagers are left impressed and oblivious to the dog-girl's nature as they bow their heads before Saili.

The flouting of appropriate female conventions for comic effect surfaces in other performances by upper-caste women in Kangra.[4] The nexus of such performances is the *giddā* which I have already mentioned. When members of the groom's party leave to fetch a bride, a wild, high-spirited mood seems to take over. (This mood may also be recreated at any other celebratory moments not associated with weddings, when women may unexpectedly bolt the doors and rush into costume). I have already described how some women dress up in their husband's clothes and strut about with mock phalluses. But other women act the part of women: women who are hilarious in their inappropriate, unrestrained behavior. "Come on, girls, let's go worship Narasingh [the deity of doorways]," sang two giggling middle-aged women as they waved lamps before the crotches of the groom's female relatives at one gidda I attended. Another woman played the stock character of Nani—the maternal grandmother—a hunched, slothfully dressed, whining character who tried to feed everyone cow dung cakes. Yet another middle-aged woman slipped her hands into her baggy *salwars*, flapping and crying out, "I'm itching! I'm itching!" as her assembled audience collapsed with laughter. Other *giddā* skits involved mocking the burdens of cooking, promiscuity in the joint family, and the tossing away of mock babies. Though I have not ever witnessed a dog-girl skit, she would seem a character practically designed for these events.

The story of the dog-girl also fits in with a larger pattern in Indian tales in which women get away with breaking norms, whether it is blamed on extreme idiocy, cleverness, or devotion.[5] The daughter-in-law described here was in the idiotic category. As Urmilaji said, "She had no sense. She had the sense of a dog. No honor (*izzat*). When you talk to a bad person like that, they might hurt you. That was why Saili withdrew her hand."

Enough sense to understand what was appropriate; enough honor to ensure that one did not embarrass oneself or one's family; enough chasteness to control one's appetites: these seemed essential ingredients for the character of a morally upright woman. To not conform was to be animal-like, or else, downright demonic. Urmilaji moved on that day to tell a long and elaborate tale of a demoness who also had unconventional eating habits, seeking out bloody raw flesh from humans and animals (chapter 18).

It was getting dark when I arrived home. Steffi the "bunny-puppy" came bouncing out to greet me. I bolted the doors behind me, shutting her in, for the hillside behind my mother's house was also home to a leopard who came out at dusk and was notorious for eating people's dogs. Urmilaji's black dog had been seized from her very courtyard. To try to prevent Steffi ending up as a sweet morsel, we locked her indoors after dark, not even allowing her out as we brushed teeth staring up at the Milky Way. (I should add that, sadly, after my return to America, Steffi slipped out one night and met her end with the leopard).

Sitting down to eat, I reported as usual on my adventures of the day. As I began, "There was an old woman, who lived alone. There was a female dog . . . ," my mother looked toward Steffi, who watched us with cocked head and bright round eyes. Ma began to smile. "Do you think Urmilaji told this story because of me?" she asked.

TEN

The Skein Woman

By early July the heat had finally broken, and the rains poured down. In some fields, maize was growing tall. In other fields, men plowed rice shoots and women replanted in their wake. Shade upon shade of green glistened in every direction. Wild pink orchids appeared in the crooks of tree trunks. The clouds hung low, swollen, hiding the mountains and drawing the valley into itself.

I had been taping other women's life stories. I had mentioned to Urmilaji several times that I would like to hear more about her life too. Urmilaji was noncommittal. On an afternoon in early July when everyone else in the house was away, she began by speaking of a woman who (like me) was an irregular visitor from "outside"—the world of the plains beyond the valley. This woman had been friendly with Urmilaji, but later had humiliated her. I felt as though in telling me this tale of an aborted friendship, Urmilaji was asking that I not betray her too.

With unadorned candor and unsuppressed emotion, Urmilaji went on to tell me about the tribulations she had experienced. My tape recorder lay between us, but I found myself unable to switch it on. This outpouring seemed to be for me as her increasingly trusted friend, not me as the anthropologist appraising cultural "data." I thought I discerned how some of the songs and stories that Urmilaji had been sharing with me played on themes she had lived through. But, instead of standing back, detached, to ask further contextual questions, I ended up with tears in my own eyes. In return, I confided painful details from my own past. Urmilaji did not seem surprised that there were even a few points of similarity between our stories.

This exchange of personal stories deepened our friendship. It made for a frankness between us that allowed me to share some research funds, an act that I had previously feared might offend her. It also enhanced the sense of relaxed rapport I felt in her presence. Sometimes, when I had spent too many days involved in other visits, I would begin to long for Urmilaji.

A fortnight later, I came back from an outing to a nearby village to be present at a ceremony marking four years since the death of a friend's father. This man

101

had been very kind to me when he was alive. Thinking about the older generation slipping away, interacting with crowds of people, spending the night elsewhere, and finally bumping through a long and crowded bus ride home, left me rattled and upset. Rain was pouring down, winds were blowing umbrellas inside out, and the roads were awash in mud. But after giving my mother the report over a hot lunch, I rolled my *salwār* up around my calves and set splashing out to seek Urmilaji's soothing company.

Urmilaji was indoors, surprised when I appeared through the rain. She said she had been thinking about what I had shared with her the previous week and was concerned about whether I could really spare funds. She wanted to confirm that I was drawing salary on leave. I said that I was lucky enough to have a fellowship.

"Hell is experienced by those who don't have anything, who are poor and vulnerable," Urmilaji commented. "Heaven is experienced by those who have everything, whose wishes are all fulfilled, who are not always worried about how they will eat. I tell you, heaven and hell are both here."

Uncomfortable about the implicit comparison between us, I deflected the conversation to a story I had learned from Swamiji.[1] In this story, a man discovered he was under a wish-fulfilling tree. After wishing up all manner of good things to eat, he wished to meet with a perfected being. A holy man appeared in a flash. The man was embarrassed for having summoned him for no good reason, and he tried to cover this up by saying that he wished to see heaven. "The way to heaven is through hell," the holy man said. In hell, they saw souls whose arms were fused at the elbow joint. When food was set out, these hungry souls could not bring it to their own mouths: they tossed their food into the air and trampled it underfoot. In heaven, too, souls had arms fused at the elbows. But in heaven, order reigned and everyone was content: each person was not occupied with getting food to his or her mouth, but rather with feeding others.

Urmilaji listened, smiling. I had already told her this story in March, after she had narrated "Heaven and Hell." But she nodded as though she was hearing it for the first time.

In turn, she too told a story.

❁ ❁ ❁

There was a Merchant's wife. A Merchant's wife, and what she did was this: she kept spinning all year long. Then, when the Five Days of Fasting came, she would wind the yarn into skeins. For five days, she wouldn't spin on her spinning wheel, but she'd wind yarn instead. She'd also light lamps and do worship for five days. She wouldn't spin, but she'd wind yarn into skeins.

Then, when she died, in her next life she became a woman again. Once again, she was born into a Merchant's family. And how tall did she grow? Just this tall [*the distance between two hands winding yarn, about a foot or so*]: she was small, really small.

Then she was married to a Merchant, and she became a Merchant's wife all over again. One day she gave birth to a son. Then she, poor thing, was just this big, and it was really difficult for her to look after the baby.

One day she went somewhere or the other, to wash clothes or something, and she left her son playing there. Someone came by. They saw that the son had been left by himself and that there was no one else around. They worried that a jackal or a dog would eat this boy up. So they tied up a cloth cradle high from the rafters and placed him in it.

When she got home, she saw that the son was up there! And she was so small. She, poor thing, was down below, and the son was high above her.

Shiva and Parvati happened to be passing by. Certainly, the woman had showed plenty of devotion in her previous life. But for five days she'd also been fixed on that one piece of work, winding yarn. Because of this, she'd been reborn small.

Shiva and Parvati asked, "Why are you crying?"

She said [*in a barely perceptible mumble*], "My son is up there and I can't reach him."

So they brought the son down from the swing and gave him to her. She gave her son her breast, and he was pacified. Then Shiva and Parvati started to set off. But she was still weeping, "Look, you were here this one time to lift the boy down. But what if this happens again? What did I do to earn this sort of fate? To be this tiny makes me terribly sad."

Then, they pulled this Skein Woman straight out, and she became tall. They were gods, right? Shiva and Parvati, they could do things like that!

She bowed low, clasping their feet, and asked, "Tell me, what action of mine made me this way?"

They said, "During the Five Days of Fasting you burned lamps, didn't you?"

"Yes," she said.

They said, "For five days, you'd be winding yarn into skeins. You did show some devotion, but mostly you kept on doing your work. You set your mind on devotion much less. You were always winding yarn, and that's why you became the Skein Woman. From now on, don't do this: when you're worshipping, fix your mind on God. Because of your devotion, we've given you this boon."[2]

❋ ❋ ❋

Urmilaji explained that there was a taboo on women spinning[3] during the Five Days of Fasting. The woman in this story, though, had tried to make the best use of her time by saving up all that she had spun and industriously winding it through five days.

"Why shouldn't people spin at such times?" I asked.

"Sometimes I sit alone and think about things like that!" said Urmilaji. "For example, you're not supposed to spin on a boy's birthday either. Then, too, when someone dies, you're not supposed to spin. But when a wedding starts, before the oil ceremony, red thread has to be spun and made into a bracelet that the Pandit will tie to a girl's wrist."

Actually, by the 1990s, when to spin was a moot question. With the spread of mill cloth, I knew no woman who regularly spun. Yet, almost every household had a spinning wheel, which just a few decades ago had whirred busily. As Urmilaji observed, the spinning wheels were dusted off and occasionally brought out for rituals.

For Urmilaji this taboo against spinning illustrated a larger point. "There are two different kinds of work (*kām*)," she said, "Work for God is not the same as other work, such as spinning." Abstaining from a particular kind of work, then, could serve to demarcate a sacred time as different; similarly, reframing work within a ritual setting could infuse otherwise unremarkable actions with sacred connotations. Explaining why Sunna the Washerwoman had not helped people with loads on their heads, Urmilaji pointed out that work dedicated to God was different from routine enterprise. She now said, "In Kali Yuga, this degenerate era, people are more involved with doing their own work: they don't turn enough to God."

Coming almost as an afterthought, many months after the earlier stories associated with the Five Days of Fasting were told, the Skein woman story did not seem to be one central to Urmilaji's repertoire. Compared with other retellings, her rendition seemed foreshortened, even sketchy. The more commonly told variant of this story features a woman born so small that her parents worry that no one will marry her, so they send her off to live in the forest. I summarize the tale as I heard it from Asha Devi Sharma.

In the early 1990s, Asha Devi Sharma was a Brahman woman in her fifties. I called her "Masiji" since she was the "Masi" or mother's sister of an old friend. Masiji was born with a crooked shoulder. She was short, stooped, and crooked, but her face was filled with radiance and her voice had a palpable, loving kindness. In her village, she was known for her enormous stock of songs, her devotion, and her sweet voice. As she once told me, she "never knew the love of a mother or a father," for her father had abandoned his first wife and their two girls in favor of a younger woman who might bear him sons. After this, her mother became mentally unstable. With this background, Asha Devi's own marital prospects were unclear, but when she was eighteen (old for that era), she was married to a man several decades older than herself. His childless and bedridden first wife had arranged the match.

I first learned about this cowife at the wedding of Asha Devi's son, when Asha Devi broke down, sobbing. A relative explained that she was weeping because her cowife was no longer alive to enjoy this happy moment. I later heard this from Asha Devi too. Apparently these cowives had grown to love one another very much, forming a close household alliance until the older woman died. She died fulfilled, having showered Asha Devi with affection and having seen her deliver two promising sons.

Hearing of my interest in stories, Asha Devi told me another story about the Skein Woman while out on her porch tending her baby grandson. (She believed this boy to be a reincarnation of her recently deceased husband and addressed him like a mature man). She told the story with relish and engagement, as though she well understood the tiny woman's plight.

In Asha Devi's variant, the Skein Woman was born into a royal family. Being that small, she seemed to have no prospects for marriage, so her parents built her a log cabin in the forest. She lived here alone, looking after herself. When a young Prince came hunting in the forest and found the cabin, she hid. He came often, and once he tossed onto her bed a flower he had been sniffing (in other versions, this is a fruit he had partially eaten or the skin of a fruit). When she later sniffed the flower, the Skein Woman got pregnant. She gave birth to a boy. When the Prince next visited, he found the baby sleeping in a low swinging crib. He again wondered who lived there, and before leaving he tied the crib up higher for safety: higher than the Skein Woman could reach. Shiva and Parvati, who were out and about traveling through the world, heard a mother and child wailing. On Parvati's insistence, they stopped. The Skein Woman hid as usual. Eventually they found her and took pity on her, stretching her out to the size of a normal woman. Later, when the Prince came again, she tried to hide but she was now too big to conceal herself. He spied her, and she told him her entire story. Then they were married, and the Prince accepted the baby as his son.

As someone who can be obsessive about her own work, I had first heard this story as an allegory of how being overly fixated on accomplishing a particular task could shrink one's emotional body. But Asha Devi's variant brought out meanings that hadn't been apparent to me. Her story highlighted how an unmarriageable daughter was a source of embarrassment to her parents, and she too was bashful, hiding away. Her son became the means through which she grew in stature. I came to see the story as a commentary on the transformative experience of giving birth to a son in Kangra. With this birth, an in-marrying daughter-in-law could finally be integrated into her husband's family, achieving a higher social standing.[4]

I could not make out the connection between heaven and hell and this story about the tiny woman. Why had my tale induced Urmilaji to tell this one? Much later it dawned on me that perhaps both stories were connected through themes of karma and self-absorption. Just as the people in Swamiji's hell all sought to feed themselves first, and so all remained hungry and unfulfilled, so the woman in this story was preoccupied with getting her own work done and bore the consequences of this self-absorption in her next life. Just as the people in Swamiji's heaven were fulfilled when they thought of feeding others before themselves, so the woman's concern for her crying child led her to being pulled out straight and tall. Yet these very parallels also showed up a world of difference. As a holy man, Swamiji extended moral advice without emphasizing family responsibility, caste, or gender-based work and ritual. As a housewife and mother, Urmilaji emphasized a high-caste woman's duty to the gods and her family.

As though following up the theme of continuity in women's experiences across lifetimes, and also the mention of Shiva and Parvati, Urmilaji started on a song about Parvati's many incarnations during which she was married to Shiva.

Shiva and Parvati traveling through the world to witness suffering mortals reminded Urmilaji of another story that she outlined. She said that this story, "Earth into Gold," was associated with a ritual in the monsoon that she referred to as "The Thunder Thread" (*garjā dhāgā*) or "The Thundering Fifth" (*panchīch gajernā*). The story and ritual, she said, were linked to a tale she had already told me in March: that of the twelve years of affliction by Honi.

The Thunder Thread

The women's ritual of the thunder thread (*garjā dhāgā*) is only observed in the Sood trader caste. From the new-moon day to the fifth day of the waxing half of the lunar month of Bhadrapad (August/September) a white thread is placed atop Goddess Saili, the sacred basil plant. When thunder crashes through a clear sky but before it begins to rain, women bring the thread indoors. The thread is broken into portions for all the female members of the family who are not widowed. Little girls get shorter lengths. Each woman attaches the thread to herself, whether wrapping it around her bangles, her chain, or a button.

Later, whenever it is convenient, women assemble indoors together in secret from men. They make dough figurines of Shiva and Parvati and set these on a small wooden platform, along with a berry bush (*barairi*) that has been brought inside. They also pat out thick rounds of dough, two for a grown woman and one for a girl. These are placed before Shiva and Parvati. In addition, a tiny round bread is made for each participant in the ritual. When Shiva and Parvati have been honored with lights, vermilion, and so on, each female crumbles part of one of the larger breads along with sugar. She sets this crumbled mixture atop the tiny bread and drapes the bit of thread on top. Then, she lifts all this in her palms. Each woman asks her companions, "Should I open up the thunder thread?" (*garjā dhāgā khōr*). The prescribed response is "Yes, open it!" (*hān khor*). When the go-ahead has been received from all women present, the little bread is placed before Shiva and Parvati. The thick round breads are eaten together by the assembled women. The little breads that have been offered, however, are given away: to another woman of any caste that is not Brahman.

Urmilaji described how men of castes associated with agriculture are also drawn into this observance. After worship has been performed, upper-caste women request a lower-caste man to pull two-and-a-half lengths of furrows with his plow. This man becomes a fictive brother and is offered tokens of kinship on days associated with brothers.

Urmilaji pointed out that the thread ritual is unique among women's rituals: it is kept assiduously hidden from men, and even a male Brahman receives no offerings. As she said, "Look at what happened to the Queen in this story when a man came upon her doing the ritual!"

ELEVEN

The Twelve Years of Affliction

Back on a cool afternoon in March, Urmilaji and I sat together on the enormous bed in the inner room. Sello lounged with her head in her mother's lap. When Urmilaji began the following story, Sello sat up to watch her tell it.

❊ ❊ ❊

There was a Brahman. If this Brahman asked for alms at one house he'd receive one measure,[1] about a kilogram, of goods, and if he begged at ten houses it would amount to just that much too. Even if he walked through the entire village, he would get one measure. There was just that one measure in his destiny.

This was how it was with him. He would go home with the things and his Brahmani would get terribly angry. She'd say, "You've never brought more; this is all that you bring home. But the numbers who eat keep growing. We now have children to feed, others to feed, and this is all that you bring home."

The Brahman felt terrible anguish. "What can I do? Even if I really exert myself, even if I go to many villages, this is all that I get, no more."

His wife said, "OK, now I'm going to show you a way out of this." She set about spinning and winding a sacred thread. Then she took a roasted garbanzo, emptied it out of its shell, and put the sacred thread into the shell. In this much space [*Urmilaji indicates a quarter inch with thumb and forefinger*]: a good and beautiful sacred thread.

Then she said, "There is a certain king, King Bhoj. Go to the fire ritual he has sponsored. He will be bathing, and his sacred thread will break."

[*With her hand motioning from her left shoulder down over to the waist, Urmilaji explains, "A sacred thread has twelve strands. If even one strand breaks, it's incomplete. Then it shouldn't be worn." She and I both understand that it is only upper-caste "twice-born" men who wear these white threads slung over their torsos.*]

"As he bathes, his sacred thread will break."

[*Urmilaji lapses again from the Brahmani's instructions to tell me, "Among these*

109

rulers of the past, if their sacred threads broke, they wouldn't speak at all until they put on a new one."]

"Then, as he looks around, here and there, as he's bathing, then you give him this sacred thread. And then his wife will be opening the thunder thread that we untie in the black month [of August/September].[2] She will have kneaded some dough for the ritual breads. You should bring back just enough of that dough to fill this garbanzo husk. Just bring dough, that's all. Fill up the husk—it's all the dough we'll need."

That's it. So the Brahman set off. He went and sat down in the King's palace. The King began to bathe. As he bathed, he set to wringing out his sacred thread.

[*"Unplug the television, the electricity might have come back," Urmilaji says, turning to Sello. "Not yet," says Sello, stretching. She lingers, then ambles out.*]

The sacred thread broke. The King was agitated and began to look around, here and there. Then the Brahman held out the garbanzo husk. The King took the sacred thread from it, put it on, and was enormously pleased. He said, "Ask for whatever riches or rewards you might want."

The Brahman said, "I don't want to take anything! I just want to fill this husk with some of the dough that your wife has kneaded."

So the King went to the Queen. She had kneaded the dough to open up the thunder thread for her own ritual. She said, "Men aren't supposed to set eyes on this dough! It's not meant to be viewed by men. This is dough meant for thick ritual breads[3] and I won't give it to him."

But the King was bound to his promise. She probably kept the dough covered in a shallow kneading pan. He sliced at it with his sword. A small amount of dough stuck to the sword. The King stuffed this into the husk and presented it to the Brahman.

❀ ❀ ❀

He presented it to the Brahman, and the Brahman went home. After he departed, then, for the King, one day an elephant would die, the next day a horse would die. In this way, everything began to be finished off. Everything began to dwindle in the kingdom.

[*Sello is back and sitting on the edge of the bed, listening in. "This is still about King Bhoj?" she inquires. "Humm," her mother nods a quick aside, gesturing at the recorder.*]

The King thought and thought about all this, and he withered, he grew thin. The Queen asked him, "Why have you become so thin and weak? What thoughts are occupying you? What is the matter?"

He said, "No, it's nothing."

She said, "No. I'm your wife. If you don't tell me what's going on in your head, then who are you going to confide in? What is the problem?"

He said, "There is a woman who comes and stands by my pillow."

[*Urmilaji motions to the head of the bed on which we are sitting, cross-legged.*]

"Every night as I sleep, she comes and stands beside me in my dreams. Then she asks, 'Should I come? Should I come?' [*in a high-pitched, strained voice.*]."

The Queen thought, "We gave the Brahman that dough, and this is the result." She said, "OK. Today you must tell her, 'Leave the four legs of the King and Queen's bed and depart.'"

That's it. Night fell and the King went to sleep. The woman came and stood there. "Should I come?" she asked. He said, "Leave the four legs of the King and Queen's bed and depart."

When they woke up, nothing was left, the entire palace and all its balconies had vanished. All that was left was the space of the bed in which they had slept.

Then the Queen said, "Let's take off, there's nothing else here. You had such a huge kingdom but now it's all gone. Honi has come to you."

Honi, you know, is a condition. It's a matter of the stars. Honi had come to him.

So they took off, poor things. As they went further and further, the Queen felt hungry. There was a partridge in the tree. The King shot an arrow and the bird fell down. He said to the Queen. "Roast this. Collect some sticks, make a fire, and roast the partridge. I'll go wash and then we'll eat, else we'll die of this hunger on the road."

"That's no problem," said the Queen. But as she roasted the bird, it revived and flew back up into the branches.

[*"What was this? Wasn't it dead?" asks Sello. "It was Honi, the condition that had befallen them," Urmilaji reiterates.*]

Bas, so the bird flew up into the trees. Then the King came. "Did you roast the partridge?" he asked. She said, "I was terribly hungry, and I ate the whole thing."

He said [*in a resigned voice*], "Well, let's go on."

They went on, and they saw a tree with mangos. The King hit at the tree with his stick so the mangos would fall down. Up on the tree, they were mangos, but when they fell to the ground they became sour citrus fruits (*rarhe*).

[*"It's a fruit too sour to eat," Sello explains, grimacing.*]

This is what happened. The King said, "Well, the day has come that when I shake a tree, mangos fall down as sour fruits. Come, let's proceed."

They went on, and at one bank of a river, a Jheer fisherman was catching fish. The King said, "Whatever you haul in with the net this time, give that to me."

The fisherman said, "No problem, I'll give it to you."

So he gave them all the fish he had caught, and the King gave it to the Queen. He said, "Cook this and I'll go wash."

111

When the King turned around, the fish all roused themselves and hopped back into the water. Nothing remained. He came back and asked, "Queen: the fish . . . ?"

She said, "I was terribly hungry and I ate them all."

[*"She lied," puts in Sello.*]

"OK, then, let's proceed."

So they took off. Up ahead, in the next state, was the place where they had given their daughter in marriage. They arrived at this place and sat down by a well.

Then his wife dispatched him, saying, "Ask someone to tell her that her parents are here, and she should come meet them at the well."

Someone went and told the daughter: "Your parents are here. They are sitting at the well and are calling for you."

The daughter was offended. "My parents would travel with many royal attendants! Why would they come sit by the well and send for me? Who knows who these people are and what family they are from? They must be some fisherfolk or field laborers.⁴ My mother and father wouldn't arrive here like this."

All the same, she filled a platter with pure pearls and put a brick of gold on top of it, and sent this with someone, saying, "My mother and father are royalty."

This was taken to them. But when the King lifted the platter and uncovered it to see what it held, the pearls and gold had become rice and black lentils.⁵ He dug a hole right there and buried the platter. Then they went on.

"Look at this, today even our own daughter sent someone else to us with rice and black lentils," the King said.

They went on and came to another country. The King had a friend there, a well-loved friend. The King took his Queen to visit the friend. They were warmly greeted, "My friend has come!"

The friend said to his wife, "My friend has come. But he's in the grips of some sort of difficulty. He's a powerful King, but some affliction has befallen him. Don't you say anything disrespectful to him."

The wife and the other one, poor thing, set about cooking, making the finest things. She and the other wife worked together in the kitchen. Everyone ate and drank. They fed the men, then they ate themselves. Then they went to sleep.

The friend's wife took off her necklace worth ninety thousand. She hung it on a hook. She hung it there, and the two of them went to sleep.

They lay down to sleep, but the poor Queen, where was sleep going to come from for her? She was dying of sorrow. Halfway through the night, she woke up and she saw that the mud peacock molded into the wall was eating the necklace. She saw this and she went to wake up the King. She said, "King, our affliction has followed us. Look, a peacock is eating up the necklace. Let's run away or we'll be ensnared, people will say we took it."

The condition had followed them there. So the two of them stood up and set off. The peacock ate the entire necklace, and in the morning, when everyone got up, they saw that those two had left. The friend's wife began to quarrel with her husband. "What kind of friend was that who would take my necklace and set off?" she said [*indignantly*].

He said, "Be quiet, be quiet, don't say anything. My friend isn't like that. Who knows what really happened?"

But was she ready to listen? Does a woman like that take heed? No, she said all sorts of bad things.

Now those two had traveled further ahead and gone to sleep under a pipal tree. While they slept, some thieves came by on their way to loot a king's treasury. The thieves made a vow there that if they were able to carry out their plan they would offer bracelets and a waistband to the tree. The King and Queen were still sleeping under the tree when the thieves returned from the King's treasury. They dressed her with a pair of bracelets and him with a waistband. Then they went off.

[*"A time of being ensnared!" exclaims Sello.*]

So the thieves left this offering there and carried on. Morning came, and there was an uproar: "The King's treasury has been looted! There was a huge theft!" So the soldiers set off to search for the thieves. Those two, poor things, were still asleep under the tree. They were nabbed while they slept.

That King had given the order that, without questions, without trial, the criminal's hands and feet should all be cut off. So the soldiers cut these off: hands and feet too.

❊ ❊ ❊

Bas. Then he couldn't do anything, he couldn't walk. His wife sat beside him and tried to tend him.

In the past, there were Oilpressers.[6] An Oilpresser woman had set out carrying a small pot on her head filled with oil to sell. As she came by, the wife said, "My husband here is a cripple with no hands or feet. Please throw a drop on all his wounds." There was no medicine there, no herbs, nothing. All the wife could do was sit there with him. "Just sprinkle a few drops of oil on him," she requested.

The Oilpresser woman felt sympathy for their suffering. She sprinkled a few drops on him, and then she went on to sell her oil. That day she gathered much more money from selling oil than she usually did. The next day she came by and said, "Here, I'll sprinkle some oil on you again." She kept this up for two or three days. She'd sprinkle some oil on the cripple and then she'd sell the rest for lots of money. She began to accumulate loads of wealth.

113

Her husband saw this and said, "You've become immoral. I give you just the same amount of oil as ever, and yet you bring so much more money home!"

She said, "There's this cripple. I sprinkle oil on him and then I get loads of money."

He said, "What? Where does he live?"

She said, "He lives under the pipal tree." She told him how this man had outraged the King of the land.

He said, "Let's bring him here and sit him down on our oil presser. He can sit there, the bullocks can go round and round, and the oil can keep flowing."

She said, "Whatever you like. If you say so, since he can't walk we'll have to lift him to bring him here."

The Oilpresser went to them. He saw them and listened to them, and he lifted the cripple to take him home. He brought the wife, too, saying, "You can stay here as my adopted daughter. And he . . ."

[*"A son-in-law," says Sello. Urmilaji laughs, perhaps because in North India, daughters are usually given away, making sons-in-law who live with their wives' parents an anomalous object of fun: the term "household's son-in-law"* (ghar jamāi), *used for a man who lives with his in-laws, is usually derogatory.*]

". . . a son-in-law is how we'll think of him." So they brought him there and sat him down on the oil presser where the bullocks circled. *Bas*, the Oilpresser became a millionaire.

※ ※ ※

Honi had come for twelve years. As they lived there, twelve years passed by. Then the stars began to move on, and the King's daughter came of age.

[*"Whose daughter?" I ask, confused.*]

The King who had ordered his hands and feet to be cut off. His daughter came of age and he said, "Let's hold a big gathering of Kings[7] so she can choose a good groom."

The drummers roamed all over, inviting all the Kings to assemble so that the daughter could choose a groom.

That's it. Kings and great Kings congregated from far and wide. She walked all around the gathering.

Now her King was supposed to have a fragment of a cloud over his head. Even if the entire sky was clear, he would have a fragment of cloud to shade his head.

She saw that all these Kings had come, but the one with the fragment of cloud was not there. She said, "I don't want any of these men." She told her father, "Call for everyone, all the common people." So drummers went out to announce that all the common men should assemble too.

[*"The lame and the crippled too," prompts Sello. "No, that's for the third day," corrects her mother.*]

So all the common people came there. She walked through the crowd, looking at the men. She looked up and saw that the one with the fragment of cloud above him had not come but had remained where he was.

On the third day it was announced, "The blind, the deaf, the crippled, everyone should be brought here. They must all assemble." The King said, "If anyone doesn't come I'll squash him and his children like seeds fed into an oilpresser. I'll execute everyone in his home."

The Oilpresser woman said to her husband, "Look, you have to take our cripple and seat him there. It's the King's order or we'll all end up pressed like seeds in our presser."

Bas. The Oilpresser lifted the cripple like a child and took him there. There was a huge heap of ash and he set him down on top of it.

When the virgin came out, she saw that the fragment of cloud was over the head of the cripple. She walked through the whole crowd and then came to where the cripple was sitting on the heap of ash. She came up to him and put the wedding garland around his neck.

She put this around his neck and all the people who had assembled began to cry, "Fie! Fie! This is a man who is guilty of stealing from your father. And he's a cripple that you've made your husband. Fie on your face! Fie on your face!"

Her father was furious too. He said, "Get out of my sight this instant. If this is the kind of groom you choose, don't ever come home again!"

She said, "Arrange for a small room for me somewhere nearby. I'll live there with this cripple. He is the groom for me."

So the King, her husband, made a room for her nearby. They began to live there. And the first wife, poor thing, stayed on with the Oilpresser.

They lived together for awhile.

❀ ❀ ❀

The King, her father, began to have a dream. Four beings would come and stand by his pillow: Dharma (or righteousness), Karma (or the fruits of action), Vidhi Mata (or Mother Fate), and Honi.[8] They would all come to where the girl's father was. They would assemble there, saying, "Judge who among us is the mightiest of us four. Who's the mightiest?"

The first would say, "I'm the greatest," the second would say, "I'm the greatest," the third would say, "I'm the greatest," the fourth would say, "I'm the greatest."

The King was mystified. He didn't know which one to choose as the greatest and why. He kept wondering, "Should I choose this one or that one?" He began to grow thin, just as the first King had. He kept losing weight, and then his wife said, "You've become so weak and thin, what's the matter?"

He said, "Dearest, how can I explain what the matter is? There are four that come and stand by my pillow. They say, 'Judge among us, who is the mightiest?' I don't understand who is the mightiest. I have no idea who it could be."

The Queen heard this, and she felt very upset. She went to her daughter. If a daughter is nearby, a mother goes to see her, this is a mother's heart. She went and told her daughter. "Dearest, these days your father is terribly troubled. He's wasting away."

"What's the matter?" asked the daughter. After all, a daughter worries about her mother and father.

She said, "Four beings come and stand by his pillow. One says 'I'm the greatest,' the second says, 'I'm the greatest.'

'Choose among us,' they say. 'Who is the mightiest?' He says that he doesn't know what answer to give, who he should judge as the mightiest."

The daughter came in and said to the cripple, "My mother was here, and she told me all this: they're really upset. Who should be judged the mightiest?"

The cripple said, "Tell your father that if he will allow me to sit on his throne for two minutes I will judge who is the mightiest. I'll decide among the four."

She went and told her mother; she didn't go to her father any more for she was scared of him. The mother told the father, "He says that if he can sit on your throne for two minutes he'll judge who the mightiest is."

The King said, "I can certainly give him my seat for two minutes so he can pass this judgment."

Bas. This is what they agreed. The cripple was brought there and settled upon the throne.

First Dharma, righteousness, arrived. He said, "I'm the greatest."

The cripple struck him like this (*arm raised at an angle*). He said, "I did such righteous deeds and you allowed my hands to be cut off." Then Dharma gave him a hand.

Next came Vidhi Mata, Mother Fortune. She said, "I'm the greatest."

He kicked her. "Was this what was written in my destiny?" he asked. "Was it written that my hands and feet should be cut off?" And she gave him a foot.

Third came Karma, the fruits of one's actions. The cripple gave him a blow of the leg too. "Did I earn this sort of karma? I used to feed a hundred people each day, and was the fruit of this that my feet should be cut off?" Karma gave him a foot too.

Then came Honi. She said, "I'm the greatest."

He walked around her and he bowed his head before her. He said, "You are the mightiest. If you come to someone, troubles cling to them and don't go away." Then his other hand was given back.

He said to his father-in-law, "I've pronounced the judgment. Honi is the mightiest. When she comes to someone, she only leaves when she's passed her time. Whether she's to stay for a little while or a long while, she'll stay out her full duration: only then does she go."

Then they performed a huge wedding with pomp and celebration for their daughter. Enormous dowry, many gifts.

He said to the King, "Now we will go to my own country. I've been here for twelve years since Honi came to me. Now her time is over. She's the greatest."

❊ ❊ ❊

So they turned around and took off. At the Oilpresser's house, great wealth had amassed. This wealth was drawn along with the the Queen. Then the Oilpresser's wife said to the Queen she had treated as her daughter, "Turn around and look back three times. See what is ours and what we're sending to your mother-in-law, see what is left behind."

Here, when a girl is going off to her in-laws' place, she turns around and looks back three times. She looks back and says inside herself: "That which is mine is coming with me, and that which belongs to my parents' place is staying at my parents' place."

They proceeded along, and they came to the country where the friend lived. The father-in-law had attendants, who came along bringing the enormous dowry and gifts. Elephants, horses, a big caravan.

That's it. They returned to the friend's house. The wife there said [*in a high-pitched, breathless voice*], "Here's that friend who stole my necklace and took off! He's back!"

The husband said, "Don't let such words leave your mouth. This is my friend. But it is not the person who stole your necklace."

But was she going to listen to him? She said all sorts of things. He, poor fellow, didn't allow this to affect his own thinking.

The King said, "We will spend the night here."

The friend thought, "This is their wish, how can I stop them? But what might my wife say?"

The King insisted on halting to stay right there. When it was time for a meal, now that he was King again, he had his own attendants make the food. It was late into the night when they finally ate everything and went to sleep, the first wife in that very room as before.

But she couldn't sleep. How could she sleep when she was wondering what they might say? As she lay awake she saw that the mud peacock was vomiting up the necklace. She woke up everyone then: she woke up the friend, the King, and the friend's wife too.

The friend said, "Didn't I tell you he had fallen into some difficulty? Look, there's the peacock, and look, there's the necklace." The peacock was vomiting the necklace.

117

His wife began to beg forgiveness. "How could I know that a mud peacock would do something like that?"

The King said, "It was Honi that came and did this. But I didn't say anything. What was there to say?"

Then they went on to the daughter's place. Then the Queen said, "Your mother and father have arrived, come meet them." The daughter came running! She said, "My mother and father are here today. There are royal attendants with them, right? Last time, it wasn't really them."

So she came and met with her mother, they exchanged all their confidences. The mother said, "Daughter, when we came here before, we were suffering hard times, but you only sent some rice, black lentils, and a little salt."

The daughter said, "Absolutely not! I sent a platter of pearls with a brick of gold on top."

The mother said, "Well, we buried it all right here."

They went and dug at that place, and there was the platter of pearls. "When Honi came to us, all these things were her doing," they agreed.

When they proceeded ahead, fish jumped out of the water and fell before them. The King said, "We're not hungry today." When they went further on, mangos on the tree started to fall to the ground. The King said, "Today we don't need this." Further on, there was the partridge.

When they arrived, everything had been restored as it was before. The kingdom, the palace, everything! So he returned to ruling his kingdom.[9]

❋ ❋ ❋

"This was because Honi came," observed Sello, yawning and stretching.

"All Honi," repeated Urmilaji.

"So Honi can come to all people?" I asked.

"To anyone at all," asserted Sello.

"It's tied up with the stars," said Urmilaji. "It's a condition (*dashā*)."

"I've never heard of this before," I said, "It's not Saturn (*shani*) or a limiting aspect of the moon (*rāhu*) is it?"

"It's a condition," repeated Urmilaji.

"So what does a regular person do if Honi comes?" I asked, still confused.

"Well, Honi can come for ordinary people for short times or long periods. This is why the King circled her, saying, 'You are the mightiest.' Once she comes, she bides her time and only then does she depart."

I felt upset by this story; disoriented, as though I'd woken from an afternoon sleep dense with troubled dreams. I wanted to think through the story, order it through transcription, before we talked more about it. Urmilaji inquired whether I would like to tape a song about the difficulties experienced by Ram and Lakshman when they were exiled to the forest along with Sita. I turned on my recorder to catch this, thinking of the parallels in wandering and suffering, even if the epic did not attribute the change of fortune to a force like Honi.

Later on I asked Urmilaji: "How does one know that Honi has come? Does an astrologer tell you?"

"An astrologer might tell you about the condition, but it's not from the stars. A person falls sick. A person suffers, their riches dwindle. Their money just finishes off. Then you say that Honi has come."

"Is there anything you can do when Honi comes?"

Urmilaji shook her head.

Honi then, appeared to be a condition that couldn't be predicted or cured, but could be diagnosed in the case of acute, unexplained misfortunes. Thinking of afflicting planets, and wondering if the word Honi might perhaps be related to Shani or Saturn, I asked again about their relationship. Urmilaji reiterated what she had said earlier: "Honi is different from Shani; different from Rahu (a limiting aspect of the moon). These are all the nine planets. You know this. But Honi is a condition. They say that those to whom Honi hasn't come don't understand anything about it."

Honi appears to be related to the root *honā* (to be) and so could mean, simply, "existence" or "that which happens." In a Hindi book of Pahari folktales, I came across a variant of this tale entitled "The Greatness of Honi." Proclaiming her greatness, the King states, "Honi is powerful. When the settlements of fortune, the fruits of karma, the destined connections of the creator all come together, then what is to happen happens. You are the greatest of all."[10] In this version, Honi emerges from the conjunction of the multiple forces shaping lives. For Urmilaji, though, Honi seemed less of a cumulative force and more the personification of arbitrary bad fortune for which other causal explanations—righteousness, fate, prior actions—fall short.[11]

Another intriguing interpretation of Honi's identity was offered by Professor Vashistha, who taught mathematics at a local college in Kangra. His wife, a professor of English, had become interested in my project on Urmilaji's tales and had taken me to visit a Panditji—ritual specialist and astrologer—so as to clarify particular details in the rituals. When we discussed Honi, Professor Vashistha observed, speaking English, "Honi is the bad part of one's actions: what you do unconsciously and do not know will come back to you." In this sense, then, Honi—questioning people in their dreams—appears to be a shadow of the conscious mind.

Urmilaji was a firm believer in things not happening until the time was ripe. Using the English word "time" she explained that time was in God's hands. She used the concept of the right time to explain why she and I were only drawn together through her stories only years after we had first met. Urmilaji also resorted to this explanation when trying to make sense of why an appropriate match hadn't yet been found for her eldest son (and in 1994, Sello too):

119

"It is a matter of the right time. Things happen only when it is the right time for them to happen."

In another conversation, Urmilaji revised her earlier position that nothing could be done to alleviate the effects of Honi. She admitted, "Well, this is a condition, after all. Sometimes certain things can be done to protect a person. Otherwise, I've told you about all the powerful reversals that can occur: hands and feet can be cut off; everything can dwindle; the elephants, the horses, the palace and its balconies, everything can decline until a person begs from door to door. Honi is the greatest."

She touched on the original transfer: "That King was a very fortunate King, but Honi came to him when he gave the dough to the Brahman. The Brahman had Honi sitting on him. He possessed nothing, no matter how hard he worked. But when the King took the dough and gave it to the Brahman, then the Brahman's Honi diminished and was finished off, and it came to the King instead.

"They say that by doing things like that, the condition of Honi can be alleviated. Sometimes, it goes and sits on someone else, and someone else suffers the force. But you shouldn't transfer it. It can even take people's lives away. It's a bad action to save one's own life by destroying another's. But sometimes when Honi settles on a person, they try to transfer it to someone else. After all, all people want to alleviate their own misfortune!"

I asked how this related to the Bujru, a low-ranking Brahman who was known to absorb inauspicious planetary influences. I had been present at a house in the adjoining village when the Bujru, wearing blue, arrived on a Saturday (*shanivār*, Saturn's day) with a staff over his shoulder from which hung a metal pot full of mustard oil. By looking at one's reflection in the oil, and putting coins into it, I was told, the difficulties produced by Saturn were reduced. Also, at a boy's first birthday ceremony in another part of the valley, I observed another Bujru (this time in a not-so traditional costume of mottled-green army fatigues) weigh a baby boy against various packages of whole grains, seeds, and lentils, each package representing a difficult planetary influence. When a Bujru took money, grain, or other whole foods with him, I was told, he also took away specific afflictions.[12]

Urmilaji's explanation matched what I had previously heard. "The Bujru probably has some special boon, some special power, so he can take on other people's afflictions and nonetheless himself stay healthy, eating and drinking," she said. "He can lift the influence, melt it, and bear it away with him."

Like transactions centered around Saturn and oil with the Bujru, in the story, the first turning point comes when the Oilpresser woman offers oil to the mutilated King and finds that she has unexpected good fortune in selling oil that day. Before this point, the story had spiraled down into tragic desolation; after this point, misfortune is gradually alleviated, until, reseated on a throne to pass judgment, the man once again takes the form of a King. Then, point by point, the story reverses itself into good fortune. The oil transaction highlights the conception of an influence clinging, bodily, to a person, and the possibility of this influence being transferred or dissolved by contact with certain substances, such as oil. Seating the mutilated king in the center of the oilpress, from which healing oil flows, the Oilpresser[13] helps effect important changes. Though Urmilaji denied that Saturn was linked with Honi, the importance of oil in alleviating the difficulties would indicate that there is perhaps a connection.[14] Further, the Oilpresser carrying the king from the center of the oil press to a heap of ash indicates another transfer of substances—after the liquid power of oil, the residue of fire associated with death and regeneration. Being chosen by the Princess, the mutilated king gains the chance to pass judgment from her father's throne.

Switching to a more psychological tone, Urmilaji observed, "Partly, it's that doing something gives people peace in their hearts. Sometimes when they have misfortunes, they're told that this is a condition and they do all kinds of recitations, rituals for it. Then some get well, but for others, no matter how much they do, their situation doesn't change."

While the suffering meted out by Honi can't always be alleviated, an unfortunate person can aspire to be like the King, maintaining inner peace despite all odds. "The cloud over his head means that he is peaceful," said Urmilaji. "Everyday that Princess used to see the cloud from the distance. The whole sky might be clear, but there would be that one cloud over his head, giving him shade."[15] Because of metaphorical associations within the English language ("an overcast mood," "clouds of gloom," and so on), a perpetual cloud over one's head might strike an English speaker as a condition of unfortunate moroseness. Yet one need only think of high, blazing South Asian skies to understand that a cloud making a spot of shade might be linked to a state of cool inner peace. As Urmilaji pointed out on another occasion, just as Kings always traveled with royal canopies over their heads, so the clouds provided shade for the incognito King.

Though this story is linked to the women's ritual of the thunder thread, it is also one that men tell. Urmilaji said that she had first learned it from her father. In July 1991, I recorded a variant from Pandit Jagannath, the Sood's charismatic family priest who had arrived to preside over a birthday ceremony for Nirmalaji's son. With a crown-like Kulu cap adorning the white hair on his head, gold hoops glinting from his ears, Pandit Jagannath sat cross-legged on the bed beside the television—completely displacing it for the moment. After everyone had been fed, Pandit Jagannath kept us captivated with a procession of tales. He told us myths of the gods, legends about the revered ascetic Shankaracharya, and finally, the story about Honi. While Urmilaji had identified the King as King Bhoj, Pandit Jagannath called him King Vikramaditya (these are both Kings celebrated widely in Indian folklore).

121

The Bujru visiting on a Saturday (*Photo by Kirin Narayan*)

"Honi came, and everything was finished in the kingdom," Pandit Jagannath began, in rapid-fire Pahari. "The King and the Queen had to go wandering." Here the introductory story about the unfortunate Brahman, the sacred thread, and the King's barging in on the secret woman's ritual of the thunder thread was omitted. As in Urmilaji's version, when the King and Queen went wandering, the ripe mango turned into sour fruit, the fish flopped back, and the felled bird flew up. Yet, these were stated as events, without the dialogue between the King and Queen. Their visit to the married daughter and their overnight stay with friends were also left out. The sequence of being set up by robbers and the King's hands and feet being cut off was the same (though Pandit Jagannath added, "The Queen had no punishment, for she was a woman"). The stay with the Oilpresser's family was abbreviated, leaving out the exchange between the Oilpresser woman and the Queen. The Princess's

122

Urmilaji's extended natal family doing a ritual to honor the sun, 1988. Pandit Jagannath (extreme right). Urmilaji's elder brother, Omkar Sood (right foreground) and Urmilaji's eldest son Raju (left background). Urmilaji second from left, background. (*Photo by Brigitte Luchesi*)

choice of the man with a cloud over his head remained the same, though her parent's outrage was not elaborated. Here, too, her father was troubled by four personified forces (though Vidhi Mata, Mother Fate, became Vidhata, the male Creator who also oversees fate). Pandit Jagannath finished off his version as though he had been conducting a ritual retelling, exclaiming piously, "Say to Krishna Bhagavan... Hail!" Getting the cue, we all joined in for the "Hail!" causing him to let out a long, roaring laugh of delight. Almost immediately after finishing the story, Pandit Jagannath went rushing down to road so as not to miss his bus home.

As Pandit Jagannath told this story, Urmilaji smiled quietly from a corner. At moments when he diverged from the way she told it, I caught her eye. Later, when I asked her about these differences, she diplomatically commented, "People tell stories differently." Perhaps Pandit Jagannath's having to catch a bus explained why his version was less elaborated than Urmilaji's more leisurely retelling. All the same, his version showed the extent to which Urmilaji's re-telling forefronted the perspective of the women involved.

Though the King is a central character in Urmilaji's version, she stresses the actions and emotions of the women around him. It is the Brahman's wife who figures out the solution to her husband's problems and sets the plot moving. It is the Queen's ritual dough that seals the transfer of Honi from Brahman to King. It is the Queen who instructs the King on what to say to the figure hovering by his pillow, who divines that this is Honi, who asks him to send a message to their daughter, who observes the mud peacock eating the necklace, and who befriends the Oilpresser woman. The Princess of the other kingdom is another strong-willed character, determined to choose the right mate for herself, even if this brings on her father's ire. Finally, the Princess's mother is also similar to the first Queen (as well as the Brahman's wife) in her concern for the preoccupations that are devouring her husband.

Another theme that recurs is that of the strong ties between mothers and daughters. Both queens hanker to visit with their married daughters. Also, the first Queen is adopted by the Oilpresser woman as a daughter. So strong is this association with the Oilpresser woman that when the adopted daughter departs with her husband, the adopted parents' possessions follow after. In Urmilaji's story then, a tale about a man's hardships becomes a tale about women sticking with their men through difficult times, and of the strong bonds between mothers and daughters who are socially destined to be separated.

An interesting feature in both Urmilaji's and Pandit Jagannath's retellings is how, once the King was mutilated, he is no longer referred to as "the King" (*rājā*) but merely as "the cripple" (*roḷā*). Without hands or feet, tended and carried around like a child, the King loses his autonomy. He is moved from oilpress to ash heap and finally to the throne. While he is unable to walk or care for himself, it is the King of the other kingdom who controls the situation and who is referred to as "the King." His visitation by four figures mirrors the first King's being approached by Honi in his dreams. When the first king is seated on the throne of the other King, he once again regains his status as a king who can pass judgment, and the other King (his father-in-law) disappears from the story.

This is one of the few stories that Urmilaji explicitly drew on to describe her own life to me. Some months later, as she was telling me about a relentlessly difficult period in her life, she said, "I went through hard, hard times, like the King and Queen who were accused of stealing the necklace that the peacock had eaten up, and to whom all those other things happened." Clasping my hands, Urmilaji looked into my eyes. "Sometimes things are bad, and they stay bad," she said. "If you wait, finally they can turn around."

TWELVE

Earth into Gold

There is another story associated with Honi. Urmilaji first mentioned this story when discussing the thunder thread in July. On subsequent visits, in response to my questions, she elaborated. I gradually pieced together what had happened. At first I hesitated to present the tale as a full-blown story for I had never heard Urmilaji tell the story sequentially. But I had been moved by its images. Urmilaji herself emphasized that this was a story in its own right, not a fragment to be incorporated into a discussion of the story of Honi.

"The same story for Honi is also there for the thunder thread," Urmilaji had said when she told me this story. "There's just this difference: when the Queen made flat breads of river loam, she threw them on the roof. This was when they were at the Oilpresser's house and had no riches left. She'd go to the riverbank and worship the thunder thread."

"And why is the thunder thread worshipped?" I asked, confused.

"Why? Open the thread, open the thread.... What's the story?" Urmilaji squinted, apparently racking her memory. "It's a ritual in honor of Shiva and Parvati."

❀ ❀ ❀

There had once been another woman who performed this worship. Her husband was plowing. She had taken food to him where he worked by the riverbank. When she got there, a snake bit him and he died. Then people began to mourn.

The Gods Shiva and Parvati happened to be passing by. Parvati was always being obstinate. Wherever they went, she'd want to assert her will.[1] "Raise up this man!" she said to Shiva. "Look at the situation. Everyone is in despair."

Shiva got annoyed. He said, "In this world, some people are suffering and other people are happy. Everyone is confined within his or her own experience. But wherever you go, you demand, 'Rescue this person! Alleviate so and so's suffering!'"

She said, "Lord, you absolutely must do this now."

125

So then they went to the woman and asked her what the story was. She said, "This and that happened, and he came here and was bitten by a snake."

Shiva sprinkled the nectar of immortality on the man, and he stood up. Then Parvati said, "In this month, from this fifth lunar day onward, worship snakes and also this thread: open up the thread." That's why Shiva and Parvati are placed there in worship, along with a sapling from the berry bush (*barairi*). Then they are worshipped and the thread is opened out.

So the woman sat under the bush and set to opening the thread, laying it out before Shiva and Parvati, and doing this worship.

In the same way, the Queen opened the thunder thread beside the berry bush at the river bank. She'd pat out round breads from muddy sand, and throw them on the roof of the Oilpresser's house. While they stayed with the Oil-pressers, this family became enormously wealthy. Otherwise, the family was so poor that the Oilpresser woman had to go out and sell oil each day. The Queen was moral and pious. She did a lot of worship and recitations. Once Honi had departed, these breads turned into gold.

When the Queen was leaving for her own home, everything—even the oil-press!—all came along with her from the Oilpresser's home.

The Queen said, "No!" She had thought of this place as her mother's home. She said, "What's mine should come with me, and everything that's theirs should stay."

Then just the gold and silver went off with the Queen. The gold on the roof, too, where she had placed the breads of river sand, all this went with her. But what was the Oilpresser's stayed behind: the house, the bullocks they used to press oil, the oilpress, and all the other things that had made him wealthy.

The Queen became prosperous once more. Her husband, King Bhoj, was after all a great King. It was just when Honi came to him that things had changed. Honi comes to some people for eighteen years, to some for twelve years . . . but it destroys whatever a person has.[2]

❋ ❋ ❋

Urmilaji commented, "This is a ritual for the time in which you and I live, but when it all actually happened, Shiva and Parvati were living beings. Now we make them of clay. The breads are of flour, and the figurines are of clay. The dough used to make the breads shouldn't be shown to men. It has to be made in secret and all the worship should be hidden. The Brahman took that dough, right?"

Though the performance of the worship is hidden, Urmilaji appeared to have no qualms about relating the details to me and a potential audience that could contain men. It was not that men should not know that this ritual was per-formed, but rather that their presence at a performance could potentially be dangerous to them.[3]

In a gender-segregated society like Kangra's, upper-caste women's symbolic life takes place mostly in spaces set apart from male intervention. Groups of women gather to worship at riverbanks, under trees, in courtyards, in inner rooms, where men are not present. In my experience, men are usually off at work or are making themselves scarce. They seem usually to keep away of their own accord because it is considered women's business. It is only with this ritual of the thunder thread that it is a women's formal responsibility to hide all traces of the ritual from men.

As these stories associated with Honi caution, if a man should violate this sphere of women's worship, misfortune will result. The King thrust his sword into the vessel of dough that men are not meant to view; overriding his wife's objections, he set the stage for the Brahman's misfortune to cling to the king instead. Later, the King lost his hands and feet (presumably also with the swift cut of a sword). Wandering destitute, the Queen lacked the materials to pat out dough breads. Yet she kept steadfastly to her ritual, replacing dough with muddy river sand. In this way, she saw through the difficult times until their fortunes shifted.

Urmilaji also pointed out that the thunder thread was associated with the worship of snakes, on the fifth day of the waxing lunar month of Bhādrapad (August/September). On this day, also called Snake's Fifth (*nāg panchi*),[4] five snakes are drawn in different colors in the courtyard, and offerings, including milk are made to them. "Be happy and stay in your own country," the snakes are told. In the story, too, Urmilaji pointed out, the husband of the original woman who performed the ritual was bitten by a snake. After the worship of Shiva and Parvati, a lower-caste "brother" is asked to pull a plow the length of a two-and-a-half furrow: Urmilaji explained that this was on account of the plowing husband bitten by snakebite in the original story. By asking a lower-caste man to plow, a woman ensures that her husband and son will not be bitten by snakebite. In other words, this transaction serves as a form of ritual transfer.

I was surprised to learn about the making of a "brother" from a lower caste (although within the bounds of touchability). I wanted to know what other ties or obligations this ritual bond entailed. Urmilaji said that you might give the man a *rākhi* bracelet or anoint his forehead with vermilion on occasions when brothers were honored. It did not necessarily mean a close tie. She said that the man who had done this ritual for her, poor fellow, had already died. She herself had long ago performed a grand finale for her own observance of the thunder thread.

I asked Urmilaji why the Oilpresser's family had become rich on account of the King and Queen's presence. She said, "It's because the influence (*prabhāv*) of wealth fell on the Oilpresser's family too. Take you and me: after meeting you, I too have some money in my purse."

❋ ❋ ❋

I have a confession to make here. Among my father's relatives, women's rituals were performed too. But with my hybrid background, I found these rituals awkward, oppressive: feeling that they did not contain the kind of woman I wanted to be, I simply stayed away and never wanted to hear the stories. Ironically, it was taking the position of an outsider in Kangra who could *choose* whether to participate or not, and of encountering these stories as Urmilaji's own gentle teachings, that led me to appreciate women's ritual stories.

This is the last story I heard from Urmilaji that was associated with women's rituals. Before moving on to her winter's tales, it is worth reflecting on themes that pervade this first set of stories.

First, all the ritual stories foreground women and their concerns. Women's desires and activities set plots rolling, women's relationships with one another (as mothers, daughters, sisters, mothers-in-law, daughters-in-law) are often highlighted. In the stories, performing rituals differentiates observant and fortunate women from nonobservant and unremarkable women or men. There are certainly sons, brothers, husbands, fathers-in-law, and saintly men in these stories, but all these men tend to play out the scripts determined by women's pious actions. As I mentioned, in the case of "The Twelve Years of Affliction," which can also be told as a nonritual tale, Urmilaji's retelling accentuated the contributions and emotions of the female characters.

Second, all these stories assert that women's rituals are powerful. They celebrate the good karma, the fruits, of performing these rituals. Worship is shown to be a potent source of transformation, of shape-shifting. Worship can bring the dead to life, erect palaces in desolate jungles, create husbands and sons out of thin air, channel forms through births, and transmute mud or feces into gold. Performing rituals redeems women from dire straits and makes for miracles in the lives of the men to whom they are related.

Third, the stories uphold the virtues of doing two kinds of work: industrious household work that involves serving others and ritual work that entails serving the gods through rituals. (Agricultural work is conspicuously absent here). Both kinds of service may yield boons. Moreover, boons are not just granted by apparent gods—Shiva, Parvati, Krishna, and Saili—but also by gods disguised as mortals (like the old visiting Brahman) or mortals with divine powers (like Sunna the Washerwoman).

Fourth, all of these stories feature ritual practices, such as lighting lamps, floating boats, or patting out breads. Many of these practices involve trees and plants. The pipal tree, the sacred basil plant, the sour berry tree, and the *barairi* berry bush, are among the flora that find a place in these stories and also in village women's natural environments.

Fifth, some older observant women spoke of these stories as true, set in a primordial earlier time, or at least in the era of ancestral memory. Younger women, though, seemed less convinced about the veracity of these stories. They did not seem to perceive continuities running between the world of the stories and their own lives in the same way that the older women did.

Without realizing it, I too became entangled in these threads of continuity between rituals, stories, and everyday life. For months, Urmilaji accompanied me along the cobbled path to the crossroads where I turned left to go home. She stood, smiling, watching me as I picked my way along the rounded stones people said were once used as the salt route up into the higher mountains. Each time, when I looked back, she was still there. The second and the third times, she was watching too. But the fourth time, just before I rounded the corner, she had turned back.

This soon became a regular practice for us. Sometimes we would share the path with a cow ambling along, a woman with bales of grass on her head, a group of girls lugging their evening load of drinking water from the spring in plastic canteens or mud pots, men in jackets and trousers trudging home after a day's work in town, a brother with an overnight bag escorting a married sister, adorned in red, home for a visit. But even if there were other people on that stretch of cobbled stones, I came to always look back three times. I had no idea why this should have any meaning; it seemed a private ritual between us. Visiting Kangra briefly during the monsoon of 1991, my sister Maya remarked on the way Urmilaji patiently stood, watching us make our way down the then muddy and slippery path.

In the course of narrating "The Twelve Years of Affliction," Urmilaji had explained, "Here when a girl is going off to her in-laws' place, she turns around and looks back three times. She looks back and says inside herself: "That which is mine is coming with me, and that which belongs to my parents' place is staying at my parents' place." The Queen had not thought to do this at first, and so her departure from her adopted parents' home drew all their wealth as well as what was rightfully hers. It was only when she stopped, looked back, and consciously articulated the rightful separation between her two homes that the possessions were sorted out. This part of the story struck me as resonating deeply with Kangra women's experience of negotiating identities between two homes: that of her parents and that of her in-laws. (I should add that when women remarked that I could enjoy my mother's company since I had no in-laws' home in which to serve, I sometimes retorted that my university was equivalent to an in-laws' home—full of feared elders, and burdened with work.)

I had taped "The Twelve Years of Affliction" within my first month of friendship with Urmilaji. But it was much later, musing over these tapes, that I connected the Queen's looking back in the story to my own looking back. It struck me that just like a daughter departing for a distant home, whenever I left Urmilaji, I was bearing quantities of gifts, of words and of wisdom, if not outright material objects. Perhaps, amid Urmilaji's generous outpouring of her own knowledge, she was also concerned that I bear away only what was due to me. Our going through these motions each day was perhaps equivalent to my saying about the symbolic materials she shared: "That which is mine is coming with me; that which is Urmilaji's is staying with Urmilaji."

When I asked Urmilaji about this, she smiled. "Yes, I watch you go," she acknowledged. She neither affirmed nor contradicted my interpretation, but she did add this: "When we watch a daughter leave we think, 'She too should flourish, green and full [as a growing plant] and we should flourish too.'"

PART 2

Winter Tales

Divining Destiny
and Rebirth

Karma, the fruits of past action, and reincarnation are often viewed as key Hindu concepts. Yet, as the stories presented so far have showed, karma may coexist with other systems to make sense of life's vagaries: for example, personified forces of misfortune like Honi or miraculous good fortune resulting from a boon dispensed by deities. Also, destiny may be written on a person's forehead at birth by Vidhi Mata, Mother Fate.

Dharmraj, "the just ruler," is a key figure in the sorting of souls after death. In Kangra folklore, he keeps files on souls, sometimes with the assistance of Mother Fate. He sends souls on to heaven or hell, according to the actions they have performed. While the existence of heaven and hell might seem to contradict the idea of rebirth, this can be resolved by seeing these as temporary stopovers before the soul moves on to a birth in the sort of womb decreed by past actions.

Themes of karma, destiny, and rebirth have already appeared in tales associated with women's rituals. Some of the winter tales expand further on these issues.

THIRTEEN

In the Court of Destiny

"I still haven't told you the story of the lion," Urmilaji said, inviting me back after our first long afternoon together.

This story with a lion turned out to be the first winter tale that I heard from her. She had learned it in childhood from her father. As she reminisced, "Every year when winter came, then we'd start to entreat my father, 'Tell us that story about the lion! Tell us that story about the Demoness! Tell us that story about such and such.'"

When her father told stories, he attracted large and varied audiences. "When he began to tell a story, then everyone who was there would come and sit around him to listen. Older people would flock there too. Adults and children alike. The workers and the coolies from the tea gardens would come and sit there too. The stories would begin, and we'd listen to them into the night."

Another woman of about Urmilaji's age, Jnanu Bhandari, also described such winter gatherings. "Now there is television, there is radio," she said. "In the past, for these long winter nights what other entertainment did we have but stories? Everyone would come and cluster in the house where they knew there was a storyteller."

Storytellers, then, became a locus for gatherings on winter nights. Usually, groups gathered near a source of warmth: a bonfire, a pan of smoldering coals, or a kitchen hearth. Jnanu Bhandari described her grandmother as a storyteller, and Urmilaji also mentioned a female neighbor in the tea gardens as a teller of winter tales. On the whole, though, most people mentioned male storytellers of winter tales. Everyone who told me of such gatherings described them as a vanished social practice.[1]

Unlike women's ritual tales, which are told in segregated gatherings of high-caste women, winter tales appear to have drawn in an audience that spanned gender, caste, and occupation. Accordingly, the tellers of these stories were also from a range of backgrounds. Among the most talented tellers I encountered was Loru Ram, a bricklayer of the basket-maker caste, who emphasized to me that though he was poor and illiterate, he too had learned the sort of stories you could find in a book. Rita, a young woman from the cobbler caste, also told wonderfully elaborate stories that she had learned from her father, a field laborer who earned extra money by entertaining in wedding bands.

Winter tales are closer to what we think of as "fairy tales." They often have an expansive, meandering quality, and are filled with strange and marvelous happenings. The didactic emphasis of women's ritual stories is absent from most of these tales. Readers who do not subscribe to the prescriptions for pious womanhood found in the ritual tales may find these stories more appealing.

Leafing through my transcriptions of songs as we first got to know each other, Urmilaji, had seen the words to a devotional song (*bhajan*) sung by a Brahman woman in her eighties. It must have struck Urmilaji's imagination, for she asked if I could bring over the tape in order for her to learn the melody. Grateful to Urmilaji for the stories she had been telling, eager to reciprocate however I might, I brought along this tape on the third long afternoon that we spent together in March.

The song was about an old woman absorbed in her housework. When a messenger arrived from Dharmraj,[2] who judged people at death, the old woman objected that she couldn't go yet since she had another two-and-a-half reels left to spin. This objection did not impress the messenger. He told her that she could finish spinning in her next life and bore her away. When she stood before Dharmraj, he wanted to know what meritorious deeds she had performed. The old woman replied that she had neither given charity nor sponsored rituals: her life had slipped away in work. She pleaded that she be allowed to go home and continue what she had been doing. Dharmraj instructed her that, now, her sons were in charge and her daughters-in-law were tending the house.

This song dramatized the distinction Urmilaji often made between household work and meritorious actions honoring the gods. The old woman also embodied well-meaning but blind attachment, which distracted a soul from awareness of flux, death, and divinity. Putting on her spectacles, Urmilaji studied the text I had brought her and sang along with the tape. She called for Sello. "I want her to learn songs like this," Urmilaji said. "Songs full of wisdom." But while Sello mouthed the words, Urmilaji was the one learning the song. Putting down the paper and without the accompaniment of my little tape recorder, Urmilaji sang again. I could see that by small shifts in the words and melody she was making the song her own.

Then Urmilaji told me the story of the lion, in which Dharmraj reappears.

❀ ❀ ❀

There was a King. He had one daughter, who was born with a mark at the center of her forehead.[3] She was raised and coddled, and she grew. When she came of age, then the King said to his Purohit, the family priest, "Go find a groom who also has a natural mark on his forehead."

In the past, a King's command was such that if he issued an order, it had to be accomplished somewhere, somehow. The Purohit [*who in this story is also called* Brahman *or* Pandit] took rations from the King and left food at his home with his wife. He set out to look for a groom. He wandered in all four directions but he didn't find a single man with a natural mark on his forehead. He turned around and came back to the King. "Maharaj, no one with a mark on his forehead can be found."

The King said, "We must give her to whomever you can find with a mark on his forehead, regardless of whether he's rich or poor. She absolutely has to be given to someone with a mark on his forehead."

Once again the Purohit took his rations, once again he delivered food to his wife at home. Then he set out through the jungle.

Deep in the jungle, there sat a lion. The lion had a natural mark on his forehead.

The Brahman pondered, "The King told me, 'my daughter will be married to whomever you find.' Well, why not give her to a lion?"

So he took out some red powder (*kumkum*) and put a ceremonial mark on the lion's forehead.[4] "A certain King's daughter will be married to you," he said.

The lion laughed hard. He said, "A King's daughter?! And you want to marry her to me, a lion? This is very odd!"

[*Urmilaji looks up drolly, lips pressed together over her missing front teeth and I laugh.*]

The Brahman said, "Absolutely. She is to be married to you."

The lion said, "What sort of empty talk is this? A King's daughter? She'll take one look at me and be petrified!"

The Brahman said, "I have the King's orders to marry her to someone with a mark on his forehead. I've wandered in four directions and I haven't found anyone anywhere who has a natural mark on his forehead. Now I've found you and I've put a ceremonial mark on your forehead.

"And there's another thing," the Brahman said. "Once the marriage date is set, how am I going to find you again? [*Urmilaji laughs, perhaps because this shows laziness on the Brahman's part*]. I'll set the date for the marriage right now. Come on such and such a day to be married. Otherwise, it's going to be too hard to locate you again out in this jungle."

The lion said [*softly, as though resigned*], "That's fine."

The Brahman turned around and went back. He said to the King, "You asked me to find someone with a natural mark on his forehead. I've performed the engagement, and I've set the marriage for this date."

The King said, "That's wonderful that you found someone with a natural mark on his forehead and that you did the engagement."

Once the King had approved this, then the "program" for the wedding was

Palanquins of a bride and groom being taken between villages (*Photo by Didi Contractor*)

underway: all the things had to be assembled, there were plenty of things to be done. Finally, the day came for the wedding. The King held a huge feast, and performed many rituals.

At the time of the wedding, a group of lions emerged from the jungle together. They had been invited, after all. They arrived and gathered together in the King's garden.

The King said. "Why are they here? Why have the lions come here—such a big gang of lions? What's going on?"

Bas. The King, poor fellow, went out to the lions. He folded his hands [*in a gesture of supplication*] and said, "What's the matter? What mistake have I made that all of you come here?"

The lion with the mark on his forehead stepped forward. He said, "Your Purohit invited me to be married and this is the groom's party I've brought with me."

The King called for the Purohit. "What have you done, going and promising my daughter to a lion?"

The Purohit said, "Great King, you said you wanted to give her to someone with a mark on his forehead. I wandered e-v-er-y-where and I couldn't find anyone like that. Only this lion had a natural mark on his forehead. He was sitting in the jungle and I put a ceremonial mark on him for the betrothal. You had said that anyone was fine as long as he had a natural mark on his forehead."

138

The King, poor fellow, was really distressed. Where is a virgin daughter of a King? Where is a lion of the jungle?

[*Urmilaji looks me in the eye for a suspense-laden pause.*]

The festivities were on. All kinds of special foods were being cooked for the feast. The King asked, "What will you lions have to eat? All the lions should be served a goat apiece!" So his orders were carried out. As many goats were brought as there were lions. Each lion was given one to eat.

Then the lion made the marriage rounds of the fire with that poor girl.

After this, the dowry and the gifts that had been gathered were shown to the lion. "Take all this with you," said the King. It was all loaded into palanquins to be sent to that spot in the forest where the ceremonial mark had been put on the lion. All the lions and the palanquin bearers went there together. The palanquins were set down and the bearers turned back. Fine.

Then that lion with the natural mark on his forehead said to the other lions, "Take all these things here that have been sent with us." Also, he said to the men who the King had sent with them to carry things, "Take these objects to your own homes. Just leave this virgin girl with me."

Then out there in the jungle, the lions all went to their own places and the people went home too. Just the two of them were left: the virgin and the lion.

The lion said, "Climb onto my shoulders, holding onto my head. I'll carry you with me this way."

She said, "No. You go ahead and I'll follow behind you."

She followed and she followed; who knows how many jungles they passed through. Then they came to a place where there was a steep climb uphill. The lion insisted, "You won't be able to manage here. This time you must mount my shoulders."

So he took her on his shoulders, and with two leaps he reached their destination. They had arrived in the City of Heaven. Here, he was Dharmraj, the King of Justice.

Dharmraj! And she became a big Queen! They began to live amid great pomp and splendor.

[*I ask, "And did he have the form of a man?"*]

The form of a man! He shed the animal skin and he became a God.

A year passed by and the girl's mother was depressed. She was always weeping bitterly, "I had just one daughter, and she was married off to a lion." She cried and she cried.

The King came and asked, "What happened?"

The mother said [*almost imperceptibly*], "Nothing."

"No," he said. "You seem very sad."

She said, "I'm thinking of our daughter. What happened to her? She was our only daughter."

Now Kings of the past, when they gave commands, they had to be heeded.

He called for the same Purohit again. He said, "You go inquire after her. Look around the jungle and see if you can find her. Then bring us news of her welfare."

Bas. The Purohit said, "Give me my rations and I'll give them to my wife at home. And I'll go off and look for her."

The King gave the Purohit rations. He took them home, and he set off on his mission. He searched and he searched in that jungle. He didn't know where to look. Then, on the path that she had gone along, on that path he saw the bride's garments; the bridal red ribbons for her hair, the ornaments for her braid, and her torn clothes were all strewn there in the jungle. These were the signs that the Purohit followed. Who knows how long it took him to get there. But he proceeded on and on, following these garments, and finally he arrived: it was the City of Heaven.

The moon was bright. Stars shone in the day. There was no shortage of anything. Diamonds, gems, pearls.

The Purohit walked through the marketplace. The Queen was sitting swinging on her balcony. She saw the Purohit and recognized him from afar. She sent her maid, "Go fetch that man."

The maid went and brought the Purohit. The Queen enthusiastically greeted him. This was a man from her parent's place, after all! He too was enormously happy. "Look at what I did and how this matter turned out: this is heaven!"

They asked each other all sorts of questions. She showed him great honor since he had found a great man for her. "He is Dharmraj," she said.

The Purohit stayed there for a few days. Then he said to Dharmraj, "I want to see your court. I want to see the place that you do your work."

"Come along then," Dharmraj said [*nonchalantly*]. "Come and see it."

They went to the court. Files were being brought out and destiny was being read aloud. Then the Purohit's file[5] was brought out. It said, "A girl will be born in the Purohit's house. And in the same kingdom a boy will be born in a Chuhra Sweeper's house. These two will be married."

[*Urmilaji explains that a Chuhra is an untouchable sweeper; the caste that cleans up human feces. In other words, he would be the polar opposite of a high-caste, pure Brahman, and a most improbable match.*]

Dharmraj noticed this and he laughed.

The Brahman said, "What was in there?"

He said, "Nothing."

"No, you'll definitely have to tell me what was in there."

Then Dharmraj said, "A daughter is going to be born to you who will marry a Sweeper boy."

The Brahman said [*indignantly*], "I'm a Brahman and my daughter will marry a Sweeper?! That's impossible!"

Bas. Then the Brahman wanted to leave at once. "I'm going home. My wife is due to deliver and I'm worried about her. Who knows how things are there?"

They said, "Since you've come so far, stay here another week."

He said, "No. Now that I know the way to this place, I'll come again some other time." Inside, the matter of his daughter was troubling him. He wanted to hurry off. "I must leave today."

So they gave the Brahman a lot of riches and he went home. He returned the same way he had come and immediately went to the King. He went right to the King's court. The King said [*softly and sadly*], "How is my daughter?"

He said, "Your daughter is rocking in a golden swing."

He had brought a gold ring as a token and he gave this to the King. The King looked at it and thought about it. "You're lying!" he said.

The Brahman said, "This is a token from her. She has been married to Dharmraj. The lion with the natural mark on his forehead was Dharmraj. And he's a really powerful, great King!"

The Queen was very happy to have news of her daughter. The King was delighted too. "Ask for anything you want," he said. "We're so pleased that we're ready to grant you whatever you would like."

He said, "I don't want anything. Just this boy that's about to be born in a Sweeper's house: that's what I want."

The King said [*leaning forward, incredulous*], "What's this that you want?" [*Urmilaji laughs.*]

The Brahman said, "I want this and nothing else." He went to the Sweeper's house and took the child. The Sweepers were happy to give the boy to him. They had had sons before. "Well, if he goes to a Brahman's house, he'll be educated, he'll learn how to write: it's good that we give him away."

So the Brahman took the child and he prepared to kill it with a sword. But women's hearts are tender, and his wife said, "Don't kill him. Float him down the river."

Bas. He took the child to the river bank. He made some sort of basket or something, he put the baby in it and set it floating down the river.

In the next kingdom, the Brahman of that King used to come down to the river to bathe at four in the morning. He saw something floating toward him. "What could this be that's floating along?" That's it. So he stood there and caught the basket. It was four in the morning when he caught that basket and discovered a beautiful newborn baby inside. He lifted up the baby. There were no children in his home. He speedily swaddled this baby and gave it to his wife. And he himself went to the shop. He woke up the shopkeeper, "Give me some medicinal herbs for my wife who's in labor!"

The shopkeeper took out the herbs and gave them to him. He thought, "We never heard she was going to have a child! How come she's having a child all of a sudden?"

So the shopkeeper gave him the medicines. And when morning came, it was announced that the Brahman had had a son. Everyone was astonished and perplexed! [*Urmilaji's nephew Amit comes in to say that there is someone outside. She disappears for few moments, then returns.*] "We never heard she was pregnant and how did she deliver this boy?"

So the child was brought up according to ways of this house: the house that people thought he'd been born in [*Urmilaji has a catch of amusement in her voice.*] He was raised and nurtured. He was taught to read, to write, and everything else good.

Now that daughter had come of age. The first King's Pandit [Purohit] started to look for a groom. Someone came and said, "This King's Pandit has a son. He's very intelligent. Very learned. He's a fine boy." So the engagement was set. The first King's Pandit gave a large dowry. The girl was married. She was married and was taken away.

The Brahman's wife began to say, "Go and ask: you said that she'd be married to a Sweeper. But she married a Brahman."

Bas. The Brahman went to the King and said, "Maharaj, It's been many years since you asked after your daughter's welfare. I'll go bring news of her." He actually wanted to ask about his own affairs, but he didn't tell the King this.

The King said, "By all means go and bring news of her, this is a matter of great happiness that you've come here of your own accord. We too had been thinking that many years had passed since we last heard from her."

"So I'll go then," said the Brahman.

He once again took his rations from the king, and left these at home with his wife. Then he set off himself. He traveled and traveled, and then he reached there. He went and met the King's daughter. He was bathed and washed, he was fed and rested: after all, that was a place of fabulous riches.

After a few days, he said, "Dharmraj, I hammered a nail into your lines of fate (*tumhāriyā rekhā main mekhā mari thiyān*).[6] I smashed a nail through what you wrote! I've come back here just after marrying my daughter to the son of a Brahman."

Dharmraj said [*in a sarcastic and indignant tone*], "Sure, I'll go right over there! I'll go look at the file and see what's in it. You say you smashed a nail through what I wrote? Well, it's all going to be brought out for me to see."

"Oh yes!" said the Brahman [*with equal indignance*]. "I'll go along with you to the court."

"Don't come with me." He said, "Don't come along with me."

"No! I'll definitely come. I want to observe this. You said she'll marry a Sweeper but I've just married her to a Brahman."

Dharmraj tried to stop him, but the Brahman came along to the court. Dharmraj said to Mother Destiny and the other person who was probably there with her, "Take out his file. Take out the file of his daughter and the Sweeper boy who she was to marry."

"Wait to have your laugh," he told the Brahman.

Bas. The files were brought out. He set to reading them aloud. He said, "Panditji, you left this place. Then the King was pleased with you and you asked him for the boy."

The Brahman began to nod his head.

"Then you began to kill the child. But your wife wouldn't let you kill him. She said, 'Don't kill him, float him down the river.' Then you took the child and put him in a basket and began to float it down the river. In this certain kingdom a Brahman picked him up. In his house there were no children. He just had this one son, that was him. Before you came back here, you married your daughter to him, didn't you?"

The Brahman died right there!

[*Urmilaji laughs.*] *Bas.*[7]

❀ ❀ ❀

"That's it?" I asked, startled by what to me seemed a sudden ending. At the same time, I was relieved on behalf of the newly married Brahman's daughter. As the Brahman had insisted on accompanying Dharmraj to his court, I had been thinking ahead, worrying about what would happen if the Brahman returned to earth with the explosive news about his son-in-law's caste at birth. I was also caught off guard by how the Brahman had started out as a seemingly minor character following a patron's orders to arrange a match, just like Brahmans in other tales. Yet the story had moved on to push him forward as a central character, boldly challenging the authority of fate. With this abrupt end, my own narrative expectations were shaken.

This story juxtaposes the marriages of two daughters to grooms who are not what they seemed. One bride is married to a lion who turns out to be a divine King; the other bride is married to a Brahman who turns out to be an Untouchable. For both marriages, the Brahman is the connecting link. The first choice of a groom for the Princess is the result of the Brahman's sly reading of his instructions to find "someone (male) with a natural mark on his forehead"; this description, after all, does not specify a human being. The second choice of a groom for his own daughter is the result of more careful deliberation, with the groom's caste in mind. Yet, despite his jubilant sense that he has outwitted destiny, it turns out that he once again was destiny's unwitting agent.

The story emphasized the perspective of a father or matchmaker in these choices. In her commentaries, though, Urmilaji highlighted the Princess's destiny—not the Brahman's choice or even Dharmraj's destiny—in directing who she is matched with. With regard to Dharmraj, Urmilaji explained, "He became a lion because it was the girl's destined union (*samjog*). If not for this story, why would he want to leave heaven? He had nobody of his own on earth. He had never lived here. But Dharmraj was in that girl's destiny. The Brahman could never have reached him otherwise. So he became a lion in the jungle and came to sit in the jungle. Then, according to her fate, he had the natural mark on his forehead. So the Pandit arranged for them to marry. Otherwise, would Dharmraj have had a natural mark on his forehead? And then, too, who would give their daughter to a lion? But it was her destiny, and he had to become a lion and arrive there."

I found that this woman-centered perspective on matters of married destiny was pervasive in Kangra (as in much of India): time and again women explained to me that one's destined match (*jorī*) was due to karma from past lives, pious actions in this life, and what Mother Fate wrote on one's forehead. This view of marriage—as destined, earned, and inscribed by fate—made the choices for arranged marriages seem inevitable. One song addressed to a bride, which Urmilaji and her sisters had sung in 1982, includes the following exchange:

han kinnī tere lekh likhe	Now who wrote your lines of fate?
kinnī kalam pheriyān	Who flourished the pen?
dharmrāj merā lekh likhe	Dharmraj wrote my lines of fate.
vidhī mātā kalam pheriyān	Mother Fate flourished the pen.

In the story Urmilaji told, Dharmraj and Mother Fate also work closely together, keeping files on people's past karma and their written fates. Yet, even Dharmraj is subservient to fate's scripts, becoming a lion to fit in with what was written for the Princess.

The daughter of the Brahman was never developed as a character, but the Princess was described from the story's suspenseful start to its happy outcome. The girl appears to have meekly acquiesced to the marriage arranged for her; she treats her new lion husband with deference, insisting on following behind him. (This position of walking several steps behind echoed a common sight on Kangra paths and roads, where wives often walked several demure steps behind their husbands if they were out together).

Like other stories featuring an animal mate, I wondered about the implicit sexual imagery associated with the lion's transformation. The jungle scene directly after the marriage would seem particularly suggestive: red ribbons and torn clothes strewn along the path, the lion's request that his new wife mount him for the final leap into Heaven. The Queen's rocking on a golden swing also seems resonant with such connotations. However, Urmilaji did not pursue this line of interpretation and I did not ask.

While the Princess is married out of the human fold, she does not seem to have been married inappropriately: after all, as a King's daughter, she is matched with the King of the jungle, and then finds herself with the King of

Heaven. Retelling a part of the story with a slightly different twist, Urmilaji emphasized the royal status of the lion.

"At first, the King didn't know that the Brahman had promised his daughter to a lion," Urmilaji said, describing the scene when the lions all arrive at the wedding. "Barefoot, he stood up, left his court, and went out to meet the lions. 'I'm the King of this place, and you're the King of the jungle. What did I do wrong that you come and uproot my garden?' Then the lion came forward and stood before him, saying, 'Your virgin daughter was given to me, and I've brought my groom's party.' It was then that they revised that feast. 'Bring 100 goats!'" Urmilaji laughed happily at the image. She went on to summarize the rest of the wedding arrangements.

The image of the King of the state greeting the King of the jungle not with war, but with respectfully bare feet and a supplicant's folded palms, moved me. It was an image of respect across boundaries, of polite petitions rather than aggression.

But, if the first marriage turned out unexpectedly well, the second marriage is so shocking that the Brahman, learning what he has arranged, falls down dead! At first I assumed that the Brahman died as punishment for so rudely challenging the authority of fate. Urmilaji's explanation, though, followed along the same lines as her depiction of women's deaths in the tales associated with the Five Days of Fasting. "He died due to mortification (*sharm*)," she said. "He was so embarrassed." Yet while the women were embarrassed when they revealed to a husband what they already knew, the Brahman was mortified when what he had never known was disclosed. In both cases, it was the public disclosure of personal humiliations which brought on death.

I found it interesting that though the Brahman died, his revelation was not revealed down on earth. In stories from South India featuring the marriage of a Brahman woman and an untouchable man, when the unsuspecting woman learns of her husband's true identity, her fury swells her into a bloodthirsty Goddess.[8] I was curious to learn if, in Urmilaji's view, being raised as a Brahman meant that the untouchable boy was acceptable as a Brahman.

"So, when a Sweeper is brought up in a Brahman's house is he a Brahman?" I asked.

"A Brahman," Urmilaji agreed.

"Does this mean that caste doesn't come from one's birth, but from the customs of the household?"

Urmilaji replied, "No, caste is set from birth, but for this boy, nobody knew about his caste."

I tried another tack. "So, if you don't know a caste then it's not in the body?"

"What, caste? Caste is in the body, but that infant was placed in the water, locked in a chest. When he was picked up in the other kingdom, they didn't know who he was, they just brought him to the home and said, 'He's ours.'"

Urmilaji went on to summarize the story, telling how, despite people's amazement at the sudden birth, the boy was raised as a Brahman. "He was raised as a Brahman, and he became a Brahman. That's how he was married to the girl, but only Dharmraj knew the truth," she said.

In other words, Urmilaji seemed to be putting forward an attitude that I had observed in village matters: in many cases and within limits, actions and alliances that went against ostensibly espoused norms might be quietly tolerated. If the parties concerned were discreet and otherwise respectable, others might gossip behind the scenes, but otherwise turn a blind eye.

"This is a tale about karma," Urmilaji summarized. "It goes with this saying, 'The movement of karma can't be stopped' (*karma gatī ṭāre na ṭāre*). You can't change karma, even if you try."

FOURTEEN

The Floating Flower

"There's another story that my father used to tell along with this one," Urmilaji announced when she had finished the last one. She launched into this next story almost without a break. In future conversations, she always spoke of these two as related: one inevitably evoked the other.

❈ ❈ ❈

There was a King. There were no heirs in this King's house; not a single child. For a long time the King and the Queen lived alone. They lived, giving and receiving. Then he became old, and he still had no son. No son. Neither a daughter nor a son.

One day the King said to his Prime Minister [*pausing weightily*], "Now I'm old and soon I'll die. This huge kingdom will be left without any descendants for the future. So do this: go out wandering tonight. And wherever a child is born, bring that child back so we can raise him."

Bas. The Prime Minister wrapped a black blanket around himself and set out. He went a long distance and there was a Sweeper's house. In the Sweeper's house, the female Sweeper had started to have labor pains. He loitered around there and called out, "What child will be born?"

Inside she was having pains, and he stood outside.

The Sweeper came out and said, "If we have a son we'll kill him."

[*"Really?" I ask, this is such an unusual inversion of the value given to sons. "Yes," Urmilaji affirms.*]

"But if it's a daughter we'll bring her up."

They probably had had two or three sons before. In the past [*her voice shifts to explanation*], among those people, if a girl was to be married, the boy's side would have to pay money. They had two or three boys and they would need a lot of money to marry them all off. This was the custom in the past.

Bas. He said, "If it's a boy we'll kill him."

147

The Prime Minister heard this and took note. He said, "If it's a boy, then give him to me. If it's a girl, then, since you don't have any girls, you won't want to give her away. But if you have a boy, I'll take him."

"That's very good," they said.

"And I'll give you money too." He was the King's Prime Minister, after all. So he sat there. After a while, a son was delivered. Then the Prime Minister took him. He swaddled him and bore him away stealthily [*voice lowered*]. He gave them 400 rupees. They were happy: with this birth, they were able to save up! [*Urmilaji laughs.*]

He came back to the palace and gave the child to the King. The King was overjoyed. He gave the child a name. He presented the child to the Queen and she too was overjoyed: "We'd grown old and felt such sorrow that there was no one to look after the kingdom: now we have a Prince."

There was a Prince in the King's house! The drums were beaten and there were celebrations. A Prince in the King's house!

So, for many years the Prince was reared. He read a lot, he wrote a lot, he was educated. Then the King was sitting in his court one day, and he said to his Prime Minister, "Now we must take this boy, this Prince, and anoint him. We should install him on the throne. He's worthy of the throne now. He's fully educated."

Bas. So he was installed with all the customs of that country. He was crowned. He sat on the throne. That's it.

Now all the servants of the King would salute him, but the Prime Minister would not. Inside his mind he had this feeling: "This is the son of a Sweeper." He knew, right? This was why he never bowed before him.

So the new King observed this again and again: "Everyone else salutes me, but this man does not."

One day the Prime Minister went to bathe, and at the riverbank a flower came floating along. An absolutely beautiful, rare flower. In the past whenever someone found a good thing they would come and present it to the King. So when the Prime Minister went to bathe and he found this floating flower, he picked it up and brought it to the King.

The King was very happy with this gift. He took the flower and gave it to his Queen. The Queen said, "I want another flower like this."

Bas. The King said to the Prime Minister, "Bring one more flower."

He said, "This flower came floating along downstream. It's not as though it was growing on a bush where I could go pluck it. How can I fetch it?"

The Queen said, "It's a question of life and death. I must have this flower or I'll die." She lay on her bed. She was overwhelmed with this desire. "I must have this flower or I won't survive."

[*Children are playing in the courtyard, shrill as they chase each other. Urmilaji pauses, listens, continues.*]

The King summoned the Prime Minister again. "You must bring this flower. You'll just have to bring it from somewhere or the other."

Bas. The King was very agitated. The King knew this whole story [that they were in]. He knew about the flower, too.

The Prime Minister pondered over all this. He said, "I'll follow the river gorge upstream. There has be a tree somewhere from which I can fetch the flower. After all, the flower came floating downstream. There's no certain place from which this flower came."

So he went. He took his rations and delivered them to his family to drink and eat. Then the Prime Minister set out. He walked and he walked and he crossed the river. When he got there, there was . . . a hut. A beautiful hut with a temple beside it and many flowers blossoming.

There were flowers blossoming and there were three fires burning. There were some Babas, some holy men sitting there in deep meditation. They were Mahatmas, great souls. Two were there, but the third space was empty, with tongs standing upright and a bag for alms lying beside it.[1]

The Prime Minister stared. Now, where the Mahatmas sat, grass had grown up all over them. They had been so involved in their devotions that they never moved. He uprooted the grass and they became conscious. Then he took a stick and hit the tree and flowers . . .

[*With an excited shriek, Sello comes dashing in, pigtails flying, her clothes splattered with rain. "Um um . . . ," Urmilaji shakes her head, lips pressed shut, motioning to the recorder. "What?" asks Sello, then she sees and is quickly silenced. She sits down for a moment, listening in.*]

They were engrossed in devotion. [*"Deep meditation," I offer, thinking of the holy men not having moved so long that grass had grown over them.*] Deep meditation. [*"The rain is really pouring down hard," says Sello, peering out into the courtyard and a world outside the story.*] Then they became conscious. When they were fully conscious, the Prime Minister said, "I want to take flowers from here." They said, "You can strike with a stick just once, and then you may take as many flowers as fall down." So he struck the tree and he picked up a flower, and he set off. [*Sello too has set off again, hollering to someone across the way.*]

He went back, he turned around and went back, and he set this flower before the King.

The King asked [*in a voice of wise concern*], "Did you go there?"

The Prime Minister said, "Yes."

"Tell me, who all were there? What was there? Tell me."

He said, "There were two Mahatmas there. They were sitting engrossed in their devotion. I plucked grass off them and they woke up."

"Was there anyone else there?" asked the King.

"Yes, there was also another place, with a bag and a pair of tongs, but no man."

149

"There was no man, right?" asked the King. Then . . . he said: "I am he."
[*"Really?!" I exclaim.*]

Then the King said to him. "I am he. You don't ever salute me because I was born in the house of a Sweeper." He went on to explain, "When my breath was leaving me, I was sitting under the tree. My breath was leaving, and above me, there was a crow sitting, who shat. This shit fell in my mouth. Because of this I was born in a Sweeper's house. But there's no Sweeper in me. I didn't eat there, I didn't drink there, I didn't even suckle mother's milk. I had earned very high karma, I had performed great devotions. But this was the only thing that was low, this thing that happened as my breath was leaving me."

This is the story.[2]

※ ※ ※

Hearing this story directly after the last, I could immediately see the interplay of themes that served to pair them. Especially in its second half, "In the Court of Destiny" has significant parallels with "The Floating Flower." In both stories there is an adoption across caste lines. Sweepers are presented as a polarized opposite of high castes who value sons and give dowries: instead, they are depicted as willing to give away their extra sons on account of bride price.[3] In both stories, the Sweeper boy is raised as a fully competent member of the caste he is adopted into. Yet, in both stories, the man responsible for taking the newborn later discredits his new caste identity: the unknowing Brahman boasts to Dharmraj that his son-in-law is a Brahman, while the knowing Prime Minister refrains from saluting the King. The wise Dharmraj looks to the files of fate in finding out the identity of the Sweeper turned Brahman. The wise King/ Sweeper/holy man sends the Prime Minister off on a journey that will later confirm the story that he is to reveal. In a sense, "The Floating Flower" adds a postscript to the last story by explaining the kinds of circumstances in a previous life which might lead to an infant being switched between castes at birth.

That a crow defecating into one's mouth at death could lead to rebirth as a Sweeper at first made sense to me only because Sweepers are in contact with polluting feces. What I did not know was that crows are themselves seen as untouchables of sorts. I later learned that when an upper-caste woman is observing menstrual taboos—sitting aside, not touching others, not handling food—the euphemism for her behavior (told especially to children) is that "a crow touched her" (*kāh cho giyā*). In another words, she was touched by an untouchable and so, until her bath, is temporarily an untouchable herself.[4] Urmilaji herself confirmed this association with the straightforward statement, "A crow is an untouchable." In regard to this story, she reiterated the King's explanation, "As I was dying, a crow shat in my mouth. A crow is low (*nīch*). Because of the crow doing this in my mouth, I was born in a Sweeper's house.

Otherwise, my karma was high (*ūnchā*), and so after my birth I came to a King's house. This was because of what came into my mouth."

"So, the King remembered his past life then?" I asked Urmilaji on a future visit.

"The King remembered his past life because he had been a Mahatma, a great soul," stated Urmilaji. "When the Prime Minister wouldn't salute him, he felt sad about it. He probably knew—after all, he knew what his past life was— so he also probably knew what was in the Prime Minister's mind: 'He thinks I'm a Sweeper and so he won't salute me.' So then he went to the bank of the river, and set a flower floating, which the Prime Minister picked up and brought to him. Then the Queen got obsessed, saying she had a stomachache. The King said, 'Go, bring another flower: where there was this one, surely there will be others. Go, find another!' "

With the retelling of this portion of the plot, Urmilaji more fully illustrated what she meant by her cryptic statement embedded in her first retelling: "The King knew this whole story." She said this after the Prime Minister brought the floating flower. Now it turned out that it was the King himself who had set the beautiful flower afloat.

Also, Urmilaji added the detail that when the Queen became obsessed, she complained of a stomachache—an excuse that women in other stories make when they vehemently desire something.[5]

"Why such obstinacy?" I asked. I meant the Queen, but Urmilaji replied in terms of the King.

"He insisted because he wanted to teach the Prime Minister a lesson. Else, how was the Prime Minister to know? He behaved this way because of the birth in the Sweepers' house."

"What do you think the meaning of this story could be?" I asked.

"The meaning of this story," said Urmilaji, "is that the Prime Minister's pride was broken. The meaning is probably that one should never judge another as lower than oneself, another person as worse than oneself. The Prime Minister, after all, had kept it in his mind that he shouldn't salute the King because he was low caste. The meaning is that one shouldn't see people as low or as bad. They might appear to be bad, but who knows why they are like that, so they should be thought of as good. This is the meaning I draw out of the story, what do you think?"

"It seems like this could be the meaning," I said, awkward with the tables turned. Who was the authority here, after all? With this summary, Urmilaji seemed to be arguing less for the rigidity of caste divisions, and more for the illusory, karma-driven quality of movements across these divisions.[6]

In stressing the need to act decently toward other people, however powerless or inferior they might seem, Urmilaji was echoing a theme I sometimes heard from other older, pious women. For example, Tayi once told me a story about a girl who married a dog and then learns he is a King. Tayi's seven-year-old great-niece, Shivani, squatted beside us along with a neighbor's little girl. Tayi instructed, "You should never judge anything from its form (*rūp*). Forms mislead. For example, holy men come to the door, and call for alms. You might want to say, 'Get lost! Go work for a living.' But always give them something, even if it is a single coin. You never know, the holy man could be God. Then, too, look at these little girls," she pointed to the two who were listening in, agog. "You might want to shout at them, but you never know what sort of Mother Goddess they might be. You can never say how one form will turn into another. That's why it's good to be nice to everyone, to speak nicely, act nicely."

When I first heard these two stories, I heard their endings as a possible challenge to the notion that caste origins were, in the end, important. Uncomfortable with caste-based distinctions myself, I was eager to see these stories as a critique of caste. But thinking more about them and talking more with Urmilaji leads me to believe that the stories do end up affirming caste. What the stories do is situate social divisions like caste within a larger framework of transitory and illusory forms, driven by karma and fate. Yet, assertions about the hidden workings of fate in these stories might perhaps have encouraged a minimal decency toward lower castes on the part of upper castes.

These two stories introduced me to Urmilaji's father, Jodha Ram Sood. In the months that followed, she told me more about him, and I began to gain a sense of the man whose presence she kept alive through retelling his tales.

Jodha Ram Sood was born in 1902. He began his career as a schoolteacher. Then he worked as a land clerk. Long before Urmilaji was born, a middle child of nine children, he became a manager of tea estates. At Urmilaji's brothers' home, I was once shown an old photograph of their father, seated with several dignitaries from one of the tea gardens where he worked. Facing forward, with a turban on his head and rings in his ears, his face had an alert intelligence that seemed to reach out, inquiring, from across the years.

Tea was brought to Kangra in 1849, soon after its annexation by the British in 1846. The foot of the Dhauladhar range proved hospitable to this imported plant, and the British managed to transform vast stretches of commons (termed "waste lands") into tea gardens. Yet the earthquake of 1905 leveled many of these gardens' production facilities, forcing European planters to depart. As the tea industry was gradually rebuilt, Indian proprietors—prosperous local people and particularly immigrants from Punjab—began to take over. By 1924, there were 421 estates owned by Indians, and only 4 owned by Europeans.[7] It was in these Indian-owned estates that Jodha Ram Sood worked.

To his children, Jodha Ram Sood was known as "Chachu," which means "Uncle" (literally, "father's younger brother"). This was because his elder brother's three children, who had lost their mother, lived in the joint family household along with his own nine children. Urmilaji remembered her father with such love that her eyes would grow moist and her voice would break as she spoke of him. "He traveled a lot, and he worked a lot, worked a lot!" she told me. "And us children—he raised us with real wisdom. He really had a way with raising us. We had no idea of how a father might scold a child. The biggest scolding we'd ever get from him would be if our mother said, 'This one hasn't done such and such, doesn't do anything at all.' He'd just look at us like this—" Urmilaji demonstrated with a solemn, fixed gaze, "and say 'Oh eh!' This was the biggest scolding. We'd never get a bigger scolding than that."

Urmilaji also explained that her mother never told stories because she had been the sole adult woman in the household as Urmilaji was growing up. She was too busy looking after the needs of the enormous family to have time left over for stories.

My impression was that, of all her siblings, Urmilaji was most actively involved in carrying forward her father's stories. She felt a strong bond with him also on account of having been married into the same village, just a few minutes walk away, allowing her to come and go with an ease that most married daughters would never have. She once told me of a dream she had had some six or seven months before he died in 1968. In the dream, four palanquin bearers brought a palanquin into her courtyard. They knocked on her door and asked for her father. "No!" she had said. "You can't take him! He hasn't met with all his sons yet." Later, as he lay ill, his sons did come in from their jobs in different parts of India, and only then did he die.

Living in different tea gardens across the valley, interacting with a cross section of people, traveling on business related to tea, may all have added to Urmilaji's father's folktale repertoire. When I asked Urmilaji where he learned his tales, she said, "I don't know where he learned these. We were just interested in hearing the stories; at that time, who would try to follow up on a story to find out where it had been learned? Why would we have asked? We'd just listen. Our main interest was wheedling, 'Tell a story, tell a story.' He'd keep telling, and we'd keep listening."

FIFTEEN

Heaven and Hell

Months later, I asked Urmilaji if she could better explain to me who Dharmraj was. She replied, "Dharmraj, well, he's in heaven. When people die, they go before Dharmraj. He decides on the kind of birth a person will have. Dharmraj sends people who performed good actions off in a good direction, but those people who've performed bad actions are sent off in a bad direction. Heaven on one side, hell on the other. Someone who's done good actions goes to heaven, someone whose actions were bad goes to hell."

Back in March, the day after Urmilaji memorized the song about an old woman being hauled up before Dharmraj, she told me a story that dramatized Dharmraj's sorting out of souls.

❋ ❋ ❋

There was a man. He died. He went to Dharmraj, who asked, "Do you want to experience heaven or hell first?" He began to think [*muttering*], "Should I say heaven?" He thought and he thought about it. Then he said [*loudly*], "I want to experience heaven first."

He went to heaven, and on the way he saw hell. There was terrible filth there and a lot of noise. And in heaven everything was peaceful.

He was told, "You have just a little bit of heaven allotted to you." He had done just a little good in his life, I don't know, maybe he gave a piece of bread to someone. That was all the good he'd done, and that was his heaven: everything else was hell.

He said, "Fine, I have just a little heaven, and I'll experience that first. After that I'll have to go fall into hell. But at least I'll have had a small experience of heaven."

So he went to heaven, and it was wonderful. There he gave lots of gifts and alms, he sponsored fire rituals. He did all these great things and he earned more heaven. He was told, "Now you have more heaven." He said, "Well, I'll experience that too, and then I'll go on to hell." Then he went back to heaven and he did even more fire rituals. All his hell was finished off and he only experienced heaven. Then he became a saint, a great soul.

It's like this: if you have some heaven, you do some good, this can grow from one side, and you can be freed from hell. Sins are quickly dissolved. And good actions . . . [1]

❊ ❊ ❊

Urmilaji paused, distracted by the arrival of Sello, who had come up to us with the tray of tea. "They keep blossoming," I offered.

"Now drink your tea," ordered Sello. After watching Urmilaji and me absorbed in intent exchanges, she seemed to have decided that we needed some practical management. The previous day, I had stood up to leave and had even walked several steps across the courtyard but had kept on talking. Urmilaji too had risen as we spoke. Sello had intervened. "Why are you standing?" she had rebuked, leading me back to the ledge. "Both of you should sit down together."

The word I have translated as "good action" here is *dharm* (Sanskrit *dharma*), but I am woefully aware of the imperfect fit between these two terms. *Dharm* is also often translated as "religion" but this too is only a partial overlap. *Dharm* is a multifaceted Hindu concept that spans many cultural domains. It can also mean virtue, customary obligations, duty, morality, righteousness, and justice.[2] It is widely understood in India that what constitutes *dharm* varies according to context, depending on the person, place, and time.

Urmilaji often spoke of *dharm* as residing within people. In a parable she attributed to her Tayi Sas, from whom she also learned this story of heaven and hell, *dharm* becomes a personification of decency and wisdom. Urmilaji brought up this parable in the course of reminiscing about her Tayi Sas—her husband's father's elder brother's widow. As she said, "My Tayi Sas, she was a very old and wise person. When I came here and was new here, people would say things that hurt me a lot. Then she'd say, 'Look here, child. This anger is a sin. And *dharm* is . . . well, it's *dharm*."

Urmilaji then went on to rephrase Tayi Sas's description of the turbulent scene wrought by anger:

> When anger takes possession of a person, then *dharm* leaves and sits outside. Anger rages inside, and *dharm* waits outside, watching the show. Whatever bad things come into the mind just get said.
> *Dharm* sits and laughs. When things quiet down, then *dharm* comes back in. Then he sternly questions, 'What was that you blurted? What is this hell you've made? Speaking badly, acting badly, seeking the worst! You're suffering yourself, and the other person is suffering too.'

Urmilaji's voice lowered, becoming calm and measured as she moved on from this tumultuous scene. "If you just keep calm and don't let anger take over, then *dharm* stays put inside you," she instructed. "People don't understand this, though, they'd change themselves if they understood. Peace is the hardest thing to hold on to. If you can make yourself peaceful, you'll have a way to cross life's waters."

Urmilaji often spoke of her Tayi Sas as an expert on all matters of *dharm*. Urmilaji recalled:

> Poor thing, she taught me a lot: "Do this, perform worship, this is all necessary. And the little time you have, portion it out: give some time to your work, some time to your devotion, your reading, your study." She knew the whole Ramayana by heart. She was a very knowledgeable person. All of *dharm*. She told such a lot of stories. She knew the words of the great saints, she knew how they'd lived. She'd show me: "You too do this, do that, in this way. Then wisdom will arise in you too."
>
> On Sundays she'd sing God's name here. Even if no one else was here, she'd light an oil lamp and sit for an hour or two hours singing, holding her beads, sitting, taking God's name.
>
> She was without selfishness. If you had come here and she'd seen that your shirt was torn, she would sit you down and sew it up. She was so selfless. Then, down at the shops, men would be smoking water pipes. She would bring down coals from the hearth for them. Or else, men would bring their pipes to her. Then she'd see that one button had fallen off. "Wait," she'd say, "Wait!" She'd bring out the needle and thread, sew it on right there. She was so selfless.

Urmilaji had mentioned this matter of Tayi Sas mending people's clothes more than once: it seemed to have particularly impressed her. One afternoon during the monsoon, when I came in wearing a torn *churidār* (tight-fitting pants), Urmilaji whipped out her needle and thread and set to mending the tear as I sat, still wearing the *churidār,* before her. This was one more concrete instance of her enacting Tayi Sas, as if bringing her to life through actions in the moment.

It was particularly moving when Urmilaji told me Tayi Sas's personal tale without a clear boundary separating herself and her aunt as speaker. For example, here is Urmilaji's retelling of the central tragedy in Tayi Sas's life, the loss of her only sons in the Kangra earthquake of 1905. This earthquake, which struck on April 4 at 6:00 A.M. registered a magnitude of 8 on the Richter scale.[3]

> Here, earthquakes keep happening, but that one [in 1905] was very big. She used to tell us about it. She hadn't given birth to the girls at that time, she just had two sons. This house was ruined, and then a new one was built.
>
> My mother was born the third year after the earthquake. My father saw it. He said that he had been about five or six years old.
>
> But her sons were killed. One of these sons would have been the same age as

the grandfather of your friend Kamal [a neighbor's daughter, now married and living in Delhi]. She used to tell us:

"I had woken up in the morning and was sweeping the courtyard. And the sons, one was bigger, about nine years. The other was six months. The older one used to go with his father to the shop [*"the one that is now rented to the basket maker," Urmilaji explains in an aside*].

He [the husband] woke up and was getting ready to go. I was sweeping. I asked, "Should I wake up the boy to go with you?" He said, "No, today, I'm going to visit a nearby village. Let him sleep." So he left and I was sweeping the courtyard. The earth shook violently, and the house fell down: all rubble.

"An old woman was killed. Everything here was buried. Then, there was another uncle, who had one girl. She had a sister, who was six months old, or maybe six years old. As she slept, a huge basket fell over her, as a cover. She was lying inside because she was sick. And she was saved. But both those boys . . . they were both buried alive. They both died."

Implicit in Tayi Sas's account was the assumption that a son is far more valuable than a daughter. Sons would be expected to stay on to care for parents as they aged; daughters would be married away. Tayi Sas went on to bear six daughters. But because she had lost her two sons, when she grew old she was stripped of immediate family. It fell to Urmilaji, her nephew's wife, to look after her. It was Tayi Sas who instructed Urmilaji on songs and stories, saying, "When you sing songs and tell stories, you understand different kinds of suffering. Then a little peace comes to you."

As the old woman grew increasingly feeble, Urmilaji's young children became increasingly demanding. It was difficult to look after them all. Eventually, one of Tayi Sas's daughters broke with Kangra conventions and brought her mother to live with her. That is where she died. I wanted to trace Tayi Sas's surviving daughters to see if they told any of the same stories that Urmilaji ascribed to her, but we were never able to arrange a visit.

Urmilaji also explained earthquakes in terms of a breakdown of *dharm*. Mother Earth became too burdened with people's sins, she told me, and every now and then would have to shake them off.[4] Earthquakes were part of people's consciousness in Kangra not just because of the terrible earthquake of 1905 (by which many older people reckoned their age), but also because of the ongoing tremors. Situated where shifting tectonic plates from the subcontinent butt toward the Himalayas, Kangra occasionally experiences lesser quakes. Several times over my years of visiting, I have been woken at night with the floor jolting, slates clattering on the roof like leaves in a storm. This motion is always followed by an enormous hullabaloo of people yelling across the valley, waking each other, warning each other that a more serious quake might follow and that everyone should rush outdoors.

Urmilaji's story about heaven and hell underlines that to perform good actions is to further *dharm*. Such good actions seem to be of two sorts. On the one hand, performing appropriate rituals, such as fire ceremonies, accrues good karma for the man in the tale. On the other hand, it was the isolated act of giving bread to someone that had brought him to heaven at all. While Urmilaji herself observed fasts and rituals, she also often emphasized generosity, kindness to others, and unshakable serenity in the course of everyday life as aspects of *dharm*.

Her story located heaven and hell in the afterlife. Yet Urmilaji also spoke about heaven and hell as metaphors for psychological or material conditions among the living. Hell was a place of strife and thwarted desires; heaven a place of serenity and fulfillment. In Tayi Sas's allegory about how *dharm* stepped outside a person when anger started a scene, *dharm* chided anger on return, "What is this hell you've made? . . . You're suffering yourself and the other person is suffering too!" Hell, then was also a site of human conflict and suffering.

The central meaning of this story, according to Urmilaji, lay not with heaven and hell but with the power of goodness. Even a bit of goodness—like the giving of bread—could triumph, transmuting the past and redeeming a soul. "The meaning of this story is that one should do good deeds," Urmilaji stated firmly. "If you do good deeds, then bad deeds from your past will also become good."

SIXTEEN

The Two Gems

By the end of July the monsoon was in full swing. In the flooded fields, young rice shot up in a fresh, sharp green that gladdened the eyes. Women from castes involved in agriculture waded calf-deep in cold, muddy water, backs bent, as they transplanted the rice. Sometimes they sang as they worked in groups. Once I was able to squat on the embankment between fields, taping "monsoon songs" from my old Rajput friend Tayi's daughter-in-law and the group of Chamar women who had been hired to work beside her. The women sang to the accompaniment of bird calls and the ripple and splash of working hands. Urmilaji listened attentively to these songs on tape, an appreciative smile spreading between headphones. "Whenever I am out walking on the road, I also stop to listen to these songs in the fields," she said. "It's so beautiful to hear women singing in the green fields!"

Rain poured: drizzles, downpours, violent crashing storms. Slate roofs gleamed with wetness. Clothes were now dried indoors—sometimes for days—leaving a sour, soggy aroma. Stagnant pools bred mosquitoes that rose in whining, biting swarms. At dusk, farming families often lit smoking heaps of dung and straw beside their livestock to chase away the ravenous mosquitoes.

But for Urmilaji and her sisters, who did not work in the fields, the rhythms of life went on much as before. In other households, I would find women complaining of backaches, of colds, of fungus between their toes. They sighed about all the *paṭoṭā*, the physical toil. Sitting with Urmilaji, dry and indoors during the wet season, I often felt our own privilege.

One of Urmilaji's younger sisters, Kamalaji, arrived for a visit in early August. The two sisters met up at the wedding of a relative, and then Kamalaji came home with Urmilaji. I came by one afternoon to find both sisters settled on the double bed. The day was dark and rainy, and the light was on inside. Kamalaji was knitting briskly; Urmilaji was carding wool from her ram. Kamalaji was a pretty, well-dressed woman, plump and exuding confidence. Like their youngest sister, Nirmalaji, Kamalaji was a school teacher. As at other times of the year when help was needed in the fields, the schools were now on vacation. I had met Kamalaji nine years before when I was a graduate student exploring Kangra wedding songs.

Urmilaji had heard a long song about the wedding of Gauran (a local name for Parvati) at the wedding she had just attended. She had gotten someone to write it down on lined sheets torn from a notebook. She triumphantly presented me with this text.

Kamalaji was curious to know what I was doing in Kangra this time. She wanted to hear all about my projects. With a faint smile on her own face, Urmilaji concentrated on the fluffed wool before her as I mentioned the plan to put together a book of stories. Then the two sisters began to reminisce about their father telling tales in the winter, around a roaring fire.

"He'd sing certain portions too," Kamalaji said.

"Like what?" I asked. I knew from reading collections of Indian folktales that they sometimes had sung verses, but I had not yet heard one of this sort.

Urmilaji began singing softly, hesitantly, glancing at her sister. Kamalaji hummed along, her hands never pausing amid the flash of knitting needles.

dhan dhan īshwara	Thanksgiving, oh Lord,
dhan bo paramātmā	Thanksgiving, Eternal Soul.
e deya ḳitīyā	May this action I've done
huṇ mata hondiyā	Never be repeated.

Recalling this song seemed to make a story come into focus. "It's the story about two gems (*lāl*)," Urmilaji announced. Knowing that lāl meant both ruby and precious son, I wondered which one the story was going to be about.

Urmilaji sketched the main strokes of the story in an undertone to her sister, who nodded, affirming. "I'll start the story then," Urmilaji said, taking hold of the microphone. Giving her sister a sidelong affectionate look, she requested, "If I don't remember, you remind me." She paused for a long time, clutching the microphone, staring intently into some inner space. Then she began.

❀ ❀ ❀

There was a Merchant. A Merchant, and a Merchant's wife too. A son was born in their house. They raised him and he grew up. Then he began to live in one of the shops that the Merchant owned. He ran the shop.

Bas. Now, this Merchant's son used to sweep the shop daily and throw all the rubbish he collected into the upper story. The father probably didn't visit the shop too often. When the boy was old enough, he managed the shop, living there and attending to all the business. The Merchant only visited once in a while.

Alright, so a holy man, a Sadhu came and visited this boy. He gave the boy two rubies. He said, "Son, store these rubies."

The boy wrapped and folded these rubies in some paper, and then—in the past we had rafters—he put the packet with the rubies into a bird's nest in the rafters.

Then the Sadhu asked, "Son, do you know how to tell the difference between a true ruby and a false ruby of glass? Do you know what a true ruby and a false ruby are?"

"No," said the boy.

The Sadhu said, "The way to identify a ruby is with a blacksmith's hammer. If you hold this over a ruby and bang hard, the ruby will remain whole. But if you should even lay a hammer down on top of a false ruby, it'll splinter and break. This is the difference between a true and a false ruby."

So the Sadhu taught him how to identify rubies. Then the Sadhu took off. He said, "When I return I'll take these rubies back from you."

[*"And both were rubies?"* I put in. *"Or was one a false ruby?"* *"Both were rubies,"* says Urmilaji.]

Bas. After the Sadhu left, probably many days passed, and then the Merchant, making his rounds, arrived at the shop. He roamed between his various shops, as he must have had two or four, or even five or seven of them.

The other shopkeepers started up, saying, "Your son is really useless. He deposits all the dirt from sweeping in the upper story, and he's managed the shop so badly there's not a thing left in it. He's filled up the entire upper story with dirt and there's absolutely nothing left below in the shop."

The father was enraged. "I worked and earned so much, I was a successful merchant, and this boy has squandered it all."

Sticks from the mulberry tree are thick and strong. The father cut a mulberry stick. He beat his son so hard that the boy died.

The boy had hidden away what the Sadhu had given him. *Bas.* So the boy died. And when the father actually opened up the shop and looked inside he saw that, inside, there were tremendous riches. All the sweepings had become rubies. The entire upper story was packed with rubies!

Then the merchant began to weep. He sang:

dhan dhan īshwara	Thanksgiving, Thanksgiving Lord,
dhan bo paramātmā	Thanksgiving, Eternal Soul.
e deya kitiyā	May what I did
huṇ mata hondiyā	Never again be done.
tūte diye simaṭiye	A mulberry stick
jāgate jo māradā	to strike a son.
lokā diye boliye	Heeding other people,
jāgate jo māradā	to smite a son.

161

"Oh God, what is this I've done? Based on what people said, I killed my son with a mulberry stick. May actions like mine never be performed!" He wept, "I had just one son who was my wealth, and I finished him off."

Then he went home and he told the boy's mother. The mother too, poor thing, was horribly upset, for this had been their only son.

Alright. So this boy was reborn in another kingdom. There too, he was brought up properly, and he came of age. There too, he began to work. There too, his father was probably some prosperous Merchant, and he too taught him how to do business.

Then, one day the Sadhu returned! He came and he asked, "Where is your son?"

The first father, poor fellow, began to weep bitterly.

Then he confessed what he had done. "People told me some truth and some falsehood mixed together, and I went and killed my son. He had amassed great wealth. I didn't go in to check for myself, I just listened to what people said and I killed the boy." And the father shed many tears, poor fellow.

The Sadhu said, "What can I do if you killed him? But I'd given him two rubies. I want those back, hand them over."

Then the father said, "You're talking about two rubies, but he earned massive quantities of rubies. Take as many as you like."

He brought some rubies down from the upper story and showed them to the Sadhu. But the Sadhu said, "These aren't my rubies. Not a single one here is mine."

The father asked, "Where should I look for yours?"

But the Sadhu just turned away. "I won't take any of these. I want those particular rubies of mine."

As the Sadhu wandered, he came to the place where the boy had taken a second birth. He caught hold of him. "Are you the same boy to whom I gave those rubies or not?"

Then the son told his story, "It was like this: my father listened to what other people told him and killed me."

[*"So he remembered this?" I ask.*]

Yes. That boy remembered everything. "It was like this: I died and proceeded here. As for your rubies, I stored them in a bird's nest. I wrapped them carefully and hid them in the bird's nest. You can go there and claim them for yourself."

So the Sadhu turned around. When he arrived, he said to the Merchant, "Look for my rubies in the bird's nest."

Truly, when the Merchant put his hand into the bird's nest he found the package with the rubies. He unwrapped them.

"These are my rubies," said the Sadhu.

So the Sadhu took his rubies, and the Merchant caught hold of him. "How did you know?" The father was filled with terrible sorrow. He wept bitterly. "Who told you about this? How did you learn this?"

At first the Sadhu wouldn't reveal anything. Then both husband and wife wept and wailed. "For the likes of us, you're God. Tell us how you learned about this."

So he told them, "In a certain place, there's a Merchant, and the boy has taken birth in that house. He's grown up all over again. He's been betrothed and married and all the rest of it; he's come of age. That's where he lives now. That's where he told me this."

[*"Turn it off," Urmilaji instructs, gesturing to the tape recorder. She confers with her sister. How did the father remeet the son? Kamalaji suggests another couplet, "What was that one about that astrologer called from Kashi?" "No, that's another story," says Urmilaji, her face brightening. "I haven't thought of that story for maybe fifty years!" She pauses and begins singing about the astrologer from Kashi, her sister joining in. Then she starts an entirely different story about a King with three Queens, one of whom bears a son. To read the son's horoscope a Pandit is summoned from Kashi. Once again, reaching the juncture of how the father and son remeet after a long separation, Urmilaji is stumped. Was it when the King was out hunting? Was it because other children asked him his father's name? She begins to sing yet another couplet in which two sets of parents claim a son. Kamalaji chimes in, and both sisters laugh. Urmilaji decides that this couplet belongs with the story she has been telling; she is back on track with what happens next. She gives me a nod, picks up the microphone and resumes.*]

Then the father and mother went to that other place, the place where the son had been reborn. They went and settled there. They got themselves a house in the vicinity of where he was, and they began to live there. At first they watched him going out, they watched him coming in. Then one day they called him to their house, saying, "You strike us as really adorable, come to our house and sit down."

He came and he sat there with them. After this when they prepared food and drink, they would feed him too. They felt solace that they had found their son and were meeting with him.

He would come every night to visit with them for a few hours. They themselves understood that this was their son. And he too knew: "This is my mother and my father from my past life. This is my wife." But now, this was his second birth, and so he had another family. He had become attached to both families. He felt attachment for the new family and attachment for old family. There was no way of being released from either the first or the second family.

Bas. After a while, the people in his new family observed, "Look, where can it be that he goes? In the past he didn't go anywhere. Now if we ask him where he's going, he just says [*nonchalantly*], 'Oh, I go sit somewhere for a few hours.' "

This went on for many days, and everyone began to be suspicious: "Where is it that he goes?"

One day his wife followed him.

[*"His new wife?" I ask. "Yes," affirms Urmilaji.*]

Bas. She watched as he went into the house. Then he began to talk inside. She listened to what he said. He called his mother "Mother" (*māu*), his father "Father" (*bab*), and his wife "Wife" (*janās*). The three of them sat chatting among themselves.

[*Urmilaji's voice is leisurely, as though exuding domestic harmony but the next sentence she starts with a semiwhisper, her voice taut with tension.*]

His new wife listened to all this. Then she came home and she told her mother-in-law and father-in-law, "This is what he's up to. He's gone and made himself some other parents: other parents and another wife too."

They wondered, "What ties does he have to those people? What's going on?"

On the second day when he took off, all three of them followed. As he began to go in the door, they grabbed him by the arm. "Where are you off to?" they asked.

The other set of relatives came out from within. They grabbed him by the other arm. They pulled him toward them and the others pulled him from the other side. One father said, "No! This boy is mine!" The second father said, "No! This boy is mine." One mother said, "No! This son is mine." The other one called from within, "No, he's mine." The wife who'd come there said, "This husband is mine." The other wife who came out from inside said, "But this is my husband."

[*"And you sing this too!" I shoot in anticipation, having just heard the two sisters rehearse this ditty. Urmilaji smiles and begins singing to a hypnotically repetitive, plaintive melody.*]

ika bāpu boldā	One father says,
putra hai meṛadā	this son is mine.
dūjā bāpu boldā	The second father says,
putra hai meṛadā	this son is mine.
ika ammā boldī	One mother says,
putra hai meṛadā	this son is mine.
dūji ammā boldī	The second mother says,
putra hai meṛadā	this son is mine.
ika nār boldī	One wife says,
kand hai meṛadā	this husband is mine.
duji nār boldi	The second wife says,
kand hai meṛadā	this husband is mine.

When the love from both sides had assembled, one side had love for a son and the other side had love for a son too. So God spontaneously split the son in half. He became two boys. He had attachment for both sides, and he was absolutely without fault. He was a son who served and a son who obeyed. So Bhagavan made him into two. One went off with one side, and the other went off with the second side.

[*"Two sons," I laugh, thinking of how* lāl *means both "ruby" and "son."*]

Two gems. The end.[1]

❀ ❀ ❀

"So, do people here ever remember their past lives?" I asked after a pause. In my childhood it was sometimes rumored that I might be the reincarnation of my father's father (to whom I bear a strong physical resemblance, mercifully minus the thick mustache). This has left me with a perplexed fascination for theories of reincarnation: How can anyone be sure?

Urmilaji and Kamalaji assured me that there were cases in which a child remembered a past life. "Even here in Palampur," Kamlaji said, referring to the nearby market town, "there was a girl who completely remembered her past life."

"Complete memory," agreed Urmilaji.

"Really, a girl?" I prompted.

"Was it a girl or was it a boy?" Urmilaji asked Kamlaji in Pahari. "The son of the people at the press? Wasn't it their son? He had complete memories of his previous life. I've heard of a girl, too, who was in school in Palampur, who had these memories. This boy though, he used to tell people, 'I died in Delhi, in an accident. My mother and father really mourned.' Someone else said that this might be true. The boy cried, 'Take me there.' Then people said to the parents, 'Don't talk about this in front of him and don't let him talk about it either. Otherwise he'll go off there and they'll remember him too and where will you be left?'"

Kamalaji took over, using Hindi instead. "Actually, he had died in Assam," she said, referring to the Northeastern Indian state. "He had been educated and was doing a Ph.D. when he died in a truck accident." She went on to corroborate the details of Urmilaji's story, adding that the boy claimed that in his past life his parents had owned a hotel in Delhi. His present parents ascertained that there were indeed such hotel owners who had lost a son in Assam, but they refused to let their boy meet up with them.[2]

Kamalaji finished by observing that it is locally believed that until a child eats solid food he or she retains memories from the previous birth.

"But how did he *remember* his past life?" I asked Urmilaji when I was visiting again the following year. This question had now become a refrain whenever Urmilaji told stories about past lives. For other stories, Urmilaji merely restated, with no explanation, that the person remembered their past life. But this time, after a long pause, she started by hazarding an answer.

"After his birth? Perhaps because he had been beaten...," Urmilaji began.

Indeed, almost half of the cases where a past life is remembered seem to include a violent end.[3]

Musing further, though, Urmilaji ended up revising her earlier retelling. Her voice became energetic as she thought aloud, rationalizing, "Actually, he probably ran away, this is what I presume. After his father hit him, you know, then he ran away and went to live in another kingdom. There, another Merchant adopted him as a son. Then there too he got married, that is how he was that old." She went on to summarize the story a second time. When the one son split into two, she ended by saying, "So then each one went off to his own kingdom."

"Why did this happen?" I pressed.

"Because of love," said Urmilaji without a pause. "He had been beaten badly and departed in sorrow. But after all, this was his mother and his father, even if they beat him. It was only because of people's gossip that they beat him." Urmilaji sang the couplet again, softly, under her breath. As she had said earlier, when the love from both sides lined up, the pull was so strong, so balanced, that the boy split into two complete selves.

In this story, as in several others from the corpus associated with the Five Days of Fasting, the setting is a Merchant's family. When I once asked Urmilaji about the prevalence of Merchants in her stories, she began by saying, "They were the ones with money." Her sister, Nirmalaji, continued with a laugh, "Anyone with excessive money is going to do outrageous acts!" Indeed, Merchants had dispatched Brahmans to find brides when they had no real son and had set about burning a daughter-in-law alive. On a less extreme note, it was in a Merchant's family that the dog-girl licked away and a Merchant's wife who tried to cut corners by rolling yarn into skeins during the Five Days of Fasting.

As with the last chapter, and also the story featuring Sunna the Washerwoman (chapter 1), it was a Sadhu, a holy man, who had insight into the workings of destiny and rebirth. Also, it was the Sadhu who stood in the position to dispense boons, for example, to make dirty sweepings into piles of glittering red rubies. "Who was the Sadhu but God taking the form of a Sadhu?" Urmilaji inquired.

"So just as the Sadhu gave two rubies, so, in the same way, God made two sons," I observed. "This is a play on *lāl* (ruby) and *lāl* (son)."

"Yes, it's a play," agreed Urmilaji.

But the ruby in this story is defined as distinct from the false ruby (*lālaṛī*). Battered by strong blows, the ruby remains whole. A false ruby, though, splinters with even the slightest weight resting on it. The value of a ruby then, is in remaining intact, instead of shattering into many fragments.

Urmilaji had referred to the boy's two homes as the "home ahead" (*agleyā ghar*) and the "home behind" (*picchleyā ghar*). These were terms that women used when delineating their home of birth from their home through marriage. For example, rattling along in the narrow-gauge train that ran through the valley, I once listened to two Kangra women exchange introductions in the ladies' compartment. "Where is your home (*ghar*)?" one friendly woman inquired of the woman sitting on the wooden seat opposite her. "The one ahead or the one behind?" the other countered, proceeding to give full details on both as we proceeded through the open countryside with the mountains rising to one side.

Though marriage involves moving from a father's home (*piyokhī*) to a father-in-law's home (*sauhre*), women maintain ties to both homes throughout their lives.[4] More than once, women told me of the contrary tugs they felt between these homes. My friend Vidhya, for example, had been married since 1976, the year after I first visited Kangra. Now, almost fifteen years later, she still talked about the difficulties of her dual allegiances as we planned a trip to her parent's village, "Hah!" said Vidhya, shaking her head. "No matter where you are, you worry about the other home. When you're with your husband, you keep wondering how your parents are. If you visit your parents, you're filled with anxiety about your husband, your children. . . . And then, there's also the cow."

By 1991 there was often at least one phone in a village, but connections were hard to get and these were never used for simple chatting. Without running water or electrical gadgets (in many cases, without gas too), housework and caring for livestock filled women's days even when they had no further burden of work in the fields. Then, too, it was not considered seemly for a woman to travel alone. Brothers, who served as escorts between the two homes, were often away, working in the plains or for salaried jobs from which they could not take breaks. Children went to school and could not miss classes. All these contingencies seemed to make it difficult for a woman like Vidhya to retain close contact with her parents across distances that were really only a matter of a few hours by bus or train.

If a ruby is a son, then, a false ruby, which has a feminine gender, appears to indicate a daughter. Sons stay whole, the story says, but daughters may splinter. Reflecting more on this story and the equivalence between sons and gems that it plays on, I thought of how sons are valued more than daughters throughout most of India. In the North Indian ideal of the joint family, sons would continue to live with parents even when they build allegiance to another set of relatives through marriage: this would be a second identity that never quite displaces the first. The story seems to say that a second family makes a son a whole, grown man who, in his roles as son and son-in-law, still remains the same person. Daughters, on the other hand, become women by being given far away in marriage, fragmented like false rubies in the demands between two homes.

Treachery, Separation, and Reunion

Strong wills, contrary loyalties, and simmering jealousies are perhaps the dark side of any extended family. In Kangra this dark side has been played out amid kinship arrangements that include arranged marriages, the acceptance of cowives, the remarriage of widowers to women who will be stepmothers, and a rivalry between in-marrying daughters-in-law and out-marrying daughters. It is also shaped by the cultural preference for sons and idealized brother-sister ties.

In the stories that follow, characters are often larger than life. Good or bad aspects associated with a particular kinship role often appear to be split and polarized. So, as fathers or father surrogates, there are rejecting kings but nurturing holy men and prime ministers. As mothers, there are long-suffering queens but cruel and destructive stepmothers. As sisters, there are lovely persecuted maidens and coarse stepsisters who impersonate them.

All the stories that follow contain the theme of relatives being separated and estranged from one another through the machinations of wicked characters. They end with a triumphant reunion, a fresh commitment, and the punishment of wicked characters.

169

SEVENTEEN

The Astrologers' Treachery

After a morning of drenching rain, the afternoon would often clear. Setting off to visit Urmilaji after lunch, I would see slate roofs steaming in the sun, greenery glistening, butterflies darting madly. Sometimes the mountains would be unveiled, black granite with only the faintest smudges of yellowed snow from the year-round glaciers. At other times, clouds collected around the mountains: brilliant white, like tall sea waves flinging themselves against the sky.

A week after Kamalaji's visit, I walked through such a dazzling afternoon, stopping first at the household where I had been taping monsoon songs. I arrived to find that the side door of Urmilaji's house was open, leading into the room where we usually sat, enclosed. Urmilaji and her sister Nirmalaji were sitting in the light and the breeze by the door. They looked up through the spectacles they so rarely wore and smiled in welcome. Between them was a pile of grayish hair from the chins of goats. They were engaged in the laborious process of extracting the coarse hair from the fine, soft hair. To me, this looked like a task as impossible as those set in fairy tales, but both sisters said that the work kept them occupied through the long afternoons. Urmilaji said she planned to spin hers into yarn, and then have it mixed with other wool from her sheep and woven into a shawl. The sisters exchanged complicitous glances as this plan was revealed.

Urmilaji announced that she would tell the story that Kamalaji had reminded her of: the story with a couplet about an astrologer from Kashi. Kashi—also known as Benares or Varanasi—is a sacred center of Hinduism, lending an astrologer from Kashi special authority. Urmilaji had skimmed through the story as an aside when she had floundered over what next happened in "The Two Gems."

Urmilaji began speaking with her usual soft, measured certainty. Listening in as we all sat together around the goat hair, I lent a hand to pulling coarse hairs from the fine ones before me.

❈ ❈ ❈

There was a King. He had three queens. Three queens, and two of them didn't have any children. The third bore a son.

Everyone rejoiced with this birth: "A son is born in the King's house! He married three times, and from these three marriages, at last he has had a son." The King was very happy. He ordered massive celebrations.

Then the first two queens thought, "She'll become a Chief Queen, and we'll be left behind as her maids, her servants. Let's think of some way out of this."

They plotted together. Then they went to the Purohit: the family priest and astrologer. "We'll give you five thousand rupees," they said. "You must tell the King: 'Expel this son from your home or everything that's yours will be destroyed. The royal state will suffer, the kingdom will suffer, and not even a blade of dried grass will be left here of your royal property.'"

Bas. The King asked this Purohit to do the horoscope of the child. It's an important occasion when a son's horoscope is drawn up and his naming is celebrated. When the Purohit set to calculating the horoscope he began to shake his head [*Urmilaji demonstrates, slowly swiveling her head from side to side*].

The King asked, "What's the matter? Tell me."

The Purohit said, "What can I say? Everything is about to be destroyed. He brings terrible difficulties to you, to your rule, and to the state too."

The King said, "Recommend a cure for this problem. Prescribe a remedy. How can such difficulties be reversed?"

The Purohit said [*slowly*], "There's no remedy, but this: You expel this child from the house. On a Tuesday, halfway through the night, the mother should gather this child to her breast and they should both be thrown out."

The King was awfully upset. In middle age, he had finally had a son. And this was the situation he faced! He said [*sternly*], "I won't accept this."

Then he called for a Pandit, a learned astrologer, from Kashi, thinking that he would cast a horoscope. The King must have sent someone to the guru from Kashi to invite him.

The queens learned of this. "Now the King has sent for a Pandit from Kashi," they said [*whispering*] to each other. They went to the Purohit. "A Pandit has been called from Kashi for a new horoscope. We'll be crushed like seeds in an oilpresser and you will too. Go quickly and intercept him on the road." They gave the Purohit, the Brahman, five or seven thousand rupees and said, "Give this to him, and tell him to say what you have already said."

Now, if the King had invited the Pandit he was bound to give him something too. But this was a handsome bribe. *Bas.* So then the King's astrologer went out and intercepted the other astrologer. He gave him the money, saying, "Repeat what I've already said, or the King will have me crushed like seeds in an oilpresser." He told him exactly what to say.

The Kashi Pandit arrived. The King came out. He was delighted to see this great Pandit. Washing his hands and feet, spreading out a seat for him, the King showed the Pandit great respect.

hathe leiyān pothiyān	You hold a tome,
kacca manjā dhotiyān	a light shawl you bring;
patareyā badalde	Pages you turn:
munda kiyān lolade	Why does your head swing?

[*As she sings, Urmilaji demonstrates the song's actions with unhurried grace: the book is two open palms set side by side, the shawl is her folded dupatta clutched under one arm, the pages turning is a repeated motion of her hand from left to right, and her head mechanically swings from side to side.*]

He began to turn the pages of his almanac, and he began to shake his head. The King said, "Oh Pandit, what's the matter? Tell me what's wrong."

The Pandit said, "What can I tell you? Terrible adversity for you, terrible adversity for your state. All your horses, your elephants, all the things you own: Everything's going to be ruined by this son."

"What's the remedy? What can I do about it?"

"The remedy is this: You must paint the mother's face black and her hands and feet blue. Hang a garland of dried dung cakes around her neck. Put the child in her arms. On a Tuesday, at midnight, abandon them in a jungle."

The King, poor fellow, was distraught. But he did as he was told. He arranged for her to be abandoned in a distant jungle that was in a different king's state.

Around four in the morning, the cast-out Queen began to wash her hands and feet in a river flowing through the jungle. Now, the Prime Minister of that other state used to bathe in that river at four in the morning too. He arrived for his bath and when he saw her, he thought, "What can this thing be in the darkness?"

"What are you?" he called out. "Are you a ghost? A spirit rustling in the trees? What are you? Say something!"

"I'm neither a ghost nor a spirit," said the Queen. "I'm just a beggar woman."

He said, "What are you doing here at this hour?"

She said [*in a low, matter-of-fact voice*], "I was wandering through the jungle and night fell."

He said, "Come with me to my house. Bring your child. I will give you shelter."

So he brought them to his house. Then he asked, "Do you have any relatives?"

She said, "No, I work for a living. I earn what I eat, and when night falls that's where I stay."

He looked at her and he could see that she was from some well-to-do family. The son too looked as though he was from an excellent family (after all he was a prince!). But she didn't reveal the truth.

She said, "Allow me to work for you."

So he gave her a measure of rice grain. He handed it to her and said, "Husk this for me."

He hid and watched as she sat down to pound this rice. She began to weep. She quickly developed huge blisters for, as a Queen, when had she done such work?

"*Bas*," said the Prime Minister. "That's all. From now on you will be my adopted sister and I will be your adopted brother."

So she began to live there. He treated her with great respect. He looked after her, and he never allowed anyone to say anything rude to her. The son grew, and the Prime Minister put him in a school to be educated.

Once, when the boy was out playing with his friends, one of them called out: "Say your name! Everyone should say his father's name." When the boy was asked, he didn't know.

He went to his mother and asked, "What's my father's name?"

She wept terribly. As she wept, she said, "Why are you asking me this? What can I tell you?"

He said, "Tell me if you're going to tell me, else I'll end my life. I'll die. Tell me or I'll drink poison and commit suicide."

Then she told him the whole story. "The King of such and such a country is your father."

"Why aren't we with him?" he asked.

She said, "When you were born, we were expelled from the house and abandoned in the jungle in the dead of night. Since then we've spent our time here."

He heard this and was really upset. He saddled a horse and set off to his father's place. When he got there he asked the King, "Do you want to fight or unite?"

The King said, "How can I fight? I'm now blind. I have no heirs, and there is no one to govern my kingdom. I have no one. If there is no one behind me, how can I fight?"

So the boy got off his horse, touched the feet of his father, and they greeted each other warmly. Now the father had grown blind from weeping, but when he met with his son, all of a sudden, light came into his eyes. He asked, "Who are you?"

"I'm your son, the very one you abandoned in the jungle in the dead of night."

Then the King embraced him tightly. They met warmly with each other. "Where were you and what happened?" asked the King. "Once we left you in the jungle, we thought: 'Who knows, they've probably been eaten by leopards or some animal: both of you, mother and son.' After all, it was midnight in a dense forest when you were abandoned."

Bas, they kept up this exchange. "And your mother?" asked the King.

"My mother is in such and such a place," said the boy. "At the home of such and such a King's Prime Minister. She has spent this time living there. That's where she is."

[*"Namaste," Urmilaji's nephew, Amit, greets us with folded palms. He must have just come in off the bus from school. Nirmalaji gets up to go prepare him a snack. Urmilaji and I are left alone.*]

Then the King arranged for four palanquin bearers and a palanquin to fetch her, and he brought her back to his house.

As for the two other queens, he heard the story from the son: how they had conspired with the astrologer to exile his mother to the forest[1] and improve their own positions. "This is how they plotted to be rid of me and my mother," the boy said. Then the King bricked up both the other queens in a pillar. As for the Brahman, he was crushed in the oilpresser.[2]

❁ ❁ ❁

The couplet that pulled out this story long buried in Urmilaji's memory was about the Pandit from Kashi. As Urmilaji said, the Pandit was called all the way from distant Kashi because people there "are knowledgeable, and also because they are known to cast the best horoscopes. That's why they brought him from far away."

While Kashi is a sacred, authoritative site for much of Hindu India, its prestige is heightened in a marginal mountain region like Kangra. For an astrologer to have been summoned all that way was to underline the importance of his task and also to emphasize the enormity of his treachery.

Yet the source of these dire predictions was ultimately not the astrologers but the Queen's two cowives. Barren themselves, these cowives were consumed by jealousy when the third Queen produced the long-awaited son. Since childlessness is the most common reason for a man to marry more than one wife in Kangra, the issue of fertility can become a charged point against which women's self-worth is measured. It is invariably seen as the woman's fault, not the man's, although evidence (like more barren wives) may indicate otherwise.

When I talked to Urmilaji about this story the following year, she brought in new angles of causality in the evicted Queen's fate. "She was saved by God," explained Urmilaji, adding a dismal detail of rain, which had not been part of her original retelling. "Otherwise she was thrown out in such darkness, amid such pouring rain. But then the skies cleared up. And she had to spend the night in the jungle. No one was there but wild animals! But in the morning she got up again and she went on her way. That's when she met the King's Prime Minister. He took her home with him. She was after all very fortunate (*bhāgyavān*), but some inauspicious influence was coming to her from the stars. Despite this unfortunate influence, the Prime Minister kept her very well, as a sister."

The Queen in this story was similar, then, to the Queen in "The Twelve Years of Affliction." Like her, she was fortunate, but when afflicted by a malevolent influence, was forced to leave her home and wander. Like her, she was adopted as an honorary relative in another home, using this home as a refuge until the bad influence lifted. Like her, she was finally reinstated as honored Queen in her own palace.

Also, like the daughter-in-law in "The Fragrant Melon," who almost ended up being burned alive, this Queen was reinstated after her false accusation by being carried home in a palanquin, like an incoming bride. This seems to indicate not just the honor given to her by her husband, but also the start of a new phase in their marriage.

While this story shows how a husband and wife may become estranged through the machinations of cowives, it is also about the separation of a father and son. The King, fixated on his own welfare, evicts the son who is said to threaten him. Yet the Prime Minister becomes a surrogate, nurturing father, and it is only when the King has suffered so much that he is feeble and blind from weeping that the boy returns and is welcomed. I could only wonder whether men hearing this story might sense in it parallels from their own experience in the joint family: feeling stymied by a father's authority, hankering for a satisfactory recognition of their worth when full grown.

As we talked about this story, Urmilaji went on to retell portions. Yet, returning to the juncture of how the son had made contact again with his father, Urmilaji floundered, much as she had when she told "The Two Rubies." "Then the King went to hunt in the forest," she began. "Then . . . how did they go back? I've forgotten . . . what did I say?"

With the story in manuscript before me it was easy to remind her that the other children had demanded to hear the name of the father. But Urmilaji's uncertainty made it clear how the reuniting of fathers and sons (and by extension, estranged wives) was a slot that could be filled in various ways:[3] being informed by a Sadhu, having no father's name to say among other children, or even perhaps encountering each other while hunting. Coming to the same turning in the plot, Urmilaji was each time confronted with a choice: What was the right motif that filled it? Each choice, it seemed would draw the story off along a particular direction, just as a fork in a path might lead to a different destination.

On the actual day of the telling, we did not have a chance to discuss the story at all. Savarna, the carpenter's daughter who helped my mother with housework in the afternoons, had appeared at the open door soon after Urmilaji finished. "Your mother is calling you," Savarna had said, handing me a note.

My mother's scribbled writing informed me that two American graduate students doing research in the valley had come to visit on a motorbike from some distance away: Could I come home for tea? Urmilaji agreed that I should set off at once.

I walked through the sunny afternoon beside Savarna, mentally reorienting myself. Using Hindi, I told her the story I had just heard. She grinned. She was studying for high school examinations, and my interest in these "old stories" told in dialect never failed to amuse her. But then I fell silent. Leaving the leisurely world of women sitting together with their handiwork in the afternoon, I tried to conjure up my American academic persona. I wondered what these two fellow researchers would make of my fieldwork situation, complete with a mother.

EIGHTEEN

The Devouring Demoness

Creaking groggily down the stairs one June morning, I came into the small kitchen and found Ma by the radio, deeply upset. She had just heard the news. The day before, in the adjoining state of Punjab, Sikh separatists protesting national elections had boarded two passenger trains. They had shot at the passengers, leaving many wounded and killed. The station, Ludhiana, was one that anyone going to or from Kangra by rail also had to pass through. Like everyone else around us, we hoped that no one we knew had been riding the train that day.

The rains hadn't yet broken. The weather bloomed hot, bright, and still. Scarlet canna lilies were out in people's gardens, and many trees were festooned with pink flowers. Yet, amid the apparent picturesque serenity, I kept thinking that over the horizon on both sides of Himachal Pradesh were two states shattered by violence: Punjab and Kashmir.

The next day, interspersed between other outings, I left Ma lying under a mosquito net, reading the papers I'd written for my conferences in America. I made my way through the shimmering afternoon heat to see Urmilaji. She started by telling about the weevils who fasted. Then she told the story about the dog girl. After this, she told me about a princess who loves her father like salt. Finally, she moved on to this one.

❊ ❊ ❊

There were two people, a Brahman and a Brahmani, his wife. They had two sons. They probably were very poor. They tilled their own fields.[1] They were always occupied with work on their land. One day when they went to till the fields, they found a goat there. She had huge udders; a milk goat.

Bas. So they brought the goat home and tied her up and tended her. She began to supply them with milk.

After two days, the Brahmani asked the son to go out and graze the goat, for if a goat is grazed properly, it gives lots of milk. Now that goat was a demoness. The son took her to the jungle. And what the goat did was—she ate the son! Then, when it was getting to be evening, she came home. She came and stood there. The Brahmani tied her up.

"Our son must have run off to his maternal uncle's house,"[2] she said. "I'd forced him to go graze the goat. He must have run off to his maternal uncle's place from there, and the goat, poor thing, has grazed her fill and come back alone." The Brahmani thought that this goat was wonderful, since she gave a lot of milk.

Two days passed and the Brahmani said to their second son, "Go on. Now that your brother has run away, you must take the goat out." The son said no, but his mother wouldn't listen. She was overcome by greed for milk. So she sent her second son off too. Within two moments the goat ate him as well. And by evening, the goat came home again.

The mother said, "This second one has probably also run off to his maternal uncle's place. Both the boys have gone off to their maternal uncle's place, and the goat, poor thing, has grazed her fill and come home." So she tied her up. Again at night, the goat gave lots of milk.

Three days later, in the morning, the Brahman said, "I'm going to the fields with the bullock; bring my afternoon meal after a while." So he went off to some faraway place where their land was, a place across the river. He started to till the fields, assured that his food would arrive.

She, poor thing, cooked the food. She put it in a basket, and she was ready to set off. But first she went to the goat, to give her grass and water. The goat ate her up.

Then the demoness took on the form of a human being instead of a goat. She dressed in the clothes that the Brahmani had been wearing and lifted the basket of food onto her own head.

Bas, she took off. The fields were at a great distance, and the Brahman was plowing the field with the bullock. He saw her from afar and thought, she's come with my food. "She's come with my food!" he said aloud. He said this, and his bullock began to weep.

He said this.

And his bullock began to weep.

"Why are you weeping?" asked the Brahman. "What's the matter?"

"Nothing's wrong," said the bullock. "I'm just crying."

"No!" said the Brahman. "You must tell me."

The bullock said, "That goat is a demoness. She's eaten up both your sons, and now she's eaten your wife too. She's coming here in the form of your wife, and she'll eat you up as well. After that she'll eat me: she's a demoness, after all."

Bas. So the Brahman sat down. He felt grief for his sons, grief for his wife. What could he do? "Give me advice," he said to the bullock. "Tell me what I should do."

The bullock said, "What advice can I give you? When she comes up to you, demand, 'What, do I eat without bathing?! First I must give the bullock water, then I must wash up myself. I'll only eat after that. Get back!' Then you must take us across the river. You can proceed by yourself and climb up to the top of any tree. That's the only way you'll escape, else she'll eat you up."

When she arrived there beside the Brahman, she said [*sweetly*], "Eat your food."

"Get lost!" said the Brahman [*with indignation*]. "Do I ever eat my food without bathing?! Do I ever eat without a bath first? I have to give the bullock water, then I'll wash up myself, and only after that I'll eat. You sit here with the food. I'll be back after bathing in the river."

Bas. He set off, driving the bullock toward the riverbank. After he crossed the river, he drove the bullock into the jungle. Then he climbed a hillside. And she saw him from the fields. "There he goes! He's running away!" She rushed after him.

There was a very tall tree in the jungle. The Brahman climbed it and sat up in the branches. She arrived, running, and sat at the base of the tree. She had become a very pretty woman, sporting adornments and airs. She sat down beneath the tree and called out: "Come down! Come down the tree. Come on down, won't you?" She wept and she pleaded. She wailed and she cried.

A King who was out hunting reached this place. He came there and he said . . .

[*"Open up, Sello!" we hear Nirmalaji cry from next door, along with a loud rapping. The kids must have locked themselves in with the television. Urmilaji listens for a moment, evaluates the situation as being under control, then continues.*]

The King who was hunting arrived. He said, "Give me this woman. A woman this beautiful ought to be kept in an enclosed courtyard as a Queen; she shouldn't be with a poor man like you. What do you want for her? How much money do you demand?"

The Brahman did this with his hand [*Urmilaji waves one hand with her five fingers outstretched, and I laugh expectantly, knowing from Swamiji's stories that gestures substituting for words invariably bring about a misunderstanding*]: he meant, you can just take her away. He was terrified, poor man, he was quaking up there. With his hand, he said, "Take her away."

The King's servant said, "He wants five thousand. Put it under the tree and take her away."

So the King put five thousand under the tree and took the woman off to his enclosed courtyard. When the King left, the Brahman came down the tree. He took the money, and he probably went home with the bullock. He had set a drama in motion. That's it. And she went to the palace: a Queen.

✿ ✿ ✿

Bas. Now, she was a demoness. She did what those of her kind do. When everyone else was sleeping, she stole off to eat the finest horses. She ate and drank, and with her bloody hands, she went to the King's other three wives. She smeared her bloody hands over their faces.

When morning came, the King said, "Today the stable of horses is empty: what's happened?"

Now the King really adored her. [*"The horse?" I ask. Sounds from the television are seeping through the wall and I'm confused. "No, the demoness," says Urmilaji patiently.*] She was very pretty, very adorable. She said to the King, "Look at your queens! They're hardly what they appear. Take a look at their faces, they've been eating horses all night."

And these women, poor things, had no idea of what it was like to eat things like that!

Bas. In this way, she ate the horses, the elephants. She proceeded to devour whatever belonged to the King.

"What can we do now?" asked the King. "What's happening is terrible."

"Put them down into a dry well," said the demoness. "All three of them."

The King said, "That's what I'll do."

Bas. All three queens were taken and they were lowered into a dry well. Now, all three were pregnant. And all three of them were in the well: they were all so hungry, poor things, what could they eat down there? [*Urmilaji shakes her head and I cluck*].

She had them lowered down, and she herself lived with great pleasure, eating and drinking.

Down in the well, one of the queens went into labor. A son was born to her. She said, "If we are so hungry, what is this child going to eat?" So she ate up the child. Who knows how long it had been since they had eaten anything, neither dying, nor anything else happening.

Alright, so a second one delivered. She too ground up her child and ate it. [*"All three of them ate their babies?!" I ask incredulously.*]

Two of them ate the babies. When the third delivered, she said, "No! I didn't eat yours, though I was dying with hunger, I didn't join you. I am going to raise my baby." And she put him to her breast, but what would there be to eat? Then God himself arranged for something to eat in the well, who knows what it was as they sat worrying: some bit of rubbish or something. So they were able to eat and drink, and care for their stomachs. So this one Queen brought up her child.

❋ ❋ ❋

Now, as she was raising this child, there were cowherds who came there and would bring their cows to graze. They heard some murmuring, as though someone was speaking in the well.

181

In the past, cowherds used to wear long pieces of cloth. They sometimes wore these on their heads. They collected all these cloths together, tied them up, and made a very long rope. Then they threw this rope into the well.

When they threw it in, the boy caught hold of it. Then the cowherds tugged the rope out: "Let's see what will come out of here, what's speaking in the well." When that boy came out, they were absolutely amazed: "How did you get in there?"

The boy said, "I have three mothers. They are all in the well."

Then the cowherds provided them all with food, poor things. After this, whenever the cowherds brought the cows out to graze, they would bring food to eat as well. They'd give the boy food. Then he would deliver food down below to his mothers too. They did this every day.

"Everyday, when we set out from home carrying our food, a radiant boy comes out of the well. He's hungry, poor fellow." Thinking this, they would bring extra food from their homes especially for him.

In this way, the boy began to understand things. The health of his mothers also improved: in the past, they had been dying of starvation.

Then one day, one of the cowherd boys was packing extra food. His mother said, "Who is this for? One of these days, bring him home with you."

"Fine," he said. "I'll bring him."

He pulled the boy and the Queen out of the well. He wanted to take them home with him.

When all the cowherds were going home that evening, the boy and his mother came along. One cowherd said, "Come to my house"; a second said, "Come to my house"; a third said, "Come to my house."

They said, "We'll go to the home of someone who's well off, who has something stocked away."

Bas. Then they went to the house of the cowherd boy. The people there fed them, poor things. The woman of the house fed them good food. Then in the evening, they were brought back and lowered back into the well.

The father of the cowherd boy said, "Ask that boy what the name of his father is. The woman seems to be of an excellent family, and yet they are in these terrible straits. Ask the boy his father's name."

A day or two later, all the children went out to play together. The cowherd boy said, "Everyone should speak the name of his father." Each boy spoke the name of his father, but when they asked the boy from the well, he didn't know, poor fellow, he didn't know who his father was.

Bas. He turned around and went to his mother. "What's my father's name?" he asked.

She, poor thing, began to weep. "What name can I tell you? You are the son of such a great King, but look what fate wrote: we have nothing to eat, nothing at all, and we're in this condition." And she wept.

He said, "If you don't tell me, I'll die. What is his name?"

Then she told him the whole story.

[*"Were the other two Queens with them?" I interrupt. "This was all in the well,"* says Urmilaji.]

"Tell me who it is," said the boy, and his mother told him the whole story: "It was like this, and you are the son of a King. But he married a demoness, and we were lowered into a well."

He said, "Is that so?"

❀ ❀ ❀

After two or three days, the boy went off to the King. As he arrived, the demoness was sitting out on the balcony of the palace [*Urmilaji laughs*]. She caught sight of him.

She said, "Hey, lad! Where are you going?"

He said, "I'm going to pay my respects to the King. Where else would I be going?"

He gave her an answer at once. She asked him where he was going; he said he was going to see the King, where else would he go? And he proceeded.

Then he paid his respects to the King. The King thought he was very hand-some and was loving to him. The demoness understood that this boy was the King's son.

Bas. When she knew this, she said, "I have a terrible pain in my stomach."

A pain in the stomach, a pain in the stomach, a pain in the stomach.

The King asked, "What will cure your pain?"

Now, the other queens had learned that this was a demoness because her parent's home was in a country of demons. [*Urmilaji pauses, as though recollect-ing: there is now piano music and the voice of a male commentator drifting in from the other room—I guess that this is a romantic advertisement for Nestle's instant coffee.*] A certain country. They must have learned this from some man who said, "Her parent's place is in a certain country and they are all demons there. The essence of her life is in the form of a parrot." The queens had told the boy about this country.

The King said, "What will cure the pain in your stomach?"

She said, "The pain in my stomach will only be cured if you send this boy to my parent's place." And she spoke the name of that country. "Rice is tilled there. The boy should bring back a stalk of rice grains. Then, there's a gray buffalo. That buffalo's milk must be brought along too. If rice pudding is made from these two ingredients, and if I eat it, then the pain in my stomach will be cured."

She calculated that since this was the country of demons, if the boy managed to get there, he wouldn't come back alive. "I'll have the boy sent off to that country. If the King learns that this boy is his son, he'll bring him into this home. Better that I have him done away with in that country."

So that was the King's order. The King still didn't know that this boy, who had emerged from the well, was his son. He sent the boy off to that country, saying, "Bring the milk of the gray buffalo, and a stalk of the finest rice. Bring these so that they can be boiled together in a rice pudding. When she eats this, her stomachache will go away."

The boy's mother objected. "I won't send him. He was raised amid such hardship. We were starving, somehow we collected things to eat: why send him off to a demon's country now?"

But the boy wouldn't listen. "No, I'm going to go," he said. "I'm off to that country."

Bas. He went to the King and said, "Give me expenses for the journey." He got money, expenses, rations. He took all this from the King, gave some to his mothers, and kept some for himself.

As he proceeded, he came to a jungle. Night fell. There was not a single person, not a soul: just dense, dark jungle. He came to a small hut. A Baba, a holy man, sat doing austerities in the hut, and sacred grass had sprouted all over him. It was a powerful austerity that this Baba had been sitting and doing, for so long that sacred grass had grown up all over him.

The boy uprooted the grass. He cleaned off the Baba's body. Then the Baba became conscious. He said, "Son, I'm very pleased with you. Ask me for a boon."

The boy said, "Babaji, what can I request of you? My story is like this: I am going to the country of the demons, and I am supposed to bring the milk of a gray buffalo and a stalk of fine rice. Tell me how I can accomplish this."

The Baba said, "Son, don't worry at all. That is truly the country of the demons, and it's difficult to get there."

The Baba gave the boy a military uniform of iron: pants and a shirt. He put roasted garbanzos into the pocket. And ... he made him into a parrot. He gave him the feathers of a parrot to wear so he could fly to this faraway place.

"Put on this pelt of a parrot and fly away. When you get there, you can take it off. But first, as a parrot, you must procure the rice that has been requested. You must bring one stalk back to where you set up camp. But there will be many other parrots squawking there. You mustn't squawk at all, or else they'll understand that you're a man. Then, when you reach that place of the demons, you must ask, "Where is my maternal uncle? Where is my maternal aunt? Where is my maternal grandmother? And grandfather? Ask about everyone." You will be offered a woven mat of thorns. This is to test you. You should sit down with great force. Since the thorns won't have pierced you, you'll be accepted as a demon too. Then you'll be offered garbanzos of iron to snack on. Sneak these into one pocket, and from the other pocket, take out your own roasted garbanzos and eat them with loud crunches: *marak-marak*. Then they'll

184

believe that you're a demon for sure: the son of that demoness and a grandson."

So the boy followed these instructions. He became a parrot and flew off. He arrived in that place. Then, at some distance he took off the parrot pelt and he once again became a man. He proceeded ahead and greeted his "grandmother" by touching her feet. He named the Queen demoness and said that he was her son.

OK, so she showed him great love:"My daughter's son is here!" She brought the thorn seat for him to sit on, and he thumped right down onto it. She was pleased. Then she brought out a handful of iron garbanzos. He stealthily put this into his pocket and taking out the other garbanzos he began to munch on them. She was assured, "He's truly a demon!"

Then he asked this grandmother, "Where's my maternal uncle?"

She said, "He's gone out." After all, he was a demon who had to eat [*Urmilaji smiles*]!

He asked about everyone: "Where's my uncle? Where's my grandfather? Where's my aunt?" Everyone.

Then they lay down to sleep, the grandmother and the grandson. They began to chat.

"What's that cage hanging up here?" the boy asked.

She said, "This cage contains the life of your grandfather, that cage has the life of your uncle, that one has mine, and that other one has your mother's. Our lives are in these cages in the form of parrots. When these parrots die, then, wherever we are, we die too."[3]

The grandson continued asking questions. "What's that hanging up there?"

"That's a warm *dhotī* to wear."

[*"A warm* dhotī," *I repeat, thinking that a* dhotī, *a long piece of cloth draped around the waist and pulled up between the legs, is usually of the finest cool muslin, rather than being warm. "There must have been a* dhotī *hanging there," explains Urmilaji.*]

"If you sleep in this you are always warm," she said.

Then there was a rope and an ascetic's staff.[4] "These are what these things are," she explained.

"I see," said the boy. He kept asking questions and she kept talking. Finally, late into the night, they went to sleep.

When he saw that this old woman had fallen asleep, he got up. In a flash, he caught hold of her cage, and he twisted the neck of the parrot inside it. So she died, this grandmother. Then he wrung the necks of all the other parrots, except for the one in the cage of his "mother": his stepmother, the demoness.

He took that cage with him. Then he plucked one hair from the gray buffalo in the courtyard: the milk-giving buffalo whose rice pudding the stepmother wanted to eat. And from the ripe fields he took a stalk of rice. He couldn't carry too much with him for the distance. He took his "mother's" cage along. Also, for the holy man, he took the warm *dhoti*. His stepmother had also said, "I must eat the rice pudding off the gold plates of my parent's home," so he brought a plate along too. He had asked the grandmother about all this and she had told him. So he took all these things, became a parrot, and set off.

When he reached the Baba, it had gotten to be night. He gave the warm *dhoti* to this saintly person saying, "You're a man who lives in the jungle and this will be of use to you." He took the rest of the things and went on his way.

❀ ❀ ❀

When he got back, he went to his mother. His mother, poor woman, had really been suffering. Who knows how many months had gone by since he'd set off? He had to get that far, and then he had to turn around and come back too. When he arrived, his mother took heart that he was back.

He said to the King, "Have the drums beaten! Call all the people to assemble. Then I'll come and give you all the things you wanted."

The King did that. Everyone assembled. The boy set down the hair and the buffalo appeared. He set down the stalk of rice, and an entire pile of rice appeared. Then he set the cage down.

When the stepmother saw the cage, she was filled with black rage. "Oh-oh, he's laid everything down, and the gold plate too. He's brought everything. How did he manage to return?" She just rushed toward him in her own form: "I'll eat him up!"

As she neared, he twisted the foot of the parrot. Then she was crippled: how could she come toward him? She began to crawl. Then he twisted the wings as well as the feet: she was truly crippled. She was in the gigantic form of a demoness. Crawling and scraping, she came toward him: she was intent on somehow eating him up. Then he twisted the bird's neck, and she died.[5]

Then he said to his father, "Oh foolish King, do queens ever eat horses and elephants? Why didn't this enter your head? Do queens eat horses and elephants? Based on what this demoness said, you had all three of your queens lowered into a dried-up well. You even ended your lineage: three sons. And you kept this demoness?!"

He went on to say, "I'm your son. I was born of one of your queens."

Then the King set him on the throne. And as for the demoness, she had died.

[*Urmilaji laughs. She starts to hand the microphone back to me, but from my perspective there is still one detail unaccounted for. "And the mothers?" I inquire. "Did they bring the mothers back?" Urmilaji goes back into the story to tie up this detail*].

The King brought the first Queen back into his inner courtyard. And as for the demoness, she died. The boy had said to his father, "You're a foolish King!

You had no understanding. You lived with your Queens, and brought her to live with you. When she arrived, your elephants and your horses began to dwindle, and you unjustly put the blame on the heads of the other Queens."[6]

❀ ❀ ❀

"Do you think there are demons around here today?" I asked.

"There are all kinds of stories about demons (*rākshasen*)," Urmilaji said. "But these days, they aren't to be heard or ever seen under the sun. A demon is a human who eats other humans. That's who a demon is. And these days, terrorists (*ātankvādī*) have become the demons!"

Urmilaji extended an upturned palm, which I slapped in acknowledgment of her black wit.

"Truly: they drink blood too!" I said.

"That's right. Those who drink blood are demons. In the past we had so many different kinds of beings here: specters and sprites (*chhal-chhaleṛe*), and this and that, here and there. That was because there were fewer people in the past. We had ghosts and revenants (*bhūt-pret*), we had specters and sprites: we had at least one hundred different kinds of ghosts. Now there are so many settlements of people, none of these beings are left. They're all finished off. Now, the terrorists have become the demons, nobody else."

Eating human flesh and the power of metamorphosis are two attributes of demons.[7] In addition, an extremely thick skin and a lack of human sensitivity are further attributes. Thinking of associations between goats and the devil in Christianity, I asked Urmilaji if goats were usually thought to be vehicles for demons.[8]

Apparently not, for Urmilaji replied, "Demons take on all kinds of forms, they can keep changing forms. The poor Brahman, his whole family was killed."

"In this story, the Brahman was forgotten early on," I observed. As in "The Twelve Years of Affliction," once the Brahman served his purpose in setting the plot rolling, he was forgotten.

"The Brahman was set free then and there," said Urmilaji, laughing.

Similarly, in the economy of the tale, the two cowives who had eaten their children were also forgotten partway through. As human beings forced through desperate circumstances to hungrily devour their own newborn children, they were revealed as being partial demonesses themselves. Their intermediary position between the nurturing Queen and the flesh-eating demoness made me think of this tale as a gradation of mothers: a self-sacrificing good mother at one end and a cannibalizing, destructive, and sexy stepmother at the other. Psychologically, this split could be viewed as a polarization in the emotional responses to the fabled Hindu mother, who could at times seem excessively devouring in her love;[9] ethnographically, this could be viewed as a commentary on heartless stepmothers who, having bewitched a father, destroy the family

187

through their whims. As Urmilaji said, "Stepmothers used to be called demonesses. They were likely to beat and scold their stepchildren. Then other women used to say, 'Stay away! She's a demoness, the way she hits them.'"

The rejecting, weak-willed, and easily enamored King can also be seen as a polarized opposition to another father figure: the kind, nurturing, holy man who has taken control of his appetites. Rather than being caught up in matters of the flesh and the kingdom, the Baba is turned so deep within that, like the holy men in 'The Floating Flower,' sacred grass has grown all over him. This sacred grass emphasizes his peaceful immobility and identity with the earth; in Kangra, another local tradition about *drub* (or *drubari*) grass says it is the Ramayana's heroine Sita's hair sticking out after she has been swallowed up by her mother, the earth.[10] On account of the holy man's practices, he has built up ascetic powers that enable him to know what is to come and the ways to get around these future events.

"These kings, you know, if they came across any beautiful woman, they'd just marry her!" Urmilaji said. "They wouldn't think about whether they already had wives in the house: no! Any beautiful woman they laid eyes on was borne off and lodged in the inner courtyards of the palace. In this way, one King could have five or six or even seven Queens. That's how it was."

Indeed, the boy rebukes his father for having believed the stepmother, and by implication, having been so enamored by her charms that he could not help bringing her home and believing all she said. He ignored the evidence that before her arrival there had been no mass slaughter of his horses and elephants.[11]

In this story, a son has the last word with his willful and misguided father, but in the next story, it is a daughter who does so.

NINETEEN

Love Like Salt

Urmilaji actually told the following story just before she told "The Devouring Demoness." It is one that Urmilaji learned as a child when her father worked at tea gardens in Garli Paragpur at the other end of the valley. She heard it from a woman who lived nearby.

❊ ❊ ❊

There was a King. A King, and he had three daughters. He raised them and nurtured them, and then he began to think about marrying them off. One day when he was sitting around, he began to cross-examine them.

He asked the first, "How much do you love me?"

She said, "Lots of love! Just as crystallized sugar is sweet, very sweet, that's how much I love you."

Then he asked the second. He asked, "How beloved am I to you?"

The second said, "Just as refined sugar that's stirred into milk is sweet, that's how much I love you. You're dearly loved."

Then he asked the third. She said, "Just as vegetables need salt, that's how much I love you."

"*Bas*," he said. "That's enough." After that, he was angry at the one who said that she loved him like salt. He thought that she didn't love him at all.

Bas. He found powerful kings for the other two and married them off. Then he took the one who said she loved him like salt and married her to a woodcutter: a very poor woodcutter.

Bas. The King married her off and she, poor thing—where is a King's daughter and where is a woodcutter?—began to live there with him. He, poor fellow, would bring wood home every day and then he'd sell it. What she'd do is embroider beautiful hangings. She'd sell these in the town. This is how they managed to make a living, poor things. They supported themselves.

They continued in this way. Now the woodcutter would bring home bundles of wood, right? Each day the value of these bundles increased. He'd get a good price for them. And she kept making her embroideries. So they got together a

189

fair amount of money. Then they opened a small shop. They made a lot of money in the shop too. When they had run the shop for some time, they started a small factory. From that too, they earned a lot of money. In this way, they went on to become millionaires. They had huge amounts of money, and they built themselves a proper house and had everything in it decorated just right.

Around that time, the Queen—her mother—said, "You know our girl who was married to the woodcutter, we haven't had any news of her. The other two come and go on visits. But we married her to such a poor man and then we haven't cared for her either; it's as though we've sent her off across the seven seas." This is a mother's heart, after all.

Bas. So it came into the King's mind to find out about her. He sent a servant or someone to bring the news. When they found her, there she was, a tremendous millionaire! Terrific splendor, many rooms all very decorated: she was like a Queen, a great Queen.

He turned around and went back. He said, "Oh King, in that particular country, they have become like royalty."

The King told his Queen what the man had said. She was really moved. "Let's go and meet her."

So they got up and set out. When they arrived at the daughter's place, they greeted each other warmly. The daughter met with her father, she met with her mother too: she showed them great respect.

They asked, "How have things been for you?"

She said, "I endured really hard times. We were so poor, and this is how we earned. We earned, and the earnings grew, and now this is where we are."

When night fell, she set to making dinner. She made a dinner in which all the vegetable dishes were sweet. There was no salt in anything.

Bas. When they sat down to eat, whatever they put their hands to, that was sweet; whatever they put their hands to, that was sweet. You can't eat a lot of sweets. The father ate just a little and then he stopped.

She said, "Oh Father, do eat!"

He said, "But you haven't made anything salty. Everything here is sweet, and I can't eat too many sweet things at once."

She said, "No! But sweet things are really loved. I said that I loved you like salt. When you eat anything salty, then you can eat to fill your stomach, can't you? If you eat sweet things, your stomach doesn't fill. I said that I loved you. Now do eat this sweet dinner to your heart's content!"

So, then it penetrated his mind that she really loved him. It's true, a person can't live without salt. A person can live without sweets, but not without salt.[1]

❀ ❀ ❀

This was the first story that Urmilaji told which I had known before visiting Kangra. I could not recall where in the fertile mix of fairy tales I'd read as a child I had come across it before: one of the rainbow-hued Andrew Lang books? The shiny gray Oxford series of folktales, each volume featuring a different part of the world? A child's retelling of Shakespeare? All these books were still on the upstairs shelves of my mother's house, and I thought of consulting them but never did.

The father's question, testing his daughter's love before he decides on their married fate, hints at an overinvolved, possessive relationship. He punishes the daughter whom he suspects of not loving him by marrying her off to a poor man of indeterminate caste. While he does not state that he wants to himself marry his daughter, he puts so much stock in the answer that he would appear to be unhealthily attached.[2] Using Urmilaji's own taxonomy for types of love in these tales, the father would seem to feel not just possessive attachment for his daughter, but deluded infatuation too.

The presence of the mother is an unusual twist to the tale. Most variants do not mention her at all, instead foregrounding the King's attachment to his daughters. The Queen only comes into focus when she is needed by the plot and fades out at other times. She serves the important function of engineering the reconciliation between father and daughter. Like the mothers in "The Twelve Years of Affliction" and "In the Court of Destiny," this mother yearns for news of her married daughter. As Urmilaji said, commenting on the tale, "This is a mother's heart, after all."

The parents going to visit a married daughter and staying with her may indicate that the story was imported; among the Kangra upper castes, giving a daughter is an ultimate gift (*dān*) for which nothing should be received in return. In several families I knew, if parents visited their daughter at all, they would be unlikely to take more than tea, and if so, would shell out a few coins at once. Cooking a full-scale meal for a visiting father and mother would not be a readily observable practice.

Urmilaji's description of the rise from poverty—from piece work to owning a shop, starting a factory, and eventually becoming millionaires—seemed to echo Hindi films that were shown on television. Also, the idea of a cement house that was well-decorated struck me as an astute depiction of what ascent into the middle class meant in Kangra. Moving out of the old adobe house with a slate roof, people built themselves flat, box-like cement houses; if this was not possible they would at least add a cement room, showing that they could afford bought material over locally made earthen bricks. Invariably, cement houses would have doorbells that played the first line of "We Wish You a Merry Christmas," "Doe a Deer, a Female Deer," or "London Bridge Is Falling Down." Since doors were mostly left open, and it was the custom to call out or cough, there was really no need for such bells. My friend Vidhya, who had recently moved into such a house with her schoolteacher husband and two sons, once reported that her teenage son was so entranced by the doorbell, so frustrated that no one used it, that he would sometimes shut the door, ring it, and then go running in through the back door to open it up.

"Why did so much wealth gather?" I asked Urmilaji the following year.

"Because of her hard work—making those embroideries and other things," said Urmilaji. "And also because of God's support. She was married off to a poor man, and she went with him. People had said, 'You are speaking with such arrogance, saying you love the King like salt: You should be married to a poor man.' And each sister who said that love was like white sugar was married to a very rich man." In this commentary then, emphasizing the will of "people" rather than the King, Urmilaji underplayed the King's possibly incestuous possessiveness. Instead, it was public opinion that turned against the Princess for frankly describing her emotion. Redeeming herself by cooking a meal rather than through outright argument, the Princess derailed further allegations that she had arrogantly talked back.

"Then too," Urmilaji observed, "this story shows you that the rich can become poor, and the poor can become rich. In that other story, a rich one became poor, didn't she, and a poor one became rich?"

By the "other story" Urmilaji meant "First Sour, Then Sweet." In both stories, the poor sister was rewarded for her industry, hospitality, and piety and so was eventually able to put poverty behind her. But in this story, the woman who emerges from poverty is less explicitly engaged in ritual practice. Her virtue lies partly in having told the truth and having stuck by that truth until she could prove to her father that she was right.

Refined white sugar is now a staple in Kangra, but an expensive one. Each month there would be long lines for rationed sugar at Urmilaji's brother's shop as people hoped to take advantage of government prices for sugar, rice, wheat, kerosene, and so on. While tea, drunk several times a day, was always amply laced with sugar, actual desserts were usually confined to special occasions. Many people of Urmilaji's generation recalled that when they were children, refined sugar was not widely available, and it was usual to drink tea with a lump of unrefined jaggery (a form of brown sugar). Salt, on the other hand, has always been available through trade, and Urmilaji's village lay on the old salt route up into the mountains. In this setting, love like sugar would be an unstable, unhealthy delicacy; love like salt, a dependable staple of which you would not easily tire.

Urmilaji's summary of this story was in nutritional rather than psychological terms. "The meaning of this story is of salt and sugar. A person can't eat too much sugar, even though it's a very lovable thing. It's very lovable, isn't it? But you can't eat too much of it—it's salt that you can eat."

TWENTY

Fair with Freckles

As the date for my departure grew closer, I was swept headlong into my research on songs. I was gone for days at a time, visiting other villages. During this time, Urmilaji was preoccupied too. Her mother was ill with a serious eye inflammation, admitted to the hospital more than an hour's bus ride away. The days that I dropped in, Urmilaji was usually not home. When she was home, she seemed racked with anxiety. As she said about her worries, "If you live far away, you don't always come to know what's happening with your family [of birth]. But I live close by, I learn everything at once. After all, happiness and sorrow are true brothers."

By late August, the rice was darkening and the corn had grown tall. Rakshabandhan, the festival in which sisters tie bracelets on their brothers, had been celebrated, bringing Urmilaji's eldest daughter home for a visit along with her two young sons. When I came by, Urmilaji introduced me to this daughter, Rama. Rama was a woman of my own age, though as a wife and mother she had the edge of seniority. She had a bright, open manner and a warm smile.

Urmilaji and Rama were about to walk over to Urmilaji's home of birth to attend a song session in honor of a birthday of one of Urmilaji's brothers. I inwardly groaned when they invited me along: The last thing I needed was yet more songs! I had already taped hundreds. But I tagged along anyway, thinking that like life itself, prolonged fieldwork could become repetitive. At the same time, I was glad to have the chance to spend time with Urmilaji in the context of her extended family.

The house where Urmilaji's brothers and mother lived was only a few minutes walk further down the cobbled path from Urmilaji's house. Houses were clustered close in this part of the village, dominated by Soods. Bamboo plumes bent over the path. We passed the village post office and turned to the left, entering a grand house built like a box around a spacious central courtyard. Urmilaji's brothers and mother lived in one of these wings.

Urmilaji's mother was home from the hospital. She was a woman of about eighty, with a serene face and thick white hair covered with a white scarf. She looked weaker, her eyes more bloodshot than when I had last seen her a few weeks before. She sat with her legs drawn up to her chin on a rope cot, smiling down at the group of women gathered on mats spread out over the floor.

The assembled female relatives and neighbors sang birthday songs, mostly led by Urmilaji. As the women sang, steadily, repetitively, their hands were all busy motion: knitting needles flashed, last year's sweater was unraveled to be remade around a bigger child, a crochet hook wove in and out, fingers flicked stones from green mung lentils. Also, my own hand moved briskly across my notebook as I attempted to transcribe what I heard.

When the standard birthday songs for a man's long life were sung, the women moved on to ballads with themes of married life and separation. Urmilaji began one song that no one could remember a crucial verse for. It involved a charming brother-in-law trying to flirt with—perhaps even seduce— his brother's wife as he escorted her from her parent's to her in-law's home. The relationship between a wife and a husband's younger brother is one of jokes and innuendos throughout Northern India. I had previously taped a variant of this song from a nearby Brahman village. Though I couldn't myself recall the exact words, I promised to look over my transcriptions and provide Urmilaji with the missing verse.

After a while most of the neighbors left, each taking a handful of sprouted garbanzos from Urmilaji's mother. Such edible sprouts distributed at birthdays represented a man's long life. Urmilaji's sons came in after a day's work as tobacco merchants in town. Another round of sweet tea in tall, steel glasses was brought out. I used this opportunity amid the gathered family to read aloud a list of stories I had taped from Urmilaji so far. I had hoped that maybe other family members would remind Urmilaji of stories she hadn't told me. But for the moment, everyone just nodded in recognition, laughing aloud when the Dog Girl was mentioned.

The next afternoon was humid and sweltering, crying out for more rain. I returned to find Rama and Urmilaji seated on burlap sacking just inside the doorway of Nirmalaji's apartments. Both were knitting different parts of a brown wool sweater for Rama's husband. Nirmalaji sat further within.

As I arrived, Sello emerged puffy-faced from a nap in the other wing of the house. "How come you have such white skin?" she asked me groggily, "Is there anything you use that I can use to become fair too?"

"Maybe this skin is because of my American mother," I replied, trying not to be self-conscious.

"There's nothing that you use? No cream or anything to become fair?" Sello asked again, as her mother and sister grinned at this display of emerging teenage vanity.

Obviously disappointed with me, Sello set off to make everyone's tea. I presented Urmilaji with the words for the verse she had been missing the previous day. "That's what it is!" she smiled. "For so long, I've been thinking about this song and wondering what she said to him in the tent!"

I had brought with me a complete, translated draft of all the stories she had told me over the months. I now hoped to elicit some general observations on these stories. Urmilaji and Nirmalaji together instructed me on aspects of storytelling, reminiscing about their father and citing the proverb about winter tales coming with the sowing of wheat. "Why do you think such stories are important?" I then asked.

Urmilaji looked deferentially toward Nirmalaji, who was, after all, the educated schoolteacher. "Tell tell," Nirmalaji urged. Hesitantly, as she added stitches to the sweater in her hands, Urmilaji began to speak. I wrote her comments on a preliminary index page. "In the old days, these stories were all told to save people from paths of wrongdoing," Urmilaji said. "Stories tell you about the value of serving others and that misdeeds are punished. They teach you about adopting good qualities and how to live a good life."

Rama broke in to prompt her mother, "What about that girl who was made into a bird? You used to tell that, remember?"

Urmilaji smiled. "I haven't told that one for a long time," she said. She sang a verse under her breath, Rama joining in.

Starting into the story, Urmilaji derailed by having the stepmother immediately transform the girl into a bird. She then stopped, asked me to turn off the recorder, and turned to confer with Rama. "What was it that happened?" she asked. Rama suggested that it was only after the girl had met, married the King, and returned home for a visit that she had been turned into a bird.

At Urmilaji's request, I erased what I'd taped so far and we began afresh.

❋ ❋ ❋

There was, you know, a Brahman and a Brahmani, his wife. A daughter was born to them. The Brahmani, poor thing, died soon after the birth. Then the Brahman married a second time. A daughter was born to the second wife as well.

The first daughter grew up. The stepmother fed her coarse corn bread, but she'd give fine wheat bread and other delicious things to her own daughter. The first daughter never got any of these good things, she'd just be fed the food left on their plates.

Now the first daughter was very beautiful. The stepmother would send her out with the cows. As the cattle grazed, the girl would sit embroidering in the company of her girlfriends.

One day, when she was grazing the cattle, a King who was out hunting came there. She had made a particularly beautiful embroidery and she gave this to the King. The King was very pleased.

"What is your situation?" he asked her.

She told him that her mother had died. Right there, he . . .

[*"Sat her down on his horse," prompts Rama with a wide grin*].

—sat her down on his horse and took her off with him.

[*"Why did she give him the embroidery?" I ask, thinking that this is surely a bold thing for a girl to volunteer. "She gave him a present," says Urmilaji, switching to Hindi. "A very fine thing as a present." Remembering the story of the Prime Minister who brought the King the beautiful white flower, I add, "And very fine things are given to Kings."*]

He saw that she was unhappy at home, poor thing, and he took her with him. In the past, Kings used to marry many times—anyone passing by might become a Queen! If a woman was very beautiful, no matter where she was from, a King could just bear her off.

When she went off with the King, there was a huge commotion. "So and so's daughter was taken by the King! The King took her. He took her, he took her. . . ." She was installed in his inner courtyards.

The stepmother's girl remained at home. Who knows how many days passed before the stepmother sent the Brahman to fetch the girl: "Even if she's gone to the King's house, we must keep meeting her, it's not as though we can't. Bring her back for a visit." This mother and daughter hadn't cared a whit about her before, but now this is what they wanted. So then the Brahman brought her home for a visit.[1]

The daughter came home. She brought along masses of gold and silver and all the finest things. She brought all of them many gifts too. She showed them respect and devotedly looked after them all, even her stepmother. She did this even though she had become a Queen.

She stayed there for a few days, and when she was preparing to return, the stepmother said, "Come, let me braid your hair for you." And she rammed a nail into the girl's head.

When the nail was rammed into her head, the girl became a bird. She flew away. The stepmother used all those clothes, those jewels, to dress up her own daughter, and she sent her to the King instead.

So the second daughter went to the King.

Now there was probably a tree, a tall tree, beside the King's palace. The girl who had become a bird flew there and perched on a branch of the tree. From there she sang:

tilkā sundar ḍāle ḍāl	Fair with freckles,
	hops from branch to branch,
charḍubotan rāje pās	Thick as four washing sticks,
	is in with the King.
fiṭe mūnh mātre tain kī kittā!	Fie on you, stepmother, for what
	you've done![2]

That's it. So for many days the King kept hearing this song. She'd sit on the branch and keep singing it. [*Urmilaji repeats the song and explains the meaning of the names.*]

The King was baffled. Everyday, she'd come settle on a branch near him to sing this. The King kept listening. He listened for several days. Then he said to his Minister, "Look, a bird comes and sits on this tree. It says this and that."

"I'll listen to it," said the Minister. So the Minister listened, everyone listened.

Then the King gave the order that this bird should be caught: "Catch this bird!" His servants set about catching it. Once they had caught it they somehow managed to put it in a cage.

Even then, she would sing this song [*Urmilaji repeats it yet again*].

That's it. The King would pet and stroke the bird [*Urmilaji demonstrates, cupping her palm in a smoothing action*]. One day when he had the bird in his hands, and was petting it, he happened to pull out the nail.

The nail came out and she became herself! The King had no idea that the sister had replaced her. He said, "Where did you come from, and where is the other one?"

Then she told him her story. "I told you that I have a stepmother. When I went there this is what she did: She stuck a nail into me and made me into a bird."

So then the King crushed the stepmother in an oilpresser. He had her daughter bricked up in a wall. And he made this girl his Chief Queen.[3]

❀ ❀ ❀

"What happened?" asked Sello, who had reappeared with tea and perched on the threshold at the end of the tale. Rama repeated the fate of the stepmother and her daughter. "Good gracious! *Hay vo!*" exclaimed Sello, rolling her large eyes. Her mother, still smiling a little, returned to counting stitches on the brown sweater taking shape in her hands.

"And where did you learn this?" I asked.

"This . . . ," began Urmilaji, "well, we used to sit together, we sisters, when we were small. I don't remember, we were all small. Maybe a sister told it, maybe it was a grandmother or someone. I heard all kinds of stories, but I don't remember them all. Certain stories that were told stay in my mind. Someone's words, and later I recall them—this happens, then that happens. After that, it's learned!" She laughed.

Urmilaji later explained the King's inability to see the difference between his wife and her stepsister as a case of their looking alike. "She was probably just like her sister: healthy and well-built. This is probably how it happened."

By "healthy and well-built" (*tagṛi*) Urmilaji was drawing on the local ideal of beauty as well-rounded: voluptuous and plump. Weight, as I knew all too well, was usually equated with strength and health. The same sort of directness that Sello had used in asking me about fairness was present in women's evaluations of each other's bodily appearances. To my perpetual chagrin, I was always being judged as "thin and weak" (*kamjor*) for what in America might be construed as slenderness.

"Then too," Urmilaji continued, "in the past when a woman was brought in marriage, she wasn't seen. Now, someone is viewed first and then she's married. It wasn't like that in the past. In the past, until someone was married, they weren't seen. That's probably what happened. Sometimes, one girl would be engaged and another girl would be sent in marriage." She paused, smiling, to add, "Now, everyone wants to see each other before a wedding: a boy wants to see a girl, a girl wants to see a boy!"

As the folklorists Stith Thompson and Warren Roberts have remarked on this tale type, "stories dealing with the Substituted Bride theme are very common in India and show a great variety in their treatment of the theme."[4] Though the King in this story chose the girl after seeing her in the field, Urmilaji's comment does make it clear why such stories would catch people's imagination in situations involving an arranged marriage with a heavily veiled bride. In Kangra, a bride and groom are allowed a glimpse of each other under cover of a scarf thrown over their heads soon after he arrives. Through the rest of the wedding, though, the bride resembles a red tent, so swathed that a female relative must lead her around so she doesn't fall: She could be anybody. Today, the theme of a substituted bride is also played out through urban legends featuring photographs: one picture was sent, another bride (or groom) substituted.

As I had learned almost a decade earlier when doing research on women's wedding songs, the metaphor of girl as bird is well established in Kangra and elsewhere in North India where village exogamy is practiced.[5] Song after song likened girls of the same age to birds who ate seeds provided in their father's courtyards and then with marriage all flew to different lands. In this story, though, the girl has already been married when she is turned into a bird: it is a second departure for her husband's home, but in a different form. It is only when the husband has shown her affection in the form of stroking and petting her that she is transformed back into a woman and they embark on a deeper level of mutual recognition. The King could not have paid very close attention to this wife if he never even noticed that she had been substituted; however, feeling affection for her bird form (that perhaps stands for a husband sympathizing with his wife's having been wrenched from her home of birth), he strokes her, breaks the enchantment,[6] and apprehends her true form. This story, then, follows the pattern of women's tales described by A. K. Ramanujan as starting with a marriage, continuing with a separation between spouses, and ending with a reunion with a renewed commitment.[7]

"This story is about the ways of a stepmother," Urmilaji informed me.

"That's why they say that stepmothers are bad. Even the good ones are bad. Somehow their habits had to be described."

The "habits" here had to do with systematically mistreating children of a different marriage while favoring their own children. To guard against this, many older Kangra women I knew who had been married to widowers were enjoined to wear amulets known as "cowife" (*saukan*) which protected a new wife from the wrath of the deceased spirit and proclaimed her identity as the same. "So you will treat her children as your own," said one older Brahman woman who had worn such an amulet through the early years of raising her husband's three sons from a previous marriage.

"It's about the bad habits of stepmothers," repeated Urmilaji. "That stepmothers shouldn't be like this."

"Or they'll be punished?" I inquired.

"That they shouldn't be like this," Urmilaji vehemently shook her head.

TWENTY-ONE

The Girl Who Went on Quests

When the last story was done, I turned to Rama and inquired, "So, when you were little you used to hear these stories from your mother? In the evenings? Did this make you happy? Tell me what it was like."

"Tell her," urged Urmilaji. "Tell her how we used to sit together in the evenings, how we used to sit together for the Five Days of Fasting."

"We used to sit together," said Rama. "We'd sit together at night. Grandmother would tell some stories, Mummy would tell others. Everyone gathered together. Sometimes it was a festival like the Five Days of Fasting, with stories for each day. We were little, we were eager to hear stories."

"I've remembered another story too," Urmilaji broke in to say. "I've remembered another story that my daughter has pulled out for me! Put the tape on."[1]

❊ ❊ ❊

There were five brothers. They had one sister. Just one sister. That's it. Their mother had died. Each one of the five brothers had married when his turn came,[2] and five sisters-in-law came to the house. Then all five of the brothers went off to work elsewhere. They went off, leaving their sister with the sisters-in-law.

"This is our little sister," they said. "Look after her."

But the sisters-in-law plotted how to kill their husband's sister. One sister-in-law said to her, "Bring me the nose-ring of a demoness. I have a terrible pain in my stomach. I'll only be cured if you bring me the nose-ring of a demoness."

[*"She wanted Hira-kuri, the Diamond Girl, to bring it," prompts Rama. Urmilaji explains, "Diamond Girl is the sister's name."*]

"If you bring a demoness's nose-ring and I put this on, this will make the stomachache go away. Otherwise it won't get better."

So she went off, poor thing, to find a demoness. Now demons, you know, eat people. She walked and she walked, all the way to the land of demons.

200

When she got there, the demoness said, "Human beings, human beings: I smell a human being!"

Then the Diamond girl addressed the demoness. She sang:

panjā bhābhiyān	Five sisters-in-law
samitā kittā nī	plotted together
hīrā kuṛi	that the Diamond Girl
kaṛi lāiyān	be thrown out.
ik nī mangiyā	One ordered
rākshas bālu nī	the nose-ring of a demoness.
dūye mangiyā	The second ordered
singhi dudh nī	milk from a lioness.
triye mangiyā	The third ordered
samundar jhag nī	foam from the ocean.
chautiye mangiyā	The fourth ordered
bālu ret nī	a nose-ring of sand
panchiye boliye	The fifth said,

[*Urmilaji switches from singing to declaim*]

hīrā kuṛi rāje rahangi	Diamond Girl if you survive,
tā kamal phul lei āyā	then bring me a lotus!

The demoness felt distressed on behalf of the poor girl. She took off her nose-ring and gave it to the girl. The girl took it home and gave it to her sister-in-law, who put it on.

Then the second one said, "I've got a pain in my stomach."

Diamond Girl asked, "What will cure your stomachache?"

"If you bring me a lioness's milk and I drink this as medicine, I'll be cured."

So once again, she set out, poor thing. She walked and she walked, and finally she spied a lioness. She went up to the lioness. She was really scared, poor thing, as she went before the lioness. Then she sang her the same song [*Urmilaji sings it again*].

Then the lioness too felt compassion and gave her milk to the girl. She took it home.

Then the third one began to say, "I want foam from the ocean."

So she went off once more, and everything happened as before, and she brought the foam home.

Then the fourth asked for a nose-ring of sand from the sea shore.

[*"A nose-ring?" I ask. "Of sand," Urmilaji assures, "sand like you get on a riverbank." "What did they want this ring of sand for?" I ask. "Nothing other than killing the girl!" Urmilaji patiently states.*]

201

So she went off, poor thing, it took her three months to come and go all the way to the sea. And she brought back this nose-ring of sand too.

Then the fifth one said, "Now I want a lotus flower."

A lotus flower was only to be found at some distance. She went off there, poor thing. Just as she was plucking the flower, her youngest brother came by, on leave from his job. Actually, all five of them had been let off on leave.

The youngest brother watched from afar, saying, "That girl who's plucking the lotus flower, she looks like our Diamond sister."

The second one probably said, "How would Diamond ever get out here in the jungle? This far?"

So, talking among themselves, they proceeded ahead, and said, "How could she be here? No! It is her!"

They came up beside her. Then they asked, "What brings you to this place? Why are you here?"

And she sang:

panjā bhābhiyān	Five sisters-in-law
samitā kittā ni	plotted together
hirā kuri	that the Diamond Girl
kari lāiyān	be thrown out.
ik nī mangiyā	One ordered
rākshas bālu nī	the nose-ring of a demoness.
dūye mangiyā	The second ordered
singhi dudh nī	milk from a lioness.
triye mangiyā	The third ordered
samundar jhag ni	foam from the ocean.
chautiye mangiyā	The fourth ordered
bālu ret nī	a nose-ring of sand
panchiye boliye	The fifth said,

[*speaking, not singing*]

hirā kuri rāje rahangi	Diamond Girl if you survive,
amal phul lei āyā	then bring me a lotus!

"They thought that I wouldn't survive. Who ever survives a demoness? A lion? Who ever finds foam or a nose-ring of sand?"

Then the brothers put her in a palanquin and they brought her home. They arrived, set down the palanquin outside the door, and asked, "Where is our sister?"

The sisters-in-law began to mix truth and lies: "She lives at a distance, she lives in the fields...."

Then they brought their sister out from the palanquin. After this, four brothers killed their wives, bricking them up in pillars. The fifth began to strike his wife, but his sister stopped him, saying, "She didn't order me in the same way as the others. All she said was that if I lived, I should bring her a lotus."

So then the two of them, the husband's sister and the brother's wife, began to live together happily.

❊ ❊ ❊

"This too is very beautiful," I said as Urmilaji finished.

Urmilaji smiled, glancing at her daughters. "To you all my stories are beautiful!" she teased.

"No, really . . . ," I began, feeling as though I'd been caught out. Admittedly, the song giving away all the quests early on in the story had not made for as much suspense as some of the tales Urmilaji told. Also, I had been disturbed by the theme in this story of women, related through marriage and in competition for the affections of the same men, being so murderously hostile toward one other. I had, though, genuinely enjoyed the image of a young girl out performing deeds of valor—fearlessly approaching a demoness, a lioness, or taking a three-month trip to the ocean. Having been chastised so heartily in Kangra for remaining unmarried, I was especially glad to see that no mention was made of Diamond Girl's marriage!

At the time that Urmilaji told the story, we did not discuss it further. Rather, Urmilaji moved on to more general reminiscences about storytelling. It was only the following year that we got to back to the tale.

"The five sisters-in-law wanted to get rid of the sister so they could live there themselves," Urmilaji said. Just mentioning the story made her sing the couplet again, and she went through the various ways that they had tried to get rid of her.

The rivalry between a brother's sister and a husband's wife was a familiar theme in the many Kangra songs I had heard. From a sister's point of view, tension resides in being packed off to another home while upstart wives born elsewhere take over the household that has been hers from birth. (In wedding rites, this is played out when a groom's sisters physically block the door, preventing a new bride from entering, until they are bribed with money). From a wife's point of view, tension resides in being an outsider who must prove herself through hard work while the daughters of the family are treated with indulgence both before marriage and during their visits home after marriage. Furthermore, the openly displayed and culturally sanctioned affection between brother and sister is in marked contrast to the demure public avoidance practiced by husband and wife. Also, a man's responsibilities to the children of his sister are emphasized during all of the children's life-cycle rituals, making for added expenses that a wife could see as detracting from the funds available for her own children. Small wonder then that the women related as sisters-in-law through one man were thought to view each other with uneasy ambivalence if not outright hostility.

The mother of the five brothers, as mother-in-law, could perhaps have kept a check on the malicious actions of her daughters-in-law, but she was dead. The motif of the brothers going off to work is reminiscent of actual patterns of male migration in Kangra, where women of the family may be left to get along together. The end of the story reaffirms the centrality of the brother-sister relationship, with the brothers having no qualms about murdering their wives when it is revealed that they schemed against their sister. It is only the youngest wife who is spared, for having set an easier task for her husband's sister. At the end, the statement that these two lived together happily erases the presence of the linking brother and husband. This story, then, seems to act out the hostility between brother's wives and husband's sisters even as it instructs them to get along.

This is an adventure story of the sort that could not be played out in most Kangra women's lives. Diamond Girl is a plucky character who will set off on long journeys all by herself and who performs what seem like impossible deeds. She confronts a demoness, a lioness, and goes all the way to the far ocean. She appears to be blissfully unconcerned about modesty, reputation, or marriage. In this collection, she is the only female figure who has not at some point, been a wife. Perhaps it is this lack of attention to the more retiring qualities appropriate to a wife that allows Diamond Girl her valor. I like to hope that a quest narrative like this keeps alternate scenarios for fulfillment alive in women's imaginations even if, given the restrictions on women's movements and reputations, such adventures aren't usually possible.

A few weeks earlier, Urmilaji described how marriage could hamper a woman. In counterpoint to all the other women who clucked about my unmarried condition, Urmilaji had pointed out what she perceived as the advantage of my own career quests. "If you were married," she said, "you wouldn't be able to do the work that you do. You'd have to always be bringing your husband tea. When you sat down to write, he would call for tea. Every time you would try to write something, he'd want his tea. How would you ever do your work?"

While a man on a quest might trick or battle adversaries, Diamond Girl accomplishes what she desires by enlisting sympathy. She does not challenge: she sings plaintively of her woes. I asked Urmilaji why it was that the demoness and others gave the Diamond Girl what she requested: did they feel compassion?

"Compassion!" Urmilaji nodded. She sang the couplet, then asked, "Don't you feel compassion too when you hear it? Don't you think, 'Why would she be singing this, poor thing?'"

I thought back to the other stories that included sung couplets. In "The Two Gems" the father sings to God not to let such an event occur again, and later, a song in which both sets of families plead for the boy. In "The Astrologers' Treachery," the King forlornly sings to inquire of the astrologer from Kashi why he is shaking his head. In "Fair with Freckles" the girl turned bird sings of her plight, exiled on a branch while her sister is with the King, and blames the stepmother for this situation. Finally, Diamond Girl sings here of her sisters-in-law's harsh demands.

In all these cases, the song is a plea for help, for sympathy. It is only in the case of the corrupt astrologer from Kashi that the song has no effect. Otherwise, in each case, singing is a potent form of action, melting hearts and altering situations. I had thought that my project on Urmilaji's stories was a detour from my "real" research on songs, but it had brought me back full circle to the emotional force of songs.

When the story was done, Urmilaji returned to wider reminiscences. "If these stories weren't continuously told, would they still be with us today?" she inquired, her voice strong. "But these days, after eating and drinking, everyone immediately wants to go sit somewhere else. When is a story to be told—?"

"—Now everyone just watches television," Rama tried to get a word in edgewise.

"—In the old days, what would happen is that we'd eat and then go lie down together. We'd all stay awake. 'Tell a story, tell a story': These kids really used to bother me!" Eyes narrowed a little, a smile puckered around her closed mouth, Urmilaji swiveled her head slowly from side to side.

"Really!" I laughed, for though she said she was bothered, she seemed to be looking back into a circle of happy memories. "And did children from other homes also come over sometimes?" I asked, trying to imagine what these sessions were like. "Your mother knows so many stories," I said to Rama.

"Oh yes," agreed Rama.

"Ummmmmm," Urmilaji affirmed with a nod. "So many used to assemble! But it isn't just a matter of children. My sister from Pattiar, my elder sister— you met her the other day. When her husband was sick, he was unable to fall asleep. So he too requested: 'Now you must give me stories.' He was ill, and so I went to them. 'Now you must give me stories,' he said. I gave him many stories too."

"Was it that you told your sister the stories and then she . . . ?" I began.

"No-oo! We used to light a charcoal burner and sit together. It was winter then. And my brother-in-law would say, 'Tell us some stories.' So I would give stories."

"I see," I said, moved that the stories I had heard had been able to divert someone who was in pain; delighted that I had testimony of this sort on tape.

Urmilaji continued, "In the past, when the Five Days of Fasting came around, women would get together and tell stories. Even now, when we go to float the lamps we walk together, and one woman says to another, 'Dear, let's hear a story.' When a Monday on the dark night of the moon rolls around, even then it's the same, 'Dear, give us a story.' "

"They all know that you're the one who tells the stories," I said. "And so it's 'give' and not just 'tell.' "

"Ummm . . . ," Urmilaji was still smiling to herself.

This was the last story that Urmilaji told me in 1991. The following day, I broke the rhythm of packing and came to say my good-byes. Urmilaji was not in the now familiar courtyard, nor in the outer rooms. "She's in bed," murmured Sello, who came out when I called from the doorway. Urmilaji stood up when I arrived, her shoulders bent, her hair uncombed. She was in a worn brown outfit with full-length sleeves and a square neck. She embraced me, her eyes glistening. Then we sat side by side on the bed.

"I am going to be so sad when you are gone," Urmilaji murmured, pressing my hand between her palms. "It's already starting. We have told each other the innermost secrets of our hearts. To me, you're one in a million."

With her two daughters looking on, she presented me with a small packet of waṛī, a local specialty made from the dried stem of a large-leafed plant and coated with spiced flour from lentils. She had prepared these waṛī herself, she said. They were for me to cook in America. "I've never cooked waṛī," I confessed. Urmilaji then led me through a recipe, starting from the heating of oil and the chopping of onions.

Urmilaji also drew out a bulky package wrapped in newspaper and put it in my hands. Sello and Rama looked on expectantly as I undid the wrapping, embarrassed. Inside was a soft, unbleached white shawl, woven by a local weaver from the wool Urmilaji had cleaned, carded, and spun, afternoon upon afternoon as we talked, mostly from her own ram's fleece. She had often told or talked about stories as she worked on this wool. Accepting this shawl, and with it the labor of uncountable hours, I felt as though I was being sent off in a mantle of soft, warming affection.

Flanked by her eldest and her youngest daughter, Urmilaji walked me partway along the cobbled path home. It was growing dark. Fireflies bobbed madly in the thickness of cricket calls rising from the fields. We paused beside a stream rippling through a tangle of aromatic mint. Showing the same generosity with which she had gifted these stories, Urmilaji showered upon me good wishes for my trip, my life, the success of every project. I assured her that I would indeed write and would try to be back soon.

"Good-bye," enunciated Rama in English.

"Bye bye," waved Sello.

Walking ahead toward the trip across continents, I looked back three times. Her daughters had turned to go home, but through the dusk, Urmilaji stood still, watching.

$$\boxed{\text{A F T E R W O R D}}$$

Back in Madison and browsing in the University of Wisconsin library, I come across a book called Indian Fairy Tales. *It is a small book, bound in indigo, with worn gold lettering on the cover. The author is Maive Stokes. This is one of a hundred copies privately printed in India in 1879. On the flyleaf an inscription in slanted, spidery writing runs:* "For my dear Maria from Maive, August 14 / 79. Simla." *Simla is a hill station, a place where the wives and daughters of British administrators were once dispatched to escape the summer heat. Today, Simla (or Shimla) continues to draw tourists. It is also the administrative center of Himachal Pradesh, the state in which Kangra is a district.*

I have returned to Madison with a thick sheaf of transcribed and translated stories from Urmilaji and am in the library trying to locate scholarly materials for the planned book. Indian Fairy Tales—*so tangibly linking Himachal Pradesh and Wisconsin—is a startling reminder that scholarship is not just a realm "out there." I wonder who Maive's friend Maria was, and how the Madison library came to own one of the privately printed copies instead of the edition released in 1880 by a British publisher.[1] There is a poignancy to standing in the library stacks holding the same compact volume that had been handed over by the author at least 112 years earlier.*

In undertaking Indian Fairy Tales, *Maive Stokes was following the precedent of another young woman in British India, Mary Frere. Mary Frere was the daughter of the Governor of Bombay. A decade earlier, in a best-selling book called* Old Deccan Days, *she had brought together the folktales of her nursemaid, Anna Liberata de Souza.[2] Maive Stokes was also the daughter of a British colonial administrator: Whitley Stokes, a jurist and Celtic scholar, based in Calcutta.[3] With her mother Mary's help, Maive Stokes compiled and translated thirty stories told to her in Hindustani by the family servants.*

207

I leaf through these stories, casually at first, but then with jolts of recognition. In the measured tones and small print of the pages I find: a devouring demoness who displaced her fellow queens, a King so severely afflicted that even his roasted fish flipped back into water, a Princess banished by her father because she loved him like salt! I discover: a newborn infant replaced with a stone, birds grateful when their chicks are saved from a serpent, a meditating holy man covered in grass. There is much unfamiliar material in the collection too, but it is the overlap with tales I have so recently heard from Urmilaji that sets my heart pumping and makes my fingers tremble.

✳ ✳ ✳

"They've remained there, settled and flourishing, and we've come home" is a formula with which some Kangra tellers end their tales. Saying that story characters are left behind, this formula underscores the imaginative distance traveled through the telling of a tale. Also, it marks a comfortable return, a sealing shut of concerns with those faraway characters. As I prepare to close down my own account of Urmilaji and her tales, I am reminded afresh that, unlike a fictional tale, an ethnography is about actual people whose lives are not settled, once and for all, at the end of an anthropologist's story. Even if their lives are momentarily trapped in time within the pages of an ethnography, real life moves inexorably forward. Similarly, a folktale collection is not just a closed set of texts, but rather a moment in the larger life of motifs, themes and plots that publication may perhaps spread further.

Through this book, I have kept close to the particularities of Urmilaji's stories and our interaction. In this afterword, my aim is to situate this project within wider issues while also retaining a narrative pace. I have three points to make. First, I emphasize the importance of giving tellers a greater role in folktale collections. Second, I reiterate the value of talking to storytellers about the meanings in their own tales, whether or not such consultations can hope to bring all dimensions of meaning to light. Third, I argue that looking more closely at the inequalities between the tellers and collectors of tales sheds light on social processes that are marginalizing folktales. Weaving through all this is my conviction that orally told stories are part of lives: emerging within relationships with other people, stories speak about relationships and their telling has an effect on relationships.

Tales And Tellers

Just as my own mother inspired my work with Urmilaji, Mary Stokes also helped with her daughter's book. In the preface to Indian Fairy Tales, *Maive Stokes introduces her two nursemaid* ayahs: *Muniya, "a very old, white-haired woman" and*

Dunkni, "a young woman."⁴ But it is in her mother Mary Stokes notes at the end of the book that these storytelling ayahs come to life.

> *Old Muniya tells her stories with the solemn authoritative air of a professor. She sits quite still on the floor, and uses no gestures. Dunkni gets thoroughly excited over her tales, marches up and down the room, acting her stories, as it were. For instance, in describing the thickness of Mahadeo's hair in King Burtal's story, she put her two thumbs to her ears and spread out all her fingers from her head, saying, "His hair stood out like this." And in "Loving Laili," after moving her hand as if she were pulling the magic knife from her pocket and unfolding it, she swung her arm out at full length with great energy, and then she said, "Laili made one 'touch'" (here she brought back the edge of her hand to her own throat, "and the head fell off."⁵*

❀ ❀ ❀

Through the last two centuries, ever since the publication of Jacob and Wilhelm Grimm's classic, *Kinder-und Hausmärchen*, collections of oral stories have poured into print from different parts of the world.⁶ Often grouped by country or by region, such collections are staples on library shelves and in the upbringing of literate children. In the vast majority of collections, storytellers are not mentioned at all. Else, they are alluded to near the start of a book or in appended notes of the sort prepared by Mary Stokes.

Tales told orally have a self-contained beauty and can stand on their own terms in print, with or without the presence of a storyteller. Most readers coming upon folktales are most likely absorbed by the narratives themselves. Why then is it worth bothering about tellers? Since my views are clearly partisan, I will here weave an argument by following the threads of personal and intellectual history that led me to value stories as an aspect of interaction with spirited storytellers.

As a child in Bombay, I consumed both oral and written stories of all sorts. I also wrote stories about imagined events. But it was my education in the United States that made for an analytic distance, transforming what was familiar into something strange and marvellous to record. After I first encountered anthropology and folklore at Sarah Lawrence College, my background became replete with interesting things to document. During visits home, I wrote down beliefs, recipes, customs, colorful turns of phrase, songs, and especially stories. I took notes as my Grandmother Ba narrated the legend of her husband's grandfather, Khimji the Devotee, who miraculously caused millet to grow amid a Kutch drought; as my family's friend Swamiji told how Hindus and Muslims were created as brothers; as a schoolmate from Kerala's father described a man who was convinced he had swallowed a lizard. Later, while the spoken idiosyncrasies were still lingering in my ears, I wrote up these and other stories in English.

Even then, as I looked through the texts, they seemed strangely bare. Where in these stories was Ba with her white sari, her emphatic, nasal tone, the fine-boned delicacy of her tattooed, gesturing wrists? Where was Swamiji with the low, rumbling kindness of his voice; the curve of his lips as he smiled, holding in tobacco juice; the laughter that shook his body? Where was my friend's father with his loud sniffs and straight-faced fizz of humor, pacing briskly back and forth, a white *lungi* wrapped around his waist and a towel over one shoulder? I could see that these stories I had written out were compelling in and of themselves, but that my renditions were strangely stripped of tellers and the settings in which the stories were told. [7]

It wasn't until graduate school at the University of California at Berkeley that I encountered theoretical positions that helped me articulate what was missing in my attempts to reproduce stories. My first year of graduate school I enrolled in classes with Alan Dundes, an internationally renowned folklorist of great charisma, generosity, and rigor.[8] Under Professor Dundes's guidance, I came across Bronislaw Malinowski's classic work arguing for the contextualization of folklore texts. Malinowski put my inchoate unease into sharp words: "The stories live in native life and not on paper, and when a scholar jots them down without being able to evoke the atmosphere in which they flourish he has given us but a mutilated bit of reality."[9] I learned that this early insight had been expanded in the 1970s into what is known as the "performance-oriented approach." Most elegantly encapsulated in Richard Bauman's *Verbal Art as Performance*,[10] the performance-oriented approach emphasizes that folklore texts emerge through creative performance in specific, situated contexts. Continuing my reading, I discovered that earlier work by Russian and European scholars also emphasized narrators as complex, creative beings. For example, in *A Siberian Tale Teller*, the Russian folklorist Mark Azadovskii argued that not just a narrator's personality, but also a narrator's artistry should be examined in folktale research.[11] Similarly, Linda Dégh's *Folktales and Society* made previous East European literature on narrators available to English readers while also providing memorable portraits of Hungarian storytellers from her own field research.[12] The Finnish folklorist Juha Pentikäinen's *Oral Repertoire and World View* ingeniously combined the study of one Karelian woman's life history, her folklore repertoire, and her world view.[13]

Though these scholarly books reunited texts and tellers, I remained unsatisfied. In the cases where storytellers emerged as vivid, memorable characters, it seemed that their repertoire of stories ended up being alluded to just by title, in fragments, or in outline. What scholars might have learned about the art of storytelling also did not appear to transfer into the structure of their own books. I was excited when I finally encountered the literary flair of Marcel Griaule's *Conversations with Ogotemmêli*,[14] a book that integrated complete oral stories into a larger story about the storyteller and his interactions with the ethnographer.[15]

Ogotemmêli, a Dogon elder from West Africa, interpreted the myths he told Marcel Griaule. This method of allowing tale tellers to actively direct interpretation was one that Linda Dégh also mentioned in passing in her preface to

Folktales and Society,[16] and which Dennis Tedlock wove into some of the path-breaking essays in *The Spoken Word and the Work of Translation*.[17] It was also a method emphasized by Alan Dundes. Professor Dundes called the elicitation of people's commentaries on their folklore "oral literary criticism."[18] He insisted that students collecting folklore items for his classes ask the people who shared these materials what meanings they themselves saw.

For anthropologists, the early to mid-1980s brought a widespread critique of the power relations embedded within modes of ethnographic writing.[19] I became especially inspired by "dialogical anthropology," a methodological and theoretical position that emphasizes how anthropologists actively construct ethnographic knowledge through the give and take of dialogue within particular, power-infused contexts.[20] I also encountered literary theories regarding reader response or reception.[21] The insistence that texts are not communicated as discreet packages of meaning, but are refashioned by audiences seemed to apply well to a multiplicity of points of view about cultural productions which, in ethnographic writing emphasizing a generalized subject, could all too often be flattened out.

Steeped in all this scholarship, I returned to India as a graduate student to work more with stories. I went back to Swamiji, the old holy man whose stories I had earlier been recording. In the mid-1980s, Swamiji lived in Nasik, my father's home town. He usually lay in a deck chair, bemusedly meeting the visitors and devotees who sought his audience, blessings, and advice. I sat with my tape recorder on the floor nearby, especially alert for the moments that his advice took the form of folk narratives. Whenever possible, I tried to learn Swamiji's or his listeners' interpretations of his stories. In my dissertation, which became *Storytellers, Saints, and Scoundrels*,[22] I presented eight of these tales within an interlinked set of larger, framing stories. I argued that oral stories are a powerful medium for religious teaching, partly because the ambiguous, multifaceted nature of narrative allows listeners, who hear the tales recast by a religious teacher, to find not just ultimate meanings, but also particularized, personal ones.

When this book was published, I returned to an earlier interest in women's folklore in Kangra and began to read more feminist writings in anthropology and folklore. In particular, I was inspired by work that emphasized the value of recording the often silenced voices of women in different societies, the power of cultural forms in shaping gendered subjectivities, the growing awareness that gender relations are themselves intersected by other relations of power, and the strategy of drawing on personal experience to think theoretically.[23]

All this was in my head, then, when I met Urmilaji. I came to her with the conviction that it was necessary to view the people about whom anthropologists write as more than "informants" spouting data, but rather as friends, teachers, and possible collaborators. Appealing to Urmilaji as an authority on Kangra folklore, I was following not just my own ideas, but also the lead of other women who viewed Urmilaji as the right person to consult for esoteric knowledge. This deferential focus meant that I came to know Urmilaji well. But our close one-on-one interaction seemed to preclude intensively involving the people around her and learning what *they* made of particular stories. (When I tried with Sello, for example, she shrugged, saying, "Ask Mummy.") Fortunately, I had the chance to observe Urmilaji retelling ritual tales in 1994, and to overhear some of the vigorous discussions generated among her listeners.

While I was in Kangra, I also began to tape women's life stories,[24] an enterprise which at first glance seemed to shift the balance of my research from shared to personal stories. I was already aware of a growing interdisciplinary literature on narrative as the medium through which human beings make sense of experience.[25] Individuals across the world appear to relate noteworthy events through stories, though what is considered noteworthy and the form narrations take transcend the personal and are culturally based. Closer examination reveals that even the seemingly most individualized story, that of a life, usually surfaces in culturally informed idioms.[26] At the same time, folktales and other narratives that appear to be collective—cultural rather than personal "autobiography"[27]— find vitality through an interaction with the lives of tellers. The cultural stories that people choose to retell with care are after all, part of their lives. It is no surprise that within the framework of life histories, more widely shared oral narratives—myths, legends, and folktales—are also often slipped in.[28]

Through the months I kept asking Urmilaji to let me record her life story. She eventually did tell me about her life, but she did not think it appropriate to disclose her life within this book. This means that I cannot illustrate my observation that these folktales cover some of the same emotional terrain as her life. In any lifetime, after all, a person hears many stories. But only a fraction are likely to be remembered and retold. A repertoire is a choice selection, assembled by chance, by occasions for repeated hearing, by aesthetic predilection, and by themes compelling to the teller. As a selective corpus lodged inside a mind and shaped by a sensibility, the tales in a person's repertoire relate to each other: they comment on, disagree with, and extend discussion on interrelated themes. Some of these themes pervaded not just Urmilaji's life but the experiences of other upper-caste Kangra village women of her generation. Also, in retelling other stories that were not centrally about women's experience, Urmilaji recast the tales to highlight a woman's perspective.[29] Contained in these stories, then, was personalized cultural wisdom that had oriented Urmilaji through the course of her life. These stories were clearly part of Urmilaji, part of what her life added up to.

At one point, Urmilaji mentioned that folktales taught about different kinds of love: deluded infatuation, possessive attachment, and nurturing affection. At another time, she said that by singing songs and telling stories, one came to understand suffering, and so gained a little peace. As she emphasized, "Yes, peace arises. Whatever happens in your life, you can remember these things [songs and stories]."

Framed by a Hindu vision that attachments inevitably bring pain, the two statements are not incompatible. Together, they yield an insight that I believe transcends the particulars of Urmilaji's social and cultural milieu. The stories, after all, are about human relationships: close and nurturing, distant and cruel. In providing a metaphorical lens to reflect on relationships between different sorts of people, folktales provide an arena of reflection outside the hurdy-gurdy of complex ongoing interactions. Providing insight into human motivations, such stories can yield a detachment and with that detachment a sense that predicaments are not just personal, but shared by others too.[30] As Urmilaji said, speaking of a relentlessly difficult period in her life, "I went through hard hard times, like the King and Queen who were accused of stealing the necklace that the peacock had eaten up." Or, as she said about the conflict between Krishna's mother and wife, "When you know that this sort of thing could happen in God's house too, it brings peace to your mind."

Since my return from Kangra, I have learned of other anthropologists who are also trying to work out what we hope will be more collaborative fieldwork relationships, and more mutually acceptable ethnographic products. The methodologies involved are being pioneered within the field of life history, which has always been characterized by an intense interaction between the anthropologist and the "subject."[31] In addition, folklorists are also working closely with single storytellers.[32] In the radical case of a collection of tales from South Africa, Harold Scheub has relinquished authorship to the woman who shared her stories, Mrs. Zenani billing himself as just the editor.[33]

The Spoken and the Unspoken

The notes prepared by Mary Stokes for Indian Fairy Tales *include some dialogues with the storytellers. Sometimes, the* ayahs *tell new versions of the stories they have already told. At other times, they issue commentary: "Dunkni says, 'All Rakshases keep their souls in birds,' "[34] "Muniya says that telling the prince he would marry a Bel-Princess was equivalent to saying he would not marry at all"[35] "Muniya sends her hero for a Garpank's feather. . . . She sent us to see a statue of a garpank that stood over a gateway in a street in Calcutta, which might be that of an eagle or of a huge hawk."[36]*

❀ ❀ ❀

I thought I was doing something very sensible, indeed self-evident, in asking Urmilaji questions about her stories. But when I told my colleague at Madison, Narayana Rao, about my project of eliciting interpretations from Urmilaji and other women I worked with in Kangra, he exclaimed with animated humor, "To ask people about meanings in their folklore is like trying to shine a flash-light into the dark, saying, 'Is this darkness?!'"

This analogy took the wind right out of my sails. Was I really being so silly as to brandish a light to explore darkness? I could see the sense in Narayana Rao's position that as a collective symbolic form, folklore's function is to express the culturally inexpressible. Folklore in this scheme is a sanctioned outlet for taboo frustrations and desires;[37] it enables people, particularly powerless people, to use veiled meanings and the cover of tradition to speak about what they are not supposed to say, do, or possibly even think. As Narayana Rao said, "You see, people may need masks to talk about certain feelings."

In Kangra too, people were well aware of the value of indirect speech. A proverb I often heard ran "Tell a daughter for a daughter-in-law to hear" (*dhiye jo kahanā nue jo sunānā*), indicating that criticisms could be spoken directly only to certain people, for example, a daughter with whom one is comfortable instead of a daughter-in-law, with whom relations could be strained. Or as a Kangra schoolteacher once said to me, "Kirinji. The person who becomes a singer or storyteller is one with a lot of pain. She wants a way to express the pain. There are some things that you can't say directly, but you can say them in this form. Songs and stories become her form of solace."

I certainly agree that shared symbolic forms can be used as masks through which people address themselves and each other about sensitive issues. Urmilaji's stories seemed to speak to emotional issues in the joint family (with the ideal of solidarity) and in intercaste relations (with the ideal of separation) which are unlikely to be elaborated in everyday conversation. These taboo emotions included: ambivalence toward mothers; anger toward fathers; competition between sisters; the shadow of a son's mother looming over sexual relations with his wife; pious women's resentment of mocking, nonobservant husbands; and women's chafing against the rigid constraints set on their appetites. Also embedded in these stories was a distrust of honored family priests and the clear possibility of liaisons across caste boundaries.

Yet, I would maintain that there is a danger to seeing folklore as expressing only the inexpressible, particularly in crosscultural research. Such a position may lead a scholar looking in from the outside to presume that he or she is better equipped to point out meanings in folktales than the people who actually live with the stories. It is also useful to consider more closely the different reasons that people may adopt symbolic masks. They may find symbolic forms safer than direct speech on account of unconscious conflicts and associations. But, equally, drawing on folktales may have the political motive of deflecting personal responsibility for subversive commentary through the use of collective, anonymous symbolic forms.[38] In addition, the storyteller's relationship to a researcher may render certain topics inappropriate for direct discussion.[39] What

214

is unspoken but mutually recognized is, in all these cases, a powerful social force.

Though I readily accept that there are powerful, concealed meanings in folktales, I would continue to insist that there are layers of articulable—and locally articulated—cultural insights that we would do well to elicit from both tellers and listeners. Folklore, I believe, is not just about shadowy darkness; it also speaks to the contours of lived or remembered experience, which may be illuminated by dialogue.

Imagine that I had simply borne off these twenty-one stories from Urmilaji without ever talking to her about them. It is unlikely that of my own accord I could have developed some of the themes she uncovered in our conversations: the distinction between household work and ritual work; the centrality of honor and shame to the actions of characters; the force of a woman's married destiny directing even the actions of gods. I would never have known that flies possessed the regenerative liquid with which Sunna the Washerwoman brought people to life, that children were likened to hopping frogs, that demons who drink blood had been updated by terrorists. I also would have had little sense of how Urmilaji associated these tales with tellers she loved, her Chachu and her Tayi Sas.

Asking questions, there is always the risk of imposing one's own communicative norms—ways of speaking, issues worth discussing—on other people to whom such questions don't make sense.[40] Urmilaji occasionally seemed puzzled by a question and at least once, in the case of "The Two Gems" it was clearly my repeated queries on the mechanics of rebirth that led her to rationalize the story as having occurred in the span of one life rather than successive ones. As she said, "Sometimes, when you ask me, the meaning comes to me in a flash. But other times, I too wonder: the meaning, the meaning, what could the meaning be?"

Aware that I could be forcing meanings into form, I tried to be deferential. If Urmilaji wanted to elaborate, I would follow, and if she preferred to dismiss a question, I did not press. I also held back from interrogating Urmilaji about issues that I sensed would be awkward, for example, my hunches about the possible innuendos surrounding daggers, animal grooms, or rocking swings. Perhaps I was too meek a fieldworker and should have been more diligent about ferreting silences into speech. But this was neither my personal style, nor Urmilaji's. I cared too much about our relationship to risk a rupture by behaving in a manner that might be construed as inappropriate or disrespectful.

The stories for which meanings came to Urmilaji "in a flash" were the ones associated with women's rituals. These ritual stories seemed best suited to exegesis since they so overtly contained a didactic element and had symbolic contents that spilled over into the ritual at hand. Urmilaji expanded with ease on the symbolic elements in these women's stories: the taboos of touching cotton, the deferred sweetness in sour berries, the floating of little boats. Her interpretations were largely along the lines of ritual practice, exemplary moral behavior, and joint family life in the past. Told among women auspiciously bathed, combed, and bedecked for ritual performance—under a tree, beside the river, indoors beside lamps or clay images—the stories also seemed to have an ordered, illuminated exterior. At the same time, the stories were inwardly lit by the powerful mysteries of divine will and human fate.

For the tales associated with winter's nights, Urmilaji had fewer commentaries. When I asked about particular stories, she would usually just retell them. The meaning, she seemed to say, was in the practice of sharing the story with absorption rather than in musing upon it from outside. It was as though these entertaining stories existed in the dreamlike, flickering light and shadows of a group gathered randomly around a fire at night; they did not seem to have a place under the glare of electric bulbs or my questions. Yet, even when Urmilaji retold these stories she usually told them a little differently, talking about episodes, motivations, and rationales in a new light, and so she helped me understand them better. For these stories, as with the others, she often emphasized a historical slant, explaining how certain practices described in the tales related to Kangra's past.

Many of Urmilaji's asides about particular practices, their value, or their historical significance, were clear cases of her cuing me in, of drawing me closer in from the border of outsiderhood at which I wavered. After all, oral stories find their form in interaction with a particular audience. Urmilaji's telling me these stories entailed not just my entertainment, but my education. I doubt that she would have made such asides if she was telling the stories to her own daughters who had already been raised with the appropriate contextual knowledge. It seems clear that as semi-socialized outsiders, researchers are more likely than local listeners to be issued interpretations of stories both through spontaneous asides and through elicited commentary.

It is useful then, to move beyond a polarization between dark and light; between deep, silenced unconscious meanings and rational, articulated conscious ones. We need to think instead in terms of layers shading into each other and needing each other. Some meanings are sensed implicitly through images, structures, and juxtapositions. Some meanings are tacitly understood by insiders. Some meanings are highlighted by particular social positions or life experience, and are explicitly spelled out. Throw in an anthropologist or folklorist and meanings emerge in dialogue with them as semisocialized outsiders. Scholars also bring meanings that derive from theoretical frameworks assembled in distant places, or from their own backgrounds. As I've found while retelling these stories to friends, sending stories out toward new audiences adds new dimensions of meaning that neither Urmilaji nor I anticipated. Rather than my having the light and Urmilaji's folktales having the darkness, I would prefer to think of us both as sharing shadow and illumination, each in our own way.

Translations and Transformations

In the preface to Indian Fairy Tales, *Maive Stokes reports the growing confidence of her storytelling ayahs.*

> *At first the servants would only tell their stories to me, because I was a child and would not laugh at them, but afterwards the Ayahs lost their shyness and told almost all their stories over again to Mother when they were passing through the press.... The stories were all told in Hindustani, which is the only language that these servants know.*[41]

In the notes, Mary Stokes reveals more about Dunkni and Muniya's authoritative involvement in the making of the book:

> *All these stories were read back in Hindustani by my little girl at the time of telling, and nearly all a second time by me this winter before printing. I never saw people more anxious to have their tales retold exactly than are Dunkni and Muniya. Not till each tale was pronounced by them to be ṭīk (exact) was it sent to the press*[42]

✺ ✺ ✺

Urmilaji sometimes mused on the differences between us. As she had said, speaking about our earliest encounters, "You seemed like such big people. I thought: What can we say to each other? I felt shy to speak." But as we grew closer, she commented with some wonder that we had found common ground. For example, in 1994, when I brought the news that a publisher was interested in this book, Urmilaji broke into a smile. "It was in God's hands that our minds met," she said. "For so long we knew each other, but had nothing to say to each other. Then it was the right time." She pointed up with her index finger and raised her eyes skyward, as if invoking a cosmic director. "The stories that were sitting inside me came out for you and you were able to do something with them. Telling these stories, my time was filled and you did your work. All this was inside me, but how else would it have come out in this way? I am just an ignorant person."

These comments point to Urmilaji's belief that a divine will threads through life, as through stories, and that events are ordered through an unfolding of the appropriate time. Urmilaji also acknowledged that we came to this project with different interests: she had her own motives, and only for me were her stories "work." In calling herself an "ignorant person" with characteristic humility,

217

Kirin and Urmilaji, 1994 (*Photo by Eytan Bercovitch*)

Urmilaji underscored the differences in our educational background and enablement.

While I am a person of mixed ancestry whom Maive and Mary Stokes surely would not have invited to tea, I, like them, am a product of British-accented education and all the attendant class privileges. Even when collectors of folktales are from the same cultural region as the tellers of stories, collectors invariably have a different class background, educational advantages, and geographical mobility.

Translating Urmilaji's stories, I bear cultural goods from a geographically, economically, and culturally marginalized region into the metropolitan world. In Kangra of the 1990s, goods, technologies, ideologies, media images, and people seep in from urban centers in India and the West.[43] Old cobbled paths in Kangra are smoothed over with cement; children in school learn to think in languages different from the dialect used at home; farmers purchase hybrid seeds that need chemical fertilizers, setting aside small corners of fields for the better-loved, lower-yielding local varieties of rice. Men and women wear synthetic mill cloth as spinning wheels gather dust in attics; dowries include pressure cookers, table fans, radios, and televisions from "good companies," that is, multinationals. Amid this relentless flooding in of the outside, bringing something from a Kangra village out into the metropolitan world seems like a small ripple of reverse flow.

Ironically, even as an out-of-the-way place like Kangra becomes another market for capitalist commodities, so too, metropolitan tastes happily appropriate "folk" or "ethnic" goods. In urban India, it is increasingly trendy for the middle and upper classes to decorate homes and bodies with glasswork embroidery from the Kutch desert, silver bangles from Rajasthani villagers, tribal designs from Madhuban; to play studio-recorded cassettes of folksongs; to dabble in regional cuisines. Middle-class Americans with a taste for the exotic can listen to haunting Bulgarian folksingers, dress in bright Guatemalan fabrics, buy New Guinea string bags at the local health food store. The wealthy adorn their homes with carved doors from dismantled South Indian temples, sacred sculpture from Africa, Buddha heads from Thailand. While all this acquisition might occasionally stimulate local economies in the source regions, it is troubling that little if no sense is retained of what these things meant to the people who made them.

A similar sort of random appropriation is rampant in the case of folklore and mythology. When, in the popular television series, Joseph Campbell tells Bill Moyers what a particular story means in Jungian terms, inserting clips from different cultures to prove a point,[44] he mostly disregards the complex layerings of indigenous meanings that such stories might hold for the people who used them to live by. Such appropriations can be seen as yet another inevitable transmutation, this time across cultures, in the transmission between storytellers. After all, aren't stories always recast around one's own concerns whenever they are retold? But I also worry that such appropriations may entirely erase non-Western (or noncontemporaneous) frames of reference.[45] Where actual people exist who are using such stories, I believe that we owe it to them to find out what they—as people of artistry and intelligence—might think. Engaging with other people's stories is to acknowledge other ways of viewing the world, even as it may underscore our inextricable connections.

The forces of change—particularly modernity and global capitalism—in Kangra today have led many people, including Urmilaji, to assert that the stories were being "finished off." Most often, tellers blamed the marginalizing of stories on the advent of mass-produced entertainment. I need hardly repeat Urmilaji's critiques of television as a disruptive force in family sociability and the sharing of tales. She spoke of the television in distant and general terms, almost as though it was some alien who had come to live with the family. She did not comment on particular programs, like the serialized *Ramayana* and *Mahabharata* epics on Indian television. My mother and I did not have a television, so I was not an expert on the programs playing during the time of my research. When I spent the night elsewhere—particularly with middle-class or aspiring middle-class families in Kangra—I saw some television, though because of the hilly terrain, reception was often hopelessly blurred. Amid the images of wealthy, urban Hindi or English-speaking people and the plethora of commodities pushed by advertisers sponsoring programs, the overwhelming impression I had was of a huge gap between imagined lives on television and the lives of Kangra villagers. It is this gap, and the suspicion that the younger generation will be seduced into crossing it, that seemed to contribute to Urmilaji's view of television as dangerous. As she had said when describing kinds of love, "Wisdom is ebbing with every generation. Television can't teach you these things."

Education was also contributing to the marginalization of folktales. I faced the regular amusement of younger people in Kangra who had gone to school to learn Hindi and English that I, a *"paṛ hi-likhī'* educated person, was learning their language and earnestly collecting "old" tales. ("She's like a child," one of the carpenter's teenage daughters giggled to the other. "Wanting to hear these stories!") Literacy had brought other kinds of narrative—either longer written forms, like novels, or shorter oral forms, like jokes—that were displacing the leisurely art of storytelling. I knew several Kangra women my age who preferred to read Hindi novels and magazines than to listen or tell Pahari stories. As Bimlesh Kanta, a storyteller and schoolteacher, said, "Now children read novels, they read about jokes and riddles. But in the past, when people were illiterate, they'd just tell stories. It was when people couldn't read. . . . Telling and listening, the stories were never finished off. But now they will be finished off."

Kangra storytellers also blamed the pervasive shrinking of "time" (using the English word) for the waning of stories. Time was perceived to be dwindling since everyone was preoccupied with making do amid the demands of the modern world: children were studying, adults were off working long hours at paid jobs, women who stayed home had more work because of the breakup of joint families and the breakdown of intercaste exchange relations. As Urmilaji said, "Everyone is constantly busy. When are they going to ask for stories? They have no time for worship, for getting wisdom through stories. Whatever time is left over, you know, it's all spent before the television."

When storytellers asserted that their stories were being "finished off," they did not distinguish between ritual tales and winter tales. But it was clear to me that winter tales were being edged out at a far more rapid pace. As people's winter evenings became filled with other activities, there was no setting for these stories to be retold and passed along. Not one of the winter tales I heard overlapped between storytellers. Lodged inside isolated minds rather than spread over communities, such folktales seemed to indeed be vulnerable to extinction.

Ritual tales, though, had a built-in system of formal transmission: as long as the rituals were performed, the tales were likely to be told. In the early 1990s, the goals of having an auspicious married life and furthering the long lives of relatives remained important to women, despite rapid social change, and so there was no sign within villages of a slacking off on ritual performance. Women who had moved to towns and cities, particularly those outside Kangra, though, appeared to be abandoning the local rituals because there was no community with which to worship.

Told at least once a year if not more often, ritual tales were widely known and remembered among village women. But it is clear that the forces of change could affect ritual tales too. As spontaneous conversations after some of Urmilaji's retellings in a ritual context reveal, educated women may participate in the ritual but subject the accompanying tales to rationalized critiques. Such critiques can show up imaginative tales as naive, old-fashioned, "empty talk." Lacking faith in the stories, it is possible that, in future, younger village women may continue to perform the rituals, but not to tell the stories. Alternatively, they may take to consulting the authority of printed pamphlets for ritual stories.[46] It is also likely that with time, younger women who recast themselves around a middle-class identity may accept the women's rituals on standardized calendars throughout North India and abandon regional traditions of worship.

The forces of modernization that are marginalizing folktales in Kangra have also shaped my own life and the lives of my likely readers. As Westernized literates—whether in the "West" the "East", or the so-called "Third World"—we too have probably been compelled to spurn folktales. For us, oral folktales have diminished in value, becoming written fairy tales fit only for children.[47] Mostly, when we want entertaining stories, we turn to novels, magazines, movies, and television.

I have nothing against these other kinds of stories, especially if they are intelligently told. Yet I believe that there is a magic in oral storytelling that is neither prepackaged nor mass-produced. A storyteller reshapes the story to the particular situation at hand, in interaction with particular listeners. Listeners shape the story by their responses and queries. Traditional narratives bring to life already shared imaginative histories; personal narratives share out past versions of oneself. In retelling stories told by other people, a storyteller also enacts past tellers and reaffirms a continuing emotional connection.

❉ ❉ ❉

If there is a central moral to this long story about Urmilaji's stories it is this: stories arise out of relationships, they are about relationships, and they forge relationships. From her I have learned afresh the value of remembering and retelling the stories handed over by loved people. Retelling their stories, we keep alive their nurturing presence and at the same time we deepen ties with the people we now address.

Once, when Urmilaji was lamenting the coming of television, she observed, "The only way that children of the future might come to know these stories is if someone like you writes them down. Then they'll read them." She paused, reflecting, then added with a rueful shake of her head, "But there's a big difference between reading something and hearing it told!"

Thinking of us and also of my previous work with Swamiji, I offered, "An affection (*prem*) grows between teller and listener."

"That's it," said Urmilaji, raising a hand to her heart. Her brown eyes were steady and her smile was warm: "Affection!"

221

APPENDIX: A NOTE ON TRANSLATION

The transformation of these stories from the moment of Urmilaji's retelling in the Kangri dialect that is also called Pahari to their English appearance in print has been a long process that some readers may be curious about. "Is this a word-to-word translation?" "How much is your translation an interpretation?" "What were your editorial decisions?" are the kinds of questions I've been asked. So I want to make my process explicit.

When Urmilaji told these stories, my tape recorder was on. If I didn't understand something at the time, I sometimes interrupted her and she would rephrase it so I would understand. Later, I would listen to the tape through the headphones, translating each sentence into English. If I needed clarification on words or idioms, I replayed portions of a story—or sometimes even an entire story—to a Kangri speaker who also spoke Hindi or English.

I then typed the translated story into my wordprocessor, adding notes on intonations and what I could remember of expressions or gestures. If the electricity was flowing that day, I would print out the translation on my portable printer. Most often my mother was my first reader, resting in her armchair as I looked over her shoulder. With the story in English, I would make notes in the margins with further questions I wanted to put to Urmilaji for her commentary. When possible, I would present a bilingual friend with the draft translation to look over as they listened to the tape.

My translation follows each sentence as precisely as possible without the idiom ringing awkwardly in an English-speaker's ear. I have taken several editorial liberties though, in the hope of making this smooth and enjoyable reading. Once Urmilaji had first introduced a character, she referred to the person as "he" or "she," identified only by the context. Where I myself found this confusing, I tried to clarify pronouns, inserting names like "the Brahman" or "the demoness" instead.

As with many oral stories, Urmilaji's sentences were often linked by repeating the end of the last sentence at the beginning of the new sentence. The basic structure looks like this: "This happened, then that happened. After that happened, then such and such occurred. Such and such occurred then something else took place...." In my translations, I tried to make this oral "chaining"[1] less repetitive.

While I include my own questions if they redirected the retelling in some way, I do not include every one of my interruptions for clarification. Also, I have edited out my own grunts of assent or outright "yesses" that marked Urmilaji's pauses, assuring her I was engaged.

I created paragraphs according to the rhythm of Urmilaji's retelling or through shifts of subject matter. In the longer stories, I added markers between sections I discerned as inaugurating new sequences of action.

So, for example, if I were to play and rewind, play and rewind, trying to catch every sound on the tape in which the story "Fair with Freckles" (chapter 20) begins, the first few sentences would look like this in Kangri:

Sai the nā brahmaṇ kanne brahmaṇī. [K: ji.] Tinhānde ghare ik laṛkī hoī. [K: hmm.] Laṛki hoī phiri sai bicharī brāhmaṇī marī gaī. [K: hmmmm.] Marī gaī phir sai tinnī brahmaṇe aur byāh karī liyā. [K: hm, hm, hm.] Aur byāh kari liyā phir tisāyo bhī hoī laṛkī. [K: hm, hm.] Laṛkī hoī be sai phir o bhī baṛaṛī hoī gayī. [K: hm, hm, hm.] Bas tisā tisāyo deṇiyā kutkī chhalliāiyān roṭīyān [K: hm,hm,hm.] kanne apniyāyo be kharā roṭī khuāṇī kharī sab kich. [K: hm, hm, hm, hmmm.] Kanne tisāyo je nī oṇa sai jhuṭā-pritā bach jāndi sai khuāṇā. [K: han.]

This is what a literal English translation would look like.

There was, you know, a Brahman and a Brahmani. [K: Ji.] In their house, a daughter was born. [K: hmm.] After the daughter was born, the Brahmani, poor thing, she died. [K: hmmmm.] When she died, then the Brahman married a second time. [K: hm, hm, hm.] When he married a second time, then to her too a daughter was born. [K: hm, hm.] After the daughter was born, then the other one grew up. [K: hm, hm, hm.] She would be given things like corn breads [K: hm, hm, hm.] and for her own, good breads, good everything. [K: hm, hm, hm, hmmm.] She wouldn't get these good things; she'd just be fed leftover food that had already been tasted. [K: Yes.].

In contrast, this is what my final translation looks like.[2]

There was, you know, a Brahman and a Brahmani, his wife. A daughter was born to them. The Brahmani, poor thing, died soon after the birth. Then the Brahman married a second time. A daughter was born to the second wife as well.

The first daughter grew up. The stepmother fed her coarse corn bread, but she'd give fine wheat bread and other delicious things to her own daughter. The first daughter never got any of these good things, she'd just be fed the food left on their plates.

The process of translation has been an agonizing set of decisions, accompanied by the sense that no matter how hard I try, the correspondence will never be perfect. In the end, I have tried to balance precision with beauty, so that in English these stories will hopefully captivate the reader much as I, listening to them, was captivated.

ACKNOWLEDGMENTS

My heartfelt thanks, with a smile and an embrace, to Urmilaji for giving me the gift of these tales. My thanks also to all the members of Urmilaji's family who have been supportive of this enterprise, in particular her younger sisters, Mrs. Nirmala Sood and Mrs. Kamala Sood, and her children Rama, Meena, Raju, Nitoo, and "Sello" Anamika. In recent years Chikoo has been especially patient in sharing her adored grandmother's attention with me.

My abiding and affectionate thanks to the many other women whose retellings have helped me set Urmilaji's stories in a larger context. Janaki Devi "Tayi" Rana first suggested that I tape stories as she cooked one day during Panch Bhikham. In her family "Bibi," Urmila Rana, and Nirmala Rana have also allowed me to share in their ritual stories. Mrs. Vimla Bhandari, eternally kind, entertained me and her granddaughter Simoo with some of these stories before we all went to sleep one night. Mrs. Sita Devi Sharma interspersed some of these stories with her enormous repertoire of beautiful songs, which she sang in her brother's sunny courtyard during a visit (and here, I must thank her ever-helpful nephew Hem Raj for making the connection). Mrs. Veena Dogra's "Mamiji" Sandhi Devi Sharma told a few stories during a happy day's visit to Sakri. Also, Veena's "Chachiji" Mira Devi Dogra was kind enough to retell for me all the Panch Bhikham stories she knew.

Mrs. Jagadamba Pandit, Mrs. Subhashini Dhar, and Mrs. Veena Dhar invited me along for their Panch Bhikham rituals, dispensing stories, songs, and details of the ritual. Their Chaudhrer household has been one of the most hospitable sites for learning about Kangra that I have known, starting from Zaildar Parameshwari Das's coaching me in sample Pahari sentences in 1980. Mrs. Bimlesh Kanta instructed me on a full sequence of Panch Bhikham tales with great generosity one afternoon that I was visiting. Also at Mrs. Jagadamba Pandit's insistence, "Buaji" Mrs. Mathura Devi told some stories. Mrs. Jagadamba Pan-

dit's sister, Asha Devi, and Mrs. Subhadra Sharma sat out in the winter sunshine, prompting me to tell them stories, which they then discussed, elaborated
on, and contributed to with further variants.

Charanjit Singhotra and his family have been extraordinarily kind and hospitable, and I most grateful to them. As early as 1980, Charanjit, a trained language teacher with a dramatic flair for telling tales, judged that telling me
stories would help me learn the Pahari dialect. "Amma" and Saroj have created a hospitable setting for my learning stories from Mrs. Jnanu Bhandari,
whose intelligence is widely respected. Saroj also took me along to Panch
Bhikham gatherings to hear more tales by Mrs. Jnanu Bhandari as well as
those told by vigorous "Dadi" Mrs. Mati Devi and her visitor Mrs. Nirmala
Devi Rana.

Pandit Jagannath generously allowed me to tape the stories he told at Amit's
birthday ritual and has instructed me with his extensive knowledge on Kangra
ritual life. I would also like to thank the "Panditji" who I was introduced to
by Dr. Vijay Vashishta. Dr. Vashishta not only checked on ritual details, but
read through this manuscript with her critical eye as someone familiar with
Kangra and as a professor of English literature.

In Kangra, my mother Didi Contractor provided not just the inspiration but
also the nourishment and support for undertaking this project. Thanks, Ma! I
am also very grateful to General and Mrs. Sarla Korla for their generous "Welcome to Korla Niwas" over the course of many years. Sarlaji's laughter has
always been renewing and her insights invaluable in bridging Kangri- and
English-speaking worlds.

If not for Sardar Gurcharan and "Mummy" Singh, we would never have
gone to Kangra at all. I thank them for their warm hospitality for two summers,
and for their kindness and company in subsequent years.

In Bombay, my thanks to my father, Narayan Contractor, who taught me to
love language, who was patient with my long trips to Kangra, and who encouraged me with this project. I also thank Ved Prakash Sethi for his kind
words on the value of such work.

In the United States, my thanks to A. K. Ramanujan who first suggested in
his gentle way that there was, after all, room for another collection of Indian
tales. Raman's early interest in this project helped make it come to pass. I also
could not have finished writing this book without the generosity of two of
Raman's close friends. In Berkeley, Alan Dundes gave me the methods and
theories with which to study folklore. My career is largely a gift from him and
my gratitude only grows with the years. This manuscript did not seem finished
until Alan Dundes looked it over. In Madison, Narayana Rao vigorously continued my education in Indian folklore. Every comment he ever made to me
about this project I noted down on scraps of paper, napkins, envelopes, my
hand barely able to keep up with the flow of ideas. His comments now suffuse

my thinking so completely that I can no longer keep track of where exactly to acknowledge him.

I am very grateful for the insightful readings given to an earlier manuscript by my friends and colleagues Mekhala Abu-Lughod, John Bendix, Regina Bendix, Kim Berry, Peter Claus, Mary Deschene, Wendy O'Flaherty Doniger, Kevin Dwyer, Ann Grodzins Gold, Margaret Mills, and Isabelle Nabokov. When I thought the manuscript was nearly ready to go, Peter Nabokov, David Shulman, and Beatrice Wright gave me comments that sent me back to the desk. Sabina Magliocco helped by insisting that I had said what I had to say and that I should just stop fidgeting with the afterword. Another invaluable person who helped provide a balance to the final manuscript was Cynthia Read, my editor at Oxford University Press.

Thanks too to Pat Williams for delighting in these stories, Gloria Raheja for sponsoring the conference at which I first talked to Ramanujan about these tales, Stuart Blackburn for inviting me to give a talk at the Association for Asian Studies, and Jack Kugelmass for twice inviting me to participate in his inspiring National Endowment for the Humanities' seminar "Telling Tales." I am also grateful to audiences at the University of Colorado at Boulder, the University of Texas at Austin, and the University of Iowa at Iowa City for astute comments on this project.

My class, "Self and Other in Anthropological Analysis," in spring 1995 also read the manuscript in its last stages. My thanks to Jen Clodius, Deborah Greenland, Karen Levitov, Diana Moran Molina, Susan Neill, Beth Nodland, Alice Oleson, Ashok Rajput, Linda Scholl, Deborah Soper and Amy Thompson for their astute written comments. Special thanks to Jen Clodius for her editing.

I am also very grateful to my friends who are not academics and who helped convince me that these stories might indeed delight a more general audience. My thanks to Cynthia Dobson, Gary DeWalt, Lizzie Grossman, Sarah Levin, Bill and Fran Reynolds, Jodo Bradbury Owens, and Nobuko Yamada whose suggestions formed a soil and water for the growing book. Marian Goad was especially forbearing in looking at the manuscript again, again and again in its different incarnations.

When I was morose, Gila Bercovitch, Maria Lepowsky, and Maya Narayan helped revive my faith by reminding me of the emotional connection to Urmilaji contained in this book. Sacvan Bercovitch valiantly read the manuscript on a fourteen-hour flight to Berlin. Thank you all!

Though this long roster of people encouraged me, it was the granting agencies that allowed me the time to work through these ideas. I did research with University of Wisconsin Graduate School Funds, an American Institute of Indian Studies Senior Fellowship, and a National Endowment for the Humanities Fellowship. Time for writing was provided by the School of American Research, a John Simon Guggenheim Foundation Fellowship, and a Social Science

Research Council Fellowship. I am extremely grateful to these granting agencies. May their endowments grow for future scholars!

Eytan Bercovitch, whom I had the good fortune to remeet soon after returning from Kangra, helped this project in myriad ways. He steadfastly read and talked over draft upon draft, helped me focus my ideas, and supported my quest to find an ethnographic form suitable to the stories. Urmilaji had once cautioned that if I married, I might spend all my time serving my husband tea, but this has not happened. Eytan's presence in my life has enhanced my work. For this gift, and for his love, I am hugely grateful.

NOTES

Introduction

1. Kirin Narayan, *Storytellers, Saints, and Scoundrels: Folk Narrative as Hindu Religious Teaching* (Philadelphia: University of Pennsylvania Press, 1989).
2. For an overview of the issues raised by studying one's own society, and a challenge to the polarization of straightforward "insider" or "outsider" identity in fieldwork, see my article, "How Native Is a Native Anthropologist?" *American Anthropologist* 95 (1993): 671–86.
3. For more on Kangra, see Jonathan Parry's meticulous ethnography, *Caste and Kinship in Kangra* (London: Routledge and Kegan Paul, 1979), and Gabriel Campbell's thesis, *Saints and Householders: A Study of Hindu Ritual and Myth among the Kangra Rajputs* (Katmandu: Ratna Pustak Bhandar, 1976). An excellent book on an adjoining region that is in many ways culturally indistinguishable—and was until recently part of Kangra—is Ursula Sharma's *Women, Work and Property in North West India* (London: Tavistock, 1980). The *Punjab District Gazetteer: Kangra District* vol. 7, pt. a (Lahore: Government Printing Press, 1926) continues to provide a wealth of fascinating detail. Culling information from earlier colonial settlement reports, M. S. Randhawa, who had a lifelong interest in Kangra folklore and miniature painting, describes aspects of Kangra life in his *Kangrā: Kalā, Desh aur Gīt* [Kangra: Art, region and songs] trans. Balakram Nagar (from the Punjabi to Hindi) (New Delhi: Sahitya Academy, 1970).

   More recent work based among Kangra's village Hindus is being undertaken in rich works in progress by Mark Baker, Kim Berry, Katherine Erndl, Brian Greenberg, and Brigitte Luchesi.
4. For an overview of Kangra folklore, see Randhawa, *Kangrā: Kalā Desh aur Gīt.* For collections of folktales from Kangra, see the prolific Gautam Sharma Vyathit's *Naulakhiya Hār: Himāchal kī Lok Kathāen* [The Precious necklace: Folktales from Himachal] (Kangra: Krishna Brothers, 1979), and *Kāgaz kā Hans: Himāchal kī Lok Kathāen* [The paper goose: Folktales from Himachal] (Kangra: Krishna Brothers, 1979)—many stories from this collection are reprinted in his *Rājkumāri aur Totā* [The Princess and the parrot] (Kangra: Krishna Brothers, 1979).
5. There are some collections available representing the state in which Kangra lies: see

Som P. Ranchan and H. R. Justa, *Folk Tales of Himachal Pradesh* (Bombay: Bharatiya Vidya Bhavan, 1981), and K. A. Seethalakshmi, *Folktales of Himachal Pradesh* (New Delhi: Sterling Publications, 1972). For an overview of folklore in the state, see Gautam Sharma 'Vyathit,' *Folklore of Himachal Pradesh* (New Delhi: National Book Trust, 1984).

6. G. A. Grierson, *Linguistic Survey of India*, vol. 9, pt. 1 (Delhi: Motilal Banarsidas, 1968 ([1916]), p. 609. For more recent work on Kangra's dialect, see Anant Ram Chauhan, *The Kangri Central Subsystems* (Shimla: Himachal Academy of Arts, Culture and Language, 1992) and Shyamlal Sharma, *Kāngari: A Descriptive Study of the Kangra Valley Dialect of Himachal Pradesh* (Hoshiarpur: Punjab University, 1974).

7. See H. A. Rose, *Glossary of the Tribes and Castes of the Punjab and the North-West Frontier Provinces*, vol. 3 (New Delhi: Abhinav, 1980 [1919]), p. 430.

8. For caste stereotyping through proverbs, see the *Punjab District Gazetteer*, vol. 7, pt. a, "Appendix 8: Proverbs," pp. lxxix–lxxxii.

9. For a succinct overview of the extensive literature and debates on caste, see Pauline Kolenda, *Caste in Contemporary India: Beyond Organic Solidarity* (Menlo Park, Calif.: Benjamin Cummings Publishing Company, 1978).

10. Though the exercise of listing numbered motifs and tale types often seems arcane and baffling to non-folklorists (even among folklorists it is widely recognized as arbitrary, biased, and incomplete), for me the primary value of the exercise has been glimpsing the larger life of tales and their constituent motifs. What can seem like a unique tale on first hearing can, through these indexes, be identified as a variant of those collected in earlier times and in other places. For someone who has not collected a tale from a contemporary teller, then looked in the indexes to find that the tale has been encountered by many tellers and collectors before, it is difficult to explain the rush of awe, pleasure, and sense of connection with the past that these numbers can bring. See Stith Thompson and Jonas Balys, *The Oral Tales of India*, Folklore Series 10, (Bloomington: Indiana University Press, 1958) for the identification of motifs specific to Indian tales, and Stith Thompson, *Motif Index of Folk Literature*, 6 vols., (Bloomington: Indiana University Press, 1955–58) for worldwide motifs. For the identification of tale types in the Indo-European tradition, see Antti Aarne, *Types of the Folktale*, trans Stith Thompson, Folklore Fellows Communications 184 (Helsinki: Suomalainen Tiedeakatemia, 1964); and for Indian tale types more specifically, see Stith Thompson and Warren E. Roberts, *Types of Indic Oral Tales: India, Pakistan and Ceylon*, Folklore Fellows Communications 180, (Helsinki: Suomalainen Tiedeakatemia, 1960); and Heda Jason, *Types of Indic Oral Tales: Supplement*, Folklore Fellows Communications 242, (Helsinki: Suomalainen Tiedeakatemia, 1989). For this collection, I have not needed to consult Laurits Bødker, *Indian Animal Tales: A Preliminary Survey*, Folklore Fellows Communications 170, (Helsinki: Suomalainen Tiedeakatemia, 1957).

   The brilliant work of A. K. Ramanujan in exploring the Indian recreations of wider known European tale types, and how these variants shed light on Hindu conceptions of self and society, exemplifies how indexes may be profitably used. See his "Hanchi: A Kannada Cinderella," in *Cinderella: A Folklore Casebook*, ed. A. Dundes (New York: Garland, 1982), pp. 259–75, and "The Indian Oedipus" in *Oedipus: A Folklore Casebook*, ed. A. Dundes and L. Edmunds (New York: Garland, 1983), pp. 234–61.

11. For more on women's rituals and their accompanying tales, see Susan Wadley's pioneering corpus of work: *Shakti: Power in the Conceptual Structure of Karimpur*

Religion (Chicago: University of Chicago Studies in Anthropology 2, 1975), especially pp. 61–89; "Vrats: Transformers of Destiny," in *Karma: An Anthropological Inquiry*, ed. C. Keyes and E. V. Daniel (Berkeley: University of California Press, 1983), pp. 147–162; "The Katha of Sakat: Two Tellings," in *Another Harmony: New Essays on the Folklore of India*, ed. S. Blackburn and A. K. Ramanujan (Berkeley: University of California Press, 1986), pp. 195–232; and "Hindu Women's Family and Household Rites in a North Indian Village" in *Unspoken Worlds: Women's Religious Lives*, ed. N. A. Falk and R. M. Gross (Belmont, Ca: Wadsworth Publishing Company, 1989), pp. 72–81. Other full-length studies of women's ritual practices, and associated narratives in particular regions of India, include Ann Grodzins Gold, *Village Families in Story and Song: An Approach through Women's Oral Tradition in Rajathan*, Indiakit Series, South Asia Language and Area Center, (Chicago: University of Chicago, 1982); Lindsay Harlan, *The Religion of Rajput Women* (Berkeley: University of California Press, 1991), and Laxmi G. Tewari, *The Splendor of Worship: Women's Fasts, Rituals, Stories and Art* (New Delhi: Manohar, 1991). For shorter case studies, see Ann Grodzins Gold, "Mother Ten's Stories," in *Religions of India in Practice*, ed. Donald Lopez (Princeton: Princeton University Press, 1995), pp. 434–48; Mary McGee, "Desired Fruits: Motive and Intention in the Votive Rites of Hindu Women," in *Roles and Rituals for Hindu Women*, ed. Julia Leslie (Rutherford: Fairleigh Dickinson University Press, 1991), pp. 71–88; Gloria Raheja and Ann Grodzins Gold, *Listen to the Heron's Words: Reimagining Gender and Kinship in North India* (Berkeley: University of California Press, 1994); Holly Baker Reynolds, *To Keep the Tali Strong: Women's Rituals in Tamilnad, India* (Ph.D. diss. University of Wisconsin, Madison, 1978); Holly Baker Reynolds, "The Auspicious Married Woman," in *The Powers of Tamil Women*, ed. Susan Wadley (Syracuse: Maxwell School for Public Affairs, Syracuse University, 1980), pp. 35–60; and Tony K. Stewart, "The Goddess Sasthi Protects Children" in *Religions of India in Practice*, ed. Donald Lopez (Princton: Princeton University Press, 1995), pp. 352–66. There are many printed pamphlets and books now on the Indian market for women to consult when performing their rituals: for an impressive compendium, see Asha Bahan and Lado Bahan, *Bhāratiya Vrata-Parva Tyāuhār aur Mahilā Sangīt* [Indian women's rituals, festivals, and women's songs] (Haridvar: Randhir Prakashan, 1991).

12. This in contrast to other parts of India, for example, Karimpur, where women's ritual tales are called *katha* but other folktales are known as *kissā* or *kahāni*. See Wadley, *Shakti*, pp. 46–47, and "Texts in Contexts: Oral Traditions and the Study of Religion in Karimpur," in *American Studies in the Anthropology of India*, ed. Sylvia Vatuk (New Delhi: Manohar, 1978), pp. 309–41.

13. There is now an extensive literature on European fairy tales and folktales, which sheds light on these Kangra stories. I have found the work of Bengt Hølbek to be most stimulating. See his "The Language of Fairy Tales," in *Nordic Folklore; Recent Studies*, ed. R. Kvideland and H. K. Sehmsdorf (Bloomington: Indiana University Press, 1989), pp. 40–62, which clearly lays out the kernel of his arguments from the massive *Interpretation of Fairy Tales*, Folklore Fellows Communications 239 (Helsinki: Suomalainen Tiedeakatemia, 1987). Also see the classic structural work of Vladimir Propp, *The Morphology of the Folktale*, trans Lawrence Scott (Austin and London: University of Texas Press, 1968). Max Lüthi's writing, especially *The European Folktale* (Bloomington: Indiana University Press, 1986), explores the formal nature of the folktale as a type, and Lutz Rohrich, *Folktales and Reality* (Bloomington: Indiana University Press, 1991), attempts to situate folktales in the context of

earlier magical worldviews of European peasants. For a stimulating sampler of analytic approaches to fairy tales as a subset of folktales, see Ruth B. Bottigheimer,
ed., *Folktales and Society* (Philadelphia: University of Pennsylvania Press, 1986). 14.
A. K. Ramanujan draws on Tamil literary terms to separate folklore into the inte-
rior, domestic (*ākam*) realm and the exterior, public (*puram*) realm. He points out
that folklore of the domestic realm tends to be performed by nonspecialists using
ordinary language, often featuring characters without names. Folklore of the exterior
realm, on the other hand, tends to be performed by specialists restricted by caste or
cult, who use formulaic language and performative props, and often feature named
characters. Ramanujan situates women's ritual tales as intermediate between the
domestic and public realms. See A. K. Ramanujan, "Two Realms of Kannada Folklore," in *Another Harmony: New Essays on the Folklore of India*, ed. S. Blackburn and
A. K Ramanujan (Berkeley: University of California Press, 1986), pp. 41–75.

15. Other rituals with stories that Urmilaji did not tell but which I heard from others
    include *Hariali, Pudh Chat, Singh Saptami*, and *Vats Dva* in the monsoon month of
    Bhadon (Bhadrapad), as well as *Karva Chauth* and *Hoi Ata* in following month of
    Asu (Ashvin).

16. A variant of this, told to me by a man of the Chamar caste, begins, *kanakā jamiyā
    tā kathā gamiyā*, "when the wheat is sown, then stories are to be enjoyed." See also
    "Vyathit" 's mention of this proverb in *Folklore of Himachal Pradesh*, p. 114.

17. For more on these delightful ending formulas from other regions of India, see A.
    K. Ramanujan, *Folktales from India* (New York: Pantheon, 1991), p. xxxi–xxxii

18. See Carl Von Sydow, "On the Spread of Tradition," in *Selected Papers in Folklore*
    (Copenhagen: Rosenhilde and Bagger, 1948), pp. 12–15.

Chapter One

1. I had first translated *hams* as "swan" but learned from David Shulman that this is
   a popular mistranslation for a goose.

2. As Mary Stokes observes in her notes at the back of her daughter's collection of
   fairy tales, "winning the gratitude of a bird by killing the snake or dragon that year
   after year devours its young birds . . . is a common incident in fairy tales" (Maive
   Stokes, *Indian Fairy Tales* [London: Ellis and White, 1880], p. 289). This encounter
   is left out of some retellings. In a retelling by Mira Devi Dogra, the theme of the
   serpent is returned to further on when the groom falls down dead during the
   wedding rites due to snakebite.

3. This story appears to be associated with Mondays falling on the dark night of the
   moon in other regions of India as well. It can be found in R. B. Gupte's *Hindu
   Holidays and Ceremonials* (Calcutta: Thacker, Spink and Co., 1919), pp. 159–67,
   within the frame of a story about the ascetic Bhishma telling the eldest Pandava
   how the long lives of sons can be secured. In this version (which may be from
   Maharashtra, as Gupte's wife was his chief informant), the characters all had names,
   with the girl called "Gunavati" and the washerwoman called "Soma." Saheb Lal
   Srivastava describes the *somavatī amāvās* ritual as observed by married women of
   upper castes in the villages he studied in Rajasthan and Eastern Uttar Pradesh. He
   mentions that a story detailing how "a washerwoman named Soma gave *suhāg* to a
   Brahman girl" is told by married women in both places. See his *Folk Culture and
   Oral Tradition* (New Delhi: Abhinav, 1974), p. 172. A manual of women's rituals

and their associated tales printed in Uttar Pradesh includes this tale as associated with Mondays in general and those that fall on the dark night of the moon in particular. Here too the washerwoman who grants the girl the boon of a happily married life is called Soma. See Bahan and Bahan, *Bharatiya*, pp. 222–23. In his collection of the tales associated with women's rituals of the Kanyakubja Brahmans of Uttar Pradesh, Laxmi Tewari groups a variant of this story (in which the washerwoman remains unnamed) with the stories told in association with Karva Chauth. See *his Splendor of Worship*, pp. 90–91.

In Kangra, I have also taped variants from Mira Devi Dogra and Mathura Devi Pandit.

Motifs include: V 228.6 Saint as prognosticator; M 341.1.1 Prophecy: death on wedding day; L 32 Only the youngest brother helps his sister perform dangerous task; Z 71.5.2 Journey beyond seven seas; Q 20.1 Reward for service of god, hero, or ascetic for a period; J 155 Wisdom (knowledge) from women; D 1766.1 Magic results produced by religious ceremony; E 63 Resuscitation by prayer; E 64 Resuscitation by magic object; E 121 Resuscitation by supernatural person; M 391.1 Fulfillment of prophecy successfully avoided.

4. In Kangri, *varh* is the word for pipal and can easily be confused with the banyan tree, called *vat*, elsewhere in India. To add to the confusion, this story is also told in Kangra in association with *varh Sāvitri*, which occurs in the lunar month of *Jeth* or *Jyesth* (roughly May/June). In other parts of India, this ritual is called *Vat Sāvitrī* and can be associated with banyan worship. All the written and oral references to the ritual of Mondays on the dark night of the moon that I have come across, though, emphasize the worship of the pipal rather than the banyan tree.

5. This association with the Mahabharata is also present in Gupte's account, *Hindu Holidays*.

6. This argument about the rebirth of the moon is advanced by John M. Stanley in his interpretation of *somāvatī amāvāsya* rituals surrounding the cult of Khandoba in Maharashtra. See his "Special Time, Special Power: The Fluidity of Power in a Popular Hindu Festival," *Journal of Asian Studies* 37 (1977): 27–43. I'm grateful to my ever generous friend Ann Grodzins Gold for directing me to this reference.

7. For more on the conceptual, emotional, and ritual importance of the brother-sister pair in South Asia, see Indira Peterson, "The Tie that Binds: Brothers and Sisters in North and South India," *South Asian Social Scientist* 4 (1988): 25–51; Susan S. Wadley, "Brother, Husbands and Sometimes Sons: Kinsmen in North Indian Ritual," *Eastern Anthropologist* 29 (1976): 149–70; Charles Nuckols, ed., *Siblings in South Asia* (New York: Guilford Press, 1993); and Margaret Trawick, *Notes on Love in a Tamil Family* (Berkeley: University of California Press, 1991), pp. 170–78.

8. Rituals for brother's welfare in Kangra included "Brother's Second" *Bhāi Dūj* (also known as *Bhāu Bīj*) on the day after *Divālī* in *Karttik* (October/November); "The Tie of Protection" or *Rakshābandhan* in *Shrāvan* (July/August); and "Lion's Seventh" or *Chi Sattā* in *Bhādrapad* (August/September).

9. For example, who outside of Kangra has heard of Chutki Manaka as the brother of the sacred basil goddess, Saili? Or Bastu as the brother of Parvati in her form of Rali? I suspect that this same sort of adding on of brothers may occur among village women in other regions of India also.

10. In Uttar Pradesh, an actual married washerwoman may be present during the ritual for a Monday on the dark night of the moon. Women take pinches of the red vermilion from the part in the washerwoman's hair, which indicates her auspicious

married state. They place this red vermilion in their own partings. In the accompanying story, Soma the Washerwoman's boon to the girl of bringing her dead husband to life causes Soma's own husband to die. On her return, the Washerwoman simply performs the ritual under the pipal tree, then sprinkles her husband with her own blood, bringing him back to life. See Bahan and Bahan, *Bharatiya*.

11. Stanley, "Special Time," p. 40, has argued that the powerful astrological conjuncture associated with Mondays on the dark night of the moon is especially associated with water as the medium for the exchange of substances.

12. Jnanu Bhandari, a Rajput woman, informed me that, actually, we had moved out of Kaliyug too and were now in Hathyug, the era of murder. The marks of this era, she said, were incest between brothers and sisters, the end of compassion and righteousness, and a lawlessness preventing women from wearing gold bangles. She assured me that this was the last era, and we were all headed toward certain destruction.

13. In contrast, Gupte's story lists cotton and radishes as taboo: he ascribes this to their being white, just as the moon is white (*Hindu Holidays*, p. 166).

Chapter Two

1. This seems to imply menstrual rags torn from old clothing, which women use, wash, and store away.

2. A necklace worth nine hundred thousand (*nav lākh hār*) is a common motif in Indian folktales. See Flora Annie Steel, *Legends of the Punjab* (London: Macmillan, 1894), p. 305.

3. This story also appears in printed variants from areas beyond Kangra: Mary Frere *Old Deccan Days* (London: John Murray, 1898), pp. 13–17; F. A. Steel and R. C. Temple, *Wide Awake Stories* (London: Trubner and Co., 1884), pp. 298–303; and Ann Grodzins Gold, "Devotional Power of Dangerous Magic: The Jungli Rani's case," in *Listen to the Heron's Words*, ed. G. G. Raheja and A. G. Gold (Berkeley: University of California Press, 1994), pp. 149–163. Peter Claus has sent me no less than ten variants of this story, all from Karnataka. I have taped variants in Kangra from Janaki Devi "Tayi" Rana, "Mami" of Sakri, Jagadamba Pandit, Bimlesh Kanta, Judhya Devi Avasthi and Mira Devi "Chachi" Dogra.

   The common thread in these variants is; the isolation of impoverished mother and daughter(s); the girl being found in the forest by a king who marries her; the girl's attempt to conceal her origins by hiding her mother; and the mother's transformation into a fabulous gold object (stool, dog, bird, image, or necklace), inciting the King to ask to see the girl's home. Through the intercession of a supernatural being—the sun, a snake, God—a splendid palace and parents manifest for a period of time. Someone from the royal party looks back or turns around, revealing it as illusion. The Queen is forced to confess. The Kangra retellings are the only ones in which the Queen actually dies by recounting what happened. The Kannada retellings, which Peter Claus has shared with me, tend to have an animal mother—particularly a dog mother. They split the central character into two sisters: one who is rejecting and murderous toward the lowly mother, the other who is loving and hospitable.

   Motifs include: N 711 King (prince) accidentally meets maiden and marries her; T 121.8 King (rich man) marries common girl; D 235 Transformation of man (woman) to golden object; N 817 Deity as helper; Q 20 Piety rewarded; D 1132.1

Palace produced by magic; (D 1133.1.1 Magic house made by prayer); T 258.1.1
Husband insists on knowing wife's secret; F 1041.1.3 Death from shame.
4. See Parry, *Caste and Kinship,* for a well-documented discussion of hypergamy in
Kangra. While high-ranking Rajputs were the most staunch practitioners of giving
women, along with a dowry, to higher-ranking families, through the last century
other castes that previously practiced bride-price have drifted toward limited
exchange and then dowry marriages.
5. This ideology of honor and modesty is found throughout North India and Pakistan
and is also present in the Mediterranean region. Ursula Sharma has described
women's veiling practices in a Himachal Pradesh region adjacent to Kangra, linking
veiling and gender segregation in general to women's lack of power in the public
domain. See Ursula Sharma, "Women and Their Affines: The Veil as a Symbol of
Separation," *Man* (n.s.) 13 (1978): 218–33; and "Segregation and Its Consequences in
India: Rural Women in Himachal Pradesh," in *Women United, Women Divided,* ed.
P. Caplan and J. Bujra, (London: Tavistock, 1978), pp. 259–82.
6. For more on veiling as creating a circumscribed space for women to do as they like,
see Margaret A. Mills, "Sex Role Reversals, Sex Changes, and Transvestite Disguise
in the Oral Tradition of a Conservative Muslim Community in Afghanistan," in
Women's Folklore, Women's Culture, ed. R. A. Jordan and S. J. Kalcik (Philadelphia:
University of Pennsylvania Press, 1985), pp. 187–213; and also Gold, "Devotional
Power," pp. 164–81.

Chapter Three

1. In Pahari, the eleventh lunar day is called *ikādasī* (in Hindi *ekādashā* and the twelfth
is called *dvādasi* (in Hindi *dvādashī*).
2. This is Tale Type 750 B, Hospitality Rewarded. Beck, Claus, Goswami, and Handoo, the editors of *Folktales of India* (Chicago: University of Chicago Press, 1987),
propose for this tale a new type—750 J, Devotion Rewarded (p. 151)—as they in-
troduce a variant from Uttar Pradesh associated with the worship of the deity Śakat.
Śakat is described as a goddess in some Uttar Pradesh variants, for example those
collected by Tewari, *Splendor of Worship,* pp. 108–9. Also, Śakat is associated with
Ganesh. See Susan Wadley, "The Katha of Śakaṭ: Two Tellings," in *Another Harmony: New Essays on the Folklore of India,* eds. S. Blackburn and A. K. Ramanujan
(Berkeley: University of California Press, 1986), pp. 195–232. All these Uttar Pradesh
variants feature sisters-in-law related by marriage as opposed to the Kangra variants,
which feature sisters related by blood. In Kangra, I also heard this story from Judhya
Devi Avasthi and Mira Devi Dogra.
    Motifs include: Q 1.1 Gods (saints) in disguise reward hospitality and punish
inhospitality; K 1811.2 Deity disguised as old man (woman) visits mortals; K 1815
Humble disguise; Q 42.3 Generosity to saint (god) in disguise rewarded; J 2415
Foolish imitation of lucky man; D 1002, Magic excrement; D 2102 Gold magically
produced; Q292, Inhospitality punished; L 50 Victorious youngest daughter.
3. The term *ānvlā* is also translated as "Indian gooseberry" (Emblica Officinalis
Gaertn.). Its worship in different parts of India under various names is cursorily
reviewed by Shakti M. Gupta, *Plant Myths and Traditions in India,* 2d rev. ed. (New
Delhi: Munshiram Manoharlal, 1991), pp. 38. Interestingly, in Maharashtra state, the
eleventh day of Karttik also marks a festival known as *Āvalibhojana* or "picnic under

the *āvali* [or *ānvlā*] tree." See Charlotte M. Underhill, *The Hindu Religious Year* (Calcutta: Association Press, 1921), p. 89.

4. Another variant of this proverb runs "eating a berry and the words of an old person: you remember them later" (*ānvle dā khādiyā siyaniyā dā gilāyā pichhue dā yād ondā*).
5. I am grateful to Kim Berry for emphasizing this point.
6. Significantly, in a male retelling of this tale from Uttar Pradesh, the defecation sequence is altogether bypassed. See Wadley, "Katha of *Śakat.*"
7. Told by Bimlesh Kanta, Vimla Bhandari, Judhya Devi Avasthi, and Jagadamba Pandit. It turned out that in 1994 when I asked Urmilaji if she knew this story she also told it. Since it was elicited by me by sketching it out for Urmilaji, and several years after the other stories in the book, I haven't included her retelling here.
8. I taped this story from Bimlesh Kanta only.

Chapter Four

1. There is a widespread taboo on speaking the name of husbands or elders, in Kangra, as in much of India. Therefore Kangra women usually refer to their husbands as "he" or "him"—*seh*.
2. *Lari* or bride, is how daughters-in-law are often addressed by elders in Kangra. Women are also often referred to as "so and so's *lari*" for years after they are a newly married bride.
3. A ceremony with oblations offered to the fire is called a *jag* in Kangra, from the Sanskrit *yagna*.
4. A *dhotī* is a long piece of fine cloth worn by men for ceremonial occasions, such as engaging in a ritual or serving food at a feast. The cloth is pleated around the waist and pulled loosely between the legs to be tucked in the back.
5. Here as elsewhere, Urmilaji uses the English word "public" to indicate a big assembled group of people.
6. This is related to Tale Type 459, The make believe son (daughter), which has recorded variants only from India. In Urmilaji's version there is no introductory section on a Queen chastised for her childlessness who then pretends she has born a child, and the daughter-in-law takes a more active role in beseeching divine intervention for producing a handsome youth. For a delightful Rajasthani variant, see Ann Grodzins Gold, "Mother Ten's Stories," in *Religions of India in Practice*, ed. Donald Lopez (Princeton: Princeton University Press, 1995), pp. 434–48.
Motifs include: T 53.0.1 Matchmakers arrange weddings; T 117.2 Marriage of girl to sword; Q 20 Piety rewarded; Q 26 Keeping fast rewarded; D 1766.10 Magic results produced by religious ceremony.

Chapter Five

1. This tale bears resemblances to Tale Type 440, The Frog King (for which no Indian variants are entered), and particularly to Tale Type 441, Hans my Hedgehog, under whose heading are grouped tales from all over India which deal with the marriage of a girl to a man in animal form. I heard versions of this tale from Nirmala Devi, Subhashini Dhar, Mira Devi Dogra, and Asha Devi Sharma.

Motifs include: T 676 Childless couple adopts animal as substitute for child; T 53.0.1 Matchmakers arrange weddings; B 645.1.2 Marriage to person in frog form; D 721.3 Disenchantment by destroying skin (covering); D 395 Transformation: frog to person; Q 20 Piety rewarded; Q 26 Keeping fast rewarded; D 1766.10 Magic results produced by religious ceremony.

2. For a classic statement on the mother-son tie and its implications for Indian male psychology, see Sudhir Kakar, *The Inner World* (New Delhi: Oxford University Press, 1981), pp. 76–103.

3. See Ann Grodzins Gold, *A Carnival of Parting* (Berkeley: University of California Press, 1993), p. 99, note 66: " 'playing parcheesi' appears in many Rajasthani stories and songs as a euphemism for sexual intercourse." Ann Gold, Gloria Raheja, and A. K. Ramanujan are among those who, in personal communications, remarked on talking as another euphemism for sex.

4. A variant of this story can be found in W. Buchanan, "Panch Bhikham—Bhiśma pancaka," *Panjab Notes and Queries* 35 (1886): 181–82. Over a hundred years later, I heard variants from Nirmala Devi, Judhya Devi Avasthi, and Shikha Dhar.

Chapter Six

1. This sort of blouse, called a *cholī*, appears to have been gradually phased out of Kangra women's dress since the beginning of the century. Women in their seventies recalled their mothers-in-law having such blouses in their possession and wearing them for ritual occasions along with a *ghagharu* or embroidered full skirt. Some older women had once worn these blouses for ritual occasions themselves, much as some will now wear the full skirts during rituals. The blouses were backless, tied with strings behind, cut to be molded around the breasts in front, and reaching down to the waist. They were beautifully embroidered. I am grateful to Mrs. Sarla Korla for showing me two of these blouses that she was able to salvage from relatives. In most households, they have been thrown away. As Urmilaji said, "Everyone thought that these were old things, and we would throw them out when we were cleaning the houses before Divali [the festival of lights in October/November]. Who could know that these old things would someday come to have a value?"

2. This is an extremely popular story, its memory rekindled through the performance of the boat-launching ritual each year. Less variation existed between retellings of this story than for any other I taped. Among the tellers I have heard are Janaki Devi "Tayi" Rana, Mami of Sakri, Jagadamba Pandit, Bimlesh Kanta, Judhya Devi Avasthi, Urmila Rana, Mrs. Man Singh Rana, and Nirmala Rana. Panditji of Palampur and a Bujru visiting Badoo also told the story in fragmentary form.

Motifs include: Q 243.0.2 Suspected incontinence unjustly punished; Q 414 Punishment: burning alive; D 1610 Magic speaking objects; N 454.2 King overhears conversation of lamps; R 175 Rescue at the stake; Q 26 Keeping fast rewarded.

3. For more on the symbolism of boats and crossings in the imagery of worldly life and spiritual redemption, see Wadley, *Shakti*, pp. 92–101. I am grateful to Ann Gold for reminding me of this discussion.

4. Clothes were given to children at *Rali Sankrānti*, in the month of *Chaitra* (March/April) and at *Divalī* on the dark moon of Kārttik (October/November).

Chapter Seven

1. For more on the Bharthari story as sung in Rajasthan, see Gold, *Carnival of Parting*.
2. Maharaj literally means "great king" and is used as a form of respectful address to men.
3. In *Folktales of Mahakoshal* (Bombay: Oxford University Press, 1944), pp. 202–4, 209–12, Verrier Elwin discusses tribal variants of this story, grouped together in a chapter entitled "The Jealous Queens." These stories mix Urmilaji's tale of the berry bush with her tale of the devouring demoness (chapter 18). In Elwin's variants, jealous cowives substitute a grinding stone for a newly born son (or children); later, the mother is identified when she presses milk from her nipples and it spurts into the mouth of her child (or children) even though a screen has been placed between them.

    In Uttar Pradesh, a variant of this story that also features jealous cowives is told in association with the worship of the Goddess Shitala. See Tewari, *Splendor of Worship*, pp. 129–30.

    In Kangra, Mira Devi "Chachi" Dogra also tells this story.

    Motifs include: N 817 Deity as helper; K 2115.2.1 Stone substituted for newly born babies; S 353 Abandoned child reared by supernatural beings.
4. This ritual is performed on the twelfth day of the waning half of the lunar month of *Bhādrapad* (August/September) by Brahmans and Rajputs. Mothers with sons worship cows with male calves, garlanding them and stamping impressions of their own hands on the sides of the cattle.
5. For more on ambivalence surrounding breast milk in Hindu mythology, see Wendy Doniger O'Flaherty, *Women, Androgynes and Other Mythical Beasts* (Chicago and London: University of Chicago Press, 1980), pp. 53–54.
6. On the domestication of mythological characters in women's folklore, see Ramanujan, "Two Realms of Kannada Folklore," pp. 64–68, and Sumanta Banerjee, "Marginalization of Women's Popular Culture in Nineteenth Century Bengal," *Recasting Women: Essays in Indian Colonial History*, ed. Kumkum Sangari and Sudesh Vaid. (New Jersey: Rutgers University Press, 1990), pp. 127–79.

Chapter Eight

1. Motifs include: Q 26 Keeping fast rewarded; E 656 Reincarnation: animal to man; E 611 Reincarnation as domestic animal; E 601 Reincarnation: former lives remembered; E 606.1 Reincarnation as punishment for sin; T 258.1.1 Husband insists on knowing wife's secret. Versions were told by Sita Devi Sharma, Mira Devi Dogra, Judhya Devi Avasthi, Asha Devi Sharma, and Mati Devi.
2. A *peru* is a large bamboo basket smeared with cow dung to seal it.
3. For a further elaboration on eleventh days and their association with the worship of Vishnu in a different part of India, see C. M. Underhill, *Hindu Religious Year*, pp. 83–91.

Chapter Nine

1. Similar tales have surfaced in the collections of A. K. Ramanujan and Ann Grodzins Gold. Ramanujan's Kannada tale is recorded in *Folktales of India*, pp. 33–38. Here, a starved daughter-in-law is gobbling down food in the temple of Goddess Kali, and in amazement, the image's hand moves to its mouth. The townspeople are upset. The daughter-in-law offers to return the statue to its previous state and does so by whacking the image with a broomstick. Gold's lively rendition of a Rajasthani story, "Ganeshji and the Brahman Girl" appears in Gloria Raheja and Ann Grodzins Gold, *Listen to the Heron's Words* (Berkeley: University of California Press, 1994), pp. 166–67. Here, a Brahman girl makes unconventional offerings to the God Ganesh each day, using coals from the cremation grounds and butter from the image's navel. He is pleased and puts his finger on his nose. The villagers are upset. The daughter-in-law asks for a curtain to be put up. Hidden behind the curtain, she threatens to break the icon with a stick. He puts his fingers down, laughs, and blesses her. She gets a land grant from the King. Gold brilliantly argues that the power of devotion may allow women to stretch social norms and constraints.

   Motifs include: E 656 Reincarnation: animal to man; W 125 Gluttony (cf. W 125.2 Gluttonous wife eats all the meal while cooking it).
2. The adoption of higher-caste practices by lower or less locally powerful castes as a form of enhancing status has been widely remarked on by anthropologists and sociologists in India. The idea owes its original formulation, in terms of the adoption of Brahmanically based customs, to M. N. Srinivas, "A Note on Sanskritization and Westernization," in *Caste in Modern India and Other Essays* (Bombay: Asia Publishing House, 1962), pp. 42–62.
3. Susan Wadley records that in Karimpur folklore, women with uncontrollable appetites are also depicted in antithesis to the controled and chaste ideal of an upper-caste woman. See Susan Wadley, *Struggling with Destiny* (Berkeley: University of California Press, 1994), p. 31.
4. I am grateful to Kim Berry for reminding me of this.
5. For other variants see Gold, "Ganeshji and the Brahman Girl," and Ramanujan, *Folktales of India*.

Chapter Ten

1. Narayan, *Storytellers, Saints, and Scoundrels*, pp. 189–207.
2. I taped variants of this story, called *terni*, the Skein Woman, from Mira Devi Dogra, Sandhi Devi, and Asha Devi Sharma.

   Motifs include: E 601.3 Punishment earned in one life paid in next reincarnation; E 604 Reincarnation in another human form; Q 20 Piety rewarded; Q 26 Keeping the fast rewarded; M 817 Deity as helper (usually in answer to prayer).
3. Mira Devi Dogra expanded this list of taboos beyond no spinning to no winding of yarn, no sewing, and no rolling of cotton wicks.
4. Jonathan Parry describes past aristocratic Mian Rajputs as not eating boiled rice from the hands of their wives until "the blood had mixed" and they had born a child. See Parry, *Caste and Kinship in Kangra*, p. 207.

Chapter Eleven

1. A *ser* is about a kilogram. Forty *sers* make a *man* or *maund*.

2. Bhadon or Bhadrapad is the official name of the lunar month that spans August/ September. In Kangra, this month, like many, has another name that is most often used—it is called *Kala Mahine* or "Black Month" partly because monsoon clouds darken the skies and partly because on the eighth day of the bright half of this month, Krishna, the Dark Lord, was born. The ritual of untying the thunder thread is usually done by women of the Sood caste (and is explained in the next chapter). However, here Urmilaji has a woman of the Kshatriya caste performing it.

3. The breads, called *roṭā*, are prepared in secret by women for the ritual of the thunder thread.

4. *Jhīr* are members of a caste that traditionally pursued the occupations of water carrying and fishing; *ghirth* are members of an agricultural caste. Both are seen as of low status and poor.

5. It is not clear to me why they do not eat this in the midst of their hunger, but I didn't have a chance to ask Urmilaji. Perhaps this is because it was such an affront from their daughter, or because the rice and lentils were uncooked.

6. The oilpresser caste is known as Kolu or Teli. With the spread of machinery for extracting oil, this caste profession has been rendered obsolete, although the caste remains.

7. A *swayamvar* is an occasion, celebrated in folklore and mythology, in which all the eligible kings assembled and a princess chose a man of her choice from among them.

8. In another Pahari variant, the four personified forces are Bhagya (Fate), Karma (the fruits of action), Vidhi Mata (Mother Fate) who is here made explicitly responsible for matches in marriage, and Honi. See Molu Ram Thakur, *Manoranjak Pahāṛi Lok kathāen* [Entertaining Pahari folktales] (Delhi: Himachal Pradesh Bhavan, n.d.), pp. 45–50.

9. This story follows along the lines of Tale Type 939, "The Offended Deity," with variants recorded only in India. It often occurs in conjunction with Tale Type 757, "The King's Haughtiness Punished," which is found in many parts of the world. The addition of the motif of the unlucky Brahman (N 264) is sometimes also appended. See, for example, Ram Satya Mukharji, *Indian Folklore* (Calcutta: Sanyal and Co., 1904), pp. 109–13).

   While Urmilaji identifies this King as Bhoj, in other variants this is King Vikramaditya, Harishchandra, or Alexander the Great: all of whom are kings celebrated in Indian folklore. In some variants, it is Saturn who afflicts the King—for example, in Mukharji, or in Susan Wadley's folktale of Vikramaditya recorded in Uttar Pradesh and reproduced in her article, "Texts in Contexts," pp. 317–23. Or it may be another planet, such as Jupiter, or even God himself (as in Stokes, *Indian Fairy Tales*, pp. 68–72, 224–33). This story also bears strong resemblances to the tale of Nala and Damayanti, recounted in the Mahabharata and existing in numerous regional variants (Narayana Rao, personal communication; David Shulman, personal communication)

   While transcribing this complex tale, separating the story into sections, it helped me make sense of the different episodes and locales. The divisions are my own editorial interventions.

   This story was also told by Pandit Jagannath in the variant discussed next. A more fragmentary retelling was from Panditji in Palampur. Portions were also told by Nirmala Devi Rana who had heard this from her late husband. In her version, the king is Raja Dholna, who has two wives, Rani Panopatali and Rani Ambakachai.

Motifs include: N 264 Whether man begs all day or for an hour he gets only a small basket of grain; N 125 Objects effect change of luck; N 250 Persistent bad luck; Z 135 Adversity personified; L 419.1 King (prince) becomes beggar; Q 451.1.1 Hands cut off as punishment for theft; Q 451.2.2 Feet cut off as punishment for theft; T 135.5 Marriage by exchange of garlands; T 52.4 Dowry given at marriage of daughter.

10. Thakur, *Manoranjak*, p. 50.

11. For more on multiple systems of explaining misfortune, as tied up with influences within or outside an individual's control (such as free will or determinism), see the essays in *Karma: An Anthropological Inquiry*, ed. C. Keyes and E. V. Daniel (Berkeley: University of California Press, 1983), particularly Sheryl Daniel, "The Tool Box Approach to the Tamil to the Issues of Moral Responsibility and Human Destiny," pp. 27–62, and Lawrence A. Babb, "Destiny and Responsibility: Karma in Popular Hinduism," pp. 163–81.

12. For a detailed discussion of the transfer of inauspicious influences through giving material things (grains, cloth, coins, and so on) and the impact of these exchanges on caste relations, see Gloria Raheja, *The Poison in the Gift* (Chicago: University of Chicago Press, 1988).

13. Urmilaji's version does not name the Oilpresser. Virendra Sharma of Varanasi recognized this story when I retold it and cited a Hindi proverb that names the King and the Oilpresser. According to him, the proverb, "Where is King Bhoj, where is Gangu the Oilpresser?" (*kahān rājā bhoj kahān gangu teli*) is used to highlight the differences between people; for example, if those of improbable status are thrown together.

However, in the variant of this tale recorded in the last century by Maive Stokes (*Indian Fairy Tales*, pp. 224–330) from her servant Muniya of Patna, Bihar, the primary King is named as "Harichand" and described as seeking hospitality from two friends: "Ganga" the Oilpresser and King "Bojh." In this variant, Ganga does not take him in on account of his straitened circumstances, but King Bojh remains a constant and supportive friend (though it is his daughter's necklace that is swallowed by the wall). The proverb that compared the Oilpresser and King Bhoj would indicate that some friends stick by a friend through misfortune, while others do not.

14. For example, in a variant of this episode associated with Raja Nal recorded by Susan Wadley in her study of the Dhola Maru epic, when Nal is undergoing misfortunes due to Saturn, he takes refuge with an Oilpresser "and because Sanicar [Saturn] cannot come into the room with the press, they are safe"; the Oilpresser (whose wife is here called Ganga) becomes wealthy. See Wadley, "Raja Nal, Motini, Damayanti and the Dice Game: Some Preliminary Thoughts" (paper presented at the Wisconsin South Asia Meetings, 1993), p. 12.

Another link to Saturn is that the *māh dāl* (the whole black lentils that the daughter's offering was transformed into) are associated with Saturn.

15. In Mira Devi Dogra's retelling of the Frog King story, the frog, too, always has a cloud over his head, which leads the Princess to choose him as a groom.

Chapter Twelve

1. Urmilaji is commenting here on a familiar motif in folklore in which Parvati coaxes Shiva into stepping in to alleviate people's suffering. See, for example, Susan Wadley, *Shakti*, p. 66, 83.
2. Motifs include: A162 Conflicts of the gods; A 171 Gods ride through the air; E 121.1 Resuscitation by a god; D 1766 Magic results produced by religious ceremony; D 465.1.8 Transformation: earth to gold; D 1641 Object removes itself.
3. In her study of Tamil women's rituals, Holly Baker Reynolds also describes a secret women's ritual called "Auvaiyar Nonpu," which is kept hidden from men in all its aspects. For men to witness or learn of any details is said to cause blindness and ruin. As Reynolds embarks on her description of the ritual, she cautions "any male who proceeds to read beyond this point." See her *To Keep the Tali Strong*, Vol II, p. 354.
4. Kangra also follows the pattern more widespread in Hindu calendars in which Snake's Fifth, or Nag Panchami, falls on the fifth day of the waxing month of Shravan in the earlier month. However, this second Snake's Fifth a month later would appear to be a regional practice.

Chapter Thirteen

1. I am reminded of Alessandro Falassi's book, *Folklore by the Fireside: Text and Context in the Tuscan Veglia* (Austin: University of Texas Press, 1980), in which he recounts the waning of folklore sessions around the fire among Tuscan peasants.
2. In these Kangra folktales, Dharmraj seems to stand in for Yama, Lord of Death. But this is also a name for the eldest of the five Pandavas in the Mahabharata epic and is the name of a folk deity in Bengal.
3. Urmilaji used the term *kudrati tilak*—a natural mark. A tilak refers to the mark in the center of the forehead, bestowed in a ritual; it is also called a *tīkā* and can be found on the foreheads of men or women. This has different connotations than a *bindi*, which is part of the attire of married women, usually red, and increasingly takes the form of store-bought felt stickers.
4. In this context, placing the ritual mark (*tīkā*) on the lion's forehead means that the engagement is being set.
5. This Urdu word *misal* for "file" connotes legal papers relating to a particular case, which is backed by the use of the term *kachhari*—which can refer to a law court— for Dharmraj's court.
6. The rhyme here between *rekhā* (line) and *mekhā* (nail) is what I first thought drove this saying. Urmilaji does not make this connection, but reading folktales from South India, I learned that the lines of fate are believed to be written with an iron nail. See Mrs. Howard Kingscote and Pandit Natesa Sastri, *Tales of the Sun* (New Delhi: Asian Educational Services, 1984 ([1890]), p. 235.
7. In *Types of Indic Oral Tales*, Thompson and Roberts group together Indic tales with an animal groom under Tale Type 441. Motifs include: M 369.2.1 Future husband (wife) foretold; T 53.0.1 Matchmakers arrange wedding; T 61 Betrothal; S 247 Daughter unwittingly promised to animal; B 647 Marriage to person in animal form—miscellaneous; T 52.4 Dowry given at marriage of daughter; T 136.6 Journey to husband's home accompanied by attendants; F 57 Road to heaven; F 167.12.1

Mortal marries King of Underworld; N 115 Book of fate; N 121 Fate decided before birth; T 22 Predestined lovers, Future spouse assigned by destiny; M 371 Exposure of infant to avoid fulfillment of prophecy; S 331 Exposure of child in boat (floating chest); N 101 Inexorable fate.
8. See, for example, A. K. Ramanujan, "Two Realms of Kannada Folklore," pp. 58–62.

Chapter Fourteen

1. Meditating beside fires is a practice of certain sects of Hindu holy men.
2. Motifs include: N 836.1, King adopts hero (heroine); P 17, Succession to the throne; H 1218, King possessing one marvelous object sends hero on quest for another like it; H 1333.4, Quest for marvelous flower; E 601, Reincarnation: former lives remembered; E 605, Reincarnation in another human form; E 602, Reincarnation in form determined at death.
3. Bride price marriage has indeed existed in Kangra and was an index of low status, but it is increasingly being phased out in favor of the more prestigious dowry marriages. See Parry, *Caste and Kinship in Kangra*, pp. 88, 237–46.
4. Over the years that I have visited Kangra, I have observed a gradual drift, in several households that I am familiar with, away from the strict observance of menstrual taboos associated with cooking. Once an older and more orthodox female relative dies, a woman may become less particular about sitting apart a full four days. Also, in situations where a husband's brothers have moved away, taking their wives, a woman may be managing a kitchen alone. If she does not have a daughter to take over the cooking, she and her husband may at some point decide that it is not worth the trouble to have a neighbor come in and cook. Professional women, obviously, cannot sit apart on a woven mat for several days each month.
5. For example, the demoness in chapter 18 and the sisters-in-law in Chapter 21 also complain of stomach ache.
6. For a dazzling discussion of Hindu narratives featuring movement across castes (with the poles Brahman/Untouchable/King a recurrent theme) and such narratives as lessons on the nature of illusion and reality, see Wendy Doniger O'Flaherty, *Dreams, Illusions and Other Realities* (Chicago: University of Chicago Press, 1984), pp. 137–205.
7. This overview of the tea industry is drawn from the *Punjab District Gazetteer*, pp. 238–52.

Chapter Fifteen

1. Motifs include: A 189.8 Accountant of god keep lists of good and bad acts of human beings; Q 172 Reward: admission to heaven.
2. See *Storytellers, Saints, and Scoundrels*, p. 34.
3. For more on this terrible earthquake, see *Punjab District Gazetteer*, p. 33.
4. In *Folklore of Himachal Pradesh*, p. 26, Gautam Sharma 'Vyathit' also mentions that sins are thought to cause earthquakes. In addition, he cites a memorable local explanation of earthquakes being "due to the movement of the sacred white bull who rests upon the Braja rock which in turn rests upon a holy lotus flower. The white

bull holds the earth aloft upon its horns and when he is tired of holding it on one horn, he shifts it to another, which causes the earthquake."

Chapter Sixteen

1. Motifs include: D 1810.10 Magic knowledge from a sadhu; Q422.0.1 Beating to death as punishment; S 11.3.3 Father kills son; N 340 Hasty killing or condemnation (mistake); E 696 Reincarnated person restored to original form.
2. For more on the phenomenon of past-life remembrance in India, see Ian Stevenson, *Cases of the Reincarnation Type: Ten Cases in India* (Charlottesville: University Press of Virginia, 1975); and also Antonia Mills, "A Replication Study: Three Cases of Children in Northern India Who Are Said to Remember a Past Life," *Journal of Scientific Exploration* 3 (1989): 133–84. While the facts in such cases have been extensively documented by scholars interested in paranormal events, for an anthropologist the truth value seems less crucial than the manner in which narratives about reincarnation are phrased in particular cultural idioms.
3. See Stevenson, *Reincarnation Type*: p. 68.
4. For more on the subject of a woman's sense of being split between two homes in other regions of the Himalayas, see Lynn Bennett, *Dangerous Wives and Sacred Sisters* (New York: Columbia University Press, 1983) for Nepal; and William Sax, *Mountain Goddess: Gender and Politics in a Himalayan Pilgrimage* (New York: Oxford University Press, 1991), especially pp. 115–26, for Garhwal.

Chapter Seventeen

1. *Vanvās dittā*—to be sent into exile in the forest—echoes the painful banishing of characters in the Ramayana epic. Not only is Ram banished early on, accompanied by his wife and brother, but later he banishes his wife Sita too.
2. Motifs include: T 145 Polygamous marriage; P 481 Astrologer; M302.4 Horoscope taken by means of stars; M 356.3 Prophecy: Unborn (newborn) child to bring evil upon land; M 342 Prophecy of downfall of kingdom; S 441 Cast-off wife and child abandoned in forest; H 1381.2.2.1.1.1 Boy twitted as bastard goes on a quest for unknown father; N 731.1 Unknown son returns to father's court; F 1041.3 Person goes blind from weeping; F 952 Blindness miraculously cured; Q 455 Walling up as punishment; QQ 469.3 Punishment: grinding up in mill.
3. In the terminology of Vladimir Propp, these diverse situations could be equated to the underlying structure of a "function." See Propp, *Morphology of the Folktale*.

Chapter Eighteen

1. Plowing is considered a degrading practice for Brahmans, though many do it. See Parry, *Caste and Kinship in Kangra*, p. 66.
2. The closeness of the brother-sister tie carries into the next generation, where a sister's sons often have warm relationships with their maternal uncles and are likely to go to them when in trouble.
3. The theme of the life-index—in which a person's life is wrapped up with a certain

object, animal, bird, or person—is widespread in Indian folklore. See Ruth Norton, "The Life-Index: A Hindu Fiction-Motif," in *Studies in Honor of Maurice Bloomfield* (New Haven: Yale University Press, 1920), pp. 211–23.

4. Translating "ascetic's staff" for *gorakh ḍandī* is a hypothesis on my part, for though Urmilaji uses this term she isn't sure what it is, saying "it's some sort of object." I assume it refers to a staff (*ḍandī*) used by members of the ascetic sect associated with *gorakhnath*. This is what the German folklorist Max Lüthi would call "a blunted or blind motif," which through transmission has been separated from its original purpose in the tale. See Max Lüthi, *The Fairytale as Art Form and Portrait of Man*, trans. Jon Erickson (Bloomington: Indiana University Press, 1987), p. 64.

5. In her study of the life-index motif in Indian folklore, "The Life-Index," p. 217, Norton observes, "By far the most popular index of all is the bird . . . but we find little variety in its use. It seems, in fact, that the bird can only be killed by having its neck wrung, and, even when the dismemberment is protracted, that is always the outcome."

6. This story has many recorded variants from all over India (and Sri Lanka). Margaret Mills reports that it was well known in Herat, Afghanistan, in the 1970s. Urmilaji's version combines Tale Type 462, "The Outcast Queens and the Ogress Queen," with Tale Type 302 A, "Youth Sent to the Land of the Ogres." Many of the variants include the sequence with the milk goat at the start. Often, the queens are blinded when thrown into the pit (or well). Their numbers may vary between two and ten. The queens who are not the hero's mother are invariably cannibals who eat their own babies. Variants similar to Urmilaji's can be found in entries of the last century in the journal *North Indian Notes and Queries*: "The Wicked Stepmother," recorded in Muzaffarnagar, U.P., *NINO* 4 (1894): 102–6; and "The Witch Queen," *NINO* 4 (1894): 116–17. See also "Brave Hiralalbasa" and "The Demon Is at Last Conquered by the King's Son," in Stokes, *Indian Fairy Tales*, pp. 50–62, 173–92. See also Lal Behari Day, "The Boy Whom Seven Mothers Suckled," in *Folktales of Bengal* (London: Macmillan, 1913), pp. 117–23; and Roma Chatterji, "The Voyage of the Hero," *Contributions to Indian Sociology* 19 (1985): 100–101. For a recent retelling, see A. K. Ramanujan, "The Ogress Queen," in *Folktales from India* (New York: Pantheon, 1991), pp. 73–79. Ramanujan's retelling is drawn from Rev. J. Hinton Knowles, *Folktales of Kashmir* (London: Kegan Paul, Trench, Trubner, 1893), pp. 42–50.

In *Folktales of Mahakoshal*, Elwin groups tribal variants of this story along with variants of what Urmilaji retells as "Under the Berry Bush," thus showing the interchangeability of some of the motifs when a mother-in-law/daughter-in-law rivalry is equivalent to a rivalry between cowives.

A variant of the story, also recorded in Kangra, appears in Vyathit's *Kāgaz kā Hans*, pp. 6–9. In Vyathit's Hindi retelling, the original sequence with a milk goat features a shepherd of the Gaddi tribe rather than a Brahman, and the adventures in the land of the demons are omitted.

Motifs include: G 351.4 Ogress in goat form (G 262.3.1 Witch in form of she-goat kills men); N 788, Incidents when wife takes food to husband in field or forest; G 405 King hunting sees girl; G312.7 Ogress devours horses (G 264.3.1 Witch disguised becomes queen, devours King's horses nightly); T 145 Polygamous marriage; S 413.1 Ogress-wife orders raja to turn out his six wives; S 435 Cast-off wife abandoned in pit; G 72.2 Babies eaten; Z 215 Hero "son of seven mothers." Seven mothers each with a child imprisoned. Six eat their children to keep from starving. Seventh does not. He rescues all the mothers and becomes hero (L 71 Only the youngest of group of imprisoned women refuses to eat her newborn child); R 141 Rescue from well; Z 215 Provides food for Queen; H 1381.2.2.1.1.1 Boy twitted as bastard goes on a quest for unknown father; N 731.1 Unknown son returns to father's court; H 919.6 Tasks assigned at instigation of queen (disguised ogress); H 1212 Quest assigned because of feigned illness; F124 Journey to land of demons; H 1364 Quest for demon-owned cow; Q 20.1 Reward for service of god, hero, or ascetic for a period; H 1233.3.1 Ascetic gives directions to hero on quest (N 844.1 Sadhu as helper; D 1810.10 Magic knowledge from Sadhu); D 641 Transformation to reach difficult place; D 167 Transformation: man to parrot; G 572.3 Ogre deceived by biting peas as stones; D 838.2 Magic object taken from ogre's house; G 251.1.1 Separable soul of witch in parrot (E 715.1.3 Separable soul in parrot); K 956 Murder by destroying external soul; P 233.9 Son chastises father for scorning mother.

7. These two attributes are noted by Steel and Temple in *Wide Awake Stories*, p. 395, as characteristic of demons, who they term "ogres": "1. Eating flesh and 2. Power of metamorphorsis."

8. In a variant recorded by Stokes, *Indian Fairy Tales*, pp. 173–75, as well, the demoness does start out as a goat found in the jungle by seven men traveling together. She proceeds to gobble up five of the men before she is discovered. The survivors find they cannot kill the goat, so they take her back to the jungle and tie her to a tree. Here she becomes a beautiful girl and is found by a King, and so on.

9. For the split between good, nurturing mother and sexually devouring, destroying mother in Hindu male psychology, see Sudhir Kakar, *The Inner World* (Delhi: Oxford University Press, 1981), pp. 79–103; and O'Flaherty, *Women, Androgynes*, pp. 105–15.

10. Also, the free growth of sacred grass would seem to suggest that the holy man is detached from his own sexuality. In Kangra, sexually active people are supposed to remove their pubic hair, and one of the euphemisms for this removal is "uprooting the sacred grass" (*drub puṭī denī*).

11. In the Kangra version reported by Vyathit in his *Kāgaz kā Hans*, p. 9, the son of the expelled Queen repeatedly takes his wooden horse to drink water. When questioned by the King as to the point of watering a wooden horse who obviously can't drink, the boy retorts, "Oh King, does a Queen ever eat an elephant?"

This same act of a son watering a horse and inquiring into a King's gullibility is found in a Bengali story associated with the Goddess Sasthi, in which a tricked King believes that his Queen has given birth to wooden dolls and banishes her. See Stewart, "Goddess Sasthi Protects Children," p. 364.

Chapter Nineteen

1. This is Tale Type 923, "Love Like Salt", Tale Type 923 B, Princess Who Was Responsible for her Own Fortune. Motifs include: H 592.1 Love like salt; L 61 clever youngest daughter; M 21 King Lear judgement. King flattered by elder daughters and angered by seeming indifference, though real love, of youngest, banishes her and favors the elder daughters. N 145 Cast-out princess prospers because of good luck.

While the story is found throughout Europe and North India, its presence in (or introduction to?) the area of Punjab near Kangra is apparent in Grierson's use of the story to document the Malwai dialect of Punjabi in his *Linguistic Survey of India*, vol. 9, pt. 1, pp. 728–30. The story also is used by Grierson to document Bihari (vol. 5, pp. 308–10). The motif of love like salt can also serve as a frame story within which very different adventures associated with other tale types may unfold. See, for example, the variant in Stokes, "The Princess Who Loved Her Father like Salt," in *Indian Fairy Tales* pp. 164–72.

The theme of the girl who says she is responsible for her own fortune is also present in other stories, see Sudhir Kakar, *Intimate Relations* (Chicago: University of Chicago Press, 1989) pp. 72–73. For a good example of the story without the salt motif, in which a father instead becomes enraged because the youngest daughter says she depends on her own fortune and not on her father, see Gupte's *Hindu Holidays and Ceremonials*, pp. 136–38.

2. Alan Dundes observes, "the 'love like salt' plot appears to be a weakened plot in which a 'mad' father tries to marry his own daughter": he interprets this as an incestuous projection on the part of the father. See "To Love My Father All: A Psychoanalytic Study of the Folktale Source of *King Lear*" in *Cinderella: A Casebook* (New York: Garland, 1982), p. 234

Chapter Twenty

1. In the absence of a brother to escort his sister home, a father may step in.
2. In the Bengali variant, "Kuku Mata," the girl turned bird sings an almost identical refrain: "Kuku Mata is wandering from tree to tree—from branches to branches, whereas Dai-matki is with the Shahajada [Prince]." See Ralph Troger, *A Comparative Analysis of a Bengali Folktale* (Calcutta: Indian Publications, 1966), pp. 95–96.
3. This is Tale Type 403, "The Black and White Bride," which has a wide distribution stretching from India to Europe, Africa, and Latin America. This story particularly follows form IV f 'The true bride is transformed (to a bird) when a pin or thorn is stuck in her head' and V d 'The King sees the pin or thorn and pulls it from the bird's head.' Variants of this story are found all over India. For example, see the nearly identical sequences in the tale "Kuku Mata" in Troger, *Bengali Folktale*, pp. 90–96.

    Motifs include: S 31 Cruel stepmother; N 711 King (prince) accidentally finds maiden and marries her; L162 Lowly heroine marries prince (King); D 582 Transformation by sticking magic pin into head; D 150 Transformation: man into bird; K 1911 The false bride. An impostor takes wife's place without detection; D 765.1.2 Disenchantment by removal of enchanting pin; K 1911.3 Reinstatement of true bride; Q 469.3 Punishment: grinding up in a mill; Q 455 Walling up as punishment.
4. Thompson and Roberts, *Types of Indic Oral Tales*, p. 58.
5. See my "Birds on a Branch: Girlfriends and Wedding Songs in Kangra" *Ethos* 14 (1986): 47–75.
6. An almost inverse sequence occurs in a story collected by Vyathit, where it is a man's wife and mother who have rammed a nail into his head, turning him into a bird. Later, a princess who he has become betrothed to after secretly following his wife and mother on a magical adventure, fondles him, removes the pin, and he is once again a man. See Vyathit's *Kāgaz kā Hans*, pp. 104–8.
7. A. K. Ramanujan, "Towards a Counter-System: Women's Tales" in *Gender, Genre and Power in South Asian Expressive Traditions*, ed. A. Appadurai, F. Korom, and M. Mills (Philadelphia: University of Pennsylvania Press, 1991), pp. 33–55.

Chapter Twenty-one

1. This is Tale Type 897, "The Orphan Girl and Her Cruel Sisters-in-Law," which has only been recorded in India, especially in tribal areas.

   Motifs include: H931 Tasks assigned to get rid of hero; H 934.2 Sisters-in-law impose tasks; H 1212 Quest assigned because of feigned illness; H 1361 Quest for lion's milk; H 1049.1 Task: Bringing the foam of the ocean in a large piece of cloth; H 1030 Other impossible tasks; H 133.5.1 Quest for lotus flower; Q 45 Walling up as punishment; L 50 Victorious youngest daughter.

2. In Kangra, it is usual for elder siblings to marry before younger ones.

Afterword

1. The book released in London in 1880 is the version possessed by most libraries, including the University of California at Berkeley, where I had previously encountered it. Maive Stokes, *Indian Fairy Tales* (London: Ellis and White, 1880).

2. Mary Frere, *Old Deccan Days*, 3d ed. (London: John Murray, 1898).

3. Though I have tried hard to track down more information about Maive Stokes, the biographical sources mention only her father, Whitley Stokes. Based in India from 1864 to 1882, he worked on codifying Indian legal and criminal codes. In 1879, the same year that Maive's book was released, he was president of the Indian Law Commission.

4. Muniya and Dunkni told twenty-eight of the thirty tales. Karim is the name of the male servant who told the other two tales. Neither of his stories overlap with Urmilaji's.

5. Stokes, *Indian Fairy Tales*, p. 237

6. The first volume of *Kinder-und-Hausmärchen* was published in 1812, and the Grimm brothers continued to add to their collection as well as to alter the tales in various editions until 1857. In English, a standard translation is *The Complete Grimms' Fairy Tales*, trans. Margaret Hunt and rev. James Stern (New York: Pantheon Books 1944). Of course, in Germany as in India, there were influential literary collections made before the Grimms' collection, which also had sources in oral traditions. Yet it seems that in these earlier collections, compilers felt no qualms in freely and creatively reworking the materials as their own. With the Enlightenment, a gap opened between the kinds of people who study stories and those who tell them. Romantic concepts of nationalism meant that the "folk" came to carry a burden of authenticity and collectors no longer felt the freedom to assert that they were reworking oral stories (even, if, like the Grimms, in practice they actually did so). In colonized countries, the gulf between colonizers and "natives" added another vector of difference between collectors and tellers, even as the colonial interest in systematizing indigenous knowledge inspired fidelity to the original spoken texts.

7. On the relation between narrated event and narrating event, see Richard Bauman, *Story, Performance and Event: Contextual Studies of Oral Narrative* (Cambridge: Cambridge University Press, 1986). Also see Richard Bauman and Charles L. Briggs's illuminating article on how discourse becomes extractable from its context as text, a process that they call "entextualization," allowing it to be recontextualized in new

settings: "Poetics and Performance as Critical Perspectives on Language and Social Life," *Annual Review of Anthropology* 19 (1990): 59–88.

8. For more on Alan Dundes as a scholar and teacher, see Regina Bendix and Rosemary Levy Zumwalt, eds., *Folklore Interpreted: Essays in Honor of Alan Dundes*, (New York: Garland, 1995).

9. Bronislaw Malinowski, *Magic, Science and Religion and Other Essays* (New York: Doubleday Anchor, 1954).

10. Richard Bauman, *Verbal Art as Performance* (Rowley, Mass.: Newbury House, 1977). Also see Dan Ben Amos and Kenneth S. Goldstein, eds., *Folklore: Performance and Communication* (The Hague and Paris: Mouton, 1975).

11. Mark Azadovskii, *A Siberian Tale Teller*, trans. James Dow (Austin: University of Texas Press 1974).

12. Linda Dégh, *Folktales and Society: Story Telling in a Hungarian Peasant Community*, trans. Emily M. Schossberger (Bloomington: Indiana University Press, 1969). For more about East European contributions, see Linda Dégh, ed., *Studies in East European Folk Narrative* (Bloomington: Indiana University Press, 1978), especially pt. 2: "The Storyteller and His Art"; and Gyula Ortutay's delightful essay, "Mihaly Fedics Relates Tales," in *Hungarian Folklore: Essays*, trans. Istvan Buyar (Budapest: Akademiai Kiada, 1972), pp. 225–85.

13. Juha Pentikäinen, *Oral Repertoire and World View: An Anthropological Study of Marina Takalo's Life History*, Folklore Fellows Communications 219. (Helsinki: Suomalainen Tiedeakatemia, 1978).

14. Marcel Griaule, *Conversations with Ogotemmêli* (London: Oxford University Press, 1965).

15. For more on ethnography itself as a narrative form, see Barbara Tedlock, "From Participant Observation to the Observation of Participation: The Emergence of Narrative Ethnography," *Journal of Anthropological Research* 47 (1991): 60–94.

16. Linda Dégh, *Folktales and Society*, p. x. Dégh also demonstrates the value of speaking to tellers about their tales in some of the essays in her latest book, *Narratives in Society*, Folklore Fellows Communications 255 (Helsinki: Suomalainen Tiedeakatemia, 1995).

17. Dennis Tedlock, *The Spoken Word and the Work of Translation* (Philadelphia: University of Pennsylvania Press, 1983).

18. Alan Dundes, "Metafolklore and Oral Literary Criticism," *The Monist* 60 (1966): 505–16. See also Peter Claus, "Folk Literary Criticism and the Tulu Paddana Tradition," manuscript; and Kirin Narayan, "The Practice of Oral Literary Criticism: Women's Songs in Kangra, India," *Journal of American Folklore* 108 (1995): 243–64.

19. See especially the influential edited collection by James Clifford and George Marcus, *Writing Culture: The Poetics and Politics of Ethnography* (Berkeley: University of California Press, 1986), and the essays, particularly "On Ethnographic Authority" (pp. 1–54) reprinted in James Clifford, *The Predicament of Culture* (Cambridge: Harvard University Press, 1988). For an overview of these issues, see Renato Rosaldo, *Culture and Truth* (Boston: Beacon, 1988).

20. See Kevin Dwyer, *Moroccan Dialogues* (Baltimore: Johns Hopkins University Press, 1982); Tedlock, *The Spoken Word*.

21. For an introduction to these issues, see Robert C. Holub, *Reception Theory: A Critical Introduction* (London and New York: Methuen, 1984). For an early anthropological statement on the important of audience response, see Melville Jacobs, *The Content*

and Style of an Oral Literature: Clackamas Chinook Myths and Tales (Chicago and London: University of Chicago Press, 1959).

22. Kirin Narayan, *Storytellers, Saints, and Scoundrels: Folk Narrative as Hindu Religious Teaching* (Philadelphia: University of Pennsylvania Press, 1989).

23. For a summary of feminist trends in folklore scholarship, see Margaret A. Mills, "Feminist Theory and the Study of Folklore: A Twenty Year Trajectory toward Theory," in *Western Folklore* 52 (1993): 173–92; and also several key edited collections: Claire R. Farrer, ed., *Women and Folklore* (Austin: University of Texas Press, 1975); Bruce Jackson, ed., *Folklore and Feminism, Journal of American Folklore*, Special Issue 100 (1987); Rosan Jordan and Susan Kalçik, eds., *Women's Folklore, Women's Culture* (Philadelphia: University of Pennsylvania Press, 1985); Susan Tower Hollis, Linda Pershing, and M. Jane Young, eds., *Feminist Theory and the Study of Folklore* (Urbana and Chicago: University of Illinois Press, 1993); Joan Radner, ed., *Feminist Messages* (Urbana and Chicago: University of Illinois Press, 1993); Beverly Stoeltje, ed., *Feminist Revisions. Journal of Folklore Research*, Special Issue 25, no. 3 (1988).

In anthropology, the literature on feminist positions is too voluminous to mention all the high points. Daisy Dwyer's *Male and Female in Morocco* (New York: Columbia University Press, 1978), is a trailblazing analysis of how gendered understandings are reproduced through folktales. Works I've found particularly useful in regard to the politics of ethnography in writing about women's expressive forms include Lila Abu-Lughod, *Writing Women's Worlds: Bedouin Stories* (Berkeley: University of California Press, 1992); Ruth Behar, ed., *Special Issue on Women Writing Culture. Critique of Anthropology* 13 (1993); Ruth Behar and Deborah Gordon, eds., *Women Writing Culture* (Berkeley: University of California Press, 1995); Sherna Berger Gluck and Daphne Patai, eds., *Women's Words: The Feminist Practice of Oral History* (New York and London: Routledge, 1991).

In South Asian studies, recent works highlighting women's perspectives in oral traditions include Nita Kumar, ed., *Women as Subjects: South Asian Histories* (Charlottesville and London: University Press of Virginia, 1994); and Raheja and Gold, *Listen to the Heron's Words*.

24. For more on anthropological life histories through the late 1970s, see L. L. Langness and Gelya Frank, *Lives: An Anthropological Approach* (Novato, Calif.: Chandler and Sharp, 1981).

25. See, for example, Jerome Bruner, *Actual Minds, Possible Worlds* (Cambridge: Harvard University Press, 1986), and "The Narrative Construction of Reality," *Critical Inquiry* 18 (1991): 1–21; John C. Hoffman, *Law, Freedom and Story: The Role of Narrative in Therapy, Society and Faith* (Waterloo: Wilfred Laurier University Press, 1986); W. J. T. Mitchell, ed., *On Narrative* (Chicago: University of Chicago Press, 1980); George C. Rosenwald and Richard L. Ochberg, ed., *Storied Lives: The Cultural Politics of Self-Understanding* (New Haven: Yale University Press, 1992); Paul Ricouer, *Time and Narrative* (Chicago: University of Chicago Press, 1984); Theodore R. Sarbin, ed., *Narrative Psychology: The Storied Nature of Human Conduct* (New York, Praeger, 1986).

26. On the traditional aspects of personal narrative, see Sandra Dolby Stahl, *Literary Folkloristics and the Personal Narrative* (Bloomington: Indiana University Press, 1989).

27. See Ruth Benedict, "Folklore," *Encyclopedia of the Social Sciences* (New York: Macmillan, 1931), pp. 288–93.

28. Julie Cruikshank, for example, who wanted to study Yukon life histories, found that the three women elders she worked with insisted that their folk narratives were

part of their lives too. See Julie Cruikshank, in collaboration with Angela Sidney, Kitty Smith, and Annie Ned, *Life Lived Like a Story* (Lincoln and London: University of Nebraska Press, 1990). Other memorable anthropological life histories in which the wisdom of elders surfaces in stories include Paul Radin, *Autobiography of a Winnebago Indian* (New York: Dover, 1920); Leo Simmons, *Sun Chief* (New Haven, Yale University Press, 1942); Barbara Myerhoff, *Number Our Days* (New York: Dutton, 1978); and Behar, *Translated Woman*.

29. On how men and women retell the same stories differently, see James Taggart, *Enchanted Maidens* (Princeton: Princeton University Press, 1990). For how men and women are drawn to structurally different tales, see A. K. Ramanujan on Indian folktales, particularly the Kannada ones collected by him, and Bengt Hølbek on European folktales from preexisting collections. Both Hølbek and Ramanujan point out that male quest narratives invariably end with marriage (unless, I should add, the teller is a holy man in which case it is usually only ridiculous tales that end with marriage). Women-centered tales, on the other hand, present difficulties as beginning with marriage. Thus, these tales often follow the structural pattern of separation, solitary suffering, and then renewed commitment between the couple. See Ramanujan, "Towards a Counter-System: Women's Tales," and Hølbek, "The Language of Fairy Tales," pp. 40–62.

30. See also my, "According to Their Feelings: Teaching and Healing with Stories," in *The Lives Stories Tell*, ed. Carol Witherell and Nell Noddings (New York: Teachers Colleges Press, 1991), pp. 113–35.

31. See especially Cruikshank et al. *Life Lived Like a Story*; Stree Shakti Sanghatna, *We Were Making History: Life Stories of Women in the Telangana Armed Struggle* (New York: Zed Books, 1989); and the articles in Gluck and Patai, *Women's Words: The Feminist Practice of Oral History*.

32. See Elizabeth Mathias and Richard Raspa, *Italian Folktales in America: the Verbal Art of an Immigrant Woman* (Detroit: Wayne State University Press, 1985) for an account that beautifully combines a sense of folktales, life history, and social change.

33. Nongenile Masithathu Zenani, *The World and the Word: Tales and Observations from the Xhosa Oral Tradition*, ed. Harold Scheub (Madison: University of Wisconsin Press, 1992). For more on collaboration with storytellers, also see Phyllis Morrow and William Schneider, eds., *When Our Words Return: Writing, Hearing and Remembering Oral Traditions of Alaska and the Yukon* (Logan: Utah State University Press, 1995).

34. Stokes, *Indian Fairy Tales*, p. 260.

35. *Ibid.*, p. 281.

36. *Ibid.* p. 288.

37. This view is particularly held among folklorists influenced by Freudian theories of the unconscious. See, for example, Bruno Bettelheim, *The Uses of Enchantment* (New York: Knopf, 1976); and the extensive works of Alan Dundes, particularly *Parsing through Customs* (Madison: University of Wisconsin Press, 1987). For a masterful study of folktale interpretation that synthesizes existing theories, see Bengt Hølbek, *The Interpretation of Fairy Tales*, Folklore Fellows Communications 239 (Helsinki: Suomalainen Tiedeakatemia, 1987).

38. For a study of obliqueness in storytelling in a situation of political repression see Margaret A. Mills, *Rhetorics and Politics in Afghan Traditional Storytelling* (Philadelphia: University of Pennsylvania Press, 1991). Also James Scott, *Domination and the Arts of Resistance* (New Haven: Yale University Press, 1991).

253

39. For example, my being unmarried through most of this work is very likely the reason that sexual issues were not openly discussed with me.
40. For an immmensely illuminating discussion of these issues, see Charles Briggs, *Learning How to Ask: A Sociolinguistic Appraisal of the Role of the Interview in Social Science Research* (Cambridge: Cambridge University Press, 1986).
41. Stokes, *Indian Fairy Tales*, p. v.
42. Stokes, *Ibid*, p. 238
43. My thinking here has been influenced by my mother, Didi Contractor, and by Arjun Appadurai's writings, particularly "Disjuncture and Difference in the Global Cultural Economy," *Public Culture* 2 (1990): 1–24; and "Notes and Queries towards a Transnational Anthropology," in *Recapturing Anthropology*, ed. R. Fox (Santa Fe: School of American Research Press), pp. 191–210.
44. See *Joseph Campbell and the Power of Myth with Bill Moyers*, produced by Apostrophe S. Productions, Inc. in association with Alvin H. Perlmutter, Inc. for Public Affairs Television, Inc. New York, 1988, videorecording.
45. Wendy Doniger O'Flaherty demonstrates the possibility of making other people's stories our own while also keeping their cultural setting in view. See her *Other People's Myths* (New York: Macmillan, 1988).
46. Although elsewhere in India there is a growing trend toward women's use of printed pamphlets for ritual stories, so far I have not observed this practice in Kangra. For an analysis of such pamphlets, which display regional variation, see Susan S. Wadley, "Popular Hinduism and Mass Literature in North India: A Preliminary Analysis," in *Religion in Modern India*, ed. Giri Raj Gupta (Delhi: Vikas, 1983), pp. 81–104.
47. For more on the transformation of folktales into fairy tales, see Maria Tatar, *Off With Their Heads! Fairy Tales and the Culture of Childhood* (Princeton: Princeton University Press, 1992); Jack Zipes, *Fairy Tales and the Art of Subversion: The Classical Genre for Children and the Process of Civilization* (New York: Routledge, 1991 [1983]).

Appendix

1. I borrow this term "oral chaining" from Mills, *Rhetoric and Politics*, p. 27.
2. The idea of juxtaposing word-for-word literal translation with a more free-form translation is borrowed from Gold's wonderful *A Carnival of Parting*, p. 31.

BIBLIOGRAPHY

Aarne, Antti. 1964. *Types of the Folktale*. Trans. and enlarged Stith Thompson. Folklore Fellows Communications 184. Helsinki: Suomalainen Tiedeakatemia.

Abu-Lughod, Lila. 1986. *Veiled Sentiments: Honor and Poetry in a Bedouin Society*. Berkeley: University of California Press.

———. 1992. *Writing Women's Worlds: Bedouin Stories*. Berkeley: University of California Press.

Appadurai, Arjun. 1990. "Disjuncture and Difference in the Global Cultural Economy." *Public Culture* 2:1–24.

———. 1991. "Global Ethnoscapes: Notes and Queries for a Transnational Anthropology." In *Recapturing Anthropology*. Ed. R. Fox, 191–210. Santa Fe: School of American Research Press.

Azadovskii, Mark. 1974. *A Siberian Tale Taller*. Trans. James Dow. Austin: University of Texas Press.

Babb, Lawrence. 1983. "Destiny and Responsibility: Karma in Popular Hinduism." In *Karma: An Anthropological Inquiry*. Ed. C. Keyes and E. V. Daniel, 163–81. Berkeley: University of California Press.

Bahan, Asha, and Lado Bahan. 1991. *Bharatiya Vrat-parva-tyauhar aur Mahila Sangit* [Indian women's rituals, festivals, and women's songs]. Haridvar: Randhir Prakashan.

Bannerjee, Sumanta. 1989. "Marginalization of Women's Popular Culture in Nineteenth Century Bengal." In *Recasting Women*. Ed K. Sangari and S. Vaid, 127–79. Rutgers, N. J.: Rutgers University Press.

Bauman, Richard. 1976. *Verbal Art as Performance*. Austin: University of Texas Press.

———. 1986. *Story, Performance and Event: Contextual Studies of Oral Narrative*. Cambridge: Cambridge University Press.

Bauman, Richard, and Charles L. Briggs. 1990. "Poetics and Performance as Critical Perspectives on Language and Social Life." *Annual Review of Anthropology* 19: 59–88.

Beck, Brenda E. F., P. Claus, J. Handoo, and P. Goswamy. 1987. *Folktales of India*. Chicago: University of Chicago Press.

Behar, Ruth. 1993. *Translated Woman: Crossing the Border with Esperanza's Story*. Boston: Beacon Press.

Behar, Ruth, ed. 1993. *Special Issue on Women Writing Culture. Critique of Anthropology* 13 (4).

Behar, Ruth, and Deborah Gordon, eds. 1995. *Women Writing Culture*. Berkeley: University of California Press.

Ben Amos, Dan, and Kenneth S. Goldstein, eds. 1975. *Folklore: Performance and Communication*. The Hague and Paris: Mouton.

Benedict, Ruth. 1931. "Folklore." In *Encyclopedia of the Social Sciences*, vol. 6, pp. 288–93. New York: Macmillan.

Bendix, Regina, and Rosemary Levy Zumwalt, eds. 1995. *Folklore Interpreted: Essays in Honor of Alan Dundes*. New York: Garland.

Bennett, Lynn. 1983. *Dangerous Wives and Sacred Sisters: Social and Symbolic Roles of High-Caste Women in Nepal*. New York: Columbia University Press.

Bettelheim, Bruno. 1976. *The Uses of Enchantment: The Meaning and Importance of Fairy Tales*. New York: Knopf.

Bødker, Laurits. 1957. Indian Animal Tales. Folklore Fellows Communications 170. Helsinki: Suomalainen Tiedeakatemia.

Borland, Katherine. 1991. " 'That's Not What I Said': Interpretive Conflict in Oral Narrative Research." In *Women's Words: The Feminist Practice of Oral History*. Ed. S. B. Gluck and D. Patai, 63–76. London and New York: Routledge.

Bottigheimer, Ruth B., ed. 1986. *Fairy Tales and Society: Illusion, Allusion and Paradigm*. Philadelphia: University of Pennsylvania Press.

Briggs, Charles. 1986. *Learning How to Ask*. Cambridge: Cambridge University Press.

Bruner, Jerome. 1986. *Actual Minds, Possible Worlds*. Cambridge: Harvard University Press.

———. 1991. "The Narrative Construction of Reality," *Critical Inquiry* 18: 1–21.

Buchanan, W. 1886. "Panch-bhikham—Bhisma-panchaka." *Panjab Notes and Queries* 35: 181–82.

Campbell, Gabriel. 1976. *Saints and Householders: A Study of Hindu Ritual and Myth among the Kangra Rajputs*. Katmandu: Ratna Pustak Bhandar.

Chatterji, Roma. 1985. "The Voyage of the Hero: The Self and the Other in the Narrative Tradition of Purulia." *Contributions to Indian Sociology* 19: 95–114.

Claus, Peter. n.d. "Folk Literary Criticism and the Tulu Paddana Tradition." Manuscript.

Clifford, James. 1988. *The Predicament of Culture*. Cambridge: Harvard University Press.

Clifford, James, and George Marcus, eds. 1986. *Writing Culture: The Poetics and Politics of Ethnography*. Berkely: University of California Press.

Cruikshank, Julie, in collaboration with Angela Sidney, Kitty Smith, and Annie Ned. 1990. *Life Lived Like a Story*. Lincoln and London: University of Nebraska Press.

Daniel, Sheryl. 1983. "The Tool Box Approach of the Tamil to Issues of Moral Responsibility and Human Destiny." In *Karma: An Anthropological Inquiry*. Ed. C. Keyes and E. V. Daniel, 27–62. Berkeley: University of California Press.

David, E. 1894. "The Wicked Stepmother." *North Indian Notes and Queries* 4: 234

Day, Lal Behari. 1913. *Folktales of Bengal*. London: Macmillan.

Dégh, Linda. 1969. *Folktales and Society: Storytelling in a Hungarian Peasant Community*. Trans. Emily M. Schossberger. Bloomington: Indiana University Press.

———. 1995. *Narratives in Society: A Performer-Centered Study of Narration*. Folklore Fellows Communications 255. Helsinki: Suomalainen Tiedeakatemia.

Dégh, Linda, ed. 1978. *Studies in East European Folk Narrative*. Bloomington: Indiana University Press.

Dundes, Alan. 1966. "Metafolklore and Oral Literary Criticism." *The Monist* 60: 505–16.

———. 1982. "To Love My Father All: A Psychoanalytic Study of the Folktale Source of King Lear." In *Cinderella: A Casebook.* Ed. A. Dundes, 229–44. New York: Garland.

———. 1987. *Parsing through Customs.* Madison: University of Wisconsin Press.

Dwyer, Daisy Hilse. 1978. *Images and Self Images: Male and Female in Morocco.* New York: Columbia University Press.

Dwyer, Kevin. 1982. *Moroccan Dialogues: Anthropology in Question.* Baltimore and London: Johns Hopkins University Press.

Elwin, Verrier. 1944. *Folktales of Mahakoshal.* Bombay: Oxford University Press.

Falassi, Alessandro. 1980. *Folklore by the Fireside: Text and Context of the Tuscan Veglia.* Austin: University of Texas Press.

Farrer, Claire R., ed. 1975. *Women and Folklore.* Austin: University of Texas Press.

Fischer, J. L. 1963. "The Sociopsychological Analysis of Folktales." *Current Anthropology* 4: 235–95.

Frere, Mary. 1898. *Old Deccan Days, or Hindoo Fairy Legends Current in Southern India.* 3d ed. London: John Murray.

Gluck, Sherna Berger, and Daphne Patai, eds. 1991. *Women's Words: The Feminist Practice of Oral History.* New York and London: Routledge.

Gold, Ann Grodzins. 1982. *Village Families in Story and Song: An Approach through Women's Oral Tradition in Rajasthan.* Indiakit Series, Outreach Educational Project, South Asia Language and Area Center, University of Chicago.

———. 1993. *A Carnival of Parting: The Tales of King Bharthari and King Gopi Chand as Sung and Told by Madhu Natisar Nath of Ghatiyali, Rajasthan.* Berkeley: University of California Press.

———. 1995. "Mother Ten's Stories." In *Religions of India in Practice.* Ed. Donald Lopez, 434–48. Princeton: Princeton University Press.

Griaule, Marcel. 1965. *Conversations with Ogotemmêli: An Introduction to Dogon Religious Ideas.* London: Oxford University Press.

Grierson, G. A. 1968 (1916). Linguistic Survey of India. Vol. 9, pt. 1. Delhi: Motilal Banarsidas.

Grimm, Jacob, and Wilhelm Grimm. 1944. *The Complete Grimms' Fairy Tales.* Trans. Margaret Hunt and ed. James Stern. New York: Pantheon Books.

Gupta, Shakti M. 1981. *Plant Myths and Traditions in India.* 2d rev. ed. New Delhi: Mushiram Manoharlal.

Gupte, Rai Bahadur. 1919. *Hindu Holidays and Ceremonials.* Calcutta: Thacker, Spink, and Co.

Harlan, Lindsay. 1991. *The Religion of Rajput Women.* Berkeley: University of California Press.

Hoffman, John C. 1986. *Law, Freedom and Story.* Waterloo: Wilfred Laurier University Press.

Hølbek, Bengt. 1987. *The Interpretation of Fairy Tales.* Folklore Fellows Communications 239. Helsinki: Suomalainen Tiedeakatemia.

———. 1989. "The Language of Fairy Tales." In *Nordic Folklore: Recent Studies.* Ed. R. Kviedland and H. K. Sehmsdorf, in collaboration with E. Simpson, 40–62. Bloomington: Indiana University Press.

Hollis, Susan Tower, Linda Pershing, and M. Jane Young, eds. 1993. *Feminist Theory and the Study of Folklore.* Urbana and Chicago: University of Illinois Press.

Holub, Robert C. 1984. *Reception Theory: A Critical Introduction.* New York: Methuen.

Jackson, Bruce. 1987. *Folklore and Feminism. Journal of American Folklore*. Special Issue 100 (398).

Jacobs, Melville. 1959. *The Content and Style of an Oral Literature: Clackamas Chinook Myths and Tales*. Chicago and London: University of Chicago Press.

Jason, Heda. 1989. *Types of Indic Oral Tales: Supplement*. Folklore Fellows Communications 242. Helsinki: Suomalainen Tiedeakatemia.

Jordan, Rosan, and Susan Kalcik, eds. 1986. *Women's Folklore, Women's Culture*. Philadelphia: University of Pennsylvania Press.

Joseph Campbell and the Power of Myth. 1988. With Bill Moyers. A production of Apostrophe S. Productions, Inc., in association with Alvin H. Perlmutter, Inc. Public Affairs Television, Inc. New York. Videorecording.

Kakar, Sudhir. 1981. *The Inner World*. 2d ed. Delhi: Oxford University Press.

———. 1989. *Intimate Relations*. Chicago: University of Chicago Press.

Keyes, Charles, and E. Valentine Daniel, eds. 1983. *Karma: An Anthropological Inquiry*. Berkeley: University of California Press.

Kingscote, Mrs. Howard, and Pandit Natesa Sastri. 1984. (1890). *Tales of the Sun or Folklore of Southern India*. New Delhi: Asian Educational Services.

Knowles, Rev. J. Hinton. 1893. *Folk-tales of Kashmir*. London: Kegan Paul, Trench, Trubner.

Kolenda, Pauline. 1978. *Caste in Contemporary India: Beyond Organic Solidarity*. Menlo Park, Calif.: Benjamin Cummings.

Kumar, Nita, ed. 1994. *Women as Subjects: South Asian Histories*. Charlottesville and London: University of Virginia Press.

Langness, L. L., and Gelya Frank. 1981. *Lives: An Anthropological Approach to Biography*. Novato, Calif.: Chandler and Sharp.

Lüthi, Max. 1986. *The European Folktale: Form and Nature*. Trans. John D. Niles. Bloomington: University of Indiana Press.

Malinowski, Bronislaw. 1954. *Magic, Science and Religion and Other Essays*. New York: Doubleday Anchor.

Mathias, Elizabeth, and Richard Raspa. 1985. *Italian Folktales in America: The Verbal Art of an Immigrant Woman*. Detroit: Wayne State University Press.

McGee, Mary. 1991. "Desired Fruits: Motive and Intention in the Votive Rites of Hindu Women." In *Roles and Rituals for Hindu Women*. Ed. Julia Leslie, 69–88. Rutherford: Fairleigh Dickinson University Press.

Mills, Antonia. 1989. "A Replication Study: Three Cases of Children in Northern India Who Are Said to Remember a Past Life." *Journal of Scientific Exploration* 3: 133–84.

Mills, Margaret. 1985. "Sex Role Reversals, Sex Changes, and Transvestite Disguise in the Oral Tradition of a Conservative Muslim Community in Afghanistan." In *Women's Folklore, Women's Culture*. Ed. R. A. Jordan and S. J. Kalcik, 187–213. Philadelphia: University of Pennsylvania Press.

———. 1990. *Oral Narrative in Afghanistan: The Individual in Tradition*. New York and London: Garland.

———. 1991. *Rhetoric and Politics in Afghan Traditional Storytelling*. Philadelphia: University of Pennsylvania Press.

———. 1993. "Feminist Theory and the Study of Folklore: A Twenty-Year Trajectory toward Theory." *Western Folklore* 52: 173–92.

Mitchell, W. J. T., ed. 1980. *On Narrative*. Chicago: University of Chicago Press.

Morrow, Phyllis, and William Schneider, eds. 1995. *When Our Words Return: Writing,*

Hearing and Remembering Oral Traditions of Alaska and the Yukon. Logan: Utah State University Press.

Mukharji, Ram Satya. 1904. *Indian Folklore*. Calcutta: Sanyal and Co.

Myerhoff, Barbara. 1978. *Number Our Days*. New York: Dutton.

Narayan, Kirin. 1986. "Birds on a Branch: Girlfriends and Wedding Songs in Kangra." *Ethos* 14: 47–75.

———. 1989. *Storytellers, Saints, and Scoundrels: Folk Narrative in Hindu Religious Teaching*. Philadelphia: University of Pennsylvania Press.

———. 1991. " 'According to Their Feelings': Teaching and Healing with Stories." In *The Lives Stories Tell: Narrative and Dialogue in Education*. Ed. Carol Witherell and Nell Noddings, 113–35. New York: Teachers College Press.

———. 1993. "How Native is a 'Native' Anthropologist?" *American Anthropologist* 95: 671–86.

———. 1995. "The Practice of Oral Literary Criticism: Women's Songs in Kangra, India." *Journal of American Folklore* 108: 243–64.

Norton, Ruth. 1920. "The Life-Index: A Hindu Fiction-Motif." In *Studies in Honor of Maurice Bloomfield*, 211–24. New Haven: Yale University Press.

Nuckolls, Charles W., ed. 1993. *Siblings in South Asia: Brothers and Sisters in Cultural Context*. New York: Guilford Press.

O'Flaherty, Wendy Doniger. 1973. *Asceticism and Eroticism in the Mythology of Siva*. London: Oxford University Press.

———. 1980. *Women, Androgynes and Other Mythical Beasts*. Chicago: University of Chicago Press.

———. 1984. *Dreams, Illusions and Other Realities*. Chicago: University of Chicago Press.

———. 1988. *Other People's Myths: The Cave of Echoes*. New York: Macmillan.

Ortutay, Gyula. 1972. "Mihaly Fedics Relates Tales." In *Hungarian Folklore: Essays*. Trans. Istvan Buyar. Budapest: Akademiai Kiada.

Parry, Jonathan. 1979. *Caste and Kinship in Kangra*. Boston: Routledge and Kegan Paul.

Pentikäinen, Juha. 1978. *Oral Repertoire and World View: An Anthropological Study of Marina Takalo's Life History*. Folklore Fellows Communications 219. Helsinki: Suomalainen Tiedeakatemia.

Peterson, Indira. 1988. "The Tie that Binds: Brothers and Sisters in North and South India." *South Asian Social Scientist* 4: 25–51.

Propp, Vladimir. 1968. *Morphology of the Folktale*. 2d. rev. ed. Trans. Lawrence Scott. Austin: University of Texas Press.

Punjab District Gazetteer. 1926. Kangra District, vol. 7 pt. A. Lahore: Government Printing Press.

Radin, Paul. 1920. *Autobiography of a Winnebago Indian*. New York: Dover.

Radner, Joan, ed. 1993. *Feminist Messages*. Urbana and Chicago: University of Illinois Press.

Raheja, Gloria. 1988. *The Poison in the Gift*. Chicago: University of Chicago Press.

Raheja, Gloria Goodwin and Ann Grodzins Gold. 1994. *Listen to the Heron's Words*. Berkeley: University of California Press.

Ramanujan, A. K. 1982. "Hanchi: A Kannada Cinderella." In *Cinderella: A Folklore Casebook*. Ed. Alan Dundes, 259–75. New York and London: Garland Publishing Company.

———. 1983. "The Indian Oedipus." In *Oedipus: A Folklore Casebook*. Ed. L. Edmunds and Alan Dundes, 234–61. New York and London: Garland Publishing Company.

———. 1986. "Two Realms of Kannada Folklore." In *Another Harmony*. Ed. S. H. Blackburn and A. K. Ramanujan, 41–75. Berkeley: University of California Press.

———. 1991a. "Towards a Counter System: Women's Tales." In *Gender, Genre and Power in South Asian Expressive Traditions*. Ed. A. Appadurai, F. Korom, and M. Mills, 33–55. Philadelphia: University of Pennsylvania Press.

———. 1991b. *Folktales from India*. New York: Pantheon.

Ranchan, Som P., and H. R. Justa. 1981. *Folktales of Himachal Pradesh*. Bombay: Bharatiya Vidya Bhavan.

Randhawa, Mohinder Singh. 1970. *Kangra: Kala Desh aur Geet* [Kangra: Art, Region and Songs]. Trans. Balakram Nagar from Punjabi to Hindi. New Delhi: Sahitya Academy.

Reynolds, Holly Baker. 1978. *"To Keep the Tali Strong": Women's Rituals in Tamilnad, India*. 2 vols. Ph.D. diss., University of Wisconsin, Madison.

———. 1980. "The Auspicious Married Woman." In *The Powers of Tamil Women*. Ed. Susan Wadley, 35–60. Syracuse: Maxwell School of Citizenship and Public Affairs, Syracuse University.

Ricouer, Paul. 1984. *Time and Narrative*. Chicago: University of Chicago Press.

Rohrich, Lutz. 1991. *Folktales and Reality*. Trans. Peter Tokofsky. Bloomington: Indiana University Press.

Rosaldo, Renato. 1988. *Culture and Truth*. Boston: Beacon.

Rose, H. A. 1980 [1919]. *Glossary of the Tribes and Castes of the Punjab and the North-West Frontier Provinces*. New Delhi: Abhinav.

Rosenwald, George C. and Richard L. Ochberg, eds. *Storied Lives: The Cultural Politics of Self-Understanding*. New Haven: Yale University Press.

Sarbin, Theodore, ed. 1986. *Narrative Psychology: The Storied Nature of Human Conduct*. New York: Praeger.

Sax, William S. 1991. *Mountain Goddess: Gender and Politics in a Himalayan Pilgrimage*. New York: Oxford University Press.

Scott, James. 1991. *Domination and the Arts of Resistance*. New Haven: Yale University Press.

Seethalakshmi, K. A. 1972. *Folktales of Himachal Pradesh*. New Delhi: Sterling Publications.

Seitel, Peter. 1980. *See So That We May See: Performances and Interpretations of Traditional Tales from Tanzania*. Bloomington and London: Indiana University Press.

Sharma, Ursula. 1978a. "Women and Their Affines: The Veil as a Symbol of Separation." *Man* (n.s.) 13: 218–33.

———. 1978b. "Segregation and Its Consequences in India: Rural Women in Himachal Pradesh." In *Women United, Women Divided*. Ed. P. Caplan and J. Bujra, 259–82. London: Tavistock.

———. 1980. *Women, Work and Property in North West India*. London: Tavistock.

Sharma, Shyamlal. 1974. *Kāngari: A Descriptive Study of the Kangra Valley Dialect of Himachal Pradesh*. Hoshiarpur: Punjab University.

Simmons, Leo. 1942. *Sun Chief*. New Haven: Yale University Press.

Srinivas, M. N. 1962. *Caste in Modern India and Other Essays*. Bombay: Asia Publishing House.

Srivastava, Saheb Lal. 1974. *Folk Culture and Oral Tradition*. New Delhi: Abhinav.

Stahl, Sandra Dolby. 1989. *Literary Folkloristics and the Personal Narrative*. Bloomington: Indiana University Press.

Stanley, John M. 1977. "Special Time, Special Power: The Fluidity of Power in a Popular Hindu Festival." *Journal of Asian Studies* 37: 27–43.

Steel, Flora Annie. 1894. *Tales of the Punjab.* London: Macmillan.

Steel, Flora Annie, and Richard Carnac Temple. 1884. *Wide-Awake Stories.* London: Trubner and Co.

Stevenson, Ian. 1975. *Cases of the Reincarnation Type. Vol. I. Ten Cases in India.* Charlottesville: University Press of Virginia.

Stewart, Tony K. 1995. "The Goddess Sasthi Protects Children." In *Religions of India in Practice.* Ed. Donald Lopez, 352–66. Princeton: Princeton University Press.

Stoeltje, Beverly, ed. 1988. *Feminist Revisions. Journal of Folklore Research.* Special Issue 25 (3).

Stokes, Maive. 1880. *Indian Fairy Tales.* London: Ellis and White.

Stone, Kay. 1986. "The Misuses of Enchantment: Controversies on the Significance of Fairy Tales." In *Women's Folklore, Women's Culture.* Ed. R. Jordan and S. J. Kalccik, 125–45. Philadelphia: University of Pennsylvania Press.

Stree, Shakti Sanghatna. 1989. *We Were Making History: Life Stories of Women in the Telangana Armed Struggle.* New York: Zed Books.

Taggart, James. 1990. *Enchanted Maidens: Spanish Folktales of Courtship and Marriage.* Princeton: Princeton University Press.

Tatar, Maria. 1992. *Off With Their Heads! Fairy Tales and the Culture of Childhood.* Princeton: Princeton University Press.

Tedlock, Barbara. 1991. "From Participant Observation to the Observation of Participation: The Emergence of Narrative Ethnography." *Journal of Anthropological Research* 47: 60–94.

Tedlock, Dennis. 1983. *The Spoken Word and the Work of Interpretation.* Philadelphia: University of Pennsylvania Press.

Tewari, Laxmi G. 1991. *A Splendor of Worship: Women's Fasts, Rituals, Stories and Art.* New Delhi: Manohar.

Thakur, Molu Ram. n.d. *Manoranjak Pahari Lok Kathaen* [Entertaining Pahari Folktales]. Delhi: Himachal Pradesh Bhavan.

Thompson, Stith. 1955–58. *Motif-Index of Folk Literature.* 6 vols. Bloomington: Indiana University Press.

Thompson, Stith, and Jonah Balys. 1958. *The Oral Tales of India.* Bloomington: Indiana University Press.

Thompson, Stith, and Warren Roberts. 1960. *Types of Indic Oral Tales.* Folklore Fellows Communications 80. Helsinki: Suomalainen Tiedeakatemia.

Trawick, Margaret. 1990. *Notes on Love in a Tamil Family.* Berkeley: University of California Press.

Troger, Ralph. 1966. *A Comparative Analysis of a Bengali Folktale.* Calcutta: Indian Publications.

Underhill, M. M. 1921. *The Hindu Religious Year.* Calcutta: Association Press.

Von Sydow, Carl. 1948. *Selected Papers in Folklore.* Copenhagen: Rosenhilde and Bagger.

Vyathit, Gautam Sharma. 1979a. *Naulakhiyā Hār: Himāchal kī Lok kathāen* [The Precious Necklace: Folktales from Himachal]. Kangra: Krishna Brothers.

———. 1979b. *Kāgaz kā Hans: Himāchal kī Lok kathāen* [A Paper Goose: Folktales from Himachal]. Kangra: Krishna Brothers.

———. 1979c. *Rājkumāri aur Totā: Himāchal ki Lok Kathāen* [The Princess and the Parrot: Folktales from Himachal]. Kangra: Krishna Brothers.

————. 1984. *Folklore of Himachal Pradesh*. Trans. Mrinal Pande. New Delhi: National Book Trust.

Wadley, Susan. 1975. Shakti: *Power in the Conceptual Structure of Karimpur Religion*. Chicago: Department of Anthropology, University of Chicago.

————. 1976. "Brothers, Husbands, and Sometimes Sons: Kinsmen in North Indian Ritual." *Eastern Anthropologist* 29: 149–70.

————. 1978. "Texts in Contexts: Oral Traditions and the Study of Religion in Karimpur." In *American Studies in the Anthropology of India*. Ed. S. Vatuk, 317–23. New Delhi: Manohar.

————. 1983a. "*Vrats*: Transformers of Destiny." In *Karma: An Anthropological Inquiry*. Ed. C. F. Keyes and E. V. Daniel, 146–62. Berkeley: University of California Press.

————. 1983b. "Popular Hinduism and Mass Literature in North India: A Preliminary Analysis." In *Religion in Modern India. Main Currents in Indian Sociology V*. Ed. Giri Raj Gupta, 81–104. Delhi: Vikas Publishing House.

————. 1986. "The Katha of Śākaṭ: Two Tellings." In *Another Harmony: New Essays in the Folklore of India*. Ed. S. H. Blackburn and A. K. Ramanujan, 195–232. Berkeley: University of California Press.

————. 1989. "Hindu Women's Family and Household Rites in a North Indian Village." In *Unspoken Worlds: Women's Religious Lives*. Ed. N. A. Falk and R. M. Gross, 72–81. Belmont, Calif.: Wadsworth Publishing Company.

————. 1993. "Raja Nal, Motini, Damayanti and the Dice Game: Some Preliminary Thoughts." Paper presented at the Wisconsin South Asia Meetings.

————. 1994. *Struggling with Destiny*. Berkeley: University of California Press.

Zenani, Nongenile Masithathu. 1992. *The World and the Word: Tales and Observations from the Xhosa Oral Tradition*. Ed. Harold Scheub. Madison: University of Wisconsin Press.

Zipes, Jack. 1991 (1983). *Fairy Tales and the Art of Subversion: The Classical Genre for Children and the Process of Civilization*. New York: Routledge.